REVENGE

A dish best served cold

BY JUNIUS RUSSELL

Revenge is a harmful action against a person or group in response to a grievance, be it real or perceived. It is also called payback, retribution, retaliation or vengeance; it may be characterized as a form of justice (not to be confused with <u>retributive justice</u>), an <u>altruistic</u> action which enforces societal or moral justice aside from the legal system. <u>Francis Bacon</u> described it as a kind of "wild justice" that "does... offend the law [and] putteth the law out of office".

CHAPTER ONE

Lillian

"Lillian." Laura called as she entered her daughter's bedroom.

"Yes, Momma?" She answered as she quickly turned to the Disney Channel thinking she would get caught watching the "Shoot 'em up" movie.

"How would you like to go visit your cousin, Katrina for the summer? We have to go out of town on extensive business and your father does not want to drag you along just to have you sitting around the entire summer. Now you and I both know that in order for him to agree for you to stay at my sister's in Harlem, this must be an extremely important trip."

"Katrina's?" Lillian couldn't believe her ears especially since her dad had let it be known plenty of times that he did not approve of her mother's side of the family. He considered most of the men to be ne'er-do-wells. *All they do is sit around drinking all day.* He would bad-talk everybody with the exception of Lillian's Aunt Barbara. *She can't help it if she's stuck in the ghetto.*

Her father's strict voice always sounded in her head whenever she had thought about doing anything wrong, nothing too bad, something as simple as sneaking to watch television after her 8 pm bedtime curfew. Lillian had become used to staying up after her parents were asleep watching action, adventure and drama programs, which her father didn't approve of at all.

Once, Lillian saw a late night movie called "The Point of no Return" about a professional woman assassin who was even as efficient as any man-killer she had seen and so it became one of her favorites. Before, seeing the woman gunslinger in action, she was a fan of the likes of Clint Eastwood and Charles Bronson, especially when he played the vigilante in "Death Wish."

The thought of hanging out with Katrina gave Lillian hope of not spending another boring summer with her mother and father, however the reality of finally visiting New York made her slightly nervous after listening to the stories her dad had told over time. Lillian thought back to the times when her cousin Katrina used to come up to Barrington, Rhode Island to spend the summer. She'd tease Lillian about being a goody-two-shoe and living in the *little house on the prairie,* although the Elliot home was far from that, costing the upper middle class couple $450,000.

Robert and Laura Elliot met in college when they both attended the University of California, Berkeley. Elliot went to work for a big advertising company while Laura set up a business at home that eventually became the vehicle for the family's success. While he struggled for position, which he never obtained, Laura's small advertising business began to thrive. Finally, when Elliot's employer started laying off he was one of the first to go. He always felt like being the only black in his department had a lot to do with it.

Now, seventeen years later the couple employed 112 people and had a dozen out of state accounts in addition to their local dealings. They sent Lillian to a private school so that she'd receive a better education and didn't allow her any freedom, which is why she was so into watching action packed movies. It was a way for her to escape the goody-two-shoe lifestyle or rebelling against her father.

Lillian had no friends except a few classmates she studied with during school and wasn't even allowed to talk on the telephone because her dad always insisted that phones were business tools. Even though Lillian had more restrictions than the average teenager did, her parents did make sure she had everything possible to keep her occupied at home. Her bedroom was full of fun stuff like the giant stuffed animals that lined her walls, video games, stereo equipment, a computer and closets full of clothes and shoes. In addition to getting whatever she wanted the family went to expensive restaurants, attended shows and took lots of vacations. One of the most memorable trips that stuck in Lillian's mind was the time they traveled to Canada and their guide, a nice blonde lady, reminded her of another no none sense woman, played by Sharon Stone in the movie "Basic Instinct." The only event Lillian could recall being a big deal in her neighborhood was when a motorcycle club showed up one summer and used the side road of the Mall as a racing strip. Apparently, the folks of Rhode Island weren't that tolerant of the noise and made a big fuss.

Suddenly the invasion of the biker boys was front-page news and eventually the group was run off but not before a having a few bikes impounded. Other than that there was nothing going on in the quiet suburb.

At 14, Lillian was the total opposite of Katrina who was a year older and seemed to know a lot about life, or so Lillian thought. During Katrina's previous visits she tried to enlighten her younger cousin about certain things concerning boys and sex. Katrina acted shocked when Lillian told her that she had never held a boys hand let alone kissed one. Before the summer was over Katrina had filled Lillian's head up with so much mess, the girl didn't know what to regard as truth or attribute to her cousin's vivid imagination. Sharp as a tack academically, Lillian was just the opposite when it came to worldly subjects. The movies she'd often sneak to watch did broaden her horizon slightly but was regarded as fantasy.

Girl I was doin' it with this boy named Rodney...
Doing what?
Havin' sex! Anyway, when I came...
Came where?
Girl you so dumb
I'm not dumb. My grade point average is 4.0
Not book dumb, street dumb

Katrina went on to tell her cousin that she had passed out during orgasm, confusing Lillian even more about the subject. It wasn't as if she had someone to deny or confirmed Katrina's teachings, being that she could never discuss anything remotely concerning boys to her strict parents. It was hard for Lillian to imagine her parents doing some of the things Katrina talked about, let alone a 15 year old. *I guess they do have sex, I had to get here somehow.*

"Lillian, why don't you give Katrina a call to let her know you'll be there tomorrow afternoon." Laura interrupted her daughter's train of thought.

"Okay. What's the number?"

Katrina answered the phone, which showed how different the two were being raised. Lillian wasn't allowed to answer phones or go outside alone.

"Hello."
"Hey Katrina, this is your favorite cousin."

4

"Who Diane?"

"No girl! This is Lillian."

"Oh shit. My bad cuz. It's just you ain't never called me before so I wasn't sure. Plus I was in a hurry to get away from momma so I can go around Rodney's house to chill."

"Well, I'm just calling to let you know that I'll be there tomorrow afternoon."

"I know, Momma told me but it's still hard to believe your Momma and Daddy going to let you come to Harlem to rub elbows with us ghetto folks."

"No matter where I go they trust me to follow their rules."

"Well, we gone have to do something about that, Ms. Goodie-two-shoes."

"What do you mean?"

"Nothing. So what have you been up to?"

"Not much, you know, school's the only thing I have to look forward to."

"Well, I hope we have some fun this year because I couldn't do shit around your nosy ass Moms. Anyway, what time y'all coming'?"

"We should get there by noon."

"Okay Cuz, I'll see you then. I gotta go braid Rodney's hair."

Lillian was always amazed how Katrina cursed at will. Profanity was never used in the Elliot residence and rarely did the white kids at her school use it, yet, it came out in every other word from Katrina's mouth.

The following morning Lillian sat at the dining room table while her mother did her hair in multiple, neat rows of ponytails with lots of colorful, rubber bands in the style she had always done.

In addition to still doing her daughter's hair (In what Lillian considered a younger kid's style) she also packed her clothes anytime they took a trip and today was no different. Lillian's suitcase and travel bag were already waiting to be loaded into the trunk of her mother's new Volvo when it was time to roll.

At the start of their three-hour trip Lillian reclined her seat a little and stared into the countryside while Laura listened to some boring radio talk show.

Either Mom is going to do my hair in a different style or I'll have to learn to do it myself. She imagined the comments Katrina would make about her third grade, ponytails. *Katrina could say anything out of her mouth with her crazy self.* Lillian recalled the time she inadvertently blurted out that she was coming on her period to her mother causing Laura to question where she learned such foul language. "Child! We don't say period. I've always taught you that women have menstrual cycles, understand?"
Of course, Lillian didn't want Katrina, not to be allowed to return the following summer so she failed to implicate her, using a student at school as the scapegoat. Katrina had also told her cousin that once a girl's period came she would become a sex fiend wanting sex every minute of the day. This almost scared Lillian to death and when her cycle started the following year she was relieved to find out that Katrina had just been pulling her leg. Most of Katrina's tales were now regarded as wild by Lillian and nothing more than forbidden stories. Lillian almost giggled to herself when she imagined the look she must have had on her face when Katrina told her about the passing out during sex story. *I always thought about a boxer being knocked out when she mentioned that and figured that it must hurt badly.*

"Lillian. Your father and I decided to let you stay with Barbara while we're gone because she is the most responsible on my side of the family so she'll watch out for you. The original plan was to bring you along but after reviewing the schedule we thought better of it. We trust you to carry yourself in the manner you were taught, and always remember New York City is like being in another world compared to where we live. My sister does alright working for the IRS and should have moved out of the city years ago but she chose to stay, I don't know why? I guess it's convenient for her and Lawrence to remain closer to work. Your father respects him as a humble, hardworking man but say's his only flaw is not being able to stand up to Barbara's dominate ways."

The mention of Katrina's stepfather Lawrence, brought back memories of the time when Lillian first realized the difference between the couple's relationship in comparison to her parent's. It seemed Aunt Barbara bossed her man around like he was one of the children and he'd just smile and do whatever he was told.

6

Whereas, it was evident who wore the pants in the Elliot household. There was never an argument, that Lillian could recall or any unrest, it was just how things were.

"Are you listening to me young lady?"
"Yes." Lillian snapped out of her daydream.

"Like I was saying. Your Aunt chose the hustle and bustle of the city instead of peace and quiet. Now you listen closely to this! Harlem has some nice areas, the block Barbara lives on is one, however, if you travel just a few blocks in either direction you could get shot. So don't leave your Aunt's sight and I mean that. If Katrina gets permission to go to any parties or streets jams, whatever they call it, I forbid you to attend. Those folks shoot guns for fun. Besides, I don't believe you're into that mess anyway. That rap music is counterproductive with all the profanity and disrespect towards women. Your Dad and I are pleased with the accomplishments you've made in school. I was smart but even I didn't make every honor roll so you can imagine how we feel about you and your future. We are comfortable with your decision-making abilities, however, your father thinks I ought to prepare you more for a place like New York. We have kind of sheltered you from things but you must understand that people from fast cities think their sharper than everybody else and you, not knowing what to look for may not foresee any danger looming your way so stay away from strangers. Understand?"

"Yes, ma'am."
"College is just four years away and most likely you'll be attending one of the Ivy League schools and living away from home so you must remain focused on your goals. We trust everything will be fine while we're taking care of our business thousands of miles away. Here is 300 dollars. Spend it wisely. Barbara will supply the necessities so you can use your money to buy some things to keep you occupied or take your cousin to a movie or something. I will allow you to go to a show if Barbara agrees to drop you guys off and pick you up. That doesn't mean you should go on a one-day shopping spree and be broke for the rest of the summer. You'll have a budget once you're away in college so this will give you an opportunity to manage your funds. Are there any questions?"

"No ma'am

For the remainder of the ride Lillian lay back processing everything her mother had said.

I'm lucky to have parents that care about me so much. Even though daddy's so strict I know he's just concerned about me. Lillian thought about all the family trips they had taken so that she could have fun. *The Disneyland trip when I was ten was nice and so was SeaWorld that was a good vacation too.* Then there were the educational trips to the Monument in Washington and visiting small museums to see artifacts in what her Dad referred to as the 15, slave states.

The Elliot's did most of their traveling in the families, 30ft RV which had adequate sleeping quarters and running water. Robert C. Elliot took pride in the traveling hotel but not as much as he did in his Mercedes Benz. If one didn't know Mr. Elliot, he appeared to never smile and was all business 24-7, never caught without a suit & tie outside of home. Even though it had been Laura's idea to start a home business, In the end it was Robert Elliot's drive and persistence that put the company in its present financial position; Elliot & Elliot Advertising was making their mark in the business world, having been featured in a couple of the cooperate money magazines. It was evident that the once small business was the pride and hard work of the Elliot's and they did not have a problem letting it be known what a success story should sound like.

Lillian noticed early, the difference between the ways her family lived in comparison to some of her relatives. Most of her Dad's people were doing extremely well but not as good as them. Everyone always made a fuss over the family's expensive home and cars. Lillian recalled the time she was being teased at a family reunion by some of her faster cousins. She was relieved when her father came to her rescue and explained to her that those kids were just mad because she was so smart and was going places. *You'll be rich and famous some day and they'll be working for you honey.* After that, whenever she was called a little brat or stuck up, it no longer bothered her.

Robert Elliot was originally from Louisiana, born to a Creole family. He spoke French fluently and was always telling Lillian about his ancestry and trying to teach her about the languages called Patrois or Patwa.

It was obvious what side of the family Lillian had gotten her looks from; everybody said that she was the split image of her father's mother, Grandma-Elliot. The elder had passed away when Lillian was four making it hard for the child to have a good memory of the high-yellow woman who she had gotten her looks from.

However, there were old photos in the family album which allowed Lillian to see pictures of her grandmother during her teens when her hair was long, beautiful and gray-less.

Like her dad, Lillian was light skinned and blessed with *dirty red*, silky hair that could have only come from Grandma, although Robert Elliot's was thinning rapidly. One thing was for sure and that was that Lillian loved and respected her father as just as much as she did her mother.

Lillian dozed off two hours into the trip which gave her an hour to rest before they finally made it to New York. They drove along the Henry Hudson Parkway, exiting Riverside Drive then taking Broadway to 145th into Harlem. As they made their way east towards Seventh Avenue, Lillian was shaken awake by the change in the grade of the streets. The Volvo's rack & pinion steering overran a few potholes as it made its way thru "The Damned Ghetto." (According to her father's description)

Lillian quickly adjusted her seat so that she would get a good view of the crowds of people walking the streets. She wondered where everybody was going as they came to a red light. The buildings bunched together reminded her of a jungle made of concrete. *These people don't look as poor as Momma made it seem.* Lillian noticed that a lot of the teenagers had on designer clothes and expensive tennis shoes. She saw a group of teens dipping in and out of traffic on expensive dirt bikes and mopeds. Just as one of the loud bikes past their car, Lillian heard the click of the Volvo's door lock, as if the sudden present of youth had reminded her mother to make sure they were safe and secured. Lillian also noticed some very expensive automobiles cruising around, finally concluding that some people were very well off in the ghetto.

They made a turn on a street lined with Brownstones called **Striver's Row,** located on 132nd street between 7th & 8th avenues. This area in Harlem had a reputation as a place where the folks strived to be the best in a neighborhood surrounded on all sides by poverty. It was referred to by some as *an ice depot in the middle of hell that refused to melt.*

"This area is alright." Laura told her daughter. "See, they even planted their own trees." She pointed to a line of freshly planted, curbside trees. Lillian noticed that this street was much cleaner and quieter than the ones they had traveled on, and it had little traffic.

"It's quiet because the Home Owner's Association is active in patrolling the neighborhood and making sure the riff raffs don't target cars and homes on their block." Laura continued. "I wouldn't mind if you played outside directly in front of Barbara's building but never leave this area. Most of the city is plagued with crime; drugs and shootings happen on a regular basis." Laura maintained eye contact with her daughter during their entire conversation. "A person can get killed just going to the corner store." They sat in front of Barbara's for a few minutes while Laura gave Lillian her final talk. Before they could exit the car, Laura's Sister Barbara came out of the Brownstown and stood at the top of the steps with her hands on her wide hips.

"Stop threatening that child and let her get out." Barbara joked with her older sister as she made her way to the car.

Barbara considered herself big boned but when everyone else referred to her they conveniently leave out the bone part and just called her big, especially her bother in-law, Robert. One thing for sure is Barbara had the biggest breast Lillian had ever seen.

"Where is my favorite brother in-law? I'm surprised he ain't drop her off in an army tank. Bad as he thinks the Harlem is."

"We're meeting in Colorado." Laura answered her sister's sarcastic question. Laura looked at her watch and suddenly had to hurry off. "Oh, wow. I better be going. I still have to make a few more stops." She hit the trunk release. "Don't forget to grab your bags. I'd sure hate to have to turn around."

"You should leave me this nice Volvo." Barbara joked.

"Girl, you don't want this thing. It's about to send us to the poor-house."

"That's even more reason to give it away and take my Caravan." Barbara continued before opening Lillian's door. "Come on child and give your Auntie a big hug."

All Lillian saw was a pair of mammoth breast coming toward her until she thought she would suffocate. Laura smiled knowing what her daughter was probably thinking about her Auntie's chest. Lillian struggled to remove her suitcase from the trunk, glad to be free of Barbra's bear hug. *Wow that woman's breast are huge.*

"Remember what I said." Laura waved goodbye to her daughter. Barbara waved her off, as if to say, *I got this.*

"
Cow." Laura jokingly said as she pulled away.

Lillian watched the Volvo disappear down the block as she followed her Aunt up the flight of Brownstone steps dragging her bags. "Where's Katrina?" She finally asked.

"That's a good question. She was supposed to be going to the store and coming right back." Barbara realized her niece was having a hard time carrying her luggage and grabbed the suitcase. "Child, now you let me know if my too strict sister's starving you to death over there. Look at your little, skinny, self. Don't worry because you're Auntie Barbara gone put some meat on then bones." Just as they were about to enter the building, Barbara noticed her daughter headed up the block. "There go that child right there."

As Katrina approached and recognized her cousin she picked up her pace. "Hey Lillian. What's up girl?"

"What's up with you, girl?" Barbara answered. "Last time I checked it didn't take that long to go to the store."

Katrina held up a small bag of candy as an alibi. "It was crowded."
"And what did I tell you about leaving' the house looking' like that?"

Lillian couldn't believe how Katrina was dressed or how much she'd grown since last summer. Her breast, hips and behind where straining at the seams of her clothes. The cutoff shorts and halter top she had on wasn't helping and the furry, bunny rabbit, slippers made her look like a little, ghetto, hoochie-momma. Lillian was glad her mother had pulled off before Katrina showed up because she would have surely burned rubber getting her daughter away from there.

"It took you almost an hour to get that little bag of candy. I know what your problem is... But if you don't go change out of that mess, you gone have some real problems. I guess you think you're cute." Barbara shook her head.

"I am cute." Katrina mumbled.
"What? I know you ain't giving' me no lip."

"No momma. All I said was that I look like you." Katrina decided not to press her luck.

As they entered the foyer, Katrina followed mocking her mother behind her back by raising her breast and mimicking Barbara's big boobs while rocking side to side as if imply the load was too heavy. Lillian wondered if her cousin's chest would eventually gain the size of her moms. Seeing how much Katrina had filled out made Lillian feel like a slow bloomer, weighing under a hundred pounds.

The young girls giggled while Barbara was none to the wise about the reason for the laughter. Once inside Katrina made a B-line to her bedroom with Lillian in tow. "Come on cuz. We got a lot of catching' up to do."

The girls talked and listened to music until Barbara showed up at the door with their dinner plates. "Time to eat." She sat the food down on Katrina's dresser. "Y'all can come get your own drinks."

In the Elliot household every meal was eaten at the kitchen table so the room service thing was new to Lillian. That's when it became evident to Lillian that things were definitely done differently in the Whitfield home. In a way she felt kind of guilty having spent the last couple of hours listening to Katrina's *counterproductive music full of profanity and degrading women.*
Lillian was experiencing a type of culture shock in the little time she had been there. Never had she heard someone refer to their own daughter as a heifer until Barbara let it roll off of her lips like it was common.

"My momma used to do my hair like that when I was like four or five."
Here we go about my kiddy ponytails. Lillian prepared herself for the teasing but it never came.

"You should let me put some braids in your head. You don't need extensions like me because you hair is already long." Katrina suggested as she helped Lillian unpack. She held up one of Lillian's training bras. "Damn. I haven't seen one of these in a long time. What cup size are you? Let me guess. Knobby." She teased. "Girl you got to start doing' some tittie exercises. That's how my mines got so big."

Feeling that she wasn't as naïve as she was when Katrina had filled her young head up with past myths she disregarded the comment about the breast exercise and attributed her cousin's breast size to her mother.

"Girl, why you bring all these Church clothes?" Katrina held up all of her garments one by one making silly comments about everything. "We really gotta' do something about this one." Katrina held up a jean skirt that went down to Lillian's ankles and shook her head. Without saying another word she removed a pair of scissors and begin cutting away until the once long garment now resembled a micro-mini.

"Hey. Why did you do that?"

"Don't worry cuz. Im'a fix you up. How could you wear all this kiddy stuff?" Amid protest, Katrina altered most of Lillian's garments, cutting the pants to short-shorts and cutting the stomach area of the shirts so that Lillian's belly button would be exposed. "I'm not wearing that. I liked my long clothes."

"You ain't goin' nowhere with me lookin' like that. You gotta loosen up, girl you're in Harlem and its summer time."

All Lillian could think about was what her mother would say if she saw her clothes all cut up, however, Katrina continued to alter the items using her old plastic sewing machine to fix the hems. When she had finished she urged her cousin to try them on.

"I can't wear that stuff now."

"Cuz, stop trippin'. I hooked everything up. Look at how neat the hem is. You can't be runnin' around lookin' like the Preacher's daughter. I didn't even cut yours as short as I wear mines. Just try it on."

"Okay." Lillian finally agreed. The skirt was shorter than anything she had ever worn and the shirt made her feel almost naked. Katrina's laughter made Lillian feel flush, causing her to fold her arms across her chest in embarrassment.

"I'm just laughing' cause your training bra is showing'. Let's see how it looks without it."

"Without it?"
"Yeah girl take that thing off. It's tacky."

Lillian had no intensions on wearing any of the clothes Katrina had *fixed up* for her and at that moment decided that she would use some of her money to replace the clothes before her mother returned to pick her up at the end of the summer. Without removing her shirt completely, Lillian pulled her arms through the sleeves and removed her bra. Katrina seem to make a fuss about that also.

"You gone have to come off that shy shit. We got the same thing and I sure ain't funny either because I like dillz-nick too much. But seriously I hope you ain't gone be actin' all stuck up this summer."

"I can't wear these clothes."
"Why."
"Cause my father will kill me."

"Cousin, your Mommy and Daddy's way in China somewhere." Katrina signed like an instructor losing patience with a stubborn student. "What you hidin' under there." Katrina playfully lifted her shirt exposing Lillian's small budding breast."

"Stop." Lillian screamed as she quickly pulled it back down, expecting it to cover her exposed stomach also, until she remembered the garment had been cut.

"Girl why you so ashamed. You got some lil cute ones." The comment made Lillian to blush. "Ouuuu, and look. Your nibbies are hard." Not used to being bra-less, Lillian's nipples hardened against the cotton fabric of her shirt. Once again she flushed in embarrassment.

You're a mess." Katrina offered. "But don't worry cuz. You gone be alright."

In the days to follow, Katrina found it impossible to convince her younger cousin to leave the house. When Katrina would return, sometimes after her 9 o'clock curfew, she would spend the rest of her night telling Lillian about her day.

"Look, I let Rodney put a hickey on my neck." Lillian looked at the small bruise on Katrina's neck and immediately thought of an insect bite.

14

"How'd you do that?"

"Rodney did it. It's a passion mark. He sucked my throat until the blood rushed to the surface."

Lillian shook her head. "Sounds like it hurt."

"Hurt so good. Anyway, what cha' been doin' all day. Watchin' the history channel? I don't know how you can watch all that mess. I don't give a damn about World War I or Hitler. Turn that shit girl."

Lillian flicked through the channels of Katrina's 13 inch television until another show caught her eye. A beautiful woman was lacing a man's drink with a white powder before handing it to him with a smile on her face. After he fell over apparently poisoned to death the woman pried a thick band of gold from his finger and struggled to read the tiny numbers engraved on the inside. Finally she removed a large estate picture and began opening the safe.

Katrina shook her head as she boldly undressed in front of Lillian. "You need to stop watchin' that secret agent shit and come hang out with your cuz. Is this how you really plan on spending the entire summer? You don't know what you're missin'. I was too cute today in my poon-poon shorts."

Lillian learned how her slick cousin got out of the house by wearing something presentable overtop the outfit she really intended to wear. *Katrina's always trying to be slick. One day Auntie Barbara's going to catch her and she'll be in for it.*

"Let me get my behind in the shower." Lillian tried not to look at Katrina's boobs bouncing up and down as she headed to the bathroom with a towel covering only her waist. Katrina was bold as anyone she had ever seen.
What if she ran into her Step-dad in the hall on the way to the bathroom half naked? Lillian couldn't believe her boldness.

Three weeks had passed with Lillian still not having left the house. Her routine consisted of watching lots of television, eating plenty of her Aunt Barbara's good food and sleeping. Katrina would bring bags of junk food and candy home along with her fantastic stories and Lillian would half listen to her talk while trying to catch the ending of the program she'd been watching. She knew watching the violence on television went against her parents' wishes but she had also began eating candy which wasn't permitted at home either. She favored the animal shaped lollipops so Katrina would bring them just for her.

Lillian received an early morning call from her mother. "How are making out honey?

"Fine."
"How much money do you have left?"
"I haven't spent anything yet?"

"Oh. What have you been up to? Have you guys made it to the movie theater or anything?"

"No. Not yet. I basically watch a little TV and eat lots of Aunt Barbara's food."

"Really? Is it as good as mine?"

"Aaaah, well. You guys are a tie." Lillian lied to her mother for the first time. Small as it was, she realized it, knowing that she had thought to herself earlier how much better her Aunt Barbara's cooking tasted than her Mom's. "Aunt Barbara say's I'm gaining some weight."

"We'll are you?"
"I guess. Yeah."
"Yeah!?"
"I mean yes ma'am."

"Watch your vocabulary. Don't come home talking like those New Yorkers."

"I won't Mom."

"Well, sounds like you're doing fine to me. I'll report back to your Dad, he's been extremely busy and I'm sure he'll be happy that everything worked out for the better because he really had second thoughts... Anyhow, find yourself a hobby."

"I miss my computer."

"It's just for the summer. Listen call if you need anything, okay?"
"Yes ma'am."
"Fine, goodbye."
"Bye."

Lillian stopped in front of the mirror to inspect herself noticing that all the good cooking, late night snacks and laying around were having an effect on her usually slim physique. *Your lil boobies are starting to Bloom like flowers in the springtime.* Aunt Barbara's words echoed in her head. Even then, she blushed. Katrina had also mentioned that her skinny tail had picked up some weight. Lillian took a quick peek in the mirror as she walked away seeing some difference.

During one of Katrina's long days watching action/adventure movies in front of the fan she decided she would write down some things she wanted to do before the summer was over. *It's getting boring watching TV all day but it beats running the streets with Katrina's crazy butt.*

She opened the sliding door of her cousin's closet and reached up to grab a composition notebook. Suddenly a bunch of junk came crashing down onto her head. The last item to hit her fleeing figure was a large, orange, plastic crayon. *I must be scared of my own shadow.* Lillian thought as she felt her heartbeat and shook her head. Lillian put the notebook on the bed and began replacing the items into the box they had been stored. Among some of Katrina's things was a pink diary with pictures of teddy bears on it. *I bet Katrina isn't writing nursery rhymes in here.*

After putting the box back on the shelf she turned to retrieve the big plastic crayon and recalled seeing one at the fair when she was younger. Curious, she unzipped it and couldn't believe her eyes. The entire thing, which almost reached her chest when stood up, was filled with condoms.

Wow! Is Katrina really having sex?

Lillian shook her head before tossing the condom filled missile back to its launching pad. She jotted a quick list of things to do:

Movies, Circus, Macy's, Park, Library

Not being able to come up with too much fun she flipped thru the channels until she found a program with guns blazing' and laid back for a few more hours of television.

Twenty minutes into the movie something began tugging at her. She tried to dismiss it but the curiosity was overwhelming. She looked up towards the shelf inside the closet where Katrina's diary was calling out to her. *Read me-Read me.* The voice urged. She fought the desire to invade her cousin's privacy but in the end begin rationalizing that there was no harm in it. Finally, not being able to concentrate on her program she jumped up, removed the diary from the box and sat on the corner of the bed. The fact that it was locked almost deterred her from proceeding however a bobby pin insight, atop of the dresser seemed like a sign for her to continue. Just like in one of the spy movies she had seen in the past, a quick turn of the makeshift key popped open the flimsy diary's lock and she was staring down at the sloppy, written thoughts of her streetwise cousin.

In 40 minutes Lillian had read the diary from cover to cover and the only reason it took that long is she had to go over several pages trying to understand Katrina's far-out slang or she was shocked by some of the admissions her cousin had made. Lillian sat in disbelief at some of the things Katrina had written about. Her heart was pounding in her chest. Her own knowledge about sex was basic and she even thought that was gross but to read Katrina's descriptions appalled her.

I can't believe someone could have sex in their behind.

Lillian locked the sex book and replaced it. She tried to continue watching television but her mind kept traveling back to the diary. When Katrina returned home for the night all Lillian could do was think of the things she had read. *This girl is c-r-a-z-y.*

"What's wrong with you?" Katrina asked. "You look stuck."
"Nothing I'm just tired."
"Tired from what? Watching' TV all damn day?"
"I'm getting home sick, I guess."

"What you need, is to get out this house all day and come have some fun."
Katrina's idea of fun flashed in Lillian's mind. *Yeah, like licking on some boys balls.* She thought to herself. When it was time to go to bed Lillian moved as close as she could to the opposite edge of the bed as if Katrina would try to rape her or something. She finally faded off to sleep with her cousins sexual exploits on her mind.

During the night after reaching deep level of sleep, she begin to dream of being in a hot and dark place. Something seemed to be constricting her wrist and then her ankles. After attempting to wiggle free she realized she was tied to a giant slab of red, hot rock. The heat was becoming so intense she thought she would melt. White, hot flames were all around her. Lillian tried to scream but nothing seemed to come out. Out of nowhere a large figure who seemed to blend with the flames was looming before her. She could tell by his pitch fork, horns and the menacing red tail that snapped and popped against the rock that it was Satan himself. Suddenly she realized her nakedness as she lay in the spread eagled position. *Oh god! Please help me.*

Satan laughed in response to her thoughts. "He can't help you! That's what I'm here for. To satisfy your curiosity." The voice seemed heavy as if it reached the pit of her brain. Lillian screamed again. This time she could feel her own cries for help in the pit of her brain.

"It's too late for all that." The demonic voice screamed. "Prepare to be deflowered!"

Lillian's eyes widened in fear as his penis grew right before her eyes into a thick, fiery, monstrosity with the head of a creature. Its face rotated angrily as an acid like fluid dripped from its fanged mouth and sizzled on the slab between her legs. As it got closer she could feel the heat on her thighs. The wicked laughter penetrated her soul as the devil's object entered   her.   "Noooooooooooooooooooooooooooo!   Oh   god, nooooooooooooooooooooooo! I'm a virgin!" She screamed. Before the excruciating, unbearable pain seemed to set her insides ablaze as it burned her in two. Suddenly Lillian felt herself being shaken until she awakened to see Katrina, Aunt Barbara and her husband Lawrence standing over her.

"Lillian-Lillian, are you alright!" Barbara asked concerned. Lillian tried to shake-off the dream and embarrassment, hoping no one heard her professions of being a virgin. "I'm sorry for waking everyone but-but I had a nightmare." "Its fine honey, long as you're okay."

"I'm fine."

Lawrence and Barbara turned to leave. Katrina stood there for a moment with a smirk on her face. "Girl you scared me to death with all that 'I'm a virgin' shit." Katrina shook her head and giggled.

The embarrassment returned, causing Lillian's face to flush beet red. Katrina just stood expecting an explanation but Lillian turned on her side pulling the covers completely over her head. Long after everyone had gone back to sleep, Lillian remained awake, staring in the darkness, ashamed at the wetness in her panties, knowing it wasn't sweat or urine.

The following day when Katrina went out, Lillian sat in front of the television trying to shake the dream. Finally during the afternoon her interest returned to watching movies but she barely got thru one before the urge to have another look at Katrina's diary begin tugging at her again. *Even having read the diary seems like a dream. Maybe I dreamed everything up.*

Lillian got Katrina's diary and after once again picking the lock, began re-reading it. Her heart was pounding like the adrenalin one feels at the approach of danger as she read each passage.

Prying into someone's sexual life could have been the reason for the guilt building... Perhaps being exposed to something considered prohibited in her household or even the breach of trust she was perpetuating against her parents who expected her to remain free of such sexual knowledge....

Once she reached midway into the tales of the forbidden, she was feeling like she had crossed into the realm of understanding... Having survived the encounter with Satan and his deadly member. Imagination begin to takeover, she reacted differently to the wet spot now forming in her underwear. Surprising even herself, she rubbed down there. As she continued to read, she slipped her hand inside her panties and for the first time touched herself. The sensation was unbelievable. It was like she was possessed. Finding a spot more sensitive than the rest, she masturbated until the sensation overwhelmed her and she blacked-out. Once she regained consciousness, all she could hear was Katrina's words. *Having sex can make you pass out.*

As if possessed by the devil, Lillian spent the following two weeks doing the same thing. She knew she wasn't ready to be with any boy but pleasing herself was becoming a fast habit. No sooner than Katrina would go out it would begin. She would feel guilty afterward, knowing her parents would be ashamed.

Am I losing my mind? I have to get out of this house. It's driving me crazy. I can't wind up some sex maniac like Katrina. I'm going to college to become something in life, not some humping bag for every guy to use.

From that moment Lillian decided to get a hold of herself and stop the daily masturbating. She knew she needed to occupy her mind, move around a little, and distance herself from that diary. Katrina came home that night more excited than usual.

"Girl, **Harlem Week** starts tomorrow."
"What's Harlem week?"

"All the rappers and singers come to the State Building and perform on stage for a whole week!"

"The State Building? How much does it cost?"
"Nothing girl. It's free. Ice Cube, Public Enemy and LL Cool J."

Lillian figured the State Building sounded like a safe place so even though she had been warned by her mother about rap concerts, she decided to go.

CHAPTER TWO

LEWIS

Lewis Armstrong ran up the four flight of stairs to his apartment and put the key in the door to find it unlocked. He had spent most of the school day thinking about the goodies he had hidden in the stewpot under the kitchen sink cabinet. He had three cans of spam, sardines and crackers, canned potatoes and some snacks. The cookies and candy bars were for dessert.

He knew no one would find it because it had been over seven months since his mother had cooked a meal. He dropped his book bag and jacket on the floor just outside the kitchen on his way to put together a quick meal having become used to fending for himself. Just has he was about to peel open a can of spam he heard noises coming from his mother's room. It was out of the ordinary for her to be home at this time of day because she usually ran the streets for days, sometimes weeks. On his way to investigate he grabbed a kitchen knife.

Lewis peeped thru the crack in his mother's door to find her on her knee's giving some guy a blow job. The sight turned the young boy's stomach. He wanted to rush into the room and drive the small steak knife into the man's back but fear prevented him from doing so.

"Slow down. You're choking me!" Debra begged. However, her cries seem to excite the local drug dealer even more causing him to tighten his grip on her head and pump harder.

"Shut up bitch and suck this dick!" Snookie growled as he rushed to climax.

"Awn-awn." Debra pulled away, breaking Snookie's concentration. "Don't do me like that! I said I'd make you cum but..."

Snookie stood there with his pants down, around his ankles seething at being interrupted. "Bitch! You done already smoked my crack so you better put this dick back in your mouth and get busy."

Lewis now recognized Snookie from his profile as one of the neighborhood dealers that stood on the corner of his block almost daily. Debra seemed irritated by the demanding drug dealer and sucked her teeth in response instead of continuing like she was told.

The slap sounded like a small caliber pistol and sent Debra reeling backward as she grabbed her face. "Bitch who the fuck you suckin' yo' teeth..." Before Snookie could finish his sentence, Lewis lunged catching him with a barrage of feeble blows to the back of the head. Snookie was more concerned with getting his penis in the safety of his pants than he was for the kidlike blows raining down on his back. Once his jeans were snapped he threw an arching, backhand, bolo-punch, knocking Lewis head first into the wall. The impact rendered the youth dazed, however, Snookie proceeded to stomp the youngster until he vomited the remains of his school lunch.

"Lil nigga! If you ever get in my business again, I'll kill you next time. Let your crack head momma take care of her own shit." He turned and spit in Debra's face before storming towards the door. "Bitch, you owe me."

Debra approached her son and kneeled to help him to his feet. "Baby, you alright?"

"Get off me!" Lewis screamed. "Don't fuckin' touch me. I hope you die!" Lewis said out of pure anger although he didn't really mean it. Actually he wished he could make things better, like they were before his father went to prison and his mother started getting high.

Four years earlier, in 1980 his father was a prominent hood-figure in Harlem. Butter, as he was known, drove a brand new Lincoln, Town Car and dressed in expensive suits and shoes every day.

Their apartment was nicely furnished plus Debra and her three kids seemed to have everything they needed. Lewis remembered going to school when he was 10 dressed in slacks and Buster Brown shoes. He recalled him and the twins never having to go to bed hungry.

In 1983, things changed... The police came for their father. All Lewis knew was he was never coming home again, something about drugs, money and murder.

Eventually, Debra packed the kids and moved into her mother's cramped apartment. Not long after, Grandmother died, and she had to get on welfare to survive. Slowly Debra begin to fold under the daily pressure until unbeknownst to her family. In 1984, she found a new boost in the form of cooked up cocaine, known as crack.

During this era it was quickly becoming known as the wonder drug. Debra was introduced to it by a new guy she had met in the neighborhood after becoming lonely for companionship. Crack is said to supply its users with a sparkling freeze. Some say they've heard bells. One things for sure, it was the most additive drug anybody had ever known.

Within six months it had consumed every aspect of Debra's life. She had sold everything Butter had left behind, including his clothes before she started on her deceased mother's possessions: TV's, appliances and anything else that could bring a quick buck. She even started selling her food stamps leaving her children hungry. Since welfare paid the rent directly to her landlord, she couldn't give it to the dope man, which is why they weren't thrown out on the street.

Lewis begin shoplifting to compensate for his and the twin's empty stomachs, stealing from supermarkets and later clothing stores.

He actually became good at it not withstanding that it became necessary for survival.

Somehow, Debra's relatives from South Carolina got wind of her predicament before child protective services and came for the children. The twins were seven and Lewis was on the eve of his fourteenth birthday and refused to go. Satisfied that the younger children were safe they didn't press the issue.

Lewis remained in school, continuing to steal to keep food in his belly and clothes on his back. He and Debra simply co-existed, with her eventually spending less and less time at home. She was becoming a Zombie. The once beautiful woman was now a night ghoul lurking about for one purpose; obtaining and smoking crack. If you stared really hard you could almost see a trace of prettiness in her face, which is probably what still motivated some to except sexual favors from her in exchange for a few crumbs of "cooked up coke." Deep down inside Lewis still loved his mother but she was far away, gone. All he could do was try to survive the mean streets of New York.

After looking in the mirror at the damage Snookie had done to his face, he wished he'd had the nerve to stab the man. One thing for sure, he didn't want to be seen in school with his black-eye and puffy jaw so he decided to spend the time off replenishing his food supply.

The following day he put on one of his grandmother's old girdles under his clothes and headed for the supermarket. He was able to fill the girdle with fresh meat and small can goods without worrying that it would fall out. After hiding his stash at home he headed to another market in the Bronx before making his final stop at the drug store to get a few items his elderly neighbor had ordered. This allowed him to have a few dollars so that he could spend at the register to cover up his thievery. Once back on the block he noticed Snookie at his normal post on the corner. He gave the ghetto poison peddler a look of pure hate.

"Boy if looks could kill, I'd be dead as Elvis. You must still be mad about that ass whippin' but you shouldn't have jumped me like that lil nigga'. I guess I'd be mad too but I ain't the one who got your Moms on crack. Plus we had a business arrangement that she neglected to fulfill."

Lewis just looked at the older teen sideways.

"You a tough lil nigga' though. I gotta' give you that. You know what? Im'a be the bigga' dude and apologized for our little misunderstanding. Here, put this in your pocket." Snookie held out a twenty dollar bill. Lewis stared at it for a minute before he took it. Lewis knew he could use any money he could get his hands on but he told himself that in no way would the gift change the way he felt about Snookie and vowed one day to pay the dealer back for what he had done to his mother and his face.

A few days later there was a knock at the door. Lewis looked thru the peephole expecting to see Debra coming to crash after a straight week in the streets but instead there stood Snookie looking like a visiting friend. Lewis reluctantly opened the door.

"What's good lil man?"
"Nothing." Lewis responded.

"Listen, I got a proposition for you so you can make some cash. Shit is getting hot on the block and since I need somewhere to keep my stash we can do business. All you gotta' do is hold it till I come for it and I'll hit you off."

That sounded pretty easy to Lewis. "How much?"
"100 dollars a week."
Lewis couldn't believe his ears. "For real?"

"My nigga'." Is all Snookie said before reaching inside his jacket and handing Lewis a plastic bag containing 1000 small vials of crack. "Put it somewhere safe and guard it with your life." As an afterthought Snookie lifted his jacket to expose a pistol. "You need this?"

"Nahhh." Lewis said nervously.

"Cool. See you later." Snookie had no intentions on giving Lewis a gun, he just wanted the youngster to know that this was serious business. A thousand vials at ten dollars a piece was $10,000 and for that amount of money Snookie had to answer to someone else so to let the police find his stash would be a severe loss...

The sixty/forty deal Snookie had with his suppliers was working out well for the street level dealer. The vials were moving so quick that he was going thru a 1000 pack in two days.

Lines had formed on the block for the product and Snookie's bankroll was growing fast. Out of the $12,000 a week he made he only had Lewis to pay a meager $100. After thirty days Lewis was excited about the $400 he had saved.

Since Lewis was still foolishly going on his stealing expeditions he hadn't spent a dime in three months and his $1,200 savings seemed like a lot to a fourteen year old.

On the fifth month Snookie dropped by Lewis' apartment to talk business. "Well lil-L, Shit is boomin'. You turned out to be a soldier so we gotta' step things up for you. You with it?"

"What'cha mean?"

"In addition to the $100 a week for keeping the stash, I'm paying' you $250 to bottle up and a bonus $50 for every thousand vials you fill. Cool?"

"I'm with it."

Snookie reached in a shopping bag and removed a brown paper bag containing a triple beam scale and another containing a block of crack with 5000 empty vials.

This is a $50,000 move so let's get busy. Oh yeah buy the way, make sure you wear the latex gloves I put in the bag with the scale. You don't want to get cracked out. That shit seeps into your pores." He slapped Lewis five before leaving.

Lewis silently calculated the money he'd make weekly which came to $1,400 without counting the $50 for every thousand vials. *Im'a get rich.* He busied himself with the task at hand, working from the time Snookie left until the wee hours of the night, then starting again the moment he awoke. In just three days Lewis finished the 5000 vials. In just over two months he had $6,700 dollars. When he had free time he would count it over and over. School had become a string of no-shows because making money had taken over his life. He had even decided to stop stealing.

When Debra would stop by to curl up on the filthy mattress in her room, Lewis would hide everything but somehow crack heads could sense the presence of drugs, smell it in the air. "Lewis baby. I know you holdin'. Give Momma something." Lewis noticed she was getting worse looking like a skeleton.

"Debra you're lookin' real bad. Why don't you get some help?"
"I know you got something. This my house! I'll call the po-lice."

"You know ain't nothing here. You trippin'." He reached in his pocket and gave her a twenty dollar bill. It was the first twenty bucks Snookie had given him to make amends. "That's all I got so don't spend it on crack."

Debra hurried out the door on a mission for her next fix. Even though she had lost her keys Lewis decided to change the locks anyway the following day.

1985, the crack business was booming. Supply and Demand. At this point Lewis was holding up to two kilos of crack at all times. Snookie had set up a house on the other side of town and hired a crew to bottle up vials and another team to pitch them to the never ending flow of crack fiends. Snookie had gotten too "large" to take the risk and he made Lewis second in command. Over time Snookie had tested him various times and each time Lewis came correct. The younger hustler had no desire to beat Snookie out of anything because he was already making more money than he ever imagined, plus he had developed a sense of loyalty to the man he had once hated dearly.

The following year Snookie brought Lewis deeper into the game by introducing him to the Dominican connection as his little brother. He also gave him a position collecting money so he wouldn't have to handle any product personally.

"You've been down with me from day one lil-L. I love you like a brother."

Whenever Snookie would buy himself something nice like a mink jacket with matching cap, he'd pick one up for Lewis. Snookie purchase a brand new 740 IL for himself and picked up a Bronco for his 16 year old under boss.

Lewis was in charge of a team of young killers who enforced Snookie's policies and dealt harshly with anyone who came up short with the bread. He had befriended a few of the hit men and they would party after business was done, dressed in the finest threads made by "Dapper Dan" and Big truck jewelry designed by "Manny the Jeweler."

With Lewis rolling around in Jeeps upholstered with Louis Vuitton and Gucci interior, he attracted the attention of older females, which he showed little interest in. He had dodged many gold-diggers, choosing to remain in his zone, making money. Seldom had he thought about girls.

By the time 1987 rolled around Snookie had come a long way from peddling vials on the corner and was quickly approaching Kingpin status. To prove it he purchased a home in New Jersey with a view of the Palisades and a red 1986, Testarossa, Ferrari to go in his second level, six car garage, equipped with elevator. Nobody in Harlem had such a ride at the time and when Lewis would borrow the Italian made machine the broads would go wild.

He knew they all just wanted him because of his drug dealer reputation and money. So he continued to shun many request to suck his dick while he shifted gears on the highway at 80 MPH. Some of the rejected chicks even began to spread rumors that Lewis was a faggot.

One day Lewis gathered his crew to help track down his mother. They finally found her at a crack house with her lips glued to a crack stem. She was dragged out kicking and screaming and shuffled away to an apartment Lewis kept uptown, then force fed and held for a week against her will. Finally Lewis took her to an upstate, New York, inpatient drug rehabilitation center where she eventually agreed to submit to recovery. If she was successful, after a 90 day dry-out period she would proceed to a follow up treatment center for another year in Utah. Lewis promised to check up on her to see what progress she was making.

By 1987 nobody barely knew who Snookie was. Lewis was the man to see in the streets. He dealt with the connect directly and made all decisions (With Snookie's approval of course). He had moved out to Jersey to live with his big brother who spent most of his time laying up with one chick or another. He had just celebrated his 27th birth day and it seemed like the older Snookie got the younger his tasted in females got. He was bedding down 16 and 17 year old girls at a rate of four to five a week. On many occasions he invited Lewis to join in on the fun but the younger boy always declined.

"Let me ask you somp'in lil-L?"
"What?"

"You don't like boys do you? Cause it sure seems like you don't like girls."

"Come on man. Quit trippin'. I'm just waitin' for the right one. I don't need no gold-diggin' chick."

"But you need some pussy boy." Snookie laughed from his gut. "Ouuu-boy, you better stop playin' and get some of this young pussy."

"I'm good." Lewis never really understood why everyone acted like being a virgin was a crime. He thought about all the times he heard Snookie in the next room slapping some young girl around because she didn't want to do something Snookie had asked her to do. Some of them would be begging and crying for him to stop doing whatever he was doing to them and he would continue to abuse them. This would always remind Lewis of the time Snookie slapped his Momma and spit in her face because she wanted to stop giving him head.

These thoughts made Lewis stay away from the house for days, only to return to find Snookie with yet another under aged girl. *Why don't that nigga fuck with broads his own age?*

In a way Lewis felt he would be abusing females by luring them with material things to have sex with them. He wanted someone who wasn't concerned with what he had or that he was a well-known drug dealer. He wanted a girl that loved him for him and that he could love for the sake of love. He thought about how corny that sounded which is why he'd never repeat it to anyone.

He certainly didn't want to be like Snookie abusing a constant flow of confused chicks wantin' to lay with the dope man in their attempts to shake something loose. *All they get is fucked and mistreated.*

Lewis' mind traveled way back when he was a small child and would get up in the middle of the night to use the bathroom to find his father and mother cuddling on the sofa in front of the TV. The way his mother looked at his father, you knew they were in love. Their greeting kisses and departing kisses... He was young but noticed every affectionate gesture. He missed the hugs from his Dad and the kisses from his Mom... The day his father was taken away, love ceased to exist. He decided to locate his father when he got the chance. It was a long time coming.

*****

1988-1989, Snookie's drug organization reign supreme. If somebody wanted weight they had to go thru Lewis. All drugs coming into Harlem came from the source and directly thru Snookie's crew. The Dominicans dealt with no one, which meant everything touched Lewis' pipeline. Lewis had pick-up routes from 112th - 129th streets and owned buildings from 130th- 146th streets, spanning east to west Harlem.

148th- 155th streets had remained untouched due to an understanding between some old school cats and Snookie that was forged some years back, however, Snookie's organization had grown and he had the solid backing of the Dominicans to expand, so things uptown were about to change.

148th between 7th and 8th avenues was always packed with customers. The lines to cop drugs were a block long. You would have thought they were giving away free government cheese or something.

"Cop and go! That's right keep it moving. I better not see nobody stopping in this block to get high." The lookout warned the customers after they got received their drugs.

Major's job was crowd control at the entrance. "Keep it moving." While the other two stood in the back of the dimly lit hallway of the tenement building. T-Bone served the addicts while Tank held the 9mm; Problem solver-Bullshit dissolver.

An impatient addict reached the server and requested a bundle. He handed T-Bone a wad of balled up bills. T-Bone sucked his teeth and quickly unraveled them. "What the fuck is this!? You twenty short! Man get the fuck outta' here."

"Come on brother."
"I said break the fuck out."
"Give me some dope or give me my money."

"I ain't given you shit. How many times I told you fiends, no shorts. Now you wasting my time." T-Bone cleared his throat of all phlegm and hawk spit in the addict's face. The thick spit covered his entire eye socket.

T-Bone laughed. "Bulls-eye!" Tank joined the laughter.

The addict turned and limped two steps before spinning with lightning speed. The laughter died in Tanks throat as the Mac-10 spit rapid fire. The first barrage of shells started low, catching the dope-house security guard in the groin area. As the gunman raised the machinegun, hot slugs drew a line along his belly and chest, splitting Tank in half. His head exploded like a Watermelon.

T-Bone stood paralyzed wishing he hadn't spit in the fiend's face. He extended the drugs, hoping this was a stick-up. The first burst of slugs crushed the bones of his hands like toothpicks. The next burst entered his chest cavity and exited his back, fragmenting his spinal cord. Shit and piss rushed to exit his dying body.

Immediately after hearing the first shots, outside, Major cursed T-Bone for firing his gun again to scare off another annoying dope fiend. *That trigger happy nigga' gone have the cops over here again.*

He held up his hand to halt the long line and turned to peer into the darkness. "Yawl fools better stop all that noise before yawl get the block hot!"

The percussion of a gunshot is the last thing he felt milliseconds before darkness engulfed him. He was dead before he hit the concrete steps. He had no idea that his brains had left his head rapidly, splattering against the building, creating a sickening abstract art, known has the ghetto's graffiti.

*****

At the same moment less than five blocks away, Gill was sitting inside his club, Blues Paradise, sipping on Johnny Walker Red, watching thru the picture glass window as Bobo the wino put the finishing touches on his 1976, two-tone, baby blue and white, Rolls Royce, Silver Spirit.

Gill was from the old school drug trade and it had taken him 23 years to make it to the level he was at, selling heroin since his early thirty's. With the arrival of crack cocaine and its increasing popularity he couldn't ignore its profit levels and the horde of jitterbug-kingpins it had spawned.

After selling heroin for most of his life he thought he had seen it all but this crack was turning folks out overnight. The desire to use this drug totally overwhelmed the habit a heroin addict exhibited. Time became no issue to a crack head's pursuit for happiness. They would stay up all night, even weeks at a time chasing their dream.

I really don't like that type of clientele but damn those youngsters are making so much bread. I'll have to find an angle to work in a few crack houses uptown.

Gill peeped at his gold stop-watch. *I wonder what's taking Jake so long.* Jake, one of Gill's two trusted henchmen had gone to the Jamaican restaurant to get his boss a take-out order of Jerk-Chicken with rice and peas. After a couple of early afternoon glasses of brown liquor, Gill was ready to get his munch on.

"Larry give me fifty bucks to pay Bobo." Gill called out to his second body guard who was knocking around balls on the pool table. "I gave Jake my last twenty." Larry reached in his pocket and gave him a Fifty dollar bill.

Gill was loaded but rarely could he be caught with more than a hundred dollars in his pockets. It was a habit he had acquired long ago after getting caught in a robbery at the gambling shack and loosing eight grand to some young punks. If he ever was short for a purchase he would simply borrow money from one of his boys.

Gill owned Harlem from 148th- Dykeman, which was beyond 155th street. He had recently deployed soldiers on the Dykeman side because the Latino hustlers were moving in and flooding his dope areas with crack so there was a small war going on. He was thinking about recruiting some more killers to add to his crew just in case things got bad on the Harlem side.

I remember when everything ran so smooth.... Gills train of thought were interrupted by the sight of a tall sexy female who strutted by in what seemed like slow motion. *Damn.* Gill figured her to be at least 6'1" without her hills. She was wearing a thigh length, black, silk dress with spaghetti straps, highlighting perfect sized breast and a beautiful ass spilling off her slim waist. "Now that's what we old timers call a 'brick-shithouse'."

Larry stood in the doorway as Gill went outside to investigate. Gill figured her to be of West Indian descent. Statuesque is what came to mind. Just as Gill was about to comment on her beauty she dropped a set of keys and bent down to retrieve them. If Gill thought her ass was nice standing erect he was definitely in awe when her behind spread like Texas. Her actions were a calling card to ecstasy. This eye candy was threatening to give Gill sugar diabetes.

Gill's mind started racing then he launched into action. "Excuse me Madame for my regretful intrusion but I couldn't help but notice you from the window of my club. I have traveled across the globe yet still have not encountered anyone with your affect and beauty. Believe it or not, I do not make habit of approaching women in the streets but your alluring quality drew me to you like a magnet. I'm sure your probably propositioned no less than a thousand times a day, however, please be assured my advances are totally sincere. Now tell me how I can become better acquainted with you?"

She looked at Gill obviously impressed by his speaking ability. It was different from the cat calls she was used to: *"Yo' baby come here, Damn Ma you got it goin' on, Can I get the digits!"*

"I don't normally stop and talk to strangers on the streets either, but being you're a business man in the community." She nodded towards Gill's bar. "I guess it's okay." Gill couldn't contain his smile.

"Anyway we can talk and I do need a ride home."

"I'd take you to the other side of midnight if you asked. Just give me one moment." Gill went back into the club and got his 32 revolver, sticking it in his ankle length, calfskin boot. "I'll be cool. Im'a take this devil in the black dress somewhere and save her soul." He winked at Larry. "It should be an hour tops but if I decide to rent a space in her pussy, I'll call. Tell Jake to keep the Jerk Chicken hot."

Gill handed Bobo the fifty dollar bill before jumping into his Rolls.

"I've never been in a Rolls Royce before. Do you tip all the wino's fifty dollars?"

"Only when they do as good of job as Bobo." Gill responded, letting his eyes travel across the smooth skin of her legs.

"Are you sure you're not the President of Zumunda or something?" She asked coyly.

"Actually I'm the President of Harlem." Gill bragged.
"Is that right?"

They came to a stop light. "So exactly how far will we be going?" Gill smiled to himself at his inadvertent use of "Pun".

"This should be far enough."

Before Gill could catch her meaning the blast from both barrels of her small 38 derringer sounded simultaneously, less than an inch from his right temple. The impact blew his brains out the left side of his head before he slumped over the steering wheel in a bloody mess. Just as the Rolls Royce began to roll forward she hopped out and jumped into the black Jeep Wrangler that had been trailing them. They made a quick right turn and disappeared into the concrete jungle.

At the same time that Gill sat slumped in his rolling coffin, leaking his life's blood, Jake, his body guard lay on the floor of the Jamaican restaurant bleeding profusely from the gaping cut in his juggler vein.

With Gill out of the way Snookie sent his shooters on a rampage maiming and killing anyone who had their sights on filling Gill's void. It has come to be known as the Crack Wars of 1990. When the smoke cleared only one kingpin emerged to control Harlem drug trade: John "Snookie" Peterson, lord of the concrete jungle.

Lewis and his crew were ghetto celebrities. When they stepped out all eyes followed. To say they were fly was an understatement. To say they caused fashion crazes was more like it.

It was Friday night and Lewis showed up at Willie's lounge in a brand new crème, 420 SEL, Mercedes Benz dressed in a Brown mink suit with a matching cap and a pair of brown Mauri gator boots with brown mink lining. A big gold medallion with the Mercedes emblem paved in diamonds swung from a heavy Gucci link chain on his neck. When he raised his hand to slap five to some of his associates they were almost blinded by the stones in his ring which read LA, his initials.

LA was the big boss and he never went out without at least two heavily armed soldiers watching his front and back. Most of the time he carried his own .380 in his hip pocket for easy access. There were many rumors circulating amongst the outsiders not sure what to think about the young hustler. Some claimed he was the son of a millionaire, others thought his crew had robbed an armored truck for millions and a few whispered that LA was gay. However those who it mattered to knew he was Snookie, the kingpin's little brother.

Still, there were plenty of females dying to catch LA's attention gay or not and the beginning of **Harlem week** was starting tomorrow and would give them the perfect opportunity.

CHAPTER THREE

HARLEM WEEK

Harlem week is a yearly event held at the State Building in central Harlem, 125th street, 7th avenue. A stage is constructed at the building's entrance and the court quickly fills with people, young and old wanting to enjoy the music. Jazz, R&B and Hip Hop groups perform for a full week of partying. The mature crowd usually were the first to be entertained by Singers like Roy Ayers, Keith Sweat and Christopher Williams. Then the teenage crowd had their show when Doug E. Fresh, Slick Rick, Public Enemy and Ice Cube did their thing. The week was usually topped off with some shooting occurrence making for a memorable event.

Beyond the music court the streets were filled with hundreds of people occupying every inch of the four way traffic intersection. Most of them came to interact with friends to show off their outfits, jewelry and cars. Barricades kept the vehicles from entering the mouth of each block so the parking areas looked like a car show, attracting as many spectators as the music court. Street vendors, weed dealers and anybody else with something to sell found great opportunity to peddle their wares to the massive crowd.

The police presence was heavy, however their job was mainly crowd control. Most of the cops seemed not to be concerned with the pungent scent of marijuana in the air but if someone was stupid enough to light-up in front of them they would surely find themselves being hauled off to one of the police trailers situated around the street concert. There had already been two gun arrest quite early on so they had their eagle eyes out for those who had decided to bring their weapons instead of their dancing shoes.

Some of the rookie cops who had been dispatched from quiet, white neighborhoods to work the Harlem event were surprised by the expensive cars driven by the ghetto youth. During this era they weren't aware that the ghettos were packed with mostly uneducated entrepreneurs driving cars normally only afforded by lawyers, doctors or gangsters. Frowns of distaste could be detected on some of the veteran officer's faces as they watched the young black men and women slamming Mercedes, BMW and Porsche doors, driving around with necks, wrist and fingers draped in expensive gold.

This was Harlem, **1990**, the year of the ghetto kingpin. Even the less expensive vehicles driven by underlings and their girlfriends were barely obtainable with the average cop's salary. Acura's, Supra, 5.0's, Jeeps and SUV's filled parking spots.

*****

Katrina got up early trying to put her hottie outfit together. She knew there would be lots of competition so she would have to dress extra sexy if she wanted to get noticed. Lillian wasn't enthusiastic about the event at all but needed to get out of the house for a change. She had picked up 8 lbs lying around. Katrina had tried to get her to wear some shorts cut extra short but she wasn't having it. She was already feeling uncomfortable with the amount of skin she was showing in the skirt her cousin had altered for her. She even felt a little self-conscience about the few bra sizes she had increased in what seemed like overnight.

They begin the seven block walk from Aunt Barbara's building to 125th. Once they were three blocks down, Katrina took off the knee length skirt she had put on so her mother couldn't see the outfit she really intended to be seen in. The shorts she had on underneath were called "Coochie-Cutters" and were so short and tight around her thighs and crotch area it appeared like she had a camel's foot down there, and her butt checks were bulging from the bottom. She was built like a full grown hoochie. Dirty old men were cat-calling from the doorway of barber shops and their automobiles. Katrina threw back her head and switched her tail as hard as she could. Lillian was embarrassed for the both of them.

They stopped at a corner candy store for snacks before continuing to the State Building. Katrina bought soda and chips while Lillian got a bag of animal lollipops.

The first thing that caught Lillian's attention was the crowd. The only time she had seen so many people in one place was on TV during the basketball games her Dad watched. Katrina was wide eyed about all the shiny cars angle, parked along the street. She pointed to a slim girl with too many gold chains on her neck and a pair of door-knocker earring sitting behind the wheel of a roofless, red Cherokee Jeep.

"I know she ain't buy all that shit. That's why I'm gonna find me a dude with money so he can buy my fine ass one of them Jeeps, Nah, matter fact, Im'a make him get me a mustang with the top down." Katrina leaned to the left like she was driving an imaginary car. "I'm gon be fly."

"Well I'm getting a job to buy my own car." Lillian was a bit taken back when saw a boy half her father's age driving a Benz newer than his. They heard the music blocks away and Katrina proceeded to tell Lillian about the scheduled. "They usually play music for the old fogies first before the rappin' starts so let's walk down to 8th Ave. where the money nigga's are."

Lillian followed her cousin, zigzagging thru the crowd. Guys were trying to holla' at Katrina, some even tugging at her arm but she just threw back her head and kept it moving.

"These are the broke nigga's. It's enough of them on my block. They look like they ain't got shit." Katrina schooled her unconcerned cousin. After strolling around for a couple of hours being fast, the first sounds of hip hop music started Katrina's neck bobbing from side to side. "Come on girl. Let's get over to the court so we can get a good spot by the stage."

Slick Rick and Doug E. Fresh were on stage performing their '80's hit single, "Loddy-Doddy we like to party." Katrina danced in place while Lillian looked on, noticeably unfamiliar with the whole scene. By the time Public Enemy hit the stage the crowd was going wild pumping their fist in the air.

"Don't-Don't-Don't, Don't believe the hype!" Chuck-D led the group as Flava' Flav danced across the stage with a big clock around his neck making funny faces and waving his arms, hyping the crowd even more.

West coast Ice Cube rapper was received wholeheartedly by the east coast crowd as he took the stage next. "Once about a time in the projects, yo!- I damn near had to slap a ho'- I knocked on the door, who is it- Ice Cube come to pay a little visit."

Most of the crowd recited every word, line for line but all Lillian could think about were her mother's words. *That rap music serves no purpose. It's counterproductive and it promotes teen pregnancy, violence and degrades women.*

This was a total new world to Lillian were people were allowed to party in the streets. After a few more Ice Cube songs she was beginning to enjoy herself although not as much as Katrina who was by now grinding against some young guys crotch.

Katrina's ass was like a bee hive with hundreds of bees swarming to taste the honey. After a break in the show Katrina wanted to head to the parking area on the south end. "There might be something we missed over there." A few bees continued buzzing around as they broke away from the court crowd trying to keep Katrina's tail in view.

As they approached yet another area with expensive, shiny cars lining the block, Katrina acted like she was some ghetto guide. "Now this is the real car show. See them guys shootin' dice on the curb? They got real dough."

Lillian barely glanced at the gamblers with hands full of money crouched in a loose circle but she was amazed at the group of police walking on the other side of the street who seemed to ignore the dice bouncing against the concrete. Further up her street there were a group of people crowded around a vehicle and Katrina headed that way to be nosy. She turned and noticed Lillian wasn't following. "Lillian!" She called for her cousin to keep up. What would I say to yo' momma if you got lost?"

They made their way thru the crowd to discover what all the Ouuu's and Awww's were all about. A bright yellow car with its doors in the air like the wings of a plane had everyone in awe.

"Damn that shit is fly. You see it's got wings." Katrina said in almost a whisper. Lillian couldn't imagine what kind of car it was. Spaceship is what came to mind. A guy standing close by was telling his friend it was a Lamborghini Diablo. "That shit cost more than a house. That's Snookie from 132nd. He's a millionaire."

Katrina was from 132nd but had never heard of any Snookie or saw such a car. She strained her eyes to get a close look at the brown skinned man getting behind the wheel of the Lamborghini. He was slim but athletically toned with short, brush waved hair. The white linen short set and thick sparkling diamond bracelet was in sharp contrast to his dark, even, skin tone.

"He's the king of Harlem." The guy continued to fill his friend in on the owner of the yellow, conversation piece. Katrina continued to ear hustle as she gazed at the handsome man and his beautiful ride. A pinky ring exploded specs of light as he gripped the steering wheel, posing like a race car driver.

For some reason her nipples became erect not knowing what to think of the feelings she was having just looking at this man and his car. Boys that interested her in the pass were either penniless or very small time hustlers with no cars. Once or twice someone had given her $20 making her feel special but now she realized how low she'd been playing herself and imagined what a guy like Snookie could do for her....

Suddenly she broke her trance and did her best imitation of a runway model's strut pass the driver's side of the Diablo hoping to catch Snookie's attention. Just to make sure she was seen and heard she turned and walked back to grab Lillian by the hand. "Come on cousin Lele lets go before I pee on myself." She did another walk by with Lillian in tow, this time looking him straight in the eye as she switched pass.

Snookie liked the attention he received from people when he brought one of his toys to the old neighborhood, which spoke of his undeniable success. To him it was like a successful businessman returning to his tenth year school reunion to say, Look at me and what I've accomplished. The first time he hit the release button causing the doors to raise automatically on the expensive car like an eagle in flight, the response he received from the spectator's was exhilarating. He thought to himself. *I should be able to trap some good, young, pussy with this piece of machinery.*

As he sat scanning the crowd for prospects he bypassed most of the gold diggers, imagining they had already been thru the ringer with some of his many, street level, workers who was capable of buying them jewelry or putting a leased set of wheels under their dick-sucking asses. There had been many times in the past when one of his underling's girlfriends had tried to get with him on the sly. Most of the time he'd shun them and report their attempts at deceit to their man, however, on a few occasions when one of his crew was in total denial, swearing that his broad was true-blue and would never do such a thing, specially one who bragged on it:

"My bitch is true to only me." "I got this bitch locked down!" "She's down for my crown."

He took pleasure in fucking and filming the trifling bitch licking his ass or something even more freaky, then playing the tape at the club on projection screen just to bring the overly confident worker down to earth.

Personally, Snookie liked his chicks young. Over the years he had acquired an unnatural taste for teenaged girls. He rationalized that they didn't expect much and did as they were told although it was much deeper than that. He wouldn't admit that it wasn't normal because in the back of his mind he felt he could do whatever he wanted without consequence.

I don't care how much money I stack, I'm not into buying cars and clothes for these lil bitches. As a matter of fact they should be happy just spending time with me.

Just as he was about to go on the prowl in another location for a Tenderoni, Katrina caught his eye. *Damn! Look at that booger with her honey bun poppin' out the back of them pooh-pooh shorts.* When she switched by then doubled back with Lillian that was all he could stand. The look she gave him was undeniable, he concluded. Truthfully he would have liked to have the younger looking Red Bone also that she had in tow but detected fear on her face and thought better of it. *The other lil brown skinned girl is a different story. She's got fast-ass written all over her face.* Snookie, being the pervert he was, if Janet Jackson stood before him naked, he'd opt for the younger Katrina instead. Not wanting to intimidate the young girl he signaled for Milton, one of his boys who was standing close by and whispered something in his ear. The young teen took off in the direction the girls had headed. He didn't have to go far to catch up because Katrina had walked slow as she could, hoping she had been noticed and had no intention of leaving the area yet.

"Excuse me Shorty." Milton called out. Katrina turned, disappointed that it wasn't Snookie stalking her.

"My friend back there in the yellow car wanted to holler at you for a minute." The words were music to her ears.

"At me?" Katrina acted coy.

"Yeah, he wanted to know if you'd meet him in front of the beauty shop on 127th Street in a few minutes."

"A-ight." Katrina agreed. "It's on my way home."

Before the invitation she had no intention on heading in the direction of her house. Lillian had a reserved look on her face as they took off walking.

Lewis who was parked two cars down knew what Snookie was up to because he had used him many times in the past to approach younger girls who felt more at ease with someone closer to their age. After seeing how his so called big brother had treated them he tried to avoid doing the dirty work as much as possible. Once Milton relayed the word that it was a go, Snookie fired up the Lamborghini and headed towards the rendezvous to meet his next victim. *Maybe I can work the lil Red Bone in after all.*

Once they reached the corner of the beauty shop, Katrina stopped to lean against a parked car while Lillian continued walking. "Hold on girl. Let's wait here."

"I'm going to the house." Lillian persisted.
"Why? All I'm doin' is talkin'."

"Well talk by yourself. I'm not getting involved with none of your stuff."

"Girl you know my Momma gon' asked where I am."
"I'll tell her I wanted to leave and you wanted to stay."
"Nah, tell her I went to Tammy's cause they ain't got no phone."
"Okay." Lillian continued walking towards Aunt Barbara's building.

Snookie smiled as he pulled to the curb at 127th to find Katrina waiting patiently for his arrival. He hit the release button and the passenger door slowly raised. Katrina walked over and slid in. He watched as the soft, Italian leather seats contoured with the shape of her round ass. One tap of the button and the door glided back into place before the exotic automobile sped into traffic.

"Hello Bubbles."
"My name is Kat."

"I was just try'na come up with a name for all that... You got it going on with them short-shorts."

Katrina blushed. "What's your name?" She asked already knowing.
"You can call me daddy."
"My father's at home."

Snookie laughed. "Snookie, lil momma."

"Oh. How old are you Snookie?"

"Do it matter?"

"Not really." Katrina tried to sound more mature.

The thought of what he had in mind for the young girl made Snookie's penis rock hard. Not wanting to make the long drive to Jersey, he headed uptown to his apartment on Edgecombe Avenue, minutes from the 155th bridge in an area known as Sugar Hill. He parked in front of the building's canopy and tipped the doorman on his way in. "Don't let the rollers give me a ticket."

Inside the lavishly furnished apartment, Snookie turned on the stereo and began rolling some weed. "You smoke?"

"No." Katrina was visibly nervous now that she was alone with the older man. She realized her past experience was limited to messing around with boys who humped her stuff for no more than twelve minutes flat before running off liked they had conquered the world.

Once Snookie had rolled and lit the blunt he took a few hits before leaning forward to blow Katrina a charge. "Just inhale." He schooled her as he put the lit end of the blunt into his mouth and blew a stream of weed smoke into her face. Not wanting to appear too inexperienced she inhaled deeply. After taking several charges, Katrina was high as a kite.

"Take off your clothes." He ordered, not wasting anytime.

Without question she begin to disrobe. Now standing before Snookie naked, her heart pounded against her chest.

"Turn around." He said more gently. She complied. *Not a scratch or stretch mark on this tender morsel, ass round and smooth. Just like a brand new car.*

After inspecting the merchandise he subconsciously rubbed himself through his pants. Once fully aroused, Snookie stepped out of his clothes. The sight of his large penis didn't help her nervousness. As he continued to rub himself, Katrina hoped he only wanted to masturbate. She had never been with anyone that big. She flinched when he grabbed her arm but fought to remain calm.

"Turn around." He whispered. Once she complied, he slowly bent her over and shook his head when images of a pecan pie came to mind while viewing her stuff from behind. He kneeled behind her and spread her lips like butterfly wings.

She thought her coochie was about to be rammed before she felt his warm breath on the back of her thighs. He placed light kisses on her pootie before allowing his tongue to explore her insides. Moments later she began to relax and enjoy the sensations. Getting ate out was another thing she hadn't experienced with the neighborhood boys. He proceeded expertly until she was shivering in ecstasy. Snookie didn't stop until a mixture of saliva and her juices were dripping down the insides of her thighs. At this point Katrina was so horny that she didn't care if his penis was ten feet long, she needed to be penetrated.

"Are you ready lil momma?"

She nodded in response and Snookie sat on the edge of the sofa, slowly pulling her backwards until her vagina was directly above his pole.

"Ease down, nice and slow." He cautioned her appearing to want to take it easy on her.

Facing away from him, she lowered herself until she felt the tip of him parting her lips. Slowly she went down until she reached her "full-limit" before she raised up and started down again. After several motions she rose up and down at a steady pace, enjoying the feeling. Snookie sat back and let her do all the work until she shook in orgasm. He pushed her off and she thought to herself that it wasn't bad as she expected it to be, almost with a smile on her face until she realized he wasn't finished yet. Snookie laid her on her back and mounted her going deeper on the first stroke than she had lowered herself the entire time she was on top.

"Awww!" She cried out as the battering ram went beyond her full limit again. "Ouch! That hurts." She shrieked. But her protest fell on deaf ears. Snookie picked up his pace causing her to cry out with each stroke. "Awww-awww-awww-awww! Ouuuuuuuuuuuuuuuuuuuuuuuuuuuuuuuu!"

Little did she know that Snookie became more excited with each scream. Pretty soon he was pounding away while he pinned her down to stop her from getting up.

"Please get off." She pleaded but he went deeper. Her insides were in shearing pain. "Oh my god!"

""Bitch! What's my name? Say daddy."
"Daddy."
"What is it?"
"Daddy!" She repeated as tears rolled down her face as he proceeded.

Katrina wasn't sure how long he had been riding her but she knew one thing for sure and that was he had gone well beyond the twelve minutes she was used to. As he continued, she just lay there, having become numb. His sweat dripped on her chest and face until finally, he spasm, jerking and stabbing her insides during his final assault before collapsing, spent. Snookie gave her $100 and dropped her off a few blocks from her house. She could barely walk. It felt like she had ridden a horse or more like the horse had rode her. She could feel a warm sensation in her panties and once she got home she discovered it was blood. Katrina headed straight for the bathroom and took a bath. The warm water stung on contact before it felt soothing. Somehow she dozed off in the tub.

*****

Once Katrina and Lillian had separated Lillian made her way to the house without looking back. Suddenly she wished she had taken heed to the warnings her mother made. As she neared Aunt Barbara's block a car slowed and began honking at her. Terrified she was about to be attacked or kidnapped she peeped in the direction of the horn and saw it was just some guy trying to get her attention so she quickened her pace.

Lewis was headed uptown to his old apartment on 132nd to visit his mother. She had been clean for three years and he had remodeled her crib because she had refused to move away from the area. Debra had won the battle with her addiction but found herself in another fight that threatened to take her life. During the years she had smoked crack and lived a promiscuous life, she had contracted HIV and was getting worst fast. Lewis had hired an attendant to care for her and tried to visit as much as he could.

Just as he was passing 130th street he noticed the slim, Red Bone girl who had been with the brown skinned girl that Snookie had left with. She was sucking on a lollipop and looking straight ahead. When he attempted to get her attention she quickly glanced and kept on walking, paying no attention to the brand new, sky blue, Porsche, 911 Carrera Speedster he was driving. Normally once they saw the car most females put on their brakes to see who was honking. *But not this one. I noticed shorty wasn't impressed by Snookie's $390,000 Lamborghini back at the State Building either. That's rare around here.*

Eager to say something to shorty, Lewis sped ahead of her into a parking spot at the curb and hopped out to say hi.

"Excuse me."
Again she only looked to make sure she wasn't being attacked.

"Hi." He tried again. "I'm just being friendly. Please don't be alarmed. I saw you earlier at the State Building. Your friend left with my big brother."

"Hi." She removed her lollipop and responded out of respect. Although he didn't seem dangerous like her mother had warned, she didn't want to be bothered.

"My name is Lewis. Look can I give you a ride somewhere?" He motioned towards his car. She didn't even look at it. *She's definitely not a material girl.*

"No thank you." She finally said. "I'm only a couple of blocks from my destination. Please excuse me if I seemed distant but I'm not accustomed to talking to strangers and I'm definitely not like my cousin. Pardon me but I have go." Lillian continued her walk without another word.

So that was her cousin. She's definitely in a world of her own. Lewis stared in her wake. *She sounded so intelligent. Damn, that's the type of personally I'm searching for...*

During the entire visit with his mother all he could think about was the girl with the lollipop who wasn't concerned with him or his car.

CHAPTER FOUR

LILLIAN AND LEWIS

Two weeks after seeing Lillian walking home, Lewis was leaving his Moms when he saw the two cousins standing outside of the corner store. He had neglected to ask her name and it was on his mind, hoping he would run into her again. He double parked where they stood and got out, smiling to himself because she was sucking another lollipop. Katrina noticed him first.

"Damn look at that cutie."
He stopped in front of the girls. "Hello Lollipop."

"Hi." Lillian remembered him from their brief conversation. "And my name is Lillian, not Lollipop."

"Oh. I just thought it was cute because you're always eating lollipops."

"Well, my name is Katrina." She batted her eyes but Lewis seemed to ignore her.

"You remember what I told you my name was." He spoke directly to Lillian.

"Not really."
"It's Lewis. Remember now?"
"Yes." She lied.
"Is that your pretty car?" Katrina tried to interrupt again.

Lewis never broke eye contact with Lillian and for once she noticed how handsome he was. Katrina, not used to being shunned, sucked her teeth and spun on her heels to leave. When she noticed Lillian wasn't following she turned and spoke with an attitude. "Come on girl. Let's go." Lillian didn't move.

"You're not from around here are you?"

"No. I'm from Rhode Island. I'm just visiting for the summer." Lillian continued to talk even after Katrina had stormed up the block.

"You staying around here?"
"Right up the street. What about you?"

"I live in Jersey but I come over here to visit my mother. She's sick. She stays on the same street as your peoples, only one avenue down. I knew you weren't from around here because there's something different about you." Lewis smiled. "Something innocent."

"So where do you work?"

"I go to night school. It's hard to explain my situation but I grew up in a dysfunctional setting, so I got into the wrong lane but I'm working on improving myself. Eventually I hope to put all the negativity behind and live honestly... Get married one day. They talked for a while before it was time for Lewis to attend the classes he had signed up for less than two weeks ago. He was studying Business Management.

Lillian had found herself telling Lewis some personal things about her life in Rhode Island because after talking for a while he seemed like a gentleman. What stuck with her most was that he made it seem that she was the only person in the universe. She giggled at the way Katrina acted when she discovered that the world doesn't revolve around her.

*****

After two weeks Katrina's coochie begin to feel better and she was back to her old self having sex with the regular group of boys from the neighborhood but strangely she couldn't get the feeling she once got. For some reason they all were unfulfilling, especially the quickies. She had gotten pass the twelve minute humping and wanted someone to hit it a little harder. She figured she was just tripping but after another week of the same thing she found herself thinking of the day she'd been with Snookie... And, he was glad to hear from her.

"Hello daddy. This is Bubbles..."

Snookie sent one of his boys already in Harlem to pick Katrina up and bring her to Jersey. After what he'd put her thru he knew if she called he had her. The following session was more intense than the last and each time he sexed her afterward, things got rougher and kinkier. Eventually he took her anally and began spanking her during sex until finally she was begging for it. "Harder daddy, spank it!" She yearned for the physical part of their relationship and they had marathon sex every day.

*****

Lillian and Lewis became the best of friends. It wasn't about him trying to sleep with her. It was about respecting each other's feelings and dreams. Lewis knew Lillian had a bright future that came with a set of strict parents and he was willing to wait as long as it took. Lillian had learned even more about Lewis' situation involving his childhood and she felt genuinely bad that he wasn't afforded the same opportunities that she had been. The thought of him losing his mother in the near future saddened her more than anything. They took walks in the park and talked about everything. Lewis finally convinced Lillian to let him replace the clothes Katrina had cut into hoochie gear.

During their nighttime discussions Lillian wasn't just the listener, she now had something to input although it was a far cry from Katrina's wild sex stories.

"I'm telling you girl. He's so nice..."
"How big is his thang?"
"I don't know. Our relationship isn't based on sex."

"Our relationship? Pleeease! That nigga' wanna' fuck just like every other mutha fucka' especially if he's Snookie's little brother. Boy, and if his dick is anywhere near the size of Snookie's, you better watch out cause he gon' rip your little, virgin pussy apart."

"He don't even try to go there..."
"Well he must be fuckin' some other bitch or he's gay."

"He's not gay. He respects my age and everything about me. He even believes a female should wait until she'd married before she has sex."

Katrina laughed like she had heard the joke of the century. "Girl you kill me with that corny ass, Rhode Island shit. 'I'm gonna wait until I'm married.' She mocked Lillian. "Shit. Fuck that! I need me some money and some dick and not necessarily in that order."

"Is that all you think about? Lillian shook her head.
"What else is there?" Katrina asked honestly.
"Goodnight girl."

The following day, Lewis took Lillian to the Museum of Natural History. They held hands as they viewed each display. Lewis remembered learning about dinosaurs from his early schooling because he was amazed by the prehistorically creatures. These were some of the only teachings that stayed in his head. Lillian was surprised at how much he recalled about the archaeologist findings and the periods of dinosaur existence.

"That's a Tyrannosaur." He identified one of the smaller dinosaurs.

Only half listening, Lillian acted on the urge to kiss Lewis on the cheek as he turned to face her.

"What was that for?"
"For being so smart."
"You're the smart one."

They spent the next couple of hours touring the large museum and talking about anything that came to mind. By the time the trip was over, Lewis had admitted to Lillian that he was still a virgin. She was surprised because she was hoping that nothing Katrina had said about him and other girls was true. This was something they had in common that really mattered to her. The look Lewis had on his face during his confession told her that he was being truthful.

*****

During one of their rough sex sessions while Snookie was pulling Katrina's hair as he banged her from behind, he asked about Lillian, out of the clear blue.

"What's up with the lil Red Bone you was with during Harlem week?
"Who my cousin Lillian? She's in love with your little brother."
"Who Lewis?

"Yep. They been going to the library and museum and shit, holdin' hands and makin' plans." Katrina giggled.

"Is that right?"
"Everyday."

"That lil nigga ain't even say shit about it to me. I was beginning to think he ain't like girls. Are they fuckin'?"

"Fuckin'? Nah, not Lillian. She wants to save herself until she's married. That girl is square as they come. I had to make her leave the house the day I met you."

"Yeah. I can see Lewis fallin' for somebody like that. The boy act like he scared of pussy."

"You mean he's a virgin too?"

"Far as I know, unless he and your lil cousin done did the hanky-panky."

"Oh shit. She said he never even tried to get it but I thought she was playin'. I guess they were made for each other."

"That nigga' wouldn't know what to do with a tender piece of pussy like that." Snookie shook his head at the thought of Lillian's untouched goodies. He fucked Katrina harder as images of Lillian played in his head.

*****

A week later Snookie was preparing to have a cookout at his Jersey home for 70 of his crew members and soldiers. He hired a barmaid named Doris to serve drinks and a cook by the name of Hot Sauce Fred along with his brother from a local restaurant in Harlem to prepare the food and man two giant gas grills he had set up in the backyard.

The day of the barbeque arrived with everybody dressed in all white and there was so much meat on the grill, they could have fed a small army. New York Sirloin, T-bone steaks and filet mignon served with southern, sweet, baked, ginger beans, potato salad and a table full of other sides was prepared for the hungry men and women. There was an endless flow of alcohol and weed for those who wished to indulge while enjoying the pool and other activities. Pretty women sat poolside in revealing swimsuits awaiting the evening fun.

By the time the last of the guest had arrived, Snookie's grounds were filled with Range Rover's, Benzes and many other foreign cars. Snookie's second floor garage was full of his own toys, which now boasted an Aston Martin, Bentley and 1969 Shelby GT 500 he used to race at 50 grand a run.

After some good food, weed and champagne, Snookie decided to invite Katrina to his little get together after she called to find out why she hadn't heard from him in a few days.

"Hey daddy. What's good?"

"Listen. I'm havin' a little cookout at the crib and I'd like for you to come over."

"For real? I am kinda' hungry."

"Well there's plenty to eat. I'll send Ed to get you. He's not far from your block, and listen, bring your cousin the Red Bone."

"Daddy. Lillian is not gonna' want to come way out to Jersey, believe me. It's hard to get her to walk to the store with me."

"Listen, I know you can get her to come. I'll tell you what. If you bring her I'll give you a little $500 to go shopping tomorrow and I'll spank that ass extra well when you get here. Tell her Lewis really wants her here."

"You should have him ask her to come then she'll really consider."

"Nah, I want to surprise him. Plus if he has to ask her you won't get the $500."

"Oh alright."
"Call me when you're ready and I'll send your transportation."

*****

"Lillian guess what? Snookie and Lewis are having a big barbeque at their house and since you've never been out there before Lewis wants me to bring you."

"I haven't talked to Lewis since last night. I've paged him from the payphone three times but he hasn't called back yet."

"Well I just got off the phone with his brother and he's waitin' for you over there. He probably don't have his pager with him."

"He never said anything about no cookout."
"He probably forgot because he had to help with setting everything up."
"Well I ain't going way to Jersey unless I hear from Lewis first."

"Damn girl, you act like you can't take my word. We're cousins. Why would I lie? They're sendin' a ride to pick us up but fuck-it. I'll just tell him you ain't wanna see him."

Lillian really wanted to see Lewis and was worried something had happened when he hadn't responded to her page. "Okay let me change my clothes." She decided to go.

Their ride picked them up on the corner of 134th and twenty minutes later they were crossing the George Washington Bridge headed to New Jersey. Lillian couldn't wait to see Lewis.

When they arrived at the house, Lillian expected Lewis to meet them at the door. She looked around nervously at all shiny cars, not seeing Lewis' amongst the group. As they entered the heavy, French doors, Katrina was gleaming like she was the owner of the spectacular home.

"This shit is fly, ain't girl."

Lillian shook her head in agreement. It was nicer than anything she had ever seen. In her presence, Lewis had down played his financial situation even parking his car to ride the train with her but the sight of the house spoke volumes about their wealth.

Snookie met them at the door wearing jean shorts, a wife beater and a pair of white Nike tennis shoes. He led the girls thru the foyer into the living room. Lillian glanced at the high ceilings and futuristic design.

"Welcome to my humble abode." Snookie spoke more to Lillian than Anybody. "Have a seat."

The moment they were seated, Lillian leaned into her cousin's ear. "Where's Lewis?"

"Calm down girl. He's around here somewhere. Look girl." Katina pointed to the back of the house beyond the wall to wall, floor to ceiling, glass windows at the chill scenery. "Everybody's havin' a good time."

"Would you ladies' like something to eat? There's plenty" Snookie's question interrupted Lillian's response.

"I'll have some steak and beans or something. What about you cuz?"
"No. I'm not hungry."

"You sure? --- Well a-ight. I'll be right back." Katrina headed to fix herself a plate.

"Can I at least get you a soda?" Snookie tried to get Lillian to ease up a little."

"Okay. I'll have a soda. Can you tell Lewis to come here please?"

"Actually Lewis had to take care of something real quick. But I'm sure he'll be happy you waited for him." Snookie went in the kitchen and returned with a cold glass of Pepsi.

"Thanks."

Lillian accepted the refreshment. The long drive had her thirsty and she really wanted Lewis to hurry up. Katrina returned with a plate filled with food and a tall drink of Bacardi and coke. "You don't know what you're missin' girl. This potato salad is da' bomb! They had mutha fucka's from Harlem come cook up a storm." She sat close to her cousin.

"Is Lewis here yet?" Lillian said in a whisper.

"You worry too much." Katrina suddenly noticed a change in Lillian. "Hey girl. You alright? Lillian had a faraway look about her.

"I feel funny." she responded.

Katrina's words began to sound faint. She tried to move but for some reason she couldn't. The place in her mind's space was The Twilight Zone.... Lillian awakened with an aching head. Her thoughts were so cloudy that she could barely remember her own name. She had never felt like this before and her young mind could not cope with whatever she had ingested. Thru a movie-like haze she could make out what she thought were voices echoing from the mist. Shadowy figures seem to lurk just a few feet away, waiting to pounce.

Lillian felt cold. Naked. A screech in her brain turned into the shearing laughter of a wicked clown.

"HA-hA-Haaaaaaaaaaaaaaaaaaaaaaaaaaaaaaaaaaaaaaaaaaaaaaaaaaaaah!!!

Changing to a low-pitch growl that sounded like the devil. Twisted, melting images of Snookie's devilish face came into view. A group of his trusty demon's stood behind him hissing with lust. The hot breath on her neck made her cringe subconsciously. She became aware of his mouth on her breast. Just like in her dream; the devil began violating her. *"Noooooooooooooooooooooooooo!!!* She screamed. A sound that never left her mouth as it's bounced around inside her head. *"I'm a virgin! Don't! I'm waiting for Lewis... Once we're married."*

The devil ignored her pleas and continued to defile her. Shearing pain shot thru her vagina. Her lungs felt swollen making it hard to even scream for help. A pressure constricted her chest and the pain increased. Suddenly it stopped but only for a moment before the pressure on her chest returned as well as the intense pain below.

It seemed her brain sensed and felt the pain happening to her body. All she could think about is how bad it hurt. Thoughts of being split in two came to fantasy. The violent probing started to numb her. Waves of pain came and went now. When the devil finished deflowering Lillian, she lay motionless, almost like a lifeless, rag doll, in a puddle of her own blood. She couldn't determine a nightmare from reality. The devil from her dreams had returned to carry out his threat. After all of the foul, degrading things he had already done, He now stood above his victim holding his bloodied penis. "One of y'all help me turn her over. I'm hitting this tail!" After Snookie finished, he motioned for one of the younger crew members to get his turn. Ronald had never done anything like this in his life but didn't want to disappoint his boss, especially at a time like this. He mounted Lillian and tried to perform in front of the group of rapist. Conscious of Lillian's glaze he barked, "What are you looking at? Turn your face." He couldn't finish knowing that he was going to hell... With gasoline draws.

*****

Lewis had been at Harlem Hospital since the previous morning after his mother was rushed to the emergency room in real bad shape. At first he thought it was another low point that she would overcome but this time her lungs had filled with fluid and pneumonia caused her to go into cardiac arrest. Debra Armstrong was pronounced dead less than 24 hrs. after she was admitted, from complications of the AIDS virus. He sat with his mother until eventually a doctor convinced him to go home and make preparations for the burial. Although Lewis wasn't really a drinker, he stopped by the liquor store on the street he grew up on before heading to Jersey. He sipped from the pint of Hennessey as he navigated the Porsche across the Hudson River's draw bridge. (GWB) Still deep in thought, Lewis had forgotten about the cookout until the cars parked everywhere brought his mind back to date. The last thing he wanted to do was party. He decided to let Snookie know about Debra's passing before heading back to the city to spend some time with his girl. *I forgot there's no signal in the hospital so I missed a gang of beeps. Lillian probably thinks something happen to me because I didn't call back. She'll understand when she finds out about Moms. Damn! This is the worst day of my life!*

Lillian could hear a familiar voice. It was her cousin Katrina. "Oh my god! Snookie? Why y'all have to do her like that!"

"What! Lil bitch! You know why I asked you to bring shorty out here. What, you want your $500 now? Well just wait till I finish takin' care of my business first. Now break out! Before you make me angry. Go downstairs and have some fun. I'll be down in a minute." After Katrina left, Snookie proceeded to finish what he started before being interrupted. "I' ma get my 500 worth of this..." Snookie penetrated Lillian's anus.

*****

Music floated from the party area along with the aroma of good food and weed. Lewis had no appetite or desire to kick it with anyone. He scanned the backyard as he approached the glass doors leading to the swimming pool area. Just as he was about to step out, Katrina bolted down the stairs seemingly upset about something.

"Hey Katrina. Is Snookie upstairs?"

Katrina placed her hand over her face trying to gain her composure as she went into the downstairs bathroom without responding. Lewis shook his head. "I wonder what Snookie did to that girl now."

He turned and headed in the direction which Katrina had come. At the top of the stairs he got the urge to turn and leave. *Snookie probably won't even give a fuck about my Moms dying.*

After tapping lightly on Snookie's bedroom door an irritated voice shouted for him to come in. "Damn bitch! I thought I told you..." Snookie was taken by surprise at the sight of Lewis entering the room. Lewis looked at the scene and realized that Snookie and the boys were running a train on some chick. Snookie had pulled his penis out of the girl's behind as Lewis approached. She was lying face down, motionless.

"Damn is she even alive." Lewis asked uneasy. "Shorty ain't even moving."

Realizing Lewis hadn't recognized Lillian in the dim lighting, he attempted to rush him out of the room. "Hey L.A give me a minute. Unless you want some of this. I'll be right down."

Lewis scanned the scene in disgust. As he turned to leave something on the floor caught his attention. He focused on the small white DKNY tennis shoe that looked so familiar. He had taken Lillian all the way to upstate, N.Y to get a pair. A glance to his right confirmed what he was fearing. Lillian's Glamour Girl, jeans outfit was lying balled up on the carpet like someone had peeled it off her in a hurry.

The feelings traveling thru Lewis were unexplainable but rage and infuriation was a start. Suddenly pure hatred rushed to the surface for the man who had once, abused him and his mother... Lillian's innocent face flashed in his mind and he snapped, charging Snookie like a raging bull. "Arrrrrrrrrh!" He yelled. "Why did you touch her!?" Snookie flew backwards. With the weight of Lewis on him he went crashing down onto the television and its heavy glass stand. The impact knocked the wind from Snookie but Lewis began whaling away at his face until he was pulled off by one of the crew. Stunned and bloodied, Snookie struggled to get to his feet until finally two of his boy's guided him to sit on the edge of the bed.

Lewis rushed to Lillian's prone body and turned her over. Tears rushed down his eyes as he cried her name. "Lillian-Lillian." He whispered between sobs. Lillian heard Lewis calling her name. Although the chemicals were beginning to wear off she was still finding it difficult to move. Her vision remained blurry but she could hear Lewis' voice more clearly.

"Lewis." She whispered.

Lewis' crying subsided, hearing Lillian say his name as her eyes blinked rapidly. "Lillian!" He shouted. He quickly retrieved her clothes and began trying to dress her regardless of the blood running from between her legs.

The blast was deafening enough to bring Lillian further from the haze... The weight of something crashing down on her jarred her awake to a painful reality. She struggled to wiggle free, sensing movement around her. Finally when she was able to focus on what was weighing down on her the nightmare she was experiencing got worse... Lewis lie inches away, blood and brain matter oozing from the crater size hole in his head.

The gunshot brought Katrina back into the room to check on her cousin. However, the familiar sound was either ignored or unheard by the partying crowd because everybody continued to jam. Katrina entered the room just in the nick of time... Snookie had raised his weapon and was aiming it at Lillian's head.

"Snookie! Noooooooooooooooooooooooooooooooo!" Katrina screamed.

Lillian was more aware and shaking like a leaf. Snookie looked around the room at the grizzly scene and for the first time in a long time he was indecisive.

"She won't say nothing. Please don't hurt her. If she tells I'll kill her myself." Katrina cried.

Snookie lowered the gun and stared deep into Katrina's eyes, he liked what he saw. "Okay, but I want you to tell me everything I need to know about lil Momma. Her Mother and Father's names, address, job location, the works."

Katrina shook her head in the affirmative. Thirty minutes later Katrina put Lillian in a big, oval shaped, bathtub full of bubbles. Under different circumstances it might have been relaxing but Lillian sat quietly, trembling as her cousin washed her sore body with a sponge. The sight of Snookie entering caused the badly shaken, child to flinch.

"I should kill you for what you saw here today but you have your cousin to thank for your life and because I'm allowing you to live, your parents, the Elliot's, have you to thank for their lives. See if you ever repeat one word, to anybody... The dog, fish nobody will live! The house, those nice cars your people worked so hard for will be gone. I guess you can tell from the way my home looks compared to yours over at 7415 Hamilton Lane that I have lots of money, and if necessary, I will use every dime to get you, if-you-snitch! Do I make myself clear?" Lillian nodded in fear.

Two hours later Snookie had someone drop the girls off in Harlem. Lillian had yet to utter a word to her cousin since regaining full consciousness. During the final stages of the chemical's affects, while Lillian was still paralyzed, she became able to hear... The conversation Snookie had with Katrina about $500 kept echoing in her brain.

Once they made it home, Lillian retreated to the bedroom where she stayed for the remaining two weeks of her summer vacation. She cried every night thinking of Lewis. Amazingly, Katrina continued to see Snookie and acted like nothing had happened. When Laura finally came to pick up her daughter, Lillian hadn't spoken to her cousin in over two weeks.

CHAPTER FIVE

HOME AGAIN

The Elliot's talked about how well their business had gone, having merged accounts with one of the biggest companies ever. "Lillian, you would have been proud of your Dad. The presentation he gave was wonderful."

Lillian had been withdrawn during the drive back to Rhode Island and slept most of the way. Her Mother had commented on her appearance as they embraced after their first summer apart but dismissed it as a climate flu. Lillian lost every pound she had gain over the summer, maybe even a few more. After a few days, her appetite still had not returned. She regurgitated until nothing was left in her stomach to discharge.

"I hope you didn't eat anything from none of those Chinese restaurants. They're known for unsafe food. You might have some type of food poisoning." Laura felt her daughter's forehead to check for fever. "Let me make you some chicken soup and crackers before you take this medication."

The soup and Ginger Ale soda gave Lillian some needed energy and she felt a little better. She actually made her entire visit sound pleasant, up until the point when she got sick.

The medicine made Lillian sleep peacefully for the first time in a couple of weeks, until visions of death invaded her rest... Brain matter sprayed her face as the gaping hole in Lewis' head leaked thick wads of congealed blood. Snookie and his goons laughed louder as the smell of death assaulted Lillian's sinuses. A liquid fire begin brewing in the pit of her belly until she experienced a series of jerks, causing her to spew partially digested noodles all over her face and nightgown. She awoke feeling sick, making the trip to the bathroom a task. Once under the stream of warm water, she proceeded to rinse the scent of vomit from her hair. A sharp pain tugged at Lillian's side before her abdomen tighten. "Arhhh." She let out a shriek before fainting forward, against the shower curtain and onto the floor where she lay until being discovered by her Mom.

Lillian awakened to the smell of starched white sheets and florescent lights. The IV lines running into each arm told her she was in the hospital although she couldn't remember how she gotten there. She was greeted by her Mother's stern stare as she became fully aware. Diverting her eyes slightly left, only to be met her Dad's grim scrutiny.

"Lillian." The words loomed her way. "Your father is devastated! I-We, trusted you to conduct yourself responsibly, but this is unheard of!"

Lillian searched her mind for an explanation of her Mother's statement. She looked back in her Father's direction to find tears quietly running down his face. *Did Katrina tell them some bull?*

"How could our daughter come back pregnant and with a sexually transmitted disease?"

Lillian's heart fell to the cold hospital floor. A feeling of shame coated her face. She could no longer look in her Dad's direction or at her Mother's face. As her Mother continued to speak trying to get information, events played in Lillian's mind like a slide show beginning from the day she exited her Mother's Volvo and ending with the threat from Snookie.

And because I'm allowing you to live, your parents, the Elliot's have you to thank for their lives. Because if you snitch...

Lillian wanted to scream the truth to her Father but instead she began shivering at the thought of them being killed like Lewis. For lack of any excuse, Lillian remained silent which made her appear to become defiant.

"So who was this... person you were with?" Laura was noticeably upset, almost hysterical. After being met with a wall of silence she welcomed the appearance of Officer Held who was from the Sex Crimes Unit to investigate the situation.

"Hello." The black female detective greeted everyone before she spoke directly to Lillian. "Hi."

Lillian diverted her eyes to the floor. She could see her Dad's shoes, shiny-black, and all business. Just as she paid detail to his laces, as if on cue, Robert Elliot turned on his soles and headed for the door. She could read the small words on the rubber taps of his heel. *Cat's Paw.*

"Lillian, my name is Officer, Casey Held and I want to ask you a few questions about your visit to New York but first I want to tell you that there is no reason for you to be ashamed about anything. Now if somebody did something to you, against your will then please tell me... Even if you did consent to some type of contact, you're only 14 and there are statutory implications. I've talked to your doctor and I'm aware of the extreme trauma your body has experienced. Vaginal and anal rupture and extensive damage that began healing improperly so apparently this occurred more than a week ago. Did a grown man do this to you?"

Lillian remained quiet.

"Was it more than one? Because sometimes these young guys...." Office Held had seen many cases in which a young victim was reluctant to talk. Some she knew were ashamed of being caught messing around and felt they were to blame when some grown man violated them, however judging from Lillian's background she had a strong feeling something else was up. The doctor had told her that the young girl would never be able to have kids.

Although Laura was a professional in her line of business, she hadn't a clue about handling drama, of any kind. Here lay her young daughter, evidently having suffered some dreadful occurrence and all mom could think about was that her daughter had did something to cause this... Given away her trust along with her panties and brought back evidence of the evilness... Disease, bastard children, disgrace. To her, the silence re-enforced her suspicions about her child's willful participation. Laura was too embarrassed to be concerned.

Officer Held left her business card. "Sometimes it takes a little time. Call me if she decides to talk."

After the abortion was completed, Lillian was discharged. It seemed her relationship with her parents was scarred for life because of her secrecy about the matter. When she returned to school it was hard for her to concentrate during class. Her teacher's instantly noticed the decline in her work. Lillian would stare into space for long periods and shake her legs continuously under the table. Laura received several concerned calls about her daughter until it came to the point where Lillian was barely making it. She even flunked a class and had to make it up in summer school where she found it hard to concentrate also.

In her second year of high school Lillian was left back. It was like the work had become too hard for her to grasp. At some point Robert Elliot's intellect kicked in, realizing it wasn't as simple as his daughter having crazy sex during her stay in New York. *Something terrible must have happened to my baby.* He tried countless times to get her to talk about it but she would say nothing whenever he asked. Robert cursed himself for allowing his princess to stay with his wife's family, knowing their background. He had called his sister-in-law, trying to get to the bottom of things and was amazed that Barbara claimed she knew nothing. *Bitch!*

The Elliot's sent Lillian to a psychotherapist who helped her with some anxiety but failed to get her to talk about her experience at any length. Robert felt a distanced from his daughter that tugged at his fatherhood. She said little as possible to most people, only enough to communicate.

Eventually, Lillian graduated close to the bottom of her class. The Elliot's dreams of medical school for their child became a nightmare on Hamilton Lane. At this point any aspirations were unidentifiable. The only thing Lillian found comforting were the late night movies on cable. Watching the clever action-adventure, characters who always prevailed was a way for her to escape reality.

CHAPTER SIX

TIME FOR WORK

After high school Lillian attended a community college for two years. The educational spark that she once had as a bright-eyed kid was long gone. Two years in the business administration class and she had enough with school. For a nineteen year old, she had a seriousness about her that said "I play no games." People avoided joking with the young, stern girl.

As time passed, Lillian was able to place thoughts of Lewis in a dark corner of her mind. Over five years had passed since the incident. She hadn't even thought of her cousin Katrina, not even in passing. Some things, she preferred to act as if they had never happened. Eventually Lillian got a job at a small law firm answering phones and scheduling appointments. This was a far cry from being a physician, she thought.

Lillian was polite to the people she worked with, however she kept to herself and spoke only when spoken to. One of the young, single partners in the firm seemed to take an interest in Lillian but after seeing the force field she had up, the tall, handsome attorney backed off. *Maybe she doesn't believe in interracial relationships.*

Less than a year later, bored with answering phones all day, Lillian took a job at the airport as a ticket agent, needing a change of pace; the brief interaction with people in a hurry to get to their destinations allowed her to observe a variety of faces and attitudes. Everybody seemed to have somewhere important to be which reduced the chances of guys sizing her up... Sometimes folks just asked too many questions.

Sixteen months later, at age 21, Lillian moved into a nice one bedroom bungalow, finally getting out of her parents abode and away from the *tension of failure,* radiating... Unspoken by the Elliot's but sensed daily by Lillian. Even if it was all in her mind, she felt her parent's disappointment and had to put some distance between them.

As a show of support, Robert Elliot gave his daughter a blank check to purchase some furniture as a house warming gift. She furnished the place modestly. Once she set in, the most comfortable spot in the house became the bedroom, in front of the television. Watching the news was just as interesting as the action/adventure/shoot-em'-up bang-bang flicks.

She frowned at a report of a serial rapist on the loose. He had already struck four times attacking single women. Although his location of operation was several miles from her area, as a female living alone, she felt slightly on edge. After years of watching gunfights on television and drama on cable, she toyed with the idea of getting a gun for protection. The following day she went to the pet shop and bought a small Scottish terrier with a loud bark to alert her of prowlers.

*****

Lillian felt a heavy hand on her neck, choking her... She gasp for oxygen before trying to pull free. Kicking and whaling away at the air, she was able to see Snookie's face, twisted, laughing. Her cousin Katrina stood close by, bugging him about paying her five hundred dollars for tricking Lillian to his house. The gun blast played over and over in rapid succession until the smell of gun powder and the taste of brain matter sickened her. She cried Lewis' name until she awakened in a pool of sweat. This was the first time in years that she had dreamed of Lewis and all of the tragic things she experienced back then. Heart beating like a kick drum, she got up and headed to the shower where her tears merged with the running water hiding her sorrow.

After what seemed like hours but really only just twenty minutes, Lillian emerged to find her dog sitting in the doorway, ears cocked, searching for the source of unhappiness. Lillian dabbed her tears with the towel before drying off. The mist of steam that accumulated on the door mirror began evaporating, giving full view of her nudeness. She found herself studying the figure in the mirror. Not really having paid attention to personal vanity, she observed the contour of her breast and hips, seeming to suddenly realize her beauty. Lillian gave the woman in the mirror one last stern look before wiping the lone tear from her eye and turning to continue on with her life and pursuit for sanity.

A feeling of... uneasiness begin to develop in the pit of her stomach as her mind unwillingly traveled back to her cousin, Katrina. The blatant acts of betrayal lay dormant, brewing in the same dark corner of her mind where she hid away memories of Lewis' last moments. Suddenly these demons were threatening to come forth.

Katrina's face flashed in her mind. For the first time she felt it was time to assign blame for her situation. *I could have gone on to become a doctor or lawyer if not for that girl's treachery. That stuff really blew my mind... The way they raped me, Snookie murdering Lewis and threatening to kill my family.* The pit of her stomach did a knot twist before she hunched over spewing vomit and hatred all over the carpet.

I fuckin' hate you Katrina! All of you-you bastards will pay one day!!!

Lillian cleaned up her mess, brushed her teeth and went back to sleep. She dreamt about a tall beautiful heroine wearing a skintight, black costume who swooped down on her nemesis, creating a deadly turbulence, like death-on-a-breeze. Her long, silky hair blew in the wind making her face visible. Much to Lillian's amazement it was her.

When she woke for work the following morning she felt like a new person. The gloom that once greeted her each day was gone. During her lunch break she went to a pawn shop and bought a gun. Not knowing much about caliber she pointed to a weapon that closely resembled the one used by the female assassin she saw in an action movie.

"That's a lotta' fire power for a lady. Lots of women choose something small like the 25 automatic or .380. I guess this rapist has gotten everybody scared." The pawn broker made small talk while Lillian said little as possible.

Back at work, her mind traveled frequently to the new package she had in her locker. Did it represent closure for her past? Revenge seemed more logical with each minute that passed since buying the gun. She couldn't wait to get home to touch it.

At the end of the day, Lillian wrote down the information from the bulletin broad and enrolled in a 120 day training class to become a flight attendant. Six months later she secured a slot at one of the big airlines. Soon she was flying the states and seeing new sights. She soon learned that her job required her to stay over in some states between flights, switch planes at a moment's notice or visit several cities in a 48 hour period.

During a layover in Denver, her slot changed, giving her 3 days to tour the state. Whenever she would get an opportunity like that she would rent a car for sightseeing, eventually familiarizing herself with different places. Soon her job became routine.

Most people who traveled on planes were polite, however a few were rude and arrogant. Those were the ones that regarded flight attendants as mile-high-maids. On one occasion some businessman who had too much to drink grabbed her ass before becoming more disruptive, screaming obscenities and calling Lillian a stuck-up black bitch. The plane landed just to have him ejected and arrested.

"Excuse me, madam." A gentleman with a heavy Cuban accent gestured to Lillian. "Is it possible that I have some water with ice please?"

"Sure." Lillian accommodated the passenger with a pleasant smile. "What time do we arrive in Miami"?

"In... exactly 33 minutes?" Lillian peeped at the digital cabin clock above the cockpit curtain. When she looked back towards the nicely dressed, older man she could see him pinning her breast. At 52, Miguel had been in the United States for 22 years. Thanks to his Columbian associates, he lived a luxurious lifestyle and was quite used to having things his way.

"Can I help you with anything else?"

"As a matter of fact there is one more thing." Miguel put his hand on hers. "I think your pretty fingers lack proper adornment. I own a jewelry store in Miami. Perhaps you can come get fitted for something nice. I think you are a very, beautiful woman."

"Do you give all women jewelry because they have pretty fingers?

"Of course not. Not too many times, I see such beauty. I am a very picky man and a very wealthy man with little time to enjoy... I have business which keeps me away. I would like your company... Please. Aside from my offer of a gift, name any price."

"You say you work in the jewelry business?"
"I have stores, but it is the produce of Columbia, coffee beans, sugar canes. The importation business is very lucrative."

He wants an airline call girl. Name any price. Sugar Cane, is this guy serious? Lillian concealed her irritation at being propositioned and remained polite. "You re so outspoken sir."

"Miguel Cosine." He smiled. "If you could be any food what would it be?" Lillian thought for a second. "A lollipop."

Miguel was expecting her to say some type exotic dish. "Hmmm, lollipop. That's nice."

When the question was posed to Lillian a voice came from that dark corner of her head. The name Lewis had given her came forth.

"Any particular flavor?" He smiled. "Well, Madam Lollipop. When my business is complete tonight, I will be in town until morning. Please call." Miguel placed his business card on her push cart. Lillian glanced around the First Class cabin before smiling politely as she walked away. Most of the other few passengers were engrossed in their own business and didn't seem to need anything so Lillian retreated to the break area. Not really knowing why herself, she put Miguel's card in her pocket.

After the plane landed Lillian was told her slot had a lay-over until 8:45 am. She checked into her room, showered, blow dried her hair, and got dressed. Her watch said 11:45 pm. She dialed Miguel's cell phone.

"Yes."
"Where are you located?"
"The LaQuita, downtown. Suite 11204.

Lillian knew from previous visits to Miami that his hotel was several miles from hers. She had arrived by cab in just 20 minutes. Miguel opened the door on the first knock, He was putting on a shirt.

"I didn't think you considered my invitation. But I am glad to see you again."

"We had a lay-over and I slept well before I stated my slot. You seemed like a nice guy... So, here I am."

"Fine." He touched her arm gently. "Please have a seat. Would you like a drink? I'm having Chives Regal."

"No thanks." Lillian remembered the drink of laced soda from Snookie.

After mixing his drink, Miguel walked over and grabbed Lillian's hand kissing it gently. "Relax my sugar cane. I would like you to call me Larose. It is what my close friends call me."

"May I use the restroom?"
"Of course, Presciosa. Make yourself comfortable."

He watched in awe as she headed to the bathroom, the one he thought wouldn't show. Lillian's heart shape behind shimmied in the knee length business suit, well-proportioned on her 5'11" frame and even more statuesque in 4 inch pumps.

Larose couldn't believe his luck when she emerged without her skirt and shirt, wearing heels, stockings with garter belt and a black lace bra, showing her firm flat stomach. In a trick of light, Lillian looked like a Cuban princess to the older man. He was fixed on the silky mane of hair flowing past her shoulders. Letting his eyes savor every curve required him to take a deep breath. After only two glasses of brown liquor, Larose was convinced Lillian was more beautiful than the young Columbian girl he had stashed away in a Paradise, Villa.

She sat looking up at the now bare chest man who was brewing with pure lust. For a man in his fifties, Larose was in tiptop shape. "You're a bad girl. You're gonna be my bad girl" He kneeled between her legs and took a big whiff. "Ah, candy. I'll lick it like a lollipop." Starting from the knees, he placed small kisses on her thighs making his way to the honey pot. On his approach, her legs opened in slow motion like the pearly gates of heaven. He kissed the fabric over her crotch before moving the G-string aside to reveal his treasure. Once her goodies were exposed he went at it like Peach Melba. His experience had him hitting all the right spots and no matter how much Lillian tried to stay focus, asking herself what the fuck she was doing there, she found herself drifting into pleasure. Succumbing to the oral attack, Lillian spread wider. Sex wasn't a familiar routine and she didn't have the control she knew she needed. In a crazy way this angered her, however at this point she didn't have the power to put an end to it, she was on her third, rolling orgasm.

With both hands on the back of his head she pressed herself against his face, riding the waves until she shook in ecstasy. Spent, she batted her eye trying to shake the last tremors. Larose felt the vibrations of her orgasms and tasted the flow of her juices, swallowing every drop. He smiled to himself, knowing he had hit her g-spot. When Lillian opened her eyes after an extended blink, she found him standing above her, his penis inches from her lips. "My turn." He squeezed his hard penis causing pre-cum leak from his head.

Although she enjoyed what he had done she cringed at the thought of putting his penis in her mouth. "Maybe we can finish another time." She realized that he may want to have intercourse also and cursed herself for going this far.

"Nonsense. That was just an appetizer. We still have the main course and dessert of course." Seeing she made no move, he grabbed the back of her head, gently at first but the sticky fluid left on her cheek made her pull away. That's when he got a firm grip on her long hair, twisting it sideways in his fist. "Now is not the time to change horses in the middle of the race. I know you like what I did with my mouth. Now you return the favor. When Lillian appeared to resist opening her mouth he squeezed her jaws together, forcing her lips apart. "Just put it in your mouth. You'll like it. I promise." He closed his eyes in anticipation. When he felt nothing his impatience was evident. "I want your cooperation!" His grip tightened.

"Let my hair go. Ok-ok, take it easy. Let me do it my way." She cupped his testicles. "Let's get in bed at least." He released her hair as she guided him into the bedroom by the balls. "Lie back." She pushed, gripping his now throbbing penis firmly. Larose closed his eyes after feeling the first sensations from her lips. "Yes my Lollipop." He chanted as her slim fingers glided up and down the length on his organ. "Put all of it in your mouth." He demanded. The pain was so excruciating that at first he thought it couldn't be real. The type of sharp pain that numbs before the nerve endings flame up. Blood squirt from the incision Lillian made from the shaft to the head of his penis. The shriveling organ looked like a hot dog split down the middle and shrinking fast in a hot frying pan. He sat up like an ejecting "Jack in the Box". Lillian moved with the speed of a frightened cat, slicing his throat with one swift stroke of the rug cutter. His scream was cut short and replaced by a gust of wind exiting his juggler vein along with a pint of blood. Lillian could hear a gurgling sound as he drowned in his own blood.

She quickly showered and dressed. After wiping anything she may have touched off, she did a last check on Larose. He didn't move. On her way out of the room she noticed a brief case behind the door. Taking a step back, she bent and picked it up on her way out.

Once she was back at her hotel, safe and sound, she took a deep breath, aware that she wasn't affected by what she had done like she should be. Instead she felt sly like a spy from her late night movies. Lillian took a long bath before sitting on the hotel bed to see what she had picked up. The combination was set on its open position so breaking it wasn't necessary. When she opened the case, she didn't know exactly how to respond to the even stacks of $100 bills staring back. There were sixty-eight, ten thousand dollar stacks. She stuffed the money in her travel bag and got some sleep. The following morning, she was on a flight to continue her weekly slot before touching down home.

CHAPTER SEVEN

NEVER LOOKED BACK

Katrina turned off 8th Ave onto 114th street and navigated the new, cocaine white, convertible, Jaguar XK into a waiting parking spot. She exited the vehicle without letting up the top. Everybody knew she was Snookie's and that said it all. The princess-cut diamonds on her finger sparkled as she gave a chick high five on her way in the building. Dressed in white from head to toe, the Prada, jean suit, jacket and boots made broads envious under their smiles. She put the keys in the lock of her chill-out-pad which was in Harlem but decorated like a five star suite. Actually, she lived in a seven hundred and fifty thousand dollar home in Westchester County and had two other expensive vehicles in her garage.

Being with Snookie since age sixteen put Katrina in the position she was today. It had been around the age of nineteen that Snookie got the hunger for something younger but instead of dumping Katrina he kept her around. She became even more helpful for his lust, recruiting a string of young, dumb, teenage girls for his dark pleasures.

Bambi was sitting on the sofa, watching cable and eating ice cream. "Hi Kat."

"Hey girl, get ready. We're going over to Edgecombe to meet Daddy." Katrina had been grooming the young girl for three days preparing her for Snookie. They all liked the cars, clothes and jewelry and hoped that if they please Snookie they could have the same. At least that's what Katrina told most of them. There had been so many at this point she lost count. Most likely, she was still around because of what she had experienced long ago with Snookie and Lewis... and Lillian. Her recruiting skills were also a big part of her success. No sooner than Bambi was dropped off, Katrina ran into another young chick in Burger King on her way home. She decided to get another one ready so she wouldn't be pressed if Snookie didn't like the last one. "What kind of car is that?" The young girl asked.

"A Jag. Why, can you drive?"

"Naw."

"Wanna learn?"

"For real?"

"What's your name?"

"Candace."

"How old are you Candace?"

"Fifteen."

"I learned how to drive when I was fifteen." Katrina lied.

"Where do you live?"

"Around the corner with my crazy Aunt. She drinks all the time."

Katrina noticed she only had a couple of cheap items. "Get whatever you want. It's on me." The teens face lit up as she went to place another order. "Want to hang out?"

"Heck yeah!"

After rolling like they were the best of buddy's, Candace found herself at Katrina's chill spot, smoking blunts and listening to the new CDs Katrina bought for her. "Thanks, Katrina."

"Call me Kat."

"Dog, I wish I could stay here."

They all do. Katrina smiled to herself, which is another reason she kept a steady flow of girls for Snookie. She didn't want him to get attached to any one, like he had with her when she was younger. So far Snookie's been using and discarding them at a steady rate for several years now. The most powerful drug dealer in New York, rarely could be caught outside his Edgecombe condo or his Jersey Mansion. Most of his time was spent in bed with some young girl. Snookie had made it in a game that rarely saw long term success. Not having touched any drugs since recruiting Lewis years ago and dealing with would-be snitches swiftly was part of reason. Paying police off also had its benefits.

Not only was recruiting part of her job but the job description also required her to make sure none of the teens that were kicked to curb made any fuss that could harm Snookie. It was possible the drug lord was grooming her for her present position even way back, when he paid her $500 to bring him her own cousin Lillian.

It had been a year since Lillian had the incident with the Cuban drug dealer, Larose. Nothing came back to her and the money was collecting dust in a storage bin at the back of her closet.

Simply, her present lifestyle didn't require a lot of money, however she had some vacation time coming and she wanted to visit some people... She was surprised to remember the number. Aunt Barbara sounded the same. "Lillian? It's been so long. Girl, I still don't know what happened. Your momma ain't spoke to me since, and my daughter claims she don't know what happened to this day. So how you been?"

"I'm doing fine. I work for an airline as a flight attendant."

"Oh, that's sounds nice. Katrina would love to hear from you. You should give her a call."

At the rate Katrina was going back then, Lillian was half expecting to hear that her cousin was somewhere laid up with ten kids or on drugs or something. Instead she listened to Barbara brag about the million dollar home, three foreign cars and the full length, mink coat Katrina bought her for her birthday.

"Yeah her and her man started some internet business and she just kept it up." There was pride in each word. It reminded her of the pride her parents used to have when they spoke about her grades... In the past.

"Wow. I'd like to see her." Lillian jotted down Katrina's number and wrapped up her conversation with her Aunt. After thinking about the whole situation, she wasn't too happy about the outcome....

Hearing about Katrina's success did something to Lillian. It wasn't jealousy, but something much deeper. She had a strange feeling this boyfriend was no other than the person who was responsible for all her pain. "Snookie." She wanted to heel kick Katrina to the chin like she saw Foxy Brown do to a cat in a '70s Blaxploitation movie on the late night. The thought of Katrina's prosperity after what she had did made Lillian want to cringe. *It's like she stole my life from me.*

Katrina had a steady stream of Cats that she used for her own pleasures. It had been years since Snookie had touched her. Even so, she would never be as disrespectful to fuck anybody that would possibly know Snookie or any of his associates. Carlton, her new fling was imported straight from the Virgin Islands. She had met him on one of her earlier visits working in one of the seafood shacks where she had eaten. He was poor and shirtless but packed a hell of a punch, she thought while making reservations for his second trip to the States. Even though she had to supply everything necessary to enjoy his company it was worth being discrete and maintaining an outward look of loyalty to her boss. By now Carlton was feeling like a Gigolo having bragged to the guys back home about his sugar-momma in the United States. It hadn't dawned on him that his buddies saw him as a sucker because he had come back broke and still shirtless.

Carlton thrust, deep as he could intending to keep up with Katrina's request. He knew from his last visit she likes it hard. Every muscle in his body tensed as he prepared to cum.

"Yeah rude boy!" She screamed as her juices met his... In mid pump. "Damn." she thought. I had to go way to ST THOMAS to get fucked like this.

Carlton wanted to put in work on Katrina, hoping he could earn a permanent spot in her pussy and her home. However, she had no intention on even letting him stay the weekend. Her plans involved freaking off with some cat she had met at the parking garage. Even now she was making mental plans for the meeting when the phone rang interrupting her train of thought. She rolled over catching the phone on the last ring.

"Hello."

Lillian almost hung up before hearing the women's voice. "Hello. May I speak to Katrina?"

"Speaking. Who's callin'?"
"Hey Cousin."
"Who dis?" Katrina ask almost already knowing.
"Lillian."

"Get the fuck outta here. Girl I thought I'd probably never hear from you again. Where you been?"

"In Rhode Island. Where else?"

"I thought you might have moved away, somewhere like Miami. Operating on peoples brains, at Jacobi Hospital or somethin'. You were always on some smart shit.

"Naw, I wound up not going to college. I'm a flight attendant for a big airline."

"Like a flying waitress." Katrina couldn't help saying.

"I guess you can call it that. It's not bad because I get to travel everywhere."

"Yeah? My friend here flies back and forth from the Virgin Islands. Maybe you can hook me up. Anyway you should come see me. I'm doing my thing, girl"

"My vacation starts tomorrow. It's been ten years..."

"Damn. Ten years? It don't feel like it's been that long."

It does to me, Lillian reflected. "Well I guess I'll be seeing you soon, Cousin."

"Do you need me to pick you up?"

"No, that's alright. Just give me your information and I'll call you when I'm on my way."

Lillian went to visit her parents after staying away in her own little world. She always felt she had disappointed them. They were glad to see her, seeming to act like nothing had ever happened. She told them about the traveling she did on the job and the many cities she'd visited. After a few hours of family time, Lillian was ready to head to New York... for what, she wasn't sure.

Before leaving, she hid a gym bag containing $600,000 deep in the back of the closet in her childhood room, which still looked as it did when she was a kid. The remaining $80,000, she planned on using during her vacation...

The plane ride from Rhode Island was barely 45 minutes. Shortly, she found herself sitting in a cab in front of Katrina's house. The Westchester County home sat far away from the curb with a beautify manicured yard and a ten foot, makeshift, stone torso of a man peeing into a bowl at center stage. Katrina was living very upper class, quiet and serene.

Wonder what the neighbors think about that. Lillian thought has she approached the white French doors. She began to have sudden shaky feelings, threatening to overcome her, thoughts that brought about bad memories of the past.

Lillian felt deeply in her heart that if Lewis' life hadn't been stolen away, that a beautiful home, filled with beautiful children, would have been their reality. She took a deep breath before ringing the doorbell. The door flew opened. She was greeted with hugs and kisses. "Lele! Come on in, Cuz." It was obvious that Katrina had long forgotten what had transpired between them.

"Let me help you with your things." Katrina grabbed the bag containing the cash and tossed it in the corner of the foyer. "You can leave your bags there for now." She motioned in the direction of the gym bag. "I'll have Carlton bring them in on his way out."

"You have a Butler?"

"Oh naw. He's my landscaper/freelance dick, straight from St. Thomas, Virgin Islands. "I'll tell you about that later." she winked

"You're still something else, aren't you?" Lillian took in the modern décor and comfortable living accommodations. "Wow, this really nice."

Maybe Katrina shook Snookie after all and really did become successful at some internet business. She mention a Carlton. So far no sign of Snookie. Wow, if she was able to pull this off...It really highlights how short I've fallen. I can't let her think I'm hurting for anything.

They sat on a plush sofa catching up and talking mostly about Katrina's shopping exclusions. Like always, Lillian let Katrina jump from one exciting tale to the next. No longer the naïve child, she listened closely, however, nothing in Katrina's dialog struck her as being business orientated. She wanted to ask Katrina about her success but thought against it, not wanting to seemingly pry.

Katrina, at 5'5" was still fine, but having money to splurge made her feel bigger than life. Somewhere deep in the back of Katrina's mind she knew she was responsible for delivering her young cousin to a sex fiend for $500. She had long ago, mentally, painted-over that canvas with the many young girls she had delivered to Snookie in the past ten years... *Lillian probably thought I would be broke with a house full of kids or a junkie or something. I bet she's trying to figure this shit out. A damn airline attendant. I thought this bitch was gonna be a doctor.*

"What's in them suitcases? Granny panties and ankle length dresses. I'm almost afraid to look."

Sure that Katrina would respect and even like her taste in clothing, she opened her suitcase and began showing Katrina a few items.

"I like that. But this!" She pointed to one of Lillian's favorite shirts. "What's wrong with this? I like it." Lillian protested.

"And this." She snatched up another garment. "Where you gonna wear that?"

"Okay. Leave my stuff alone."

"Don't make me go get my scissors." Refereeing to the time she cut all Lillian's cloths into hoochie wear. Lillian declined anything to drink but Katrina was on her fifth flute glass of champagne and was feeling a lil tipsy. "Let's make some moves." Katrina intended on taking Lillian shopping, feeling her cousin couldn't afford to shop expensively, she wanted to show off a little by footing the bill.

They headed out into the garage through a kitchen side door where Karina kept two cars. The girls entered the white on white Jag just as the garage door begin to raise. "What kind of car is that?" Lillian nodded towards a vehicle with a cover on it.

Katrina almost said, that's Snookie's car, before she caught herself. "That's my Sunday car, when I want to get religious on folks." She lied knowing she wasn't allowed to touch it.

"I've been saving for a car. I figured I'd have enough time during my vacation to find something nice. Where do you buy cars...?"

"I copped my Jag from COLERIDGE EXOTIC CARS, but their prices are kind of' steep. But we can go to this used car lot in Queens tomorrow."

They wound up downtown at the Gucci store. Katrina was surprised that Lillian insisted on paying for her own things.

The following morning, after breakfast, they dressed comfortably, Katrina wearing items she'd purchased the day before, a bright, white, short, skirt-set looking like she was on her way to Wimbledon. Lillian kept it simple with jean shorts, form fitting tee and sandals. As usual Katrina's goodies were attempting to breech the seams. Her boobies, were saying, Here we are..................

"So what did you have in mind? A Civic, or how about a Camry?"
"I was thinking something more like your car or maybe a BMW."

"I mean I can take you to our- my spot, but I'm telling' you, they're not cheap. Even the pre-owned cars..."

"Let's see what they can do for me."

"Alright. We have to head to Pennsylvania to Coleridge. It's about three hours away." Katrina got on the highway heading towards the New Jersey Turnpike. *I guess she gotta see for herself. I know she can't afford to roll nothing from here on her air-maid salary. There's a used car spot about five miles from where were going. She'll probably have to grab something from there when it's all said and done.*

Once they arrived at the showroom they were greeted by a tall, white salesman wearing an expensive suit. "Is Xavier around?" Katrina asked, not recognizing anyone.

"Ah. He's busy closing a big sale and won't be available for a while." He lied not wanting to blow a commission. "Don't I know you?" the salesman continued to reach.

"We bought a lot of cars here, I usually deal with Xavier."
"I thought I recognized you. What can I do for you today?"

"Well." She leaned in to whisper. "My cousin was looking for something... Affordable. She works at the airport...Where are your pre-owned options?"

The salesman interpreted it as a potential waste of his time. He glanced over at Lillian who had headed towards a row of brand new Mercedes Benz'. He rolled his eyes having become used to selling cars to people whose only problem is choice of color, not price range. "You know, maybe I should run and find Xavier for you after all. His sales team also heads the pre-owed section and should be able to give you much better assistance. Just give me a moment." He headed in the direction of the employees office, knowing good well Xavier was on vacation.

Lillian was mesmerized by a powdered blue 4-door Mercedes Benz sitting in line with a matching red, black and white one. But all she saw was light blue. The butter soft, leather seats, white with sky blue piping seemed out of her reach. Katrina appeared by her side.

"Let's go wait for Xavier in the customer lounge. I need a bottle of water. Damn! I like that white Benz." Katrina popped open the door and sat behind the wheel. "I'm bout to get me one of these next year." She bragged.

"I like the blue one." Lillian insisted

An older, pretty, black woman approached smelling like $60 an ounce. "I love that fragrance." Katrina chirped.

"Thank you. It's Opium. May I be of some assistance to you beautiful, young ladies?" Verona was finding it hard fit in at Coleridge Exotics since being hired 3 months ago. She was learning that most rich people were biased when it comes to dealing with women and expensive cars. Actually, she was being polite about her approach. She didn't actually believe the young women before her could do anything to help her sagging sales. When you're asked to do jobs outside of your title and pay grade, it's only a matter of time before you're let go... For the second time this week, Verona had been running back and forth between the parts department and mailroom.

"Thank you, but we're just looking here. My cousin needs something more used."

"I see. Well, how about something like a used Volvo wagon."

"How much is this one?" Lillian pointed to her dream car. Completely ignoring her cousin.

"Oh. Umm, let me see." She calculated by memory almost like clockwork. $68,909, including tax and title."

Katrina wanted to tell Lillian to stop wasting everybody's time.

"I'll take it." Lillian said, without blinking.

Verona did a double take checking the seriousness of Lillian's face. She looked all business.

Katrina still wasn't sure of what was going on... *I know this bitch can't afford this car.* Something about Lillian having a car two years newer didn't sit well with her. Even as Lillian followed Verona to her desk, Katrina was still skeptical. However, once she saw Lillian reach in her bag and pull out a stack of bundled hundreds she was suddenly overcome with envy & jealousy.

Verona agreed to submit the cash in a manner as to not alert the IRS, happy to have snagged such a nice commission. At the conclusion of the purchase, Lillian handed Verona a wad of 50, one-hundred dollar bills under the table. Delivery fee was included so all Lillian have to do was wait the following afternoon. "You're rolling for real now?" was all Katrina said the entire ride home. She was too busy trying figure Lillian out.

Back at the car spot Verona ran into Harold on the way to the financial office. "Damn. You made a flat-out sale. I must have been crazy to sneak off for a long lunch." *There's no way she would have made that commission if I was here.* He was actually pissed that Verona made a sale at all. "Whose arm did you twist, some senile old lady with a blank check?'

"Actually, when I returned to my desk from the parts department, you were talking to the customers."

"What customers?"
The two, young black girls."

"Whoa. They bought a Mercedes?" A pure feeling of ass-hole-ides ran across his face. "Fuck!"

Verona was more than happy to deliver the good news to the smug car salesman. *Damn creep.* She smiled to herself as she thought about the tax free, five grand in the bottom of her purse.

The following morning, right before noon, a flatbed truck arrived with Lillian's car. The beeping sound of the truck's reverse indicator, awaked Katrina from her slumber. She planned on being a little nosey today. *She had insisted on paying for her own clothes even after I offered...* When Katrina emerged from the shower, Lillian had already prepared them a small breakfast.

"I see they dropped off your vehicle." Karina said between bites of toast. 'You're gonna have to take me for a ride in that baby." She had never seen anyone make a straight-out purchase like that except Snookie. *There's something she's not telling me.* "Damn shit must be really good for you at the airport." She began to pry.

"I've been saving forever, it seems. Over the years Daddy's been funneling the money that was supposed to be for my college education to my bank account. I never touched it." She lied. "My life is very simple. My paycheck takes care of all my needs."

Knowing the Elliot's had money, Katrina was satisfied with her answer. "Shit. Ain't you glad you didn't go to School?"

Lillian was thinking that with grammar like that, there was no way her cousin suddenly launched a scheme of grand entrepreneurship. "Look at this house girl. You're the one doing great, big, things. Tell me about this business you started." Now it was her time to pry.

Katrina realized she had opened the door for the early morning inquisition. Not daring to credit anyone for her good fortune she built onto her previous lies. "I got the idea to start a referral service. There are lots of aspiring, young, black girls in financially challenged areas that can't find their way... There are powerful entities that control wealth and exposure. I bring these elements together. Magazines, TV Studio's, you name it.

Adult films, Movie extras... with the help on the Internet, everything just took off."

The truth was, everything belonged to Snookie. Her Jag was a four year lease. Her spending money was based on how happy she could make Snookie by recruiting young girls for his sick fetishes. Although she had been able to remain relevant, a little voice constantly reminded her over the years that it all could come to a screeching halt one day.

As Katrina spoke, Lillian let her words process. She could feel the untruthfulness lingering. She hoped the look on her face didn't expose her true feelings. Voices from long ago entered her thoughts as she tried to concentrate on the future. 'You knew what I wanted when I asked you to bring little mama over... Here's your $500...' Snookie's voice was burnt in her mind. *Referral Service. Yeah fuckin' right! We'll see.*

The phone ringing interrupted Katrina's web of lies. Her mood automatically changed as she headed into another room to speak in privacy. When she returned, she sighed as if she were tired, having just gotten out of bed an hour ago. "I have to make a few runs." Katrina went into her bedroom to get ready. Lillian grabbed the phone and quickly glanced at the New Jersey number, memorizing it instantly. *Most likely, Snookie!?*

"Oh yeah. If a fine chocolate guy shows up, let him in. That's my boy-toy, Carlton." Katrina stated on her way out.

*****

Snookie was anxious for some fresh-meat. He was becoming more & more impatient. To keep up with his demands, Katrina begin setting up young girls in advance. She sped towards Queens where she had stashed the latest victim. Her mind traveled back to Lillian and the way her cousin just popped up and upstaged her. She felt her success had a watered down effect on Lillian because she was expecting her cousin to be broke. She began trying to figure out how she was gonna convince her boss she needed to upgrade her driving situation. She called ahead. "Diamond. I need you to be ready... I'm on my way...

Remember the guy I told you about? It's time..." Katrina knew all the promises she made to her young victims helped convince them to agree to meet Snookie. The only thing they ever got was abused. Over the years there were only a few close calls. However, the young victims were kept so confused about names and locations that nothing became of the complaints. Katrina was so convincing that they thought when it was said and done that they too would have a house, cars and unlimited cash to spend. After being spoiled by Katrina prior to meeting Snookie, they were ready. Katrina had been lucky. She was coming to the realization that if it hadn't been for the incident with Lillian that she may have still been back in Harlem, living with her Mother.

The moment Katrina's car left the garage, Lillian headed to her bedroom to look around. She searched every corner, finding nothing specifically incriminating. There was three thousand in cash in her underwear drawer and a thick leather diary. Reaching for the book, she thought, hard habits are hard to break. She removed an earring and picked the lock like a champ. Lillian reclined on the loveseat and began reading... Her heart raced as everything came to light. She was seething with pure hatred as she read on about Katrina and all the young girls she had played on... delivering them to Satan. *Like she did me!* Fighting to control the firestorm building within her, she was overcome by a surge of self-empowerment. All the resentment and pain of what had happened to her as a child no longer threatened her future. She regained her composer and finished reading. On the back page, bottom, corner, she noted a username and pass code. Lillian booted up the computer. After entering the info she went into the personal files and located pin numbers, pass codes and other personal things. Katrina used the same pass code for her email Kattscan@aol.com, and everything else that required one. *SNK. That's got to be him.* Lillian wrote down every address and number associated with the initials.

*****

The doorbell caused Lillian to get out of the shower before she really wanted to. "Katrina must have left her key." She quickly wrapped in a towel and headed for the door. Startled to see the handsome, young man in the doorway, she almost slammed it in his face but didn't want to obstruct the view. *He's fine as hell.*

"Hello." She chimed. Figuring this was Carlton. "Katrina told me to be on the lookout for you. I'm her cousin, Li--, Lollipop."

Carlton finally broke his stare and extended his hand. "Glad to meet you. I'm Carlton." Lillian shook the tip on his hand noticing how smooth they were. She turned and headed to get dressed with Carlton following. He was transfixed on Lillian's sexy, long legs. She could feel his eyes on her back as she disappeared into the guest room.

Lately, he felt things were changing between him and Katrina. She showed less concern each trip. In the beginning she would pick him up at the airport and wine & dine him. But now he has to cab-it, laying up a few days, no more shopping sprees and dinners... Then it's back home with barely enough rent money. As of lately, he wasn't feeling like too much of a gigolo. He felt more like he was getting played out of a lot of dick.

A women's voice calling his name brought his mind back to present. He followed it down the hallway into the guest room. "I don't mean to disturb you but would you be kind enough to put a little moisturizer on my back."

"I don't see a problem with that." Carlton couldn't believe his luck. In direct contrast to Katrina's short frame, and bulging goodies, Lillian stood close to 6ft tall in a pair of 4 inch heels. She held an air of confidence that made her appear statuesque. Lillian let the towel drop to the floor exposing her flawless, redbone body. "Kat never mentioned having a runway model for a cousin."

She turned allowing him to apply the cream to her back. He massaged it in gently, eyes transfixed on her beautiful figure. "Why do they call you Lollipop?"

"Why don't you find out for yourself?" She sat on the edge of the bed, opening her legs wide in an inviting manner. Without delay Carlton dropped to his knees and ate greedily, her sweet nectar. Lillian had multiple orgasms drenching his face with cum. No longer able to wait, he was ready to feel her warm insides but Lillian got up and headed for the shower.

"Wait, let me finish..."
"You already have."
"Huh." He looked puzzled

"Now you know why they call me Lollipop." She disappeared in the bathroom.

"Damn!" Carlton cursed his hard dick. He would have to wait on Katrina to get home.

Lillian quickly dressed and left, missing Katrina's arrival by only a few minutes. She spent the entire day driving to each address connected to Snookie's initials, documenting the locations. In Harlem there were two other apartments besides the Edgecombe address, and a high rise on the lower eastside of Manhattan. In New Jersey, Lillian became anxious as she approached the Fort Lee home where Lewis had been murdered and she was raped, 10 years ago. She struggled to maintain her courage. One flash of Lewis' image was all she needed to stay strong. The last was a home not far from Snookie's mansion. It's was in an upper middleclass neighborhood much like the one she had grew up in. *I wonder what Satan has going on at all these locations. Most likely this is where he violates his victims. Wouldn't be too smart to bring them to the mansion.* The location that really interested Lillian was the one in the quiet neighborhood just 4 miles from the crime scene.

*****

After her little reconnaissance mission, she returned to Katrina's in time for dinner. Carlton had prepared a spicy West Indian dish. The meal was met with long bouts of silence in-between spurts of small talk. Everyone seemed to be withdrawn in ponder, you would have thought someone was trying to create a cure for cancer. Everyone retired to their bedrooms after dinner. Lillian turned on the TV but was asleep within five minutes of her head hitting the pillow. She was awaked by a presence in the room. She turned towards the door to see Lewis, smiling at her. He was older and looked very handsome in the expensive suit. "I love you." he whispered. Lillian was overcome with excitement. "I will always love you... Lewis" She stood, her nude body radiating.

She reached out as if in slow motion, needing to touch his face. The explosion ripped through the silence, blood and brain matter splattered her entire body. A metallic taste of blood lingered on her lips. Lillian stood, staring at the headless torso in a trance. Suddenly, a series of thuds, banging violently against the wall, like someone was trying to knock it down, shook her out of her stupor. She dived on the bed before rolling off the side, onto the floor, where she crouched in fear. The thumping became clearer as Lillian realized she had fallen off the bed and was sitting on the floor. Bang-bang Bang-bang-bang! Katrina could be heard panting and moaning as the headboard banged violently against the wall. Carlton let out a salvage howl as he came, thrusting the headboard against the wall with one final bang. The impact sent items from the dresser flying all over the place. Lillian sat in the dark, confused, attempting to distinguish between reality and fantasy.

The next day Lillian revised her thoughts in the shower before emerging with her game face. The girls spent the day riding In Lillian's new car, underwear and shoe shopping in Manhattan. Lillian also   purchased one of those new technical cell phones so she'd be able to store all the info she had obtained. Katrina asked to drive so she could get the feel of the new German-made machinery. She navigated expertly through traffic, flushed with envy. Lillian called her Mother, immediately sensing something was wrong. As she received the bad news she struggled not let it show on her face. The remaining ride was serene.

Images of her father played in her mind. She knew that he was having health issues but her parents always insisted it was nothing major. Lillian had received devastating news that Robert Elliot, her Dad, had passed away last night from complications caused by pancreatic cancer. She felt there was no need to relay the news to Katrina. Lillian certainly didn't expect any empathy from her.

"I'm gonna drive up to Rhode Island for three days then come back so we can shop my vacation away. Have to see Momma... and Daddy real quick."

"We barely touched the tip of the iceberg, but I'll see you when you get back. I have a few stores in mind." Katrina planned on putting her quest for a new car in play. *I'll have to deliver something extra special to Snookie.*

*****

The funeral was attended by a tight group of Robert Elliot's family and friends. No one from Laura's side of the family was invited. After the quiet service, Lillian planned on convincing her Mother to put the house up for sale and relocate somewhere nice. The Elliot family shed quiet tears as they buried a loved one. During the ride home, Lillian got the impression her mom didn't want to remain in the big house alone. When everyone had departed the small family gathering, Lillian helped her mother with the cleanup and dishes. "I was thinking you consider Florida as a possible place to settle... It's one of the hubs on my airline's route so I'll be able to stop by often."

"Your father's sis, Diane, lives in Pensacola, Florida. She's been telling me how nice and sunny it stays. I'm really thinking about it."

There it was. Lillian knew that she could convince Laura to relocate and started making arrangements at once. She used $100,000 of the remaining $600,000 she'd taken from the Brazilian drug dealer to put everything in motion. The event seemed far away in her mind, like recollecting a scene from one of the violent, action-adventure movies she'd grown up watching. Once she was sure her Mother would be out of harm's way when the shit hit the fan, she breathed a sigh of relief.

On the drive back to New York, that second house of Snookie's in Fort Lee, NJ, tugged at the back of her mind. The house looked like all of the other homes on the street blending right in with all of the strivers. She recalled the Honey Well alarm company's insignia posted and realized she'd need keys and a code.

Chapter Eight

No Pain- No Gain

Lillian attempted to call Katrina a few times to let her know she was headed back to New York but received no answer. *She probably left her phone behind.* Three hours later, she was pulling into Katrina's driveway beside her Jaguar.

Lillian entered the unlocked door and called out to her cousin. "Katrina, I'm back."

Carlton emerged from the bedroom shirtless and slightly out of breath. "Ah, hey Lillian. I didn't know you were coming back..."

"Hey there Carlton. Yeah, I went to take care of some business back home." *Katrina couldn't even get off of the dick for a few minutes to answer the phone. Damn.* "Would you tell Katrina I'm back? I need to take a long, hot shower after that hectic ride." Lillian went directly to her room before getting in the shower. As the relaxing stream or water pitter-pattered against her skin, she slowly oscillated her face, attempting to get the full effects of the massage. A sudden breeze could be felt in contrast to the steamy shower when the bathroom door was opened.

"Katrina." She figured her cousin came to greet her but was surprised to see Carlton standing there completely nude. "What the hell are you doing!? Get the fuck out Carlton. And where's Katrina?"

"Kat's gone." He said in a monotone voice. "Me and you have some unfinished business." He continued, advancing toward her.

"Are you crazy? Get the fuck away from me!"

He snatched the shower curtain from its rings, grabbing a hand full of her hair. "Bitch! You like to play games... Think ole Carlton's one of your toys?' He grabbed her firmly by the neck, stopping any chance she had to scream. "I will choke the life out of you if you open your mouth." He whispered.

Lillian found herself being dragged into her bedroom. Once inside he slung her across the bed knocking everything to the floor including her purse. "You think your little lollipop joke was cute. Well I don't like to be made fun of, bitch!" He grabbed a head full of hair. "Suck it." Lillian turned her head before his penis could make contact with her lips. The slap sent her flying to the floor amongst the debris from her pocketbook. Carlton kneeled within inches of her face and whispered thru clenched teeth. "If you don't suck it I will kill you right now."

"Okay. Don't hurt me." She pleaded.

The sudden, shearing, pain was too great to fathom. Almost unexplainable to the human brain. Excruciating deformity by a twisting force comes to mind... Carlton's package hit the floor with a sickening wet thud. The straight razor that seemed to magically appear in Lillian's hand, right in the nick of time, sliced completely through, severing his penis and testicles. Instant shock withheld what should had been the loudest scream in history. He dropped to his knees, wide eyed, grasping at the empty area that had once been his family jewels. Without hesitation Lillian mounted his back, cutting his throat in one motion. Carlton slumped to the floor, face just inches from his mangled organs.

Lillian tried to contain herself. Her mind was moving rapidly. She would have to change her plans. She jumped in the shower quickly needing to remove the scent of his blood. *Where the fuck is Katrina?* She shut her bedroom door and went to dress in Katrina's room. The room was a mess like someone had been rummaging through the closets and drawers. The cash she usually kept around was gone and Carlton's bags were all packed as if he was leaving in a hurry. Sensing something was even more awry, she headed towards Katrina's bedroom-bathroom. Her cousin's body was nude, submerged in a tub full of water. She stared up at Lillian with wide, dead eyes. Even though she had her owned plans for her cousin, somewhere, deep, down, inside she could have felt sympathy for Katrina, until images and the taste of Lewis' brain matter on her face flashed across her mind.

Chapter Nine

Revenge

After deciding how to approach the situation, Lillian took a deep breath before dialing...

"Hello." She recognized the voice immediately.
"Hi Snook." Lillian said in her immature voice.
"Who the fuck is this?"
"Lollipop."

"Lollipop? I don't know a damn Lollipop. How'd the fuck did you get this number!?"

"This story goes back sometime around, ten years ago..."
"Listen, whoever you are, you should know; I don't play games!"

"What happened was... I lost my virginity to you ten years ago and have not been with anybody since."

This was no big hint to Snookie who had been with so many young girls in the last ten years... However, the thought of the ten year virginity thing kept him listening.

"I was very young at the time and didn't really know how to cope with the situation. Eventually my parents sent me away to a boarding school in Colorado where I received extensive counseling. Over the years I've come to realized that I could never be with anyone until I was deflowered by the person who took my virginity on my terms."

Snookie didn't usually play around but was drawn in by the prospect of something different. "How old are you?"

Knowing he had a fetish for young girls she didn't want to shift the mood by mentioning an age out of his fetish range. "My pussy is as young as the day you first tapped it."

"Okay. Enough of the bullshit. Who the fuck is this?"
After a short pause. "Lillian."

"Lillian." He repeated to himself. Suddenly an image appeared in his head. The little redbone thing. Katrina's cousin. "Who gave you my number?"

"I stole it from Katrina."
"Why?" He decided to be careful what he said.

"I don't know. I know this sounds crazy but it's like I'm obsessed with you and the way you made me feel. I've had the same re-occurring dream for the last ten years and haven't had the desire to be with anyone else. Finally I left and returned to Rhode Island and used the money my parents had put aside for my college to buy a car and find you.

It wasn't lost on Snookie that Lewis' name was never mentioned at all. *This bitch could be trying to set me up. But maybe my dick does have her stuck in sexual-mental-limbo after all. It's apparent she hasn't told on me. Why now?*

"So you're telling me there's been no one else since me?"
"Promise." Which was the truth.
"You saw Katrina, when?"

"I saw her days ago, before I went to visit my parents. I tried to call today but didn't get an answer."

Snookie had been trying to reach Katrina since last night, needing her to bring find him something fresh. "Your parents still at the same place in Rhode Island."

"Yes." she lied. "I'm sorry how I went about it but I was kind of desperate."

Looks like Lillian will have to do for tonight. "Do you remember where my house is?"

"It's been a while but I think I can find it."
"Don't keep me waiting." was all he said before hanging up.
I won't.

Snookie's dick was in battle with his common sense. He was definitely surprised by Lillian's call but was so caught up with his own ego he felt untouchable. *If she mentions Lewis' name or anything about the incident, she'll have to be dealt with.* No one had been out to Snookie's residence but Katrina, since Lewis' murder. He held his freak sessions at one of his many other locations.

If she can find the crib then that means she could have led the police here long ago. He began to feel better about the situation. *She just needs some more of this...*

Lillian experience a ping of fear as she pulled up to Snookie's driveway. She wanted to be brave like the women on TV who were spies, gold diggers and killers. It seemed her strength didn't appear until she was threatened in some way. She wanted to be able to turn it on. Like Sharon Stone in "The Point of No Return," or Pam Grier in "Sheba Baby."

Snookie watched the baby blue Benz pull up on his security camera. *She's rolling' better than Katrina. Bet ole Bubbles don't like that one bit.* He tucked his 380 automatic in the small of his back before answering the door.

Lillian was dressed like an innocent school girl, wearing pigtails and tennis shoes. The short cut, white skirt-set capped off her youthful look. She could tell the pervert was pleased. "Hi." she said shyly.

Snookie became instantly erect. "I hope you're not playing any games with me Lillian." He approached, sticking his hand beneath her skirt. The feel of her hairless crotch further aroused him. He attempted to slide his finger inside of her but was met with a familiar resistance. *Damn! This bitch is tight as fuck.* Just to be sure he licked the same finger and tried again. *She was for real... like a virgin.* He grabbed her by the hand and led her into his bedroom.

He wasted no time removing his clothes, placing the gun atop a CD shelf.

"We have to use condoms. I've never started taking birth control." She produced a box of magnums from her purse.

That last thing Snookie wanted from all the fun was a baby. He just wanted to get to plowing away at her tight snatch. Grabbing the box of rubbers he tore away at the package hungrily. Without any foreplay he went to work like a starved sex fiend, pumping away until he bust a quick nut, collapsing onto top of her.

Lillian tried to conceal the pain but couldn't help shrieking with each thrust. It was like being raped all over again. She fought to bear with it until he finished and was amazed at how quick it had been.

Snookie wanted to last longer but couldn't resist ejaculating once he heard Lillian shrieking in pain. "Don't worry, the first one is always quick but we have the whole night." He rolled off of her tossing the semen filled condom in a nearby waste basket.

During the course of the night, Snookie repeated the violent session several times with no regard for the pain he was causing. He didn't finish until the entire box of condoms were used. It seemed like hours had passed for Lillian who was at this point in excruciating pain. Finally Snookie grabbed his gun and headed to the shower. Once she heard the water running and Snookie singing out of tune, she struggled to get up. Quickly she grabbed two of the cum filled condoms and quickly tied them in a knot and put them in a toothbrush case in her purse. While waiting for him to emerge from the bathroom, she opened the nightstand drawer. Lillian bypassed the wad of cash for a small black address book, immediately putting it inside her make-up case.

Soon as he emerged she entered. Once he heard the water running, Snookie glanced in her purse, seeing nothing suspicious, he checked his cash before headed to the living room to prepare a drink. *Everything's cool and easy.*

Lillian entered the living room wearing his robe.

"Something to drink?"
"No thanks. Can't handle alcohol."
"Shame. So what's your plans? You're gonna be around?"
'Should I?"

"Maybe you can retire Katrina, become my new... public relations person."

"I don't think she'd like that. Besides I have a few ideas about my own online business."

"Is that so?"

"That's so. Do you have a computer?" She already knew he did because she'd seen his info on Katrina's.

"Sure. In there." He pointed to his office before mixing his third drink.

Once the computer booted up, she quickly opened his email account and composed a letter, sending it to Katrina's email address. Then she quickly opened a few business opportunity sites just in case he checked to see what she'd been up to. He practically made her promise to come back soon.

Before she left he asked if she needed anything. "You already gave me everything." She smiled, before driving off.

Lillian headed straight to Katrina's. Back in Westchester, New York the street was dark and serene like a wake. She quickly entered the residence unseen. Once inside she wiped away any existence of her presence. Lillian removed the condoms from the toothbrush case and placed Snookie's DNA in obvious places on both Carlton and Katrina so that it would appear that they were both sexually assaulted by the same person. She wiped her finger prints from the straight razor, dipped it in Carlton's blood, then placed it inside of a black trash bag along with Katrina's diary and Carlton's severed penis and testicles. She turned around and made the two hour drive back to Snookie's. She parked on the dark road and walked to his trash dumpster east of his property. She placed the black bag containing the incriminating evidence inside, knowing that trash pickup was three days away.

Monday morning 9:00 am, Lillian placed a call to the Westchester County Police Department, from a pay phone in Harlem.

"911. What's your name and the nature of your emergency?"

"Hello, my name is Ebony Green," borrowing one of the names of Snookie's many victims from Katrina's diary. "I think this man I'm messin' with killed somebody," she said in a young teen's voice."

"What's your location, ma'am?"
"This is all I know. I was at his house in New Jersey…"
"Then you must contact Jersey authorities…"

"No, no. She began to piece together a tale about being recruited as a sex slave by Katrina, and Snookie coming back bloody and blabbering about doing something bad to her."

"What did he say?"
"I snuffed the cheating' bitch or something like that."
"So you think this crime took place in our County?"
"Yes. He said he was going to her house when he left."
"What's the location of the alleged crime scene?"
She gave the operator Katrina's location.
"Have you observed any weapons?"

"He has a lot of guns… There was a black trash bag. I saw him take it to the dumpster."

"What is the suspects name and address?" Lillian gave her the information. "How old are you young lady?"

"Sixteen."

"Okay. What I need you to do is wait right where you are so my command post can notify an officer in your area to pick you up…"

Before dispatch could finish her sentence, Lillian was already pulling into traffic, headed home.

Patrol officer, Joanne Ford was the first on the scene. "All quiet on approach." She notified dispatch. When she had gotten the call, it sounded most likely a hoax.

Over the years, she couldn't remember anything more serious than a theft by one of the wayward, rich kids that didn't need to steal anyway. As she entered the drive she immediately called the tag in on Katrina's Jaguar. Still sensing nothing awry, she routinely checked the premises. After receiving no response after several knocks at the door, she turned the knob and entered.

"Westchester County Police Department. Is there anyone home?" She shouted as she towards the rear of the home towards the bedrooms. "I have been dispatched to do a warfare check." She opened the bedroom door and gasped in shock. The amount of blood which had leaked from the gaping hole in Carlton's crotch was enormous. Her breakfast was already making its way back up her throat, spraying against the hallway as she made her way outside. "Oh god." She wasn't prepared for such a horrific scene.

Within minutes, the area was flooded with police and State Troopers. Katrina's body wasn't discovered until the arrival of Detective, Josh Fleming, who worked 16 years at robbery & homicide, Red Hook, Brooklyn before landing the laid back position in Westchester. The confirmation of a murder had him speeding to the scene. He was used to bullet-riddled-bodies, bleeding in the mean streets of Brooklyn... As soon as he surveyed the home, instantly, Crime of Passion came to mind.

Once Katrina's body was discovered, a forensic team converged on the property and began picking apart every aspect of the victim's deaths. The medical examiner collected evidence including what was believed to be semen on both victims. A computer specialist discovered an email sent to Katrina from Snookie's computer, which basically gave light to the entire situation and so they continued to connect the dots.

Things were coming together fast with the discovery of the email and a search/arrest warrant was issued for John "Snookie" Peterson, under suspicion of double homicide. With the two states working together, a team of heavily armed, special tactical force, officers raided Snookie's mansion. Detective Fleming hadn't seen cases come together this quick in the ghetto unless there was a confession from the actual killer.

It hadn't taken the judge long to issue several warrants after reading the email. "You really fucked up this time, bitch! I'm gonna cut off his fucking balls, right after I choke the life out of you, Kat!"

With the discovery of the black trash bag containing Carlton's genitalia and the murder weapon along with Katrina's diary in the dumpster, the case against Snookie was becoming concrete. Never knowing what hit him, he was sure there was some kind of mistake, not yet putting together that he had been set-up expertly by one of his long ago victims.

Not until he found himself fully charged, facing inescapable DNA evidence did it begin to sink in that he had been played. The best legal team that he could summon still could not convince the jury of Snookie's conspiracy theory. In the end, the physical evidence, computer science, and DNA left behind, sealed the deal.

"Jonathon 'Snookie' Peterson. You are hereby sentenced to two-consecutive life sentences without the possibility of parole to be served at a New York State maximum security prison."

Have you ever saw the look on an innocent man's face as he's being carted away for something he really didn't do? Snookie could not summon "the look of innocence". He may not have committed these murders, but for all the many crimes he did commit, there was a guilty spot on his face...The diary itself was a detailed description in chronological order involving 340 young victims. Every juror felt great about their decision, knowing they had put a very dangerous and disturbed man away for good.

Chapter Ten

A Million Reasons

On the day of the raid, Lillian was inconspicuously nearby. On her way to Fort Lee, she placed a call to the locksmith. Her next move was based on information she received from the black address book she had taken from Snookie's nightstand. While skimming through the pages, she noticed a sequence of numerical codes in addition to a lot of important addresses and phone numbers. A set of three capitalized letters (FTL) led by a series of numbers, which coincided with potions of the Ft Lee address let Lillian know it was connected. Taking her time, she played with the sequences until everything seemed to match up. Once she put it all together, it came time to put it all in play.

She arrived before the locksmith, parking her expensive car in the driveway. It fit right in the upscale area. Dressed in a navy blue pinstriped business suit, she looked like she'd had better luck at work.

"Can't believe I was irresponsible enough to leave my entire travel case back at my last location. Don't have anything I need right now. Lord, I hope your day's been better."

Roy was slightly taken back by Lillian's politeness. Normally, a black woman with a little money, locked out, after 8-10 hours on the job; Shear stinking attitude. However, there was something pleasant about this young lady and he wanted to be helpful. Hearing part of her story about leaving her things behind, he immediately went to work without asking for proper identification. "You've chosen the right man for the job. These are some real good locks here... I can breech the premises, just be ready to enter your alarm codes promptly."

Roy was just glad she realized it was all her fault. Normally, "these type" blame everyone but themselves. "Go." He urged her to hurry before the siren started blaring.

She took off, a warning signal beeping in the background. Beep-beep-beep. She didn't know if it was set to go off in 30 sec or what. Lillian's heart skipped a beat when she didn't find the alarm-key-pad directly behind the front door. Trying not to seem unfamiliar with the layout, she followed the beeping, towards the kitchen, Roy not far behind. A sign of relief as she caught view of the illuminated numbers. Just as she reached out an automated voice chimed, "Alarm Activated." The howling sound of the snitch-siren screamed bloody murder.

Roy was surprised to hear the alarm. Instantly, Lillian entered a six digit code. "Alarm Deactivated." Only then, did she exhale, she'd been silently praying that the codes she deciphered were correct. Roy was rewarded with a hefty tip and pleasant handshake. His best call of the month.

Lillian stepped out of her heels and removed her jacket before heading upstairs. She began carefully searching the bedrooms, lifting pictures and tapping for hollowed sections in the wall. As she made her way into a guestroom, Tap-tap, Tap-tap. She listened.

Bam-Bam-Bam, Boom-Boom-Boom-Boom. Lillian nearly panicked to the point of no return. When the loud bangs overrode her light tapping, it sounded like someone was trying to knock down the front door. *Maybe I underestimated Snookie and he had somebody in place to come roll things up for him nice and neat.* Wishing she could become invisible, she eased over to the window and peeped through the curtains. The two Fort Lee patrol cars in the drive said it all... "Damn it." Lillian had to pee.

She darted down the hallway making a quick left. A small victory issued has a trained, stream of urine trickled into the toilet bowl, relieving some pressure of fear from her bladder.

When the door opened, all four officers instantly relaxed when Lillian appeared wrapped only in a towel, instead of desperate robber. Her hair was soaked, apparently from the shower before being interrupted. Half of the group of happily married police officers couldn't help keeping their eyes trained on her firm breast, nestled below an inviting neckline and beautiful face. The other two men seemed transfixed on the legs that seemed to go on... all with lovely wives at home... life on the force, one day at a time.

A few months back a routine call for the same four officer's turned into a midnight pussy run for two of them and a night of boredom for the remaining having to hang-tight to cover the lucky men's backs.

Officer Kenneth Bargainer, jokingly called Ken-Doll by friends because he resembled Barbie's companion, Ken, had been the only one to score outside the racial core when he turned an 90mph speeding ticket into a day off with a young, hot, Oriental woman who talked about how cute his blonde features were the entire time.

The crime rate in Fort Lee is slow & low, sooooo tagging cuties seemed next best game... Lillian was aware of the four white officer's stares, causing her nipples to harden against the terry-cloth fabric. The danger of being caught and the power of maintaining control of the situation, gripped her like an action-packed (mutha'-fuckin') drama... She was on clue.

"We're responding to an alarm company call."

"Yes. I had a locksmith come out." She reached down, barely catching the towel before exposing her nipple, showing them the locksmith's receipt.

All smiles. "No problem ma'am. We just have to do a cancellation confirmation and should be out of your hair shortly." He turned to his partner Brandon Potts. "Give me the clip board." He had to tap his chest to get his attention. He refocused his attention on Lillian. "Please enter code on record with Alarm Company, date and sign."

Lillian quickly filled out the form and handed the clip board back. Finding any reason to hold her up would seemed pushy they all figured, so they bid her a great day. Once back inside she wasted no time heading back to the spot where she had heard the hollow section. The entire wall along the length of the closet had a different sounding thud than the others. She removed all the suit bags from the rod and stacked them on the bed before doing the same with the shoes. Grabbing the edge of the carpet, she snatched, exposing a row of removable planks. As she shifted one to the left, the green, cold, cash could be seen peeking through the plastic layer.

The doorbell followed by a series of knocks, sent her back to the curtain. Lillian couldn't imagine why the police where back. Did she get too cocky and now was on her way to jail... Reluctantly she opened the door, now wrapped in a huge man's robe.

"Yes?"

"I'm sorry. MS..." Brandon peeped at the clip. "Peterson. But we have a problem. Seems that you entered your personal alarm code which is only six digits. We need your ten digit, cancel-code for this call-out. Lillian's mind raced, she frantically searched until finally, the ten digit number that had followed the six digit sequence, appeared on her mind's chalk board.

"I'm so sorry. It's been a long week." She entered the correct numbers.

"No need to apologize. It's my job to keep you safe and protect your property."

"You're such a pleasant person. Don't you have a card? In case I need assistance..."

"Sure. No problem." He handed her his card.

Officer Brandon Potts, Fort Lee, Police Department, Cell..., Message...

At this point she felt she had them so convinced that she could practically move in. Lillian located a wall safe behind a fake bathroom mirror filled with jewelry and a bible sized, brown leather book. After dressing, she backed her car into the garage and began loading the trunk with luggage she had found in the home to hold the money. It was filled to capacity. As she entered her car about to drive off into the sunset, an olive green, Range Rover slowed her departure, partially blocking the driveway. "Hey there,' a middle aged, Caucasian man called out. I'm Stan. I live in the cul-de-sac. I was so surprised to see so much activity over because there's been no occupants at this house in the entire four years I've been here."

Lillian fought to maintain her polite exterior, so anxious to leave now that she almost ordered him the fuck out of her way. Fake smile flashing, "Live in Florida. Ya' know. Second home always feels less loved. Nice to meet you though, I'm Ms. Peterson, and I'm about to be late for my flight." She glanced at her watch giving him the cue to skidoo. Once on the expressway, she drove non-stop, until arriving at her own, quiet apartment back in Rhode Island. After stepping over the set of Louis Vuitton Luggage for two days, Lillian finally decided to take inventory. She sat on the edge of her comfortable bed and began counting for hours before breaking for a nap. When she awaked, the counting continued, realizing she hated counting money. When she was finished, she shook her head, feeling rich? Not one bit. 1.7 million dollars in one-hundred dollar bills and where to hide it was a problem.

<h1 style="text-align:center">Chapter Eleven</h1>

Back to Work

Monday morning, Lillian's vacation seemed like a crazy adventure at Warner Bros. Studios or something... She reflected on the events, like a program she had watched over the break. Back at work, she received her schedule and prepared for a month of crisscrossing the country. The airline she worked for had recently merged with a larger one and she found herself jotting around from to state to meet the overflow of business. When her scheduled was pushed, she would have to change flights at a moment's notice, staying at different hotels between layovers. Some of the flight attendants would pair-up during over-stays. Lillian was casual with some of the other women, but for the better part, kept to herself. In most cities she visited, all she had to do was turn to the news to see drama. Lillian never realized how bad things were until she heard the different events, from different news reporters, telling the same story; murder, rape, drugs...

"Good evening, this is Lamont Briggs at Fox 32, Chicago reporting... One of the two children shot in the crossfire during a shootout between rival gang has died."

"Two men opened fire at a local nightclub in little Haiti, just north of Miami's downtown..."

"Today marks the third day six-year-old Jessica Constance has been missing after being abducted from her bedroom in the middle of the night. Citizens of Portland, let's come together..."

"Blood fills the streets of Long Beach."
"Hello, Littlerock. Bad News for the people of..."
"An entire family was murdered last night in Newark, New Jersey..."

Tired of the murder stories without positive endings, she avoided the news stations, scanning the TV until she found a good movie. She eventually dozed off only to awake to a quiet, lonely hotel room. The clock on the nightstand read 1:30am. With three hours left before take-off, she turned on the nightlight, removed the brown leather book she had taken from Snookie's nightstand and began reading. When she was finished, Lillian highlighted ten cities from the thick book before showering and getting dressed in the cute flight attendant uniform. Lillian looked stellar as a Hollywood actress playing a role of a flight attendant, or airline stewardess as they used to be called, only she was the real deal. She appeared taller in heels, moving gracefully as she entered the plane, rolling her traveling bag. After greeting the Captain and two other flight attendants, she went about her duties as she had been trained:

- At least one hour before each flight, attendants are briefed by the captain--the pilot in command--on such things as emergency evacuation procedures, coordination of the crew, the length of the flight, expected weather conditions, and special issues having to do with passengers.
- Flight attendants make sure that first-aid kits and other emergency equipment are aboard and in working order and that the passenger cabin is in order, with adequate supplies of food, beverages, and blankets.
- As passengers board the plane, flight attendants greet them, check their tickets, and tell them where to store coats and carry-on items.
- Before the plane takes off, flight attendants instruct all passengers in the use of emergency equipment and check to see that seat belts are fastened, seat backs are in upright positions, and all carry-on items are properly stowed.
- In the air, helping passengers in the event of an emergency is the most important responsibility of a flight attendant.
- Flight attendants also answer questions about the flight; distribute reading material, pillows, and blankets, and food and beverage items; and help small children, elderly or disabled persons, and any others needing assistance.
- Prior to landing, flight attendants take inventory of headsets, alcoholic beverages, and moneys collected.
- Lead, or first, flight attendants, sometimes known as pursers, oversee the work of the other attendants aboard the aircraft, while performing most of the same duties. Major airlines are required by law to provide flight attendants for the safety of the traveling public.
- Because airlines operate around-the-clock, year-round, flight attendants may work nights, holidays, and weekends.
- In most cases, agreements between the airline and the employees' union determine the total daily and monthly working time.

- On-duty time is usually limited to 12 hours per day, with a daily maximum of 14 hours.

-

- Attendants usually fly 65 to 85 hours a month and, in addition, generally spend about 50 hours a month on the ground preparing planes for flights, writing reports following completed flights, and waiting for planes to arrive.
- They may be away from their home base at least one-third of the time; during this period, the airlines provide hotel accommodations and an allowance for meal expenses.
- Flight attendants must be flexible, reliable, and willing to relocate.
- Almost all flight attendants start out working on reserve status or on call.
- The combination of free time and discount airfares provides flight attendants the opportunity to travel and see new places. However, the work can be strenuous and trying. Flight attendants stand during much of the flight and must remain pleasant and efficient, regardless of how tired they are or how demanding passengers may be. Occasionally, flight attendants must deal with disruptive passengers. Flight attendants are susceptible to injuries because of the job demands in a moving aircraft. In addition, medical problems can arise from irregular sleeping and eating patterns, dealing with stressful passengers, working in a pressurized environment, and breathing recycled air.
- Airlines prefer to hire poised, tactful, and resourceful people who can interact comfortably with strangers and remain calm under duress.
- Applicants usually must be at least 18 to 21 years old.
- Flight attendants must have excellent health and the ability to speak clearly.
- Applicants must be high school graduates, and those with several years of college and experience in dealing with the public are preferred.
- Flight attendants for international airlines generally must speak one or more foreign languages fluently.
- Once hired, all candidates must undergo a period of formal training which can last between 3 to 8 weeks, depending on the size and type of carrier. Training takes place at the airline's flight training center.
- In addition, airlines usually have physical and appearance requirements. There are height requirements for the purposes of reaching overhead bins, and most airlines want candidates with weight proportionate to height. Vision is required to be correctable to 20/30 or better with glasses or contact lenses (uncorrected no worse than 20/200). Men must have their hair cut above the collar and be clean shaven. Airlines prefer applicants with no visible tattoos, body piercing, or unusual hairstyles or makeup.
- Some flight attendants become supervisors or take on additional duties such as recruiting and instructing. Their experience also may qualify them for numerous airline-related jobs involving contact with the public, such as reservation ticket agent or public-relations specialist.

Chapter Twelve

The Blue Lagoon

"Excuse me. How long before we land in Miami?" a pleasant woman asked before ordering another drink. She knew close to landing time alcohol was discontinued.

"We're do to land in approximately 60 minutes, ma'am." Lillian responded with a smile. She headed to her cubby where she kept her travel items and sat in an attached chair. Sweet juices from the peach exploded in her mouth as she took an alligator size bite. The Captain's voice over the intercom brought her head up from the brown leather book she was reading, thirty minutes later. "Landing at Miami International Airport in approx. twenty-five minutes. Please fasten your seatbelts..."

Once the plane touched down in sunny Florida, Lillian taxied to Miami-Dade Porsche and rented a 996 Cabriolet, blending with the rest of the well-to-do Floridians. She went over her plans during the twenty minute drive to the Hilton Hotel, where she planned on spending a lot of time in a warm shower. After emerging from the aqua massage, feeling clean and relaxed, she opened the brown leather book and dialed the number of the first name she'd highlighted.

"Good evening, you have reached Senor Rafael Mignon. How can I assist you?"

"Greetings amigo. My name is Alameda, an associate of Snookie. I have just arrived in Miami and was hoping we could get together to discuss some particulars. As you know, Mr. Peterson has met with some unseen obstacles and was hoping to patch up loose ends on this side."

"Ah yes, Senor Snook, I hear has made some bad decisions, which has rendered him unavailable. Ms. Alameda, was your trip comfortable?"

"Yes."

"Good. Do you enjoy dancing?"

"Dancing? Well, I hadn't planned..."

"We can meet at my club, the Blue Lagoon on the strip. Ten o'clock. See you then." Mignon had heard about Snookie's predicament and knew it was only a matter of time before he sent someone to bring him his notes. *Hopefully they have someone in place to fill the void. I've already lost millions since that whole New York thing... If these wannbe black gangsters treated this more like a business, everything would work out.* Mignon headed to his Jacuzzi, where his young lover, Antonio awaited.

*****

Lillian whipped the Porsche into a tight parking spot, noticing the packed Blue Lagoon. The entire strip was crawling with people moving about the different clubs that lined the street. In key with the weather, most folks were scantily clothed, making Lillian feel overdressed in a beige linen skirt & vest. The open toed, soft leather heels exposed her perfectly manicured toes. After checking her make up in the overhead mirror, she stepped into the party traffic.

She notified the muscle-bound bouncer of her name and was immediately whisked past the long line into the Blue Lagoon. Loud music assaulted her ears as they made their way into the thick, blue fog. Each side of the dance floor was lined with a row of stages occupied by half naked dancers, mostly men, dancing provokingly and not necessarily to the beat. It was becoming apparent from the dance floor full of men, vogue and twirling that this was a gay club. There was one woman for every ten men. The preparations she had made to engage in seductive conversation with Mignon was seeming to have been a waste of time. As she sat down at the VIP table, her suspicions were confirmed by Mignon's carefully arched eyebrows.

"Ah. I should have known you were so beautiful." He extended the tips of his fingers to shake. Mignon was a 56-year-old, gay, accomplished club owner and drug lord. "Would you like some champagne?" He gestured to a muscular guy in a tight black shirt. Within minutes their table was full of chilled bubbly.

"None for me, thanks." Lillian declined, conscious of the 25 automatic pressing against the fabric of her laced panties. She had wrestled with the thought of bringing a gun on an airplane but was amazed how easy it had been. She concealed it in the food cart which was loaded onto the plane from the lower tarmac.

Mignon filled a glass and downed it in one gulp. "Ah. This is rich man's soda pop." He proceeded to refill. Mignon reached inside his white jacket and removed a package of cocaine, pouring it onto a silver platter on the table. A different man from the group of tight shirts sitting at the nearby table handed Mignon a small, velvet box containing five small coke spoons. His pinky ring gleamed as he stuffed each nostril heavily before holding his head back and taking a deep snort. The high grade coke exploded into his brain, sending his molecules into overdrive. He needed to get his head right before he was ready to talk business.

Lillian's mind was racing. She was hoping to eventually lure Mignon somewhere more private with the hopes of some good pussy but it was apparent that wasn't his bag. In addition, his body guards were always nearby. In order to get close enough to use her razor she would have to get him away from the table alone... Then she got an idea. "On second thought, I will have a glass of champagne."

Mignon poured her a full glass. "That's more like it. Enjoy life."

Lillian took a sip and surveyed the area. Mignon continued to snort while she pretended to enjoy the music. He motioned his men to the bar not far away, where they kept a watchful eye.

"Now, let's talk business."

"Yes, as soon as I use the restroom." Lillian got up and headed to the ladies room she'd noticed on the way in, still holding her champagne glass.

Mignon signaled for one of his men to search the purse she left hanging from the arm of her chair. After a quick inspection, finding no weapons or listening devices, he gave the nod of approval. Mignon really didn't like dealing with blacks unless there was a lot of money involved and he certainly didn't do business with women because he felt he knew how they thought. He felt they were all vulnerable.

Lillian entered the last stall. She used a linen napkin from the table to wrap the glass, smashing it against the hard bathroom tile. She begin crushing the glass pieces, grinding it into small particles with the heal of her shoe. She returned to the table seemingly, drying her hands with the napkin. Now all she had to do was wait for the right time...

"Excuse me one second." Lillian couldn't believe her luck as Mignon stood up and headed towards the bar with all eyes on him, especially his body guards. With one fluid motion she opened the napkin, letting the crystallized substances blend perfectly together.

The first thing Mignon did when he returned was pour a fresh drink before filling his nostrils for a big toot. He took another big snort before addressing her. "So where do we gotta go to get my shit!" The question took her by surprise and the politeness seemed to disappear from his voice. *Wow, she realized, Snookie must have had something that belonged to Mignon before he went to jail.*

"I make it snow in the summertime. Keep smiles on the faces of my costumers with the finest product in the U.S." As Mignon talked on a strange feeling came over him. It started as a faint throbbing at the top of his head, eventually working its way towards the front.

Lillian was thinking of how to respond when she saw a thin stream of blood leak from his left nostril. Mignon squinted as the sudden headache rush to his temples causing him to grab his face in pain. "Damn," was all he said before his face slammed against the table with a violent thud. Cocaine flew everywhere. Blood oozed from the corner of both eyes as he suffered multiple, aneurysms caused by his lungs introducing the ground-glass into his blood stream. The labored breathing of someone drowning in their own blood could be heard as Mignon gasped for air.

The body guard in the tight, black, shirt was the first by his side. This wasn't the first time his boss had passed out after a night of partying. He saw no blood at first and motioned for the others to assist. Lillian stood up and stepped back as more of his people arrived. Once they had him up, only then did they notice the blood leaking from his nose and eyes. In a final quest for air his body let out a death cough, spraying a mist of blood everywhere.

Now the mode turned frantic as the stunned body guards called for more assistance. "The girl! Where is she?" One of the men yelled. A quick search found her gone.

Lillian had made her exit during all the commotion and was already on the entrance ramp to the freeway before anyone had realized she was gone. Once back at the Hilton, she crossed out Mignon's name before taking another shower and crawling into bed for some much needed sleep.

Chapter Thirteen

The Wild, Wild West

Lillian followed the crème colored, convertible Rolls Royce towards the Dallas city limits. It had been a month since her stop in Miami and it took thirty days for her schedule to fall in line with the location of her next target.

This was her second day watching Bone, number two on her list. She'd learned from watching movies that if you're following someone more than once, change vehicles. Apparently Bone saw the same movie, she thought, because the following day he made all his pickups and deliveries in a Dodge minivan in Oak Cliff and all around south Dallas. From eight car lengths behind she followed the Azure into the downtown area as night fell upon Texas.

Bone exited on Forest Park Lane, the Rolls creeping along the dimly lit streets. Lillian noticed a flock of prostitutes clear a path as he yelled something in their direction. It sounded like he said. "You bitches better get yourselves a real pimp. Mr. Bone, for the record. Restin' Dressin' and Progressin'. Breakin' Honeys and Countin' Ho' Money." He continued shouting at every prostitute he encountered until he seemed to tire and move on. Several blocks later he pulled into a parking lot next to a group of men and exited his car, greeting the other pimps. A line of Benz' and Cadillac's lined the area. Not far away on Harry Hines Blvd, no less than 100 ho's moved up and down the street catching dates from cars and on foot. Lillian had never seen anything like it in her life. Chicks in nothing but G-strings and heels, ass exposed. Police drove by as if it was legal, arresting no one. The well-dressed men continued on without a care in the world.

Lillian parked the Honda, Accord in a lot across from Bone and watched. The entire area was a concession of night clubs and adult video stores. She observed prostitutes driving around in new cars, making contact with dates before pulling to the back of one of the many parking lots and taking care of their business.

After thirty minutes or so, Bone got in his car and drove a half block away into the lot of an adult video store. Moments later, a white SUV pulled up and three prostitutes got out and got into Bone's Rolls.

Lillian watched from a few cars away as each one of them handed Bone some money before getting back into the vehicle and driving off. After leaving he drove into another parking lot not far away and pulled next to a brand new S500 Mercedes. There were four women inside, however only the driver got into the Rolls. After only a few minutes the tall, sexy prostitute got into her Benz and pulled off. Bone headed back to the lot where his pimp buddies waited. Once he returned, a hand full of the men went into one of the bars.

Lillian, sure they would be awhile drinking, drove down the strip watching the movements of the women moving about the parking lots. There was a line of cars in one lot, all waiting on the same ho'. The silver Benz that Bone's ho's was driving sat in the rear of a sushi bar. The four women, not far away, waving at traffic.

Lillian pulled into the front of the same parking lot, put on a black wig and stripped down to her white G-string panties before getting out the car and heading towards, Bone's tallest ho'. Before she made it halfway across the lot a white man in red, pickup truck cut her path. "Hey gorgeous." His Texas accent reverberated off the building. "How much for sex?"

Thinking fast, she leaned into his window. "Listen, Bud. You're lucky my shift just started or I'd take you to jail and tow your nice truck."

"Are you a cop?"

"Now be a nice boy and scat before I signal for my back up to move in…" The trick wasted no time getting out of there, probably home to his wife.

Lillian approached the group of ladies of the night. "That fool must be crazy trying to get this half price. I'm new but not that new."

The mention of being new alerted her Ho-senses. "I know that's right. Shit. I got a Pimp to pay. My name is Kiwi. Where you from with that accent Girl?"

"Philly." she lied.

Just then, one of Kiwi's wife in-laws called out. "We're going to the hotel. Be back in three hours." Two of the women got into a Camry, heading to meet a few regulars at the Days Inn.

"You got folks?"

"Huh." Lillian had no idea what she was talking about.

"Don't you have folks? A man. Who's your pimp?"

"No... Well, I just... This is my first time."

"What's your name?"

"Ah, Lollipop."

"Girl. You're a renegade. These pimps will be all over your ass if they find out you don't have no Man. You need to fuck with my folks, Bone. He's an international, Mack with the most stacks. In fact, bring me the money back, from the blow-jobs and flat-back, so I won't have to ride home alone. Then you can take-yourself and break-yourself to Mr. Bone."

Lillian had seen many movies but none of them prepared her for this Lingo because she had no idea what Kiwi had just said. She did focus on the words home and Bone.

Kiwi continued her spiel. "We gotta' dream-team. Seven deep. Number eight, evens the squad. And, you're pretty as hell. We all have our own shit. None of Bone's ho's stay in motels... I got statues and shit at my spot. That's my S500 over there." She pointed to the Benz. Every ho is rolling."

Lillian needed a little more information about the game. "So how do I join Bone's... stable?" She found the word somewhere in the back of her head.

"You gotta' choose by breaking yourself, which means to give him all the money you make. Believe me, you will be well taken care of."

Lillian had an idea. "Well before I came over here I was working down on Forest Park Lane. Did pretty good actually but once all the other girls started coming out I decided to come up to Harry Hines."

"How much did you make?"

The last guy gave me $900. So I have a little over $2,000."

Not skipping a beat, Kiwi engaged the new recruit. "Where is the money now?"

Lillian walked to her Honda, Accord, returned with the money and handed it to Kiwi. "This is a good start. Welcome to the family."

Kiwi felt like a pimp herself for a few seconds, having recruited yet another ho' for Bone's stable. She was excited about the praise and extra attention she'd be receiving from her pimp. No sooner than she put the money away, tires screeching, alerted the women to trouble. Kiwi's remaining wife-in-law, Fancy, watched everything unfold from a trick's car nearby and called Bone before calling her other wife-in-laws. "When you get off your dates don't come back to the track. Their picking up. They got Kiwi!"

Both women's train of thought was interrupted by the two white men with badges handing from the necks, pointing and shouting. "Dallas Vice. You ladies are under arrest for solicitation."

"Damn. I knew that last guy I priced was a cop." was all Kiwi said. She had been through the routine plenty of times. Lillian, at this point had to pee. *How in the world am I going to get out of this? I can't get arrested for prostitution.*

"I didn't price anyone." was all Lillian could think to say.

The girls were cuffed and driven a few blocks away to a waiting patty wagon, hidden behind one of the closed businesses. To Kiwi it was just a little bad luck but she could see Lillian seemed genuinely concerned. "Don't worry Lollipop. You're with Bone now. We'll be out first thing tomorrow."

"You're the first two birdies to get bagged. So sit tight, you're in for a long night." Officer Manchester teased before shutting the gate. The police radio indicated that more girls were being picked up. Two hours later the patty wagon was filled to capacity and on the way to jail.

During the booking process, Lillian discovered that she wasn't being charged with solicitation but impersonation. "I'm sure there's some terrible mistake." She protested until the man in the red, pick up, truck who'd she'd threatened to take to in appeared with a badge around his neck. "I would have let you slide because you didn't price me and you have no prior prostitution arrest, but you threatened to take my pickup truck, and that's my baby."

Lillian gave a fake name and address. Her mind traveled back to her rental car back on Harry Hines and the 25 automatic in the trunk. The rental information was in the name of Katrina Whitfield and could not be connected to her.

"That's good none of the other wife-in-laws got busted," Kiwi said to Lillian when she returned to the holding cell after being finger printed. She always carried a set of cover-up clothes in her bag in case they were ever arrested so she or her sable mates wouldn't be paraded in front of the judge in a G-string. "Here, put this sundress on so you won't piss off the Judge. She's a real bitch."

The holding cells were filled to capacity. Ho's were lying on the floor and under the benches, cell block smelling like armpits and pussy. Lillian and Kiwi sat on the bench talking, until they eventually dosed off, huddled together against the cold, jail-house, wall.

In the morning they began calling names for Court. It was a long, slow process. The judge was giving out $1,000 bails and a lot of the girls with broke pimps were going to the County Jail. Lillian couldn't imagine what the bail would be for her charge. Finally after hours, Kiwi heard her name called.

"Don't worry. I got your info. Daddy will have you out in no time." Kiwi assured her as she pranced out of the holding pen like a runway model. It seemed like they waited to call Lillian last. After calling her alias twice, she realized they were talking about her and scurried out of the cell.

Kiwi had been sitting in the courtroom since she had been released, waiting for them to call Lillian's name and decided to step out for a quick smoke break. As soon as she made it outside the building they called Lillian's alias.

"Sandra Collins. The charges have been dropped. You may leave."

"Next on the docket. Rhoda Clark. Charged with solicitation for prostitution. Bail $1,000!"

Lillian quickly exited the courtroom and ran right into Kiwi on her way back inside. "Oh shit. You're out. What happened?"

"I don't know. They just said charges dropped."

"I told Bone you never priced no cop. Come on, he'll be glad to finally meet you." She grabbed Lillian's hand and led her towards a white, Hummer, parked at the curb.

"This is Lollipop." Kiwi beamed with pride as she presented her new catch to Bone. He nodded with approval as he took in Lillian's innocence and beauty.

"Let's get to the property room and get your things before getting something to eat. I know some good food is in order after a night in jail." Lillian observed Bone from the backseat of the big SUV as she listen to Kiwi continue on like she was the Queen of England addressing the King.

The women retrieved their property including the cash taken during the arrest. In Texas, if the money is not directly connected to the case at hand, it's returned upon release. After Bone received the money Lillian had given Kiwi, only then, did he begin addressing her as his...

"Welcome to the family, Ms. Lollipop. "Shake-a-hand/ meet-a-man pretty." Bone extended his hand for her to touch. His tall, athletic, frame fit his name. His hair was in a shoulder length, perm like Snoop Dogg. The diamonds from his platinum ring sparkled, throwing rainbow specs against the entire interior. "No need to feel left out or alone because you've found, a man with a plan, in Bone." He smiled, exposing a mouth full of neat, white teeth. She thought about her 25 automatic.

"Oh. I left my car at the place where we got picked up. Would it be possible...?"

"No problem. The girls picked up Kiwi's Mercedes last night as soon as the squad left." Bone headed to the track. The Honda was parked where she had left it. "Lucky you parked up front. Had it been in the rear, the business owners would have had it towed away. Let Kiwi drive it so I can talk to you little bit."
Kiwi hopped out and got behind the wheel of Lillian's car, while she got into the front seat with Bone. Kiwi followed the Hummer to Bone's home in the Colony. During the ride, he questioned her a little about her past and determined she was not a cop but, green as hell, just how he liked them. "After you guys shower and we have a bite to eat, I want you to take a ride with me so I can get to know you a little better and explain some important things you need to know." Bone informed her. A few hours later, Bone pulled his Navigator out and sent Kiwi to have it cleaned, inside out. In anticipation of her ride with Bone, Lillian retrieved the small caliber gun from the rental and concealed it in the crotch of her panties. Shortly after Kiwi returned, Bone told Lillian it was time to roll.

Bone drove to several different locations in South Dallas, making pick-ups. He would enter empty handed and return with a saddlebag or backpack, emptying the contents into a gym bag on the 3rd row seat of his SUV. During the drive he gave Lillian detailed instructions about her duties and expected conduct. "And when it comes to representing my pimping, a Ho' must be in-pocket at all times..." He was talking a hundred miles an hour. Lillian appeared to be listening, however, she was thinking of a way to get Bone to go somewhere a little more secluded.

"I got one more stop before we head back. Kiwi's waiting for you at her pad. You guys can prepare for work tonight. Yeah, I'm sure she has something real sexy for you to wear. I'll drop you off there after I go see a friend of mine's."

Bone guided the Lincoln, Navigator towards the highway ramp and headed 30 miles out of Dallas, exiting on a quiet, county road. After traveling another fifteen minutes, they came upon a shabby ranch.

"Bone. I really have to use the restroom. I've been holding it since..."
"From now on, call me Daddy. Understand?"
"Yes."

"And never speak out of turn or make direct eye contact with any man unless it's a trick at work or a police interview. Understand, bitch?"

"Yes."
"Yes. What?"
"Yes. Daddy."
"Good bitch."

They were met at the door by a short, dark-skinned, man who looked like a bulldog in the face. "Mr. Bone." The men slapped five. "Sid, let my folks use your restroom." They followed the little muscular man into the cluttered house. Lillian noticed he had a gun in the small of his back. Sid motioned in the direction of the bathroom. Lillian headed that way, really having to go. The men proceeded to conduct business as Lillian made her way down a hall and into the bathroom.

"Oh my god," she exclaimed having walked in on the young girl wiping herself down below with a washcloth. The young teen was visibly shaken with a look of pure fear on her face. "I'm sorry honey, I didn't know anyone was in here."

The girl scrabble to put her clothes on. That's when Lillian noticed the welts on her back. "Oh my god. What happened to your back honey?" The child didn't respond, brushing past Lillian in a hurry. Lillian saw Sid coming down the hallway, from the corner of her eye as the scared, girl whisked by. As she hovered above the toilet, not wanting to sit on the nasty stool, she could hear Sid walk past the bathroom in the direction of the girl. She glanced at the gun resting on her panties, crotch area and quickly wiped herself.

She could hear angry murmured voices as she exited the restroom. Inches closer to the door, she could hear Sid more clearly. "What did you say to that bitch?"

"I didn't say nothing." The girl pleaded. The slap knocked her to the floor.

"Who told you to leave this room? Didn't I tell you to never leave this room...? When I finish taking care of my business, I'm gonna beat your fucking ass. Take off all your clothes and wait for me. Who the fuck told you to get dressed anyway, I wasn't near finished. Bitch, you just wait!"

Lillian was appalled at what she was hearing, bringing back so many bad memories. She wanted to bust in, gun blazing, but knew she was dealing with dangerous men and this wasn't a movie. She made her way back to the living room before Sid wrapped up his threats.

That girl can't be no more than fifteen. She's scared-- real scared. A chill ran down her spine as she recalled the look of fear on the young victim's face. *Please help me, please help me!*

After handing Bone a suede pouch, the men shook hands, business as usual. Bone headed for the door, Lillian at his heels and Sid not far behind. He was checking out Lillian's ass and legs, imagining what he was about to do to the young girl.

Bone reached for the door knob as Lillian quickly, spun 190 degrees. The two rapid shots caught Sid right between the eyes, killing him instantly. The gun fire caught Bone by surprise. He turned wide-eyed, clumsily reaching for his 9mm before realizing he'd left it in the SUV. He tried to regain his composure when he realized Lillian was the shooter. "Ho'. What's going? Did that nigga try to rob me? Bitch, you saved my life! Give Daddy the gun!"

"I'll keep the gun. You... can have these."

Lillian raised the 25 automatic and emptied the clip into Bone, turning his white, Nike, sweat-suit and Jordan's into a red, bloody mess. Lillian returned to the bedroom to find the frighten child, hiding in the closet, shaking like a leaf.

"Don't worry. No one will ever hurt you again." The girl got up and hugged Lillian so tight, she had to pry her loose. "Grab some clothes and let's get out of here. Lillian removed the Navigator keys from Bones pocket and grabbed the suede pouch. Leading the girl by the hand, they got into the vehicle and headed towards the main highway. She tossed the cleaned weapon in some thick bush along the service road.

"What's your name?" Lillian asked.
"Renee. She responded.
"I'm Lillian."
"Thank you, Lillian." Renee began to cry.

Lillian headed straight to Bone's house, knowing Kiwi wouldn't be there. She quickly wiped everything down, placed the gym bag from the backseat of Bone's, Navigator into the trunk of her rented Honda, Accord and headed back to her Hotel room. During the ride Renee stared out the window like she was from another planet.

"When is the last time you've been out of that house?"
"Three years, I think."
"How old are you?"
"Sixteen."
Who was that man?"
"He was one of my momma's boyfriends, he got her hooked on dope.

One day momma disappeared and he never let me leave the house since. He kept hurting me. I think he killed her. He used to choke her a lot."
"Do you have any family I can take you to?"
"No, it was just me and momma."
"An aunt, uncle, cousin?"

"Maybe in Denver. I think. I don't know." After a long pause, she said. "I want to go with you."

"I'm leaving Texas, today."
"Me too."

Lillian stopped at her hotel briefly before heading to the Fort-Worth International Airport, where they hopped a flight to the East Coast.

Chapter Fourteen

Sister I never had

Back in Rhode Island, Lillian and Renee sat around the table talking like big sister/ little sister. She discovered, Renee had a hard life, having moved around from place to place after her father was sent to Death Row for murdering a man he caught with his wife. Louise, her mother, began drinking heavily and laying up with different men. She eventually became hooked on heroine when she hooked up with Sid. The night before Louise disappeared, Renee heard Sid arguing with her. "It sounded like he was choking her." After listening to Renee tell her the things she'd been through, Lillian wanted to protect the young girl with all her heart. Having come from a home with caring parents, she was unaware of the plight of some young children, until she spent a summer with her cousin Katrina and was victimized by a man just like the one who was abusing Renee. Like Lewis, Renee couldn't rely on the people who are supposed to support, nurture and protect... her parents.

Just thinking about all the young people being abused and subjected to the hardships of adults made Lillian want to cast a giant net, trapping all the predators and *ne'er-do-wells*, borrowing a term from her Dad. Right then and there, she decided to use whatever money she'd taken from her targets to help children like Renee... And Lewis. The $125,000 from Bone's gym bag was added to the rest of the money. She would decide exactly how to apply it to her future-cause soon as she finished wrapping up some loose ends... Eight to be exact. She crossed out Bone's name in the book.

*****

Lillian responded to a request on the post-board for a facilitator, training new arrivals. The 3-month position would give her time to spend with Renee, daily after the three hour classes were over. She raced home each day to spend time with her new friend, more like a baby sister. Lillian tried to make Renee forget about all the past negative events by inserting some joy into her life. They went everywhere; beach, carnival, movies, circus, Water Park, shopping, eating and more shopping. Renee got her first perm and a lot of personal pointers concerning hygiene and many other things a parent on drugs neglects to teach. Renee never had anyone take the time to show her, even some of the most simple things required to maintain her health and hygiene, having used tissue instead of sanitary napkins since she started her period four years ago. The woman and young girl began to form a bond in such a short period of time because they both were yearning to be loved and accepted. Lillian felt she'd let her parents down by not going to college and becoming a doctor. Renee had never been told by her mother or father; I love you. Yet, after being around Lillian, she felt a motherly connection and abundance of gratitude for this women who'd rescued her from hell.

It had been a long time since Lillian had been roller skating and it was Renee's first time. They had as much fun falling than they did skating. It was a pitiful sight, the two holding up the flow of traffic, grasping and falling into one another. "You did worse than me." Renee teased. They laughed and shared a hug. "I love you like a little sister, Renee." The words meant more than anything to Renee. The feeling left behind was uplifting. She could feel her heart beating rapidly in happiness, instead of fear, like whenever Sid was around...

"Thank you for taking me away from that place. The man you came with been there lots of times with another lady, but no one tried to help me. Once, I talked to her when she came to use the bathroom and she told him what I said. He beat me up and broke three of my fingers. Thank you, thank you, and thank you." She was almost in tears. Renee's gratitude was sincere.

"I'm glad I went there."

Three months went by quickly in the mist of all the fun. Sunday, they had a quiet dinner at home and watched a good movie before going to bed. It was back to her normal flight schedule, come Monday morning. "I have vacation time coming up next month and we're going to California." She notified Renee.

Chapter Fifteen

Double Trouble

Lillian's flight touched down in the Windy City at 10:45pm. She had made arrangements ahead of time for the car rental, always using Katrina's information. The gun she carried belonged to her deceased father and had served as home-protection for his family. It had never been fired and only out of the case once. The 380 caliber, automatic made its way to Illinois via the food cart and now rested snuggly in her crotch.

The station wagon was perfect for her next encounter because it was as low-key as one could be. The target that brought her to Chicago turned out to be two brothers, Ronald and Stanly Chambers. Ronald was a former member of Snookie's crew from New York who fled to Chicago to avoid a drug case, staying on the Southside with his father and younger, stepbrother Stanly. Even though Ronald was six years older, it was Stan's explosive nature and violent temper that held a grip on the ghetto drug trade.

A former member of a violent street gang, Stan as he's called, was tied to several murders, however after spending a short time in the county jail, he was released due to insufficient evidence, four times. With his ranking in the street and the drug connection his brother had back in New York, over the years, the two amassed an empire, managing some of the deadliest gangs in the city.

Ronald grew up for the most part in New York with his mother, a hard working home attendant with a second part-time job cleaning offices at night, which is how her son found time to get in trouble, eventually being recruited to work for Snookie. He was kind of a momma's boy before hitting the streets and was less prone to violence, unlike his brother, who preferred a knife or baseball over a gun because it was more up-close and personal. The only thing the men had in common was a father and a love for fast cars, rumored to own twenty-five between the two. The brother's had solidified a network of connections in Miami, Texas, California and New York.

When it came to women, Stan would call Ronald Saint-Trick, instead of Saint Nick because Santa Claus only came around once a year but he'd say Ronald comes around every day. The main reason is that whenever Ronald would get pussy whipped, she was a keeper. He'd set her up in a crib, buying washers and dryers, leasing or buying her a car, depending on the depth of his lust. The problem is, he gets whipped every other week and had seven different chicks, stashed at seven different locations. He's paying seven different car insurances on several different cars and several different rents on several different cribs. Electronics, appliances and whatever it took to keep them happy. "I don't have no problem doing a little gifting now and then," he'd say.

"Mother Fuckin' Saint Trick, will pay a bitch, quick. Making all decisions with the head of his dick." Stan teased. "Nikka, let me borrow a dollar, before the ho's get to-ya'." He chuckled at his own humor.

Stan on the other hand was cold when it came to women. He couldn't give two fucks about helping some chick with her light bill or car note, let alone buy her something nice. Once a female asked for some money to get her hair done, after they had been fucking all day and he went off. "Bitch you try'na play me like a trick? Stan the Man don't gotta pay for no pussy, you funky bitch." He hawk spit in her face before slapping her to the ground. As she lie there stunned, Stan pulled out his dick and peed in her face. He had a reputation all over Chicago for being feared, supplying drugs to rival gangs and daring them to step on each other's toes. He had been shot on five different occasions during his gang banging days and was legend to be unstoppable in the streets. Southside, Westside it didn't matter Stan went wherever he pleased without a care in the world.

*****

Ronald sat way in the back of the bar enjoying the loud music while a hand full of people danced to the final song. He had planned on taking Sharon, a chick he'd met who was visiting from Philly, to the motel for a nightcap. She kind of reminded him of the girls from New York. However, once Sharon's cousin, a local girl, discovered his plans, she instantly warned her family about "bad company," putting a monkey wrench in Ronald's plans. *Nosey ass ho' need to mind her own business.* Ronald realized he would have to settle for one of his regulars tonight.

"Lock up the liquor in the basement before you leave." He ordered James on the way out, as he was dialing Travera's number to let her know he was on his way. Ronald exited from the rear, where his car was parked out back. The shiny, black Dodge Viper was the latest toy in his car collection, looking like a space machine in comparison to James' Chevy Impala. The first thing he noticed was the broken window on the passenger side of James' car. *Damn. I can't believe somebody broke in James' car back here. Fuckin'dope fiends. Just wait till I catch....* As he approached he could see his car sitting low from a flat tire and cursed his luck. "Damn!" He called Travera back. "Baby I got a flat. I'll have James change it for me. Be there in little bit. Keep it warm for Daddy." He hung up thinking about pussy.

Ronald kneeled to take a closer look. "These tires are worth $500 a piece." *They should be lined with titanium or something.* He never saw the shadowy figure step from inside the dumpster's enclosure. Lillian had a clear shot at the back of his head. As she stood about to pull the trigger, knowing this type of ambush required the victim to be shot in the back of the head while changing the flat, she still couldn't do it.

"Turn around."

The sound of a woman's voice startled Ronald but not as much as the sound of a man's would have, until he saw the gun. "Who the fuck are you? W-W-What'd I do?"

Micro-seconds before she pulled the trigger... (The signal had already been sent from her brain, to the nerves in her pointy finger, tendons prepared to retract. The next sound would be the percussion of the hammer striking the shell casing, releasing a projectile traveling at a high rate of velocity, destroying everything in its path.) However, Lillian was suffering from some type of computer glitch in the brain. The boom from her gun didn't come as intended. Instantly her mind went into another mode. From deep within, somewhere in the back of her mind, a ping of recognition surfaced. Her brain was receiving signals, attempting to process and decipher the input. Then, all at once she realized she had heard that voice before. Her mind traveled back to the most horrible day of her life when she was lying in a pool of her own blood almost dying in pain, praying it would stop... But it didn't. A face began to emerge through her foggy memory, until the face standing before her and the face, now burned in her memory forever, were the same. Like the robotic lenses on a high speed camera everything came into focus in high definition.

Ronald cursed himself for not carrying a gun. Stan warned him all the time about staying strapped. He could hear his brother's voice now. *I'd rather get caught with it, than without it.* Not really knowing what this was about, he decided to try to talk to the pretty woman holding him at gun point. "What's going on sweetheart? I'm sure there must be some type of mistake."

Lillian stood quietly, mentally taking in all of his facial features. Her glare made Ronald uneasy. "What are you looking at?" Lillian's heart began racing. *What the fuck are you looking at*, was the way he had worded it years ago when he was raping her.

The computer glitch in her brain had subsided and now it was time to blow this scumbag away. The signal again left her brain in route to the muscles in her trigger finger, when the process was interrupted by the arching blow that sent her reeling backwards. Lillian hit the ground with a thud causing her gat to slide beneath James' Impala, out of her reach.

"Crazy ass bitch." Ronald was trying to figure out what he had done to this chick. Not being able to place her face, he thought about what Stan would do in a situation like this. "Bitch, do you know who the fuck I am?" Right then he was promising himself to never get caught slipping again. "I should kill your punk ass, maggot."

Lillian found herself on the ground momentarily stunned, she saw the gun slide in the direction of the Impala but couldn't see it in the shadows. Ronald stepped over her, kneeled and retrieved the 380. "I guess I got me a new gun." He stuffed it in the back of his jeans and stood over Lillian, pulling out his penis. The warm stream of urine spattered against her face causing her to spittle, trying not to drown in piss. Ronald had heard his brother brag about humiliating females by peeing on them but never knew it felt so relieving. *Damn, I had to piss badly. This bitch scared the shit out of me.* Feeling victorious, he let out a sign of relief, putting his head back has he shook the last droplets of urine on her clothes.

The edge of the straight razor caught the skin-line at the center of his scrotum causing his nut sac to split open with a violent tearing noise. With no support, his balls dropped like two hangman on a noose, sentenced to death. The next swing severed both nuts simultaneously. As they fell to the ground, Lillian stepped on one, crushing it, in her haste to get up.

Ronald's scream was ear-piercing as he fell to the floor next to his balls. She had to wrestle the gun from his pants as he rolled around on his back screaming in obvious pain. Just as she retrieved it, James appeared at the rear door swinging a golf club. The solid, metal, driver missed her head by inches, it was definitely a death swing. Falling back to avoid the blow, she fired twice just as he raised the club to strike again. She then focused her attention back to Ronald.

"Remember when you and Snookie raped that innocent, young girl? Well that was me... Remember Lewis?" She waited until she saw the surprise register on his face before pulling the trigger. The hot shell from her father's gun landed right between his eyes. She inadvertently stepped on his other nut, smashing it flat as she fled into the night.

*****

The loud collision shook Stan from his sleep. Alert to anything out of the ordinary, he grabbed his gun from the nightstand before heading to the window. From the second floor of his townhouse, he could see the station wagon awfully close to his car and a woman standing by with her hands over her mouth. "What's going on baby?" The naked woman asked, awakened from her dick-induced-sleep.

I know this bitch didn't hit my car. Without responding, Stan slipped into his boxers and headed downstairs to investigate, taking two steps at a time. By the time he emerged from the front door he had totally forgotten about the gun in his hand. Lillian took a step back. "I'm sorry. It was an accident." She cupped her face for emphasis. The look on his face told it all.

"What the fuck did you do bitch!" It's bad enough when somebody hits your car but when they're driving a piece of shit, it makes it worst. The station wagon had raked the entire side of Stan's $200,000 Bugatti EB 110 Sports, destroying the finish.

"I have insurance." Lillian's old rental had minimal damage.

"Bitch! Your mutha' fuckin' insurance can't cover this." He glanced over at her station wagon in disgust. Stan kneeled for a closer inspection, running his fingers along the sheared grooves. *She wrecked my baby.* "Stan, watch out!" The warning from Stan's bedroom window was muffled-out by the 380 automatic's report. **Blak-Blak.** His 9mm hit the pavement with a metallic clink, while portions of his brain matter, sprayed a hideous design on the Bugatti's door. For some reason she had a change of heart about headshots from behind. The last time she had made that mistake she got pissed on. Lillian got into the still running wagon and pulled off. As she entered the freeway's entrance ramp, she could hear sirens racing towards the direction from which she was fleeing.

Chapter Sixteen

Grand Daughter

Renee jumped from the couch to greet Lillian the moment she heard the key in the front door. The two embraced. "I missed you." They said in unison. Renee giggled. "Jinx. You owe me a soda."

"What? Jinx? What's that mean?"

"When two people say the same thing at the same time, the first one to say Jinx wins and the loser owes them something; I like soda."

"Oh. That's cheating. How was I supposed to know to say Jinx?"
"Because you were a kid before."

"Okay. You win. But you have to run out to the car and get the groceries." Renee shot outside to get the bags. When she returned, Lillian gave her a box. "This is for you."

Renee quickly opened her present. "Oh thank you." She hugged Lillian's waist. The necklace had a small panda pendant and was made of 14k gold. Renee instantly fell in love with it.

"Oh, I got you something." She bolted into bedroom, returning with a box displaying a set of crystal figurines."

"Wow, where'd you get these, they're beautiful."

"I took a taxi to that strip mall we passed on the way here. I brought a few items for the house too."

"Wow. You're quite observant." Lillian decided at that point she would teach Renee to drive. "Let me hop in the shower." As the warm water sooth her muscles the scent of turkey bacon could be smelled coming from the stove. When Lillian entered the kitchen the table was set and Renee was just finishing the eggs.

"Where'd you learn to cook like that?"
"I used to have to cook for Mommy and her boyfriends."

Lillian filled their glasses with orange juice, just as the toast popped up. "We have a full scale breakfast menu going on here." The conversation was non-stop, each one happier than the other. "Let's get dressed and do a little shopping for our vacation."

After breakfast, they headed to the mall. "Start paying closer attention to every sign we come across while driving around town. Signs are information one needs to process. While your attention may be diverted, your mind can navigate between what's relevant and what's not. When to veer left or merge right... Just like in life."

The girls emerged from the mall with bags, full of items for their trip. Lillian had to get most of Renee's clothes from the Junior Misses department, because even though she had gained a little weight since being at Lillian's, she was still small at 5'4, 105 lbs. Lillian purchased two large travel bags and filled them to capacity with cosmetics, clothes and other items.

They spent the next two hours in the parking lot of an abandon restaurant. Lillian only had to show Renee a few times how to coordinate the brake and gas pedals before she was driving the Benz like she'd been driving for months. "Most people get a little nervous driving on the highway because of all the fast moving cars, but you'll do fine."

Renee beamed with confidence. 'Thanks."

"Let's try on the service road." Renee followed the service road along the highway until Lillian told her to make a right on route 27, where they traveled along a quiet road for 40 minutes. Renee could see the airport in the distance.

"You stopping by work?"
"I want you to meet someone."

When they arrived at the airport, Renee was expecting to meet a supervisor or co-worker/friend but was surprised when Lillian parked in long term and they boarded a plane headed to Pensacola, Florida.

The taxi traveled slowly along the winding road as they took in the assortment of beautiful flowers spawned by sunshine and happiness. They came to a stop at a modest home on the beach-line as the ocean's chatter sang a duet with the birds and sea creatures.

"It's so peaceful and quiet out here." Renee took a deep breath.

"I'm so glad momma decided to move to Florida. It's beautiful out here." Lillian planned on one day moving to Pensacola to be closer to her mother and hoped Renee liked it out there as well.

Before the door could fully open, Laura had her daughter in a bear hug. "You made it" She released her, sensing the child was in need of a hug too. "And, you must be Renee." She wrapped her arms around Renee. "I couldn't wait to meet you." Lillian had briefly filled her mother in on their new guest, not being specific about anything.

Instantly Laura fell in love with Renee and immediately began calling her, my grandbaby. The three women spent the next three days enjoying the beach and some good Floridian food. Renee tried to store all of the information she was receiving from the women in her young mind. She was feeling accepted and loved. It was like her birthday became the day she was rescued and she was just getting to know her mother and grandmother.

At the conclusion of their visit, Lillian made travel arrangements for the trip to California, including hotel and car rental. They bid Laura love and farewell before hopping on another big-metal-bird headed to the West Coast.

Chapter Seventeen

Osiris

The Polynesian inhabitants of the Samoan Islands in the South Pacific are called Samoans. These people are recognized as the best representatives of the remarkable and interesting Polynesian race, and their traditions hold that these islands were the center from which the race spread to other Pacific Islands. The Samoans have long "best" famous as sailors and boat builders, and they have many legends and tales of great beauty and interest.

Presently, most Samoans are Catholic and have been transplanted along the coastal regions of the United States. Having a solid tribal background keeps them close-knit and supportive of each other. The Samoans have long been famous as hard workers, and they have many legends and tales of great beauty and interest. Back home the Samoan people have up to twenty dwellers in their homes at the same time; all family, these people do not concern themselves with privacy. Everything is done together and as many ancient cultures do, the elders are the most respected and highly regarded members of the family.

In a melting pot like California, USA the Samoan culture has experienced a metamorphosis, infusing its brazen work ethnic into efforts to succeed by any means available. The youth began mimicking California's gang culture, partaking in the fast paced, hustle and bustle in an attempt to avoid financial struggles. The gang was formed in the 1980s to protect the immigrant Samoan community from established Hispanic gangs in the impoverished suburbs of Long Beach, California. It has since spread to other Southern California cities as well as other states with a large Samoan community. The gang adopted the Cripps culture and has since aligned themselves with the larger Afro American gang. Originally formed as a means of protection, Sons of Samoan sets have since emerged in every impoverish neighborhood with a substantial Pacific island community.

They are involved in violent crime, which is mostly committed by younger members, as well as organized crime, which is mostly the business of older and ambitious hardcore members of the gang.

The sons of Samoan are heavily involved in extortion, contract killing and the manufacture and distribution of methamphetamine. They are also known for the taxing of other Meth distributors, as well as ripping them off. More organized members are involved in heavy cocaine trafficking rings as well as the trafficking of weapons.

*****

Amosa Feresa came to the United States from Samoan in the 1988, when he was six-years-old. A tribe had arrived four years earlier to become established so that they could send for other family members. Amosa's father and three uncles obtained jobs, while banding with other Samoan families to establish strong ties and a solid Samoan community. By the time Amosa was ten, he was aware of the power in numbers, living in a household with his Mother, Father, Little brother Apineru, and twelve other relatives. Everyone chipped in to lessen the cost of living.

Being viewed as intruders by the neighboring Mexican Gangs made it difficult to for the young males to move about without being targeted. One day, a young Samoan teen was robbed and beaten within an inch of his life, on his 13th birthday, all for a jacket and seven dollars. That's when Amosa's uncle, Kisona, decided to do somebody about it. He called for all male, able bodied Samoans to form together.

Shortly after, the **Sons of Samoan** were born the war was on. Becoming in sync with another natural enemy of the Mexican Gangs, the sons of Samoans adapted the CRIPS blue flag. The gang was able to establish territorial boundaries, forming borders along their neighborhoods, assuring that anyone caught out of bounds, be dealt with harshly. Over the years Amosa had witnessed more Samoans die in the streets of Long Beach than at home, including two cousins, one a 13-year-old girl caught in the gunfire.

Amosa grew up attuned to gang life, being known in school as Kisona's little nephew. When Amosa was in the tenth grade, Kisona was arrested for murder and members began setting up other factions on the eastside of Carson, adapting red as their flag like the bloods.

Scotts Park Pirus spread through-out the Westside, where the Westside Pirus were growing fast in numbers, practically taking over the entire Scottsdale Housing Projects. Another cousin of Amosa, Levi was O.G of the Westside Boo-Yaa Tribe where another part of his family had landed during the migration from the Pacific islands in the late 80's. School had become irrelevant to Amosa about the time his uncle was convicted and sentenced to life in prison. The only thing that had interested him was math and Egyptian Mythology. Something about the Egyptian culture had captivated him since he was a kid. Amosa had put-in-work, during the transition of the SOS, having three silent kills under his belt already. His fascination with Egyptian Mythology prompted him to the take on the name Osiris.

"Osiris is the Egyptian God of the underworld."   Was the only explanation he offered. Demanding to be called Osiris by all his cohorts, the 6'3", 280 lb. Samoan was considered a person not to disagree with. The tattoo of Osiris the god, on his 23 inch bicep, above ominous lettering; Osiris told his story. He once beat Joker, a fellow member, down for not getting his name right, and taking his correction lightly. The man had to have reconstructive surgery to repair his facial cartilage. That ended all playing around with Osiris and he was taken serious at all times.

One day, Amosa was called to Lompoc Federal Maximum Security Prison to see his uncle Kisona. Things had changed since his conviction and he knew his nephew would be the one to set everything straight. The two huge men sat across from each other, neither smiling. Visitors milling about gave the room a real family feel as prisoners hugged their mothers, kissed their wives, and bounced their children around.

"Osiris. True Samoans recognize no separation of our families. The Sons of Samoan were formed to unify our race. To power-up with numbers, strength and posterity. Community support, family support. Our brothers on the Westside flying red flags must realize that we will fall as a people if we rival fellow Samoan's. Blue against red is the blacks beef. Those Samoans in Carson, everybody! Scotts Park, Westside, Scottsdale, are brothers. I have made arrangements with Levi to bring his Boo-Yaa to the table. I am green lighting the murder of OG Tone and anybody who refuses to tie blue and red flags at the end to show Samoan Unity & Loyalty. Tone's family came from Hawaii and may have lost some Samoan values along the way. After you take care of this you will be given the 'Key to the Chest'. Head-Man, with only two remaining elders as confidants. Total control of the SOS's business and sole decision maker; Double O.G answering only to me."

Osiris said very little, nodding in acceptance at his promotion to Double-OG status. At the conclusion of the visit the men embraced speaking more with their eyes. Osiris knew that he had been handed a very important position and was more than up-for-the-task.

In the months following, OG moves were made, starting with the consolidation of all Samoan business interest from Long Beach to Carson. Finally, Osiris set up his main hub in L.A and opened several Auto Restoration and detail shops throughout the city. Classic Custom Restorations at the 3900 block of Fountain Ave was headquarters for Osiris and several trusted family members. Most of his business was conducted at Classic Custom from an office in the rear. The other locations were ran by family and well trusted soldiers. The restoration business was very lucrative, however, nowhere near as lucrative as the steady stream of cars, vans and RVs moving to-and-from, filled with drugs and weapons headed to destinations unknown.

Within a ten-year period, the Sons of Samoan had climbed to the top, trafficking guns and drugs. Cocaine, Heroin, Methamphetamine, Ecstasy and Marijuana was just some of the substances they dealt in. Osiris' underworld connections spanned from California to New York and was growing with every new deal brokered. Pretty soon everybody had to see the Samoans, making Osiris one of the most powerful kingpins on the West Coast. With his younger brother, Apineru, as his most trusted soldier the Sons of Samoan became filthy rich and well respected. Apineru having finished high school before fully joining SOS, had been responsible for organizing the group's financial and strategic upgrades and became known as Thoth; Egyptian god of writing and knowledge.

"You have bold wisdom beyond your lifetime on earth so I will call you Thoth." And so Thoth he became, only called Apineru by his aging mother or at church.

Osiris was a force to be reckoned, larger than life. Living on top of each other in a one bedroom apartment was a thing of the past for Osiris, making sure every Samoan family had their own homes whether it was in the hills or in the projects. If you worked you got paid. Everybody was making money so everything was running smooth.

Looking back on his decision to make Osiris Double OG, he glowed in his genius. Kisona was the number one shot caller in Lompoc and could have a rival killed in almost any prison across the country with one word. He made powerful connections thru prison contacts, establishing new opportunities for his crew. Although he knew he'd never be free again, he was content knowing that his family; wife, son and three daughters were safe, sound and living the American dream. Even in prison he was rich and powerful.

Chapter Eighteen

Vacation in Cali

When the plane landed at LAX, Lillian wasted no time picking up the Dodge, Caravan rental and loading their luggage. Renee was excited about the trip and was looking forward to having some fun. "I can't believe I've been on a plane three times already. I don't think nobody in my family has ever been on an airplane before." Renee scanned the city on the drive to the hotel. "This place looks like where the movie stars live." She pointed to a gated community with huge houses off in the distance. Lillian could imagined how everything looked so beautiful and alluring to Renee after being trapped in Sid's filthy room for years.

"Yes. It's lovely out here. We'll try to see everything."

Silence fell across the minivan as they each thought about what was to come. A little while later, they were pulling into the Hyatt Regency-Central Plaza at 2025, Avenue of the Stars, Los Angeles, California. A valet sped away in the rental while a bellhop loaded their bags onto a cart. "I feel like one of them rich kids on T.V." Renee wasn't used to the livery service.

"Yes, madam, your room is prepared as you asked." The hotel clerk was even more polite. "Please enjoy your stay. Your luggage will arrive promptly."

After showering and changing into something comfortable, the two headed out the door, destination... fun, fun, fun mode. Their hotel was located on the fashionable, Westside adjacent to Beverly Hills. Renee stared in awe at the huge mansions, some with guest houses bigger than Lillian's mother's home.

"Wow. Who needs that much space?"
"The rich and famous." Lillian offered.

"You could move ten families in that house and still have plenty of room."

"Sometimes these homes are occupied by some rich bachelor."
"What's a bachelor?"
"Oh, a bachelor is a man who has never been married."
"Oh. Okay."

As they arrived in central L.A, Renee took in the splashes of colorful landscaping and buildings. "This is Universal City Plaza. First we'll grab a bite to eat then... Universal Studios, here we come." Lillian was just as anxious as Renee, always wanting to visit Hollywood as a child. "This place looks like it will be fun." Lillian pulled into a parking spot nearby.

As soon as they entered the Flintstones Bar-B-Q restaurant, they knew they had made the right choice. The place was decorated like bedrock with life sized characters of the whole crew. There was even a giant statue of Dino at the bathroom's entrance.

"We'll have two Pterodactyl burgers and a slab of Tyrannosaurus Rex ribs with Raptor sauce, baked beans, potato salad and a tray of volcano chips. Oh and a pitcher of soda."

They ate like cave women, devouring everything but the bones. "Let's just sit here for a while. I'm stuffed." Lillian had never eaten so carelessly, always watching calories.

"Me too. My belly's gonna pop."

"We need to do this more often." She paid the bill, leaving the waitress, dressed like Pebbles, a handsome tip.

They left the restaurant walking. On the way to Universal Studios, they passed through the Universal City-Walk of Hollywood. The spectrum of neon signs and colorful people was overwhelming. Laughter blending with the vendors themes and music made the whole scene feel like a movie clip. A world far away, this was... From the humid, Texas shack she had been rescued from. Renee, still couldn't believe she was here, with Lillian for good and away from harm...

She became extremely, emotional until she couldn't stop the tears from flowing forward. Slowly they crept to the corner of her eyes, suicidal, like a distraught person, threatening to jump from the office window. As they rolled down her cheeks she licked the side of her mouth, tasting the salty tear drops.

Lillian had been so caught up in her own thoughts, she hadn't noticed Renee was crying. "Oh, my god. What's wrong honey?" She asked, grabbing her shoulders gently. Renee wiped away a tear with her sleeve. The only reason she could come up for the tears was being grateful. She hugged Lillian tightly. "Thank you." She said between sniffles. "I thought I was gonna die there... Like my Momma."

Lillian tightened her grip. Now it was her time to cry. Standing in the middle of pedestrian traffic, they cried silently, oblivious to the people passing. "I have your back." Lillian assured her. After getting it all out they walked hand in hand to Universal Studios. The sight of the giant silver globe surrounded by a water fountain, wrapped in bold lettering that said Universal Studios, let Renee know she was really in Hollywood.

"Whoa, look at that thing. It's huge." Renee said happily, tears long gone. They spent the rest of the day touring the studio and picking up items from the gift shops before heading back to the hotel.

"That was the bomb. Wow, did you see the pictures of all the movie stars hanging everywhere? I saw a lot of them on TV before I just don't know their names."

"I could name quite a few. I think I've seen every made-for-TV show there is. Loved the crime dramas and mission impossible type flicks. A lot of them shot right at Universal Studio's."

"You should have been in the movies." Renee suddenly remembered how heroic Lillian had been when she had dealt with Sid and the other man called Bone. She could tell a lot of people were terrified of the man and his guns, but Lillian, her savior, had put his lights out without hesitation.

Once back at the hotel, they showered and sat on their beds, watching movies on cable before ordering snacks from room service. "I can't believe I'm still eating." When she got no response, she turned to see Renee fast asleep. Lillian smiled. *The fun's just begun. It gets greater later.*

The following morning, Lillian was up bright and early. She figured Renee would be sleep for a couple of hours and needed to make some runs. She scribbled on a note pad. **Back shortly, went to run some errands, order breakfast from room service. Should be good, at $300 a night.** ☺ **Lillian**

Lillian took a taxi, waiting curbside to Eagle-Rider, motorbike rental on South, La Cienega Blvd. She entered, noticing the line of Harley's and huge racing bikes.

"I'd like to rent a scooter type bike for a week."

"Sure. Straight ahead, then a sharp right." A salesman directed her to the scooters and mopeds at the rear. "Hello, how may I help you?" she was greeted by another salesman with bad case of acne.

"I was looking for something to rent for the week. Something with no gears but not too slow."

"Oh okay. Well we have several choices." He went down the line of scooters pointing out different features. "This nice yellow and black one is the Yamaha Zuma 50p, has a top speed of 40mph." Moving along, "This one here is the Vespa GTS 300 super, 278cc with a top speed of 80 mph."

"And what about this one?" Lillian approached a misty blue, scooter with the look of a sports bike. "This looks fast." It was a newer model with saddle bags aerodynamically situated on the back making it look futuristic. She noticed the BMW badge on the molding.

"That's the BMW C650 GT, 647-CL. We call that the High Roller, max speed 120 mph. "This is real nice." She ran her hands against the butter soft seat. "I like this one."

"Fine. Let's go take care of the paperwork." She also rented a helmet and purchased a pair of nice leather gloves. "You know, I could get you this bike at a good price if you decide to buy one." He offered.

40 minutes later she was headed towards East Los Angeles to Fountain Avenue. She pulled the bike into one of the stalls at Wimpy Burger House, directly across the street from Classic Custom Restorations. **We restore all cars back to original factory specifications…**

She glanced at her watch before pressing the intercom button. It was 10:45am. A young Latino girl's voice rang out. "Welcome to Wimpy Burgers. What would you like today?"

"Yes, I would like a Wimpy Burger, cheese-tatter-tots." She squinted, attempting to read the small lettering on the posted menu, in the glare of the sunlight. "Give me a cherry-limeade also."

She sat watching the shop, while waiting on her food to arrive. A worker in a brown uniform was moving cars from inside a fenced area in the rear to a parking lot at the right of the business. Every time the fence opened, Lillian could see men moving about and sparks flying from the grinding.

A pretty teen appeared with a tray and hooked it to the small stationary tray. Lillian took her time eating, watching as expensive cars and motorcycles came and went. Just as she was finishing the last of her tatter-tots a misty blue, Customized, 1933 Ron Beard, Ford convertible pulled out of the garage and pulled into a parking spot in the front. It had a full body custom paint job, airbrushed in an Egyptian theme, with an iconographic image of Osiris, his lunar god-crown encompassing the moon. The Ateh crown had two curling ostrich feathers at each side and he was carrying a crook in one hand and a flail in the other. In Egyptian lettering it read OSIRIS across the trunk. A worker hopped out and headed inside the front office. Moments later, a hulking figure emerged looking like an Aztec Indian on steroids, with his long, silky, black hair parted down the middle, braided in two ponytails.

Lillian watched Osiris get into the Classic Ford and ease into traffic. She counted eight vehicles before putting on her helmet and pulling out into the heavy traffic. Thirty minutes later he pulled off of the Expressway onto a road leading to a gated community in Hidden Hills. Lillian continued passed the road and made a U-turn at the next junction, heading back in the direction she had come, stopping at a 7-11 to purchase a pre-owned, automobile buyers magazine.

Renee was dressed and ready to go when she returned to the hotel. "I just have to make a few calls and were on our way." Lillian browsed the car magazine until she found what she was looking for. "Yes, I'm interested in the '65 Ford Mustang for sale in the buyer's line."

"The '65 Ford... Ah, you are aware that these cars are in need of restoration and are sold as is...?" The gentleman on the phone stated.

"Yes, sir. I'm having the work done by Classic Custom Restorations. Are you familiar with their work?"

"I've seen some of their work. Very nice... very expensive!"
"I hope they'll do great. Is the car available now?
"Yes. Sure. You can come down..."

"Okay, so I'd like to stop by in the morning to drop off the money..."
"It's $7,000, out the door."
"That's fine. I'll will send a tow truck to pick it up in the afternoon."

Once she wrapped up her conversation they headed for the door. Lillian glance over at the BMW, scooter in the next parking spot as she whipped the minivan out of the lot into traffic, thinking she wouldn't mind owning one of the sleek bikes. "Are you hungry?"

"Nah. I had a big breakfast, then when you didn't come back by eleven I ordered a burger and fries. It was so big I couldn't eat all of it." Renee patted her belly. "I'm gonna get fat if I keep eating like this."

Lillian smiled. "After all the activities today, I guarantee you'll be hungry as a hostage. I found the perfect place to go for dinner. Let's go to the boutique and get a few outfits before we go have some fun." After spending an hour buying garments the headed to Sherman Oaks in the South, San Fernando Valley. "This is one of the biggest laser tag places in the Country. Ultra Zone Laser Tag. It sounds exciting."

"Can you shoot?" Renee asked before remembering the sound of gunshots back in Dallas. "L-Laser guns."

"We'll just have to see."

The line was pretty long as it snaked around to the booth. Lillian noticed that they were the only African Americans on line. She smiled.

Black folks don't play laser tag. They like real guns with loud bangs.

"Lucky we dressed for the drama." Lillian strapped Renee into the target harness before fastening herself in. "The sensor at your heart will begin flashing like a red beacon when you've been killed. Try to stay moving and practice aiming at the sensors. Every time you're hit, a different part of your harness will illuminate. Stick with me no matter what."

Once they entered the dark maze, Renee was hit immediately causing her wrist to light up. "Oh shiii." Lillian grabbed Renee's arm, while sending a few laser shots in the direction of the shooter. "Damn!" She exclaimed as he disappeared around a corner, leaving her open. **Ping-ping,** her harness lit up as she took two shots in rapid succession causing both wrists to illuminate. "Let's go." She urged Renee to follow her to cover. Hiding behind a makeshift rock formation, Lillian tried to come up with a strategy. "We're getting hit too much already. We'll be fully illuminated soon." She peeked from behind their hiding spot to find a group waiting to ambush them. "Whoa. I see what's on. It's open season on soul Sisters today." She alerted Renee. "They want to get rid of us so be careful. Let's split up. You go the opposite way and come back around the way we came in. Soon as you see me start shooting."

"Okay." Renee waited on Lillian to bolt to the right, before she headed left. A group went after Lillian trying to cut her off while Renee slipped behind a canvas and made her way around. "Aw." A young white teen startled her as he jumped out screaming die-die-die, like this was Vietnam and he was a dog-of-war.

Ping-ping-ping. In all the panic she inadvertently pulled the trigger. The laser gun spit three quick shots lighting up his death beacon.

"Damn." He couldn't believe it. "What the fuck!" Although he had planned on ending Renee's game time, he was genuinely upset when she ended his. Billy was a breath away from calling the black teen a Fucking-Monkey but remembered the last time he had made a racial remark at the mini go-cart track, he got his ass kicked and robbed by a group of Latino kids from Compton.

By the time she reached Lillian, she was lit up to the shoulders. "Hey mom." Renee said in her best white voice causing Billy's mom to turn around. **Ping-ping.** Renee caught her twice before she realized she had made an error.

"Shit." Billy's mom turned quickly, only to get shot three more times, twice by Lillian and once by a family member attempting to come to her aid. Mom, now illuminated to the neck, was pissed, going from no hits to being almost eliminated. It had been her idea to team up against the black women.

Lillian jetted towards Renee, slapping her five. "Good work. Now let's go get the daddy and the rest of the family. Billy's Dad was a sharp shooter in the army but a crap shooter in laser tag. From his vantage point, he aimed directly at Lillian's sensor and pulled the trigger... Nothing happened. So he aimed and retried. Still nothing. "What the?" Irritated, he leaped from cover and laid on the trigger. **Ping-ping-ping-ping. Ping-ping.** No illumination. Evidently he had been given the one laser gun that didn't register pings out of the sixty available. What luck?

The girls looked at each other surprised and returned fire, each hitting him several times until his harness lit up indicating multiple deaths. **Ping-ping-ping-ping. Ping-ping. Ping-ping-ping-ping. Ping-ping. Ping-ping-ping-ping. Ping-ping. Ping-ping-ping-ping. Ping-ping.**

Renee really getting the hang of it began zigzagging around hitting sensors until the group was shaved down to just a few. "Watch out." Lillian pushed Renee out of the way just in time to avoid another hit but was lit up herself. The harness exploded with red lights. "Man." Lillian wasn't happy about being eliminated. "Go get 'em girl."

Like a drone that had been given orders to eliminate the enemy, Renee begin picking the remaining players off meticulously. She proved to be too fast and when finally she was the last soldier standing, Lillian ran excitedly to Renee and hugged her tight in victory. "You did it."

Billy's mom had a sour look on her face, like Renee had spoiled their family outing. Billy actually looked like he wanted to cry and his dad was at the counter complaining about defective equipment. "I was a fucking sharper shooter in war..."

Renee did the victory dance on the way out. **Ping-ping-ping-ping. Ping-ping. Ping-ping-ping-ping. Ping-ping.** They laughed all the way to the minivan.

"Wow. You was knockin' 'em off like flies."

"I learned that from you."

"Yeah, right. I got killed early. But you!--You held down the fort-apache and saved the day. Renee is the hero. Yeahhhhhh." Renee blushed not used to praise. "You drive, sniper."

Renee got behind the wheel and readjusted the mirror and seat. "Where to?"

"Get on the highway and keep driving until I say exit." Lillian wanted to surprise Renee. "I found a good place to eat while we watch a show." Renee couldn't wait. "You hungry now?"

"Starving."

Renee's excitement mounted as they drove into the parking lot of Medieval Times, Dinner & Tournament. "Wow," was all she could say. The restaurant's towering, white walls stretched the entire block, fashioned into the King's Castle with Draw Bridge and moat. "It looks like a real castle and everything." They looked like lost tourists in a big city, eyes following the ceilings and medieval décor.

Lillian began reading the scribe on an arch. "Surrender to an age of bravery and honor. A spectator in the Kings Court, observing epic battles of steel and steed. Feast your eyes, and appetite, enjoying the live Jousting tournament, Horsemanship and Falconry as you devour a four course meal fit for Royalty."

They were seated at a huge wooded table that extended the length of the wall, making a U-turn to the other side of the room. Sitting a few feet away was a large group of people appearing to already be having a boat load of fun. People were seated around the table surrounding a huge battle court. Renee was looking at the weapons menu describing all their names and uses.

"I'd use this one." Renee pointed to a Mace for Armor crushing.

"I'd probably pick this one." Lillian pointed out the Mandoble, a two handed sword. "Swish."

Finally the food began to flow. Lillian decided on roasted chicken, garlic bread, herb basted potatoes, and tomato bisque soup. Renee ordered the same except she preferred the spare ribs. Renee was looking for her utensils. "They didn't bring any forks."

"Oh, I forgot to tell you. There were no spoons and forks during that period... So get those fingers greasy."

"What about the soup?"

"Slurp-slurp." Lillian drank from her large soup bowl mimicking a cave woman.

One of the men in the nearby group apparently had too much to drink before arriving and was getting louder by the minute. The rest of the folks in his party, probably used to the drunken outburst, continued enjoying their meals without saying a word. When the show started, the crowd became captivated as armored clad gladiators performed a show of battles, fit to entertain many kingdoms. There were several shows, each one better than the other. During an intermission, they dipped into one of the gift shops on the premises, happy to get away from the drunk for a minute.

"If that man don't shut up." Lillian warned. "And his wife, or whoever that woman is holding his shoes like somebody might steal them."

"I thought you had to have on shoes to eat in a restaurant." Renee asked.

"You need brains too." They laughed.

When they returned, the show had already started and big mouth was heckling the horses. Apparently somebody had complained because a security guard posted against a wall directly behind the drunk. "My cock is bigger than yours Mr. Ed." He shouted at a white stallion.

"Stop that." His wife finally spoke up. The security guard did nothing.
'What. My cock is bigger..."
"Shut up. No its not!" She said, waving him to be quiet.

The man rolled his eyes, at the same time his head rolled back in a neck wobble before he jerked it back to attention. "That horsemeat's making me sick," he declared.

"I think it's about that time..." Lillian gathered her things.
"I had so much fun and the food was the bomb," Renee added.

No sooner than they exited their seats the woman placed her husband's shoes in the chair and another person ran from further down the table and hopped in the other one like they were playing musical chairs or something. Children under three entered free as long as they sat in an adult's lap. Since there were at least four kids, three years old or younger, in their group, the extra seats were a relief.

Just as Lillian and Renee exited, they heard a loud gasp from the entire audience before awkward silence. They looked back to see the entire family out of their seats with shocked looks on their faces.

"That fucking horse pissed on me." The drunk had gotten the worst of the powerful, stream of horse pee. They all began cursing in Spanish while management scrabble to qualm the problem. One of the smaller children couldn't stomach all the excitement and threw up his dinner all over the managers shoes.

Lillian and Renee spent almost a full ten minutes in the minivan crying tears as they laughed so hard, Renee's side was cramping. "Oh my god." She tried to regain her composer before bursting out in another fit of laughter.

"I can't believe that just happened."
"That horse knew what he was doing. You see he waited until we left."

Finally, after the laughter turned to a few giggles, Lillian pulled off. During the ride home, Renee sang along with some of the songs on the radio, even the older ones.

"How do you know the words to them old songs? Some of them are before my time."

"I used to listen to the radio all day. That how I learned a lot of songs."

"You have a nice voice too."

"Thanks."

Just then, an old Minnie Rippleton song came on. "I love this one." Renee joined in.

"Loving--you, is easy, cause you're beautiful. Cause every day of my life-- is filled with loving you. La-la-la-la-la, La-la-la-la-la, La-la-la-la-la--la-la-la-la-la, Do-do-do, Do-do, Ah...,"

They laughed when Renee attempted a high note like Minnie. "That was more like a scream for help." She admitted.

Lillian observed Renee as she sang, feeling like a proud mother at her daughters first recital. It was evident, Renee was happy and comfortable. Lillian wondered what it would have been like if her and Lewis had gotten married and had a beautiful daughter like Renee. "Sing it girl." She encouraged her to continue.

Back at the room, Renee watched television while Lillian sat in a recliner reading Snookie's brown leather book. She jotted down several names and addresses before joining Renee at the TV.

"What are you watching?"
"Set It Off."

"Set It Off. That's kind of violent." She caught herself sounding like her mother. "But it's a good movie. I've probably seen it ten times."

They couldn't get through the entire movie without ordering room service. After snacking on German chocolate cake, and milk & almonds, Lillian made a suggestion.

"How about we start doing a little workout routine every day, starting with some sit ups tonight? We eat like a football team." They both had gained a few pounds.

"I'm with it. Right after I eat one more piece of cake." Renee wolfed down the slice, having the time of her life. She held down Lillian's feet, counting each sit-up. "How many do we have to do?"

"About ten or twenty if you can."

They were able to manage several sets before deciding to start fresh another time. Exhausted from a long day of excitement, they slept like stowaways.

Lillian grabbed a small plastic container of orange juice from a breakfast cart as she passed by, peeling back the foil top and downing it in one gulp.

She pulled into a Shell station to gas up before heading off. Traffic was light during the early morning ride to the San Fernando Valley. Folks on the early shifts were making their way to work as Lillian pulled the minivan into the neighborhood of modern upper class homes.

She located the house she was looking for, a company restoration van in the driveway. **Eastside Restorations, Turn a bucket of rust, into a car you can trust.**

One of their other shops on the eastside.

There was a car next to the work van under a cover. From the custom wheels and lower potion that was exposed, she could tell it was another classic antique car. She surveyed the area taking notice of a line of shrubs along the surrounding landscaping. After getting a good look around, she noticed a Wrangler Jeep with no top and one of those metal 5 gallon gas tanks attached to its rear hatch. It was partially concealed in the shrubs. She wondered if it had any gas in it as she made a U-turn, headed to the eastside of LA.

She drove to three other locations around east LA. *From the looks of all the cars, these must be hangouts.* There were several cars, motor-cycles, SUVs, and pickups at the locations. The last house had a restoration van, a military hummer and three other vehicles including a '64 and '65 Chevy Impala parked side by side, across the lawn.

Lillian stopped by Ray's pre-owned cars and paid $7,000 cash for the Mustang. It was in need of some serious work. The interior was worn and torn, the paint peeling and faded.

"The strong point of this old baby is the motor and transmission." The owner tried to highlight something about the bucket, hopping she wouldn't change her mind about buying it. In fact, he spoke the truth. The engine and transmission were in great running condition. She paid without hesitation, not really caring if it ran or not.

"For another $150, I can have it delivered by a flatbed tow truck."

"That sounds good." She paid the tow truck fee. "Can you have it dropped off around 3:00pm?"

"No problem." He stated, grateful for her business.

Lillian wrapped up her business and went back to the hotel to have lunch with Renee before getting on the bike and heading to Osiris' shop. She was dressed in a pair of black, form fitting, cutoff shorts, and tank top, with a pair of black, Hi-Tech boots. The few pounds she had gain had her looking sexy, filling out in the right places. Her Creole background, light complexion and long, dirty-red hair gave definition to the term Red Bone. The fingerless riding gloves gave her superior grip as the BMW zipped through traffic, her mane blowing in the wind from under the helmet.

She whipped the bike into a space in front and dismounted, carrying the helmet under her arm. A worker on his way out of the office backed up to hold the door open for her.

"Thanks."

"You're welcome," he said politely, knowing better to harass a customer. He watched as she headed across the office. *My goodness. I'd like to ride on the back of her bike.*

"Hello. How may I help you?"
"Yes. I need to talk to someone about having a vehicle restored."

"Oh sure. I can help you with that." The short chubby woman handed her a clip board. "Fill out the form and I'll have someone come talk with you in a moment."

Lillian filled in the year, make, model, etc...

"Go down to the last office on the right next to the shop doors. It's one right before the garage. You'll hear all the sanding and grinding going on." She smiled and continued eating from the Styrofoam tray hidden under the counter, after Lillian proceeded towards the back. Just as she was about to knock one of the double doors leading to the shop flew opened and there stood Osiris.

"Well, hello." His voice sounded light coming from such a big body. Of course there were times when he sounded like thunder but there is something about the sight of a pretty female that calms the savage beast.

Lillian wasn't fooled by the mellow tone of his voice. She knew exactly who she was dealing with, and as long as he thought she was nothing but a customer she'd be fine.

"Hi." She hit him with the close-up smile. "I want to restore my mustang. It's a '65, given to me by my favorite uncle before he passed away... So I want to have it restored, like it looked back when he first bought it."

Osiris smiled at Lillian, thinking to himself that she reminded him of Pocahontas, only with reddish, brown hair. He dealt mostly with Samoan women and sometimes Latino but had never been with a black girl. Not really sure, by sight, he thought she might have been mixed.

He led her into an office. "Have a seat." Lillian sat down, placing the helmet on the floor between her feet. "I'm Osiris, the owner." She watched his huge figure settle into the leather office chair. "My name is Lollipop," she replied.

His desk was cluttered and unorganized. There was a security monitor connected to eight surveillance cameras placed strategically around the building so he could keep an eye on his operation.

"Are you interested in full restoration or just paint and interior?"
"I'd really like it totally new."

"We'll you've come to the right place. As a matter of fact, we just completed a 1964 mustang. It's in the paint oven drying. Let's go have a look. See if you like our work."

Lillian followed him through the double doors leading to the shop's work area. The air was filled with sounds of air hoses hissing, fiberglass being sanded and metal grinding. Sparks were flying in all directions as they proceeded farther into the garage towards the paint room. There were at least 15-20 sets of eyes on Lillian's long legs and round ass causing production to slow down 9% the moment she had entered.

"This belongs to a customer from Canada. He elected to ship it way to Cali to get done because we have a reputation for doing excellent work." The '64 mustang was painted burnt orange with vanilla racing stripes on the hood, crème colored, ostrich skin seats and crème suede headliner. Lillian had to admit to herself, it was nice.

"We change every nut and bolt, hose and bushing. Refinish the frame and covers. Um, suspension system, engine and tranny. Interior and exterior. I mean, we do the whole shebang. For a car like yours we charge 30k. For you I'll do everything for $26,000. So that'll be $6,000, to get started." He always made positive eye contact when he spoke, a sign of someone being truthful.

"Can I have it brought in today?"
"Need a tow truck? I also own a towing service."
"Um, no actually I have access to a flatbed."

"Let's do it." Osiris found himself glazing, until he refocused. "What kind of bike do you drive?"

Lillian had seen the row of Harleys and Fat Boys in the garage. "I wouldn't really call it a bike in the terms of real motorcycles but it's pretty fast."

"Come, this way." They headed up an isle passed the doors in which they had entered. There were cars, SUVs, trucks and motorcycles on racks and stands being worked on simultaneously. "We have three shifts here, meaning work is done 24/7. We have the fastest turn around rate in the world. Once your car hits the dismantling rack, we'll have it completely striped within 12-18 hours. So you could very well have your car back in 3-4 days. How's that?"

"That sounds great, O-Osiris."

He smiled, glad she had gotten it right. "I notice your accent. Where are you from, Ms. Lollipop?" He couldn't help licking his lips.

"I'm from New York."

"New York? Is that right? The city?"

Lillian was thinking she should have said Philly. "I'm from a little town upstate called Oneida."

"Oh yeah, I've never been upstate before. My people were from Harlem." Osiris replied.

"Harlem? I heard about that place." The look on her face indicated that the things she had heard weren't good.
    They continued towards the front of the shop. "We enter a lot of our customized cars and motorcycles in an annual show in the San Fernando Valley. You know, trophy, big cash prize, lots of publicity for the business... BMW?" He suddenly said upon exiting the garage and seeing her bike. "This is more, that, east coast hybrid; half motor bike, half bicycle thing... It's cute. Pretty good Germen Engineering. But if you ever want to take a ride on a real American dream, come roll with me."

Lillian smiled, figuring this was an indirect attempt at an invitation, of sorts. "What kind of motorcycle do you drive?"

Osiris thought she would never ask. "Check it out." He headed towards the parking lot on the right of the building. When Lillian rounded the corner she saw Osiris' pride and joy. The customized Harley Davison XL, sat bold upon the concrete. Chrome features, making love to the rays of the sun. There was an image of the Egyptian Goddess Isis wearing a head dress shaped like a throne, holding a Ankh in her hand. The background was an explosion of brilliant colors of indigo and fuchsia. The detailing was unbelievable, looking like something that was made for display only.

"Wow. It's like a work of art."

"How about if you be my guest at the bike show. I'm entering this bike for the first time. We just got it finished recently."

Lillian thought he would never ask. "Ah, I'm... When did you say it was again?" She asked not wanting to sound anxious as she headed back to her BMW. Osiris' eyes stayed glued to her backside. *Sexy as they come. Maybe Isis has completed her journey in search of her god...*

It's in two more days on Saturday. Show starts about 3:00pm. Lots of food, booze and fun. We setup a tent-line and basically have a real good time."

"Sounds nice. Count me in."

"You could meet up with us here about noon. We start heading out about 12:30, 1:00 or I can send someone to pick you up."

"Oh, that's not necessary. I'll meet you here. I'll notify my tow service about delivering my car so it should arrive sometime today."

Once back at her bike she removed her key and opened a compartment on the left side saddlebag and removed a flat stack of hundred dollar bills. "That's a hundred c-notes, leaving me a balance of $16,000." She extended her hand accompanied by a sweet smile. His large hand engulfed her tiny fingers as he accepted the handshake. Lillian admitted that under other circumstances, Osiris would pass as professional business man and law bidding citizen, and noted that the large handsome Samoan possessed a charismatic personally.

Wonder why I've never met any chicks like this in LA? Lillian struck him as independent and about business. *I wonder what kind of business she's into.* Osiris had a Latino girlfriend named Precious, referred to as his crew chick because she was part of his gang scene and was allowed to hang out with him and his boys along with their crew chicks, unlike his wife, Lunuola, who had been his high school sweetheart. She was home at all times attending his three children 24/7. Over the years, keeping house and having babies, Lunuola's cute little figure began to expand on her small frame so as of lately she was short and stout like a female midget wrestler.

One thing was for sure and that was that when Precious found out she wasn't going to the bike show, she was gonna be fuming. Samoan women were more docile and obedient in their household positions, however, on the other hand a Latino woman will poison your rice and beans if she thought you were even thinking about giving away some of her dick.

The minute Lillian got on her bike and sped away, Osiris pulled out his cell phone and turned it on. He dialed, Precious' number. "Hello."
"Hey, Presciosa-mommy."

"Hi O. I was just thinking about you earlier. Are you stopping by tonight?"

"Maybe. Look something important came up and I need you on a flight to South Beach tomorrow night."

"Tomorrow night? Then I'll miss the bike show Saturday!"

"Damn! I almost forgot about that. Well this is much more important so there's always next year." Precious was still cursing in Spanish when he hung up. He then dialed one of his couriers. "Listen Rory, I have somebody to fill in for you on the South Beach pickup so you can take care of another load headed to Canada. It's a '64 mustang, fully loaded."

Osiris walked into the building just as his cousin Teuila was dipping another tortilla chip into a bowl of guacamole. She was one of his uncle Kisona's three daughters.

"Rook called. I plugged him in to your office but it just kept ringing. He said your cell was going straight to voice mail and he was worried." She dipped another chip. "Oh yeah. Do you want me to forward the paperwork on that last job to Pennsylvania before five?" She buzzed him in.
"Ah, yeah. Sure." He replied barely listening, entertaining fleeting images of Lillian and trying to scroll his cell for Rook's number. Just as he sat down at his desk the faint sound of a motorcycle could be heard over the sanding and grinding, roaring outside. Osiris watched on the security camera as Rook parked his Red, Ducati sports bike next to the Harley and head inside.

"Did he show up?" Rook brought the scent of weed smoke in with him. Hoping he hadn't made a slip up and let something happen while he was laying up with some chick smoking and drinking all night.

"Calm down, cowboy. He was taking care of business with a pretty lady." Teuile took a big swig of diet soda.

"What pretty lady?"

"A customer, stupid. Get out of my face, already." She buzzed him through the heavy metal door.

Rook shook his head. *What the fuck is diet soda gonna do when you eat all fuckin' day.* He always wanted to ask her about it but thought better of it, knowing Osiris would come to agreement with her no matter what. *She needs a man, or a woman. Something.* The two disagreed most of the time but it was all love. Big sister and little brother forever.

When Kisona went to prison, his son, Atini was just one-year-old. Now seventeen, he was Osiris' shadow. He was appointed the position a few years back when drama was brewing between neighboring gangs and shooters were dispatched to Long Beach, Atini was eager to prove himself, but Osiris dissuaded his young cousin from jumping into the murder game so fast by keeping him around. Kisona had made him promise to keep his only son alive and out of prison. Osiris made the position sound mysterious and important.

"You're the son of Kisona, Sons of Samoan royalty. We got soldiers trained to handle the messy stuff. You will learn to move in silence."

"Come on Osiris. I grew up listening to the gangsters praising you and the work you put in..."

"That work got put in during a period when we were on the mission to get where we are now. Now that it's established who's in control there's no need to place someone so important to this family in unnecessary danger. So no, you can't roll with the hit team but you can have this new position in the crew if you want it."

"What new position?"
"Rook."
"Rook?"

"On a chess board the rook comes in order after the queen. The rook also participates, with the king in a special move called castling- **king and rook:** in chess, to move the king two squares to the left or right and move the nearest rook over the king to the adjacent square on the opposite side. The rook moves horizontally or vertically, through any number of unoccupied squares. As with captures by other pieces, the rook captures by occupying the square on which the enemy piece sits."

"So, I should move along with you capturing any enemies by occupying any space they sit? Did I get it right?"

"When I move, you're not far behind. Just far enough to watch my back. Or if we're not rolling together, you're always 3 to 4 cars in the rear. Like a shadow."

"So where's my gun?"

"Slow down." Osiris reached in his inside pocket and tossed him a cell phone. "Right now, you phone in anything suspicious, like an early warning. Maybe later the gat. I'll even get you a bike with a hidden gun box. Oh, take this too." He gave Atini a switch blade. "This came in handy when I was gang bangin' and dope slangin'. From now on your name is Rook."

That was almost three years ago. Osiris had kept the promise about the bike minus the hidden gun box. For a while young Rook had taken the position serious as a CIA agent would his job, trailing Osiris everywhere, poised for at all times. However, after some time with no attempts made, he came to realize that nobody was crazy enough to try to mess with Osiris and he was missing out on a lot of pussy, playing spy all day so he began slacking at his duties and tailing more booty.

"Where you been all morning?" Rook was checking to see if he had missed something.

Osiris leaned back in his office chair. "You need to a meal or two." He rubbed his stomach. "Samoans have a minimal weight requirement and them 150 lbs. you're sporting ain't cutting' it."

"150! I'm 180 all day, maybe 185 now! Oh, so I should start eating like Teuila. I bet if you check her desk, she's got a grocery store..."

"Hey, keep her out of this..." Osiris warned.

"Yeah! Keep me out of your shit, bitch ass nigga." Teuila appeared in the door way. "Don't worry about what the fuck I eat. Fucking Atini!"

"Oh shit. You set me up. I wasn't talking about you Sis."

"Yes you were. I heard you say my name."
"Did I say your name? You sure?"

"Fuck you. Shut up. Sorry, Osiris, for cursing in your office. But there's a flatbed dropping a car out front."

"Oh yeah, that's the '65 mustang. Write up the paperwork, have them put it on the rack and get started on it now. Tell them I want to roll it out of the paint booth by 9:00am Monday morning."

"Is it this job a special order?" Rook asked, after his sister left the room.
"Something like that." He said, knowing Rook meant a narcotics transport order. "Special order for a special lady."

"Hell you talking about? Oh, that's the lady customer that made you turn off your phone all morning?"

"I didn't turn off my phone, I just didn't turn it on until I got ready. Anyway this young lady put down $10,000 cash."

Rook did a double take, sensing that Osiris was liking somebody.

"Young lady? Oh shit. No bitch? Man you better stop. Precious gonna buy a gun you don't know about. I'm warning you..."

Osiris laughed. "You don't even like Precious, cousin, so you should be happy I think I found my Isis."

"Oh-oh shit. You're trippin' now Osiris. I remember you saying, quote, 'There is no bitch on earth that meets the divine qualifications,' or some shit like that, 'to take on the title of the beautiful goddess' of something."

"The goddess of fertility." He enlightened Rook. "This one is real close," he smiled. "Don't worry, you'll get to meet her." He watched a dismantling crew pushing, Lillian's mustang to the rack in the rear of the garage from the security monitor on his desk. "She's riding to the show with us Saturday."
Rook couldn't believe his ears. "I want to see you pull this off. I've seen you perform miracles but the only way I see you getting away with this is if you knock Precious off and that's out of the question because you're whipped. Other than that, the crazy bitch is killing you." He was bent over, laughing. "Make sure I get that Harley XL in the will."

"Might be a time to change flavors. All Precious does is wreck cars and spend money on shoes and clothes."

"Change flavors? She's white, Chinese?"
"Looks like she might be mixed."
"Mixed with what?"
"Black and white."
"You been fucking around in Compton?"
"She's from New York."

The phone ringing interrupted Rook's next response. "Hello. Yeah. Okay. Fine. I'll start getting the room ready. Okay cool. See you then." After hanging up, Osiris was back in business mode. "We got a big load going out Monday. It's traveling to the coast via RV transport then to Hawaii before it makes its way to the Samoan Islands. Make sure Parachute has the correct time and have him bring the RV in tonight so it can be loaded tomorrow."

"Got it." Rook was out of his seat, on his way out the door to take care of orders. He got on his bike headed to east LA to Parachutes crib.

*****

A big, greedy, grey, rat scurried along the edge of the catwalk racing against the approaching daylight, trying to locate any crumbs left behind by his brethren who had long ago retreated back into their dark hiding places at Lompoc Penitentiary. A prison issued work boot, smashing against the drab, wall directly above his head sent the rodent darting in several directions before deciding to take cover.

"Damn! I almost got the mutha' fucka'."

"Shut the fuck up," somebody screamed from under a blanket, up the tier.

"Ah, shut the fuck up yourself." Clarence mumbled, had he began brushing his teeth, preparing for his early morning shift in the mess hall.

At 5:30 sharp, like clockwork, the morning officer cracked his cell.

"Let's move it Clarence!" the corrections officer yelled.

"Alright, alright. I'm coming," Clarence spit into the combination sink-toilet, before heading out of his cell, stopping to put on the boot he had launched at the Rat. Once at work in the kitchen he began making preparations for breakfast, loading the mixing vat with enough oatmeal to feed the entire prison population. Before the rest of the kitchen crew arrived he had the containers of concentrated orange juice ready to be poured.

"Let's get the boxes of potatoes from the back and loaded onto the peeling table." He ordered Crawford and Morrison as they entered with a C.O. "Need to get into the knife cage boss. Got a lot of peeling to do today," Clarence said as he left the kitchen headed out into the mess hall area to begin filling the two inmate water pitchers on each table. Once he reached the second table in the tenth row he paused, quickly checking to make sure the C.O was still busy counting and documenting the knives. Clarence reached under his apron, quickly placing the crudely, fashioned shank under the metal, bench-made table with a strip of duct tape. He returned to the kitchen to help get started with the potato peeling and slicing.

At 7:45am, inmates began filing in by cell location, each one taking a seat with their click. Federal inmates travel in clicks referred to as "cars." Which identifies what state one originates from. In no time the tables were filled with hungry inmates eating and chattering about jailhouse politics.

Breakfast normally went on like clockwork at Lompoc; in and out. The two guards at the entrance immediately retreated into the C.O break room directly across from the mess hall as soon as the last cell block had been seated.

Kisona sat one seat away from the edge of his table waiting for his special tray of smoked sausage, eggs with diced green peppers, and onions, home fried potatoes, cinnamon cream of wheat and toast with jelly & cream cheese. His number two man, Juan seated to his right in the first seat of aisle ten, had already began devouring his oatmeal and toast along with the other four men at the table. A kitchen worker appeared with Kisona's food and he wasted no time digging in.

The guard, positioned in a fiberglass enclosed tower directly above the mess hall entrance, peeped up long enough from the Sports Illustrated swimsuit addition magazine to see the food server heading back up the aisle, towards the kitchen. He downed the rest of his diet Pepsi before getting up and going into the tiny bathroom to take a shit. From his spot on the shitter, C.O Wilson could hear the buzzing background chatter of a hundred, lying prisoners talking at the same time. At the same moment, the kitchen officer was called to the back by Clarence. "I think we have a knife missing."

The officer automatically called all the guys together. "Where's Morrison?" He asked when the inmate didn't appear quick enough.

"What's going on?" Morrison rounded the corner holding a basket of sliced and peeled potatoes. "Trying to get an early start on the dinner batch." The C.O sucked his teeth before retrieving the missing knife from atop the basket as Morrison headed to the sink to rinse. "Don't scare me like that. Shit, wouldn't want one of these to get into the wrong hands."

"Let's get these locked up." He proceeded to secure the rest of the utensils, as everyone continued with their duties. "Get this placed cleaned up." He ordered on his way out.

Just then, C.O Wilson was wiping his ass with the last sheet of tissue on the roll, hoping it would be enough. "Damn." He cursed his luck. After finding a piece of cloth hanging on a nearby hook, he double wiped and flushed, leaving behind a foul smell and without washing his hands. Once back at his post, he reached into his bag of mesquite, barbeque chips and tossed a handful into his mouth, suddenly aware of the extreme silence that had fallen on the mess hall. The kitchen officer noticed the same eerie silence that could only be attributed to jailhouse tension. There was a small group of inmates filing through the line, dumping their trays, all apparently from the almost empty table on row ten. The officer did a double take at the image of the large man, faced down on table two, bleeding profusely from a gaping hole in the side of his neck. "Fuck!" He shouted as he pulled an emergency pin from his communication unit, alerting the special tactical unit. Within minutes the mess hall was under siege and the prison on full lockdown.

News began to travel quickly about the murder of the founder of the Sons of Samoan and number one shot caller at Lompoc. During the course of the day and into the evening, the investigation continued.

Officials were running into problem after problem from no eye witnesses in a mess hall full of people and discovering the security camera that records the mess hall run had been reported nonfunctional one day before, and had a work order pending.

After answering standard questions for most of the day, the correction officers on duty during the incident where more than happy at the end of their shifts. Most of the bunch, aware that their lax attitudes about security may have contributed to the events, exhaled with relief. The first thing Wilson did when he got into his old, Ford, Explorer was pull out his cell phone and dial a 1-800 number. The automated teller asked for a series of numbers before giving him the information he wanted.

"Your account balance is...twenty-thousand, one-hundred and nine dollars." He smiled. Happy the $109.00 in his account had some company. Now, all he had to do was give his wife's brother, Clarence, two grand and call it a day. Although Wilson had been employed by the Bureau of Prisons for eight years, he still maintained ties with his old buddies in Compton and often did favors for the homeboys passing through for a little extra cash here and there.

*****

At the same time, that life as we know it was fleeing Kisona's body, miles away at a four star hotel, Lillian was taking a hot shower while singing the song that had Renee attempting to hit a high note in the car. Ever since Renee had sung, it was suck in her head.

"Loving--You, is easy cause you're beautiful. Cause every day of my life-- Is filled with loving you. La-la-la-la-la, La-la-la-la-la, La-la-la-la-la--la-la-la-la-la, Do-do-do, Do-do, Ah...,"

She emerged from the bathroom feeling fresh and clean. *Renee should sleep until about noon. That will give me enough time to take care of a few things.* Lillian made plans for them to visit the speedway and Ranch Park Archery Range later today. She wanted to spend the entire day having fun with Renee, knowing she'd be busy at the bike and car show with Osiris on Saturday.

Lillian glanced at her watch before backing the minivan out of its parking spot. *9:15 am. I'll swing by Classic Custom Restorations to see if they started on the Mustang like he said they would, and have another look at the place.*

When she arrived at the shop there was a huge delivery truck parked directly in front of the garage, blocking several parking spots so Lillian had to park on the street and walk about 200 feet to the building. She found the door to the front entrance locked before walking around to the gate leading to the garage.

"Hello." She spoke to a man standing inside the gate. "Is your boss around?"

Recognizing her from the previous day, the garage worker smiled. "Good morning, ma'am. Yes, he is in the office. You can go straight back, all the way, then to the right until you reach the double doors."

"Oh yes. The same way we came from yesterday. Okay, I remember." Lillian returned the smile and began walking the route she and Osiris had taken when he had escorted her to her bike in the parking lot. The workout outfit she wore hugged every curve of body as she made her way into the noisy garage. The shop wasn't as crowded as it had been during her last visit.

When Lillian reached the shop doors leading to the offices she could hear voices faintly in the background. Osiris office was the first one on the right. "Hello." She spoke through the partially opened door with no response. "Osiris," calling his name softly, she pushed opened the door and peeped inside to find an empty room. The voices she heard were coming from security monitors. Lillian ducked inside moving behind the desk until the screen was in view. The monitor was filled with several camera views from around the building. On camera view #8, Osiris was standing above several men including, Parachute, working on a RV.

"The best spot in these things are behind the sink panels and interior wall-wells. This is a heavy load... Thirty million. It's got to be secured properly." After pointing out several areas, Osiris directed the men to start loading the packages of US currency from a pallet on a nearby fork lift. He stood by with his arms folded, watching them load the Recreational Vehicle with his hard earned cash. Suddenly, he nodded to Parachute to manage the situation before turning to leave the room.

Lillian panicked, not wanting to get caught in his office, she darted out, into the corridor not knowing how close the room from camera view #8 was to her location.

Just as she was about to leave thru the shop doors she had come in thru something told her to head in the other direction towards the receptionist desk. She could see the lobby beyond the door where she had entered on her first visit. The lights were off as she turned the knob to discover it was locked. "Damn." Then she suddenly remembered having to get buzzed in.

Relief, when she located the button under the counter. Lillian barely made it into the dark lobby before Osiris entered the shop doors. He sat down at his desk watching the RV being loaded and reassembled, finding himself thinking of the pretty girl who had walked into his shop the day before... He even thought he could smell the scent of her sweet perfume in the air. *Can't wait until tomorrow to get Ms. Lollipop on the back of my bike. Maybe I might get a chance to taste that candy.*

Lillian was able to get the last of three heavy locks unengaged before exiting through the front door of the business and cutting across the parking lot where she had parked her scooter during her previous visit, headed to her minivan parked up the street.

Rook had overslept as usual, knowing he was supposed to be at the shop early on Fridays to open the offices and man the desk until Teuila arrived at 2:00pm. He looked over at the shop from across the intersection where he was stuck at a stop light on his motorcycle, trying to see if Osiris' car was in the lot but the big delivery truck was blocking his view. *Maybe Osiris ain't here yet.* He knew better even as the thought crossed his mind, figuring he had probably arrived bright and early. When Rook thought about it, he decided it was worth the drama because as far as he was concerned man can't survive without money and pussy, not necessarily in that order. *Damn, I got to slow down on these e-pills and Lucinda's addictive pussy.*

The light finally changed green. "Shit, that's a long ass light." Rook made the left and prepared for a sharp right into the parking lot, when he noticed Lillian darting across the parking lot. She walked quickly along the sidewalk, until she reached her minivan. Once she started it up and pulled away she began to relax. *That was a close call. I'm sure Osiris would kill to keep that type of money safe. 30 million.* Lillian's mind begin to wonder thinking about all the possibilities. *I could build a whole school house with that and more.*

Who the fuck is that? Rook wasn't sure but he thought he'd seen her exiting from the front of the building, knowing it was supposed to be locked until he arrived. *That didn't look right. Maybe I'm tripping.* His shadow instincts kicked in. *That pretty ass chick was moving kind of sneaky like.* He bypassed the shop and followed the minivan to the expressway continuing to follow from several car lengths behind. Lillian's mind was racing trying to fit her new found discovery into her plans. She decided to head back to the hotel to think some things though before heading out for the day.

As Rook followed he suddenly begin to wonder if the pretty, sneaky woman was the one Osiris talked about all day yesterday. *Shit, maybe Osiris was hitting it in the office and had her sneak out to avoid being seen. I'm might be wasting my time, making myself even more late for work.* Rook reached for his phone only to discover he didn't have it. Suddenly, an image of his phone appeared in his head, lying on the edge of Lucinda's sink where he had left it when he took a leak on the way out. *Damn, she might not wake up until after 3:00 pm. Fuck! I'll have to go way back to the Eastside.*

Lillian eased the minivan into a parking spot and hopped out without looking around and entered the building. The air conditioned lobby of the hotel made her realized how humid it was outside, feeling a drip of perspiration roll from her underarm.

Rook watched Lillian disappear into the Hyatt Regency Century Plaza hotel as he bypassed the driveway, making a U-turn at the next meridian and jumping on the highway headed back to Lucinda's to retrieve his phone.

*****

Renee was awake eating lunch and watching TV when Lillian returned. "Boy, it's hot out there today." She greeted her as soon as she saw the great big smile on her face. "Are to ready to make it a nonstop day of adventure and excitement, little one?"

"Sure am, can't wait. I already have my clothes laid out." Renee jumped up to hug Lillian before going to get prepared. Lillian decided another shower wouldn't hurt.

Within the hour, the two were secured in their seat belts headed to the Cotner Ave, speedway, the home of Gotham Dream Cars. The sound of engines accelerating could be heard from the parking lot of the race track. Renee's excitement was building as she realized that these were real cars on a real track.

"Driver's License, please." The tall freckled faced man gave Lillian change from the two admission tickets she purchased. "Someone else might ask to see your license again. So have it ready."

They walked to the service counter thru a carpeted corridor. "Hello ladies." Another man greeted them. "Will you both be driving today?"

"No, she will. I'm riding shotgun." Lillian said.
"Okay. I just need to have her license."

Lillian handed the man her license and two folded hundred dollar bills. "Fine. Please enjoy your stay and drive responsibly," was all he said before turning over the keys. Up ahead another employee was waving them forward. "This way."
They approached the yellow & black Ferrari like it was a spaceship that had just landed in their back yard. "Dang." Renee couldn't believe she was about to drive it.

"This is the Ferrari Spider, 490 hp, V8 0-60 in 4.0 sec. She's a real beauty. There's an empty track, just follow the blue road out of the chute."

Vrooooooommmm, Vrrrooooommmm! The engine fired up with authority. Renee climb behind the wheel, all smiles. Lillian buckled her seat beat. "Take it easy. This is way more power than the Mercedes Benz you learned to drive with."

The Italian-made Ferrari lurched as she applied too much pedal. "Whoa. I feel the difference. Okay let me get it right." She applied just enough pressure and they were on their way, traveling along a strip of blue roadway that let out into a full blown race track. Renee cruised along getting the feel of the power beneath her behind, until she was ready to open it up a little bit. Glancing over at Lillian she got the okay to open it up a little.

Vroooooommmm, Vrrrooooommmm! Renee punched the exotic sports car along the straight-away slowing for sharp turns and curves.

"Yeah." She felt free moving along at such a high rate of velocity. Lillian put her head back and took a deep breath feeling fast and free also. Renee spent at least thirty minutes navigating to speed way before building up an appetite. "Let's get something to eat from the snack bar and then come back so you can drive."

"Whatever you say, speed racer."

They had a quick bite and spent a couple more hours taking turns running the quarter mile race, comparing times. Lillian only beat Renee a fraction of a second in their fastest run. "Girl, you're getting too good." She praised her young student driver. After wrapping up their fun at Gotham Dream Cars, Lillian headed right to the next event.

"This should be interesting." Lillian said as they entered the Rancho Park Archery Range. Renee remained attentive during the quick orientation.
"Archery lessons start in 20 minutes in the armory. Any questions." The Instructor addressed the small crowd of customers.

They signed up for the lessons and where assigned an archery range where they spent the next thirty minutes learning the proper use of the equipment before they shot the first arrow. Within the hour Lillian and Renee where hitting the target gradually closing in on the bull's eye area.

"Oh yeah, you saw that one." Renee nearly hit a bull's eye.

"You mean like this." Lillian lined up her sight on the bow & arrow and let the go. It sailed towards the target like a guided missile hitting the bull's eye. "Booyah." She exclaimed.

"Wow. You're good. Let me get just one and I'll be happy." Renee attempted several more times, coming pretty close but failing to hit the intended target.

"I know what you need." An instructor passing by suggested. He disappeared and appeared moments later with a long black case containing two crossbows with scopes.

"Try these. They're very sturdy and accurate. Gives you the feel of a gun the way you aim and squeeze." After quickly showing them how to operate the crossbows he handed them over.

"Now this is what I'm talking about." Renee looked through the scope until she had the bull's eye lined up. Steady, she took a deep breath and held it pulling the trigger before she exhaled. It found a direct path to the dead center of the target. "Yes!" She jumped for joy.

Lillian hit several areas of the bull's eye but never dead center like Renee had. "You're a quick learner and that is a blessing."

Renee was glowing. "I'm learning from the best."

Before they knew it hours had passed and dinner bells were ringing in the heads. They began packing the equipment. "Did you guys enjoy yourselves?" The instructor inquired.

"Absolutely." Lillian replied. "I want to thank you for putting us up on the crossbows, they are really very easy to handle."

"Well I'm glad to have been of some help to you. If you're interested we have several affordable models for sale in our archery shop. You can stop by on your way out. It's on the other side of the reception counter."

Lillian entered the shop with Renee not far behind. "Let's check out some crossbows. This could be a great sport to take up." She smiled at the sales lady. "Hi. We just spent a few hours at your archery range having a great time practicing and one of your instructors recommended your shop here..."

"Sure. I'll be glad to assist you. Now what I recommend for a novice is the Barnett Banshee 1075, comes with scope, arrow kit. It's one of the least expensive... Goes for $231.94 a piece." She took the crossbow out of its case.

"What about that one?" Lillian asked, pointing to an all-black, sleek looking crossbow on a rack display."

"That is the Barnett Ghost 410. It retails for... Ah, $999. Comes with night vision and all that stuff. For somebody that's more into tactical crossbows."

"Give me one of each."

After loading her purchases in the trunk of the minivan they headed to the Cheesecake Factory to stuff their faces. Lillian devoured a plate of baked halibut with potatoes and asparagus while Renee had fried jumbo shrimps, baked potato with sour cream & butter, creamy corn and garlic bread. The dinner hit the spot, satisfying the appetites they had built up in the mist of all the fun.

"I'm going to dive in the bed when we get back. That's how worn out I am. I don't know about you but I'm thinking... Good night, sleep tight and don't let the bedbugs bite." Renee could remember staying up all night afraid to fall asleep because of the bedbugs lurking in the cracks and crevasses waiting to feed off of her blood like hundreds of vampire roaches. She issued a sigh of relief silently thanking the lord once again for Lillian.

During the drive to the hotel the sound of Renee snoring lightly could be heard over the music playing softly on the radio. Lillian's mind was deep in thought about tomorrow's bike show and the best way to get Osiris to let down his guard. She was pretty tired and decided to valet the van instead of parking it herself. "Renee. Get up. We're here." She handed the valet a ten dollar bill and proceeded to help Renee, who was still half asleep. They both were too pooped to shower and headed straight to bed.

Rook lie staring at the ceiling, wondering how Lucinda could slept so well after popping e-pills all day. He sat up, shaking his head as he headed to the bathroom to relieve his bladder.

"Ouch!" He shouted, jumping around on one foot. "My fuckin' toe." His eyes focused on the object responsible for his pain. "Damn dumbbells. She never fuckin' works out anyway." Lucinda continued to sleep like a baby even with all the noise he was making.

His throbbing toe was the least of his worries. Earlier that evening Osiris had chewed him up so bad that he was feeling low with a lingering sense of failure. He knew it was his fault because instead of retrieving his phone and going straight to work he wound up butt naked, knee deep in pussy. Plus, it didn't help that he tried to go on the defense.

"Come on. Opening up the office and manning the phones... That's chick business. I want to bust some heads open, make some big moves for the crew, you know? Plus I figured since you were packing a big load it would be better to keep the traffic down in the offices..." The truth was his dick got the best of him, again.

171

"You figured? It's not your fucking job to figure shit. Far as you not showing up on a day when the extra security was needed... Anything could have happened. I needed somebody on that security monitor 24/7. Rook you've lost sight of your whole purpose. The only thing you shadow is Lucinda's ass! Well, I'll tell you what mutha' fucka,' you ain't riding with the crew to the bike show. You're running the shop Saturday and delivering the RV to my house on Sunday."

Rook felt the heat. This was the first time Osiris had spoken to him like that and he was feeling small, unproven. Inadequate and unreliable.

I have to show Osiris I'm not a fuck up. Shit, I can handle myself better. I don't want him thinking I'm some buster. I have to get on the ball.

Rook realized it was time to get back on his job, keeping watch over the family. Since he was in charge of the shop today he'd make sure nobody was slacking because the boss was off. He glanced at his watch, *6:05am, deciding* to shower now and get dressed so he'd be at work bright and early, even before Osiris arrived with the crew to prepare for the bike event. It was time to show the boss he was serious about his job.

Osiris fastened the last strap on his bike trailer just as Lillian was pulling up on her BMW scooter. He smiled before making sure all three bikes were secure.

"Glad you could make it. You can pull your bike into the garage in the first stall."

"Hi." She continued towards the gates. After parking her bike inside she checked her appearance before getting in the huge, military style Hummer with Osiris. He was checking her appearance also. "Wow this is big. Fits you just right." She added.

"Good morning beautiful lady. Looking like a real biker babe today. I like it. Very sexy."

Lillian had Google some of the past events viewing pictures to check the dress code so she'd fit in much as possible. She was wearing a sheer wife beater under a black leather vest, with a pair of form fitting jeans and riding boots. Her hair was in a long ponytail, sexy, even in road gear.

"My crew headed out at 8:00 am this morning to set up the tent and get the grills fired up. Hope you like to eat because my grill man, Cyclone is the best. He claims he can barbeque a moose in a minute."

"Moose? I don't know about no moose meat."

"Don't worry, no moose. I don't really know what that means but he'll tell you that every time. You'll meet some of the guys when we get to the sight. They're managers at a few of the other shop locations and some of their girlfriends will be there. Everybody's nice and mellow."

Osiris turned the big hummer onto the road leading to the fairgrounds pulling the trailer carrying his three prized bikes. Soon as he pulled up to the area where his crew had sent up tent, four men hurried to the trailer to start unloading the motorcycles.

"I'm entering three bikes in the competition this year. We worked really hard on the custom Harley XL... Looking to take first place."

Lillian was half listening, checking out all the people milling about the area. Tents lined the rear of the field. Cars, trucks SUV's and big-rigs filled the massive parking lot. *A person could get lost in this crowd.*
"I peeped in on your car and it's coming together. Two of my shops stay open 24 hours. I have like...elves working around the clock to get peoples toys ready for the world. When you see your Mustang on Monday, you'll be happy."

"Monday? Wow, now that's putting in work. I can't wait to see it."

"I put the word down to the crew to make it a showstopper." Osiris smiled, exhibiting his pearly whites. "If I put my name on it, it's gonna be correct."

Smoke bellowed from two huge grills manned by a tattooed covered Cyclone. The smell of roasting beef and pork filled the air as the camp ground transformed into a biker's domain.

"Let me introduce you to a few of the guys. I've already mentioned our famous chef, Cyclone. That's his girl Nadia..." He continued, Dantana and Floridata, this is Eva, Diablo's woman, one of my shop foremen. I wanted you meet my cousin Rook, he's more like my son but he had to work today so he couldn't make it."

Lillian mouthed hello has she waved to everyone, not missing the funny look from Nadia. Osiris introduced her to several more of the crew and their girlfriends and it became obvious that the female she was filling in for was one of their friends.

Lillian remained cordial. *I'm not here to make any friends. You bitches better stay in check.* "Nice to meet everyone. My name is Lollipop." Now she watched the other women's different responses... Exaggerated breathes, eyes cutting left and right. Although they knew they were just the girlfriends, not wives, having their circle violated by the, the... Lollipop, was cause for attitude.

Osiris threw back a bottle of beer as he barked instructions to his men, barely noticing the interaction between the girls. "Take the bikes to the pit and get everything ready for show time. I want everybody on their jobs, no bullshit. We'll celebrate after we win the prize."

Everyone fell into position like a well-oiled machine. Lillian found herself a spot in a padded beach chair and sat back watching everything from behind her dark sunglasses as she pretended to read a motorcycle magazine.
She observed Cyclone pass Nadia something in a small plastic package before she and the other women got up heading in the direction of the fairgrounds and restrooms. They never looked in Lillian's direction letting her know an invitation to join them was not pending. The air was suddenly void of tension and catty sighs and signs from the girlfriend clique.

The loud speaker broadcasted the start of the show within the next 30 minutes, causing a lot of movement in the crowd. People began leaving the tent sites making their way to the fairgrounds at least a quarter miles walk.

Just then, Diablo pulled up in an opened top, jeep followed by a big, loud, Ford Bronco. "Let's go." Osiris helped Lillian into the vehicle before climbing aboard followed by Cyclone. All but one of the group of men hopped into the Bronco and followed. War-hog had been dispatched to watch over the pots of food simmering to flavor on the gas grills, then load it up and truck it over to the pit area. Much as he enjoyed bikes, he enjoyed food even more. At close to 360 lbs., he figured he could relax all day, listen to gangster rap and sample all the different types of meats, and other tasty things to enjoy. No sooner than the crew left he began piling up his first plate of the day...

The Jeep and Bronco kicked up dust as they sped along the dirt road. "Yeah-baby." Cyclone yelled as they approached their pit area. The three bikes, all done by Osiris Restorations were done at three locations, One at Classic Customs and the others at the shops managed by Cyclone and Diablo. This year it was like a competition with a competition. (e.g., Best prize bike out of the best shop project.)

"I love my brothers, but this year my crew put the whammy on... If the world can see what I saw when we put this bike together..."

Diablo interrupted. "All the visions and dreams can't help you. What I put into play with my bike is nothing short of a buckets of nuts, bolts, fiberglass and kick ass..."

Before Osiris could offer his declarations of success he was interrupted by the ring of his cell phone. He peeped at the screen before turning it off. *Thought I powered it down already. Sure don't want to talk to Rook right now.*

From the pit area, Lillian could see how huge the fairgrounds were, estimating at least 10,000 people in attendance. All of the crew had arrived at Osiris' pit area including the girlfriend clique. Most likely under the influence of alcohol, and probably cocaine, considering the looks of the package they headed to the bathroom with. Upon returning they tried to look through Lillian instead of at her, letting her know she had been the topic of discussion between snorts. One thing for sure, each of them knew their place and dared not make a public issue out of it. Osiris wouldn't tolerate it and would check his crew member who would in return check his girlfriend and from a past incident it became evident that girlfriends were definitely checked hard. After a while, Lillian realized there would be nothing more than an occasional sideways look from them. They were all good friends with Precious but not enough to get beat down for.

As the men scurried about, preparing their crews and projects, a picture and plan began to emerge, of three necessary targets...

Osiris became extremely busy almost forgetting Lillian was there, however an oversexed Cyclone had smiled in her direction more than once as everyone was moving about readying one thing or another. Even the women were shining and polishing their particular shops' bikes.

Once the show began, everyone headed to their pits. The crowd applauded some of the better looking bikes during the introductions, showing a high level of enthusiasm.

"Hear that crowd? I fucking love it!" Cyclone slapped Nadia's ass hard. "Ouch, fuckin' Cyclone! Stop."

"You don't never say stop, before..." He laughed along with his boys. "Go get more beer," he ordered her.

At some point Lillian begin to realize how hard it would be to get Osiris alone for even a minute under these circumstances. *He's feeling me so getting me alone is somewhere on his list I suppose.* Lillian's thoughts were interrupted by the announcer calling for all judges and contestants to get ready.

The sound of bang flashes and other fireworks along with thousands of screaming fans filled the sky, setting the stage for the event. Several American muscle bikes roared in unison as enthusiastic bikers laid on their throttles. The noise was so loud an elephant could hide behind it. During the first stage only one bike from Osiris' group, Diablo's project, went thru against several other shops. All attention was on the parade of exotic motorcycles. "That's an orgasm of chrome and paint," someone shouted.

Osiris' Classic Customs bike was up during the second round and the crowd had reacted almost equally to the first group that went thru. He was deep in the mix of the show when Cyclone got up to relieve his bladder after what must have been his 10th beer, impatiently waiting for his bike to get called in the next round. Lillian watched him miss a step on his way out of the pit. No one seemed to notice his departure, not even Nadia who was in a tight circle seemingly conspiring with her friends.

After a quick ten count she got up and headed in the direction he had gone, spotting him ahead as she weaved through the crowd of people occupying the path to the restrooms. She stopped at the water fountain separating the men's and women's bathroom and took a long sip waiting for him to exit.

The first thing Cyclone saw when he walked out the pisser was a set of long legs connected to a symmetrically, sculpted ass in form fitting jeans and rider boots. His neck muscles tensed as he flexed subconsciously at the sight of her.

"Cyclone. Hey there." She said softly.

"Oh so you do talk." He looked around. "Had to take a trip to the ladies room too, huh. I mean, I went to the men's room..." *Am I making any sense?*

Lillian smiled seductively, changing the subject. "Do you work out?" She had no way of knowing that this was a question often asked of Cyclone and that he took pride in talking about the work he put in making his muscles rock hard.

"I work out every day. When I'm at work, I'm working out. It's what I do. Fix cars, call shots and work out."

"Can I touch one?" She reached out and touched his arm as he tensed. The fibers in his triceps felt like titanium steel. His ego was clouding his judgment more than the alcohol at this point. Sure Osiris was big and strong but Cyclone thought himself more worthy of a Greek god when it came to statue and girth.

At this point his muscles weren't the only thing rock hard. Cyclone grabbed Lillian by the hand and led her to a foot path leading behind the building where the bathrooms were housed.

"We used to set up at the picnic tables back here a while ago when we first started our shops." Cyclone's breathing became intense as he approached the picnic area, feeling like a thief about to steel his grandma's last eleven dollars, or should I say, feeling like he did as a kid the day he stole his grandma's last eleven dollars. Even remembering the tears it caused, and the way he pretended to help look for it. *"I saw Bobby coming out of your bedroom."* Then trying to frame one of his cousins for the deed...

Knowing he didn't have time for a full-fledged, fuck fest, the implications of her name (Lollipop) made him want to take a good taste of her sweaty, crotch. He imagined himself feasting, greedily as she was perched atop the edge of the picnic table with her ass in the air.

Cyclone sat on the bench with his back against the picnic table, pulling her by the hips so that her crotch was against his nose and took a deep breath. "Um. I love to drink the sweet nectar." he whispered, more to himself.

The nearby trees cast a shadow over the area, simulating bedroom lighting to facilitate his fantasy. Cyclone closed his eyes as a vision of Lillian climbing slowly atop his face appeared on his minds-movie-screen.

Have you ever seen a movie where at the conclusion, after lights on, a looming, silhouette comes busting through the back of the screen, leaving a gaping hole?

Unbeknownst to Cyclone, the flash of pain that appeared white-hot on his mind's movie-screen was blood and brain matter mixing together on impact from the galvanized ice pick tearing its way into his left ear canal, into the brain and out of the other side, leaving a gaping hole in his mind.

Osiris entered the pit area just as Lillian took a sip from her water bottle. She caught his eye and issued a warming smile. He couldn't wait to get her into his bed after all his business was settled. He gave her a wink.
"Tell Cyclones he's up." He called to the group huddled in the rear mixing drinks and taking low key, snorts. War-Hog, was on his 5th plate of beef.

"I haven't seen him for about ten or fifteen minutes." Nadia recalled. "I'll run to find him right quick if you want," she said, realizing it was possible that her no good man may have bumped into some slut-ass, biker bitch on the way to the bathroom and was in some old RV in the parking lot doing the daddy-long-stroke.

"Bike up!" Cyclones number one shop man, Manny, ordered his men to roll out their masterpiece. Everyone sprang into action, happy to finally get called. Hardcore biker music was blasting as the judging began. The noise level peaked as the crowd went crazy at the sight of Cyclone's project. Osiris could feel the rumble as nearly 10,000 fans stomped and applauded. The response was definitely different from the rest of the day. The cheering proceeded as the announcer highlighted some of its specifications.

Behold this Bourget Python Chopper, sporting a 113 cubic inch, fully polished S&S motor. Remarkable black, silver and purple air brushed on a stretched one piece carbon fiber frame with dual nitrous tanks, Eddie Brook-Nasty carburetor, all chromed. Check out the 15" massive back tire and 12" Jessie James rear fender.

Wow this front end is chromed out, were talking Triple tree Springer, S&S billet rockers, viper covers. Has a dot instrument package, stitched boss seat with extra suction and a Primo open belt drive.

Without the official decision it was evident from the response of the entire fairground with bike was the winner...

"Okay, quiet people. We have an official winner. Osiris Customs, Bourget, Python Chopper!" The place went numb with noise. For Osiris it was a victory either way, however losing to his second in command was a bruise to his swollen ego. He had high hopes for his Harley XL. "Where the fuck is Cyclone anyway?"

As the sun began making its exit and the last of the equipment was being loaded, still no one had seen Cyclone or had been able to contact him on his cell phone. Nadia had formed the conclusion that she had been dumped for the night for a different pussy and was silently pissed as she climbed behind the wheel of her Camaro. She tried his cell a few more times before cursing in Spanish.

Osiris, on the other hand began to immediately explore the possibility of a rival having done something to Cyclone regardless of the long standing agreement not to bring any beefs to the fairground's bike and car events. *It's not like Cyclone to disappear like this, especially when he wanted to win so badly. There were several possibilities as far as enemies but the climate was anything other than tense, nobody flying colors or flags. Everybody was family-family, kids, cats and dogs.*

He turned to Manny. "Keep two of your men here until we hear something. I mean until the place shuts down and every paper cup, snot tissue, and bloody condom is picked up."

Lillian could tell from all the hushed conversation and delayed movement that they were looking for Cyclone. She checked her face in the passenger side mirror of the Hummer, just as Osiris opened the driver's door and got in. He didn't seemed disturbed by anything and went on like all was well.

"No need to check on that pretty face. It's an example to the gods. Beauty is etched in eternal stone and you're worthy of a Greek goddess' magical lair."

WTF

Osiris caught her puzzled look and spent most of the ride back to the shop explaining his ramblings about Greek gods and astronomy, attempting to sound intelligent.

Lillian kept watch in the mirror on the convoy of vehicles in Osiris' entourage. *No chance for a quick strike.* She would have to keep with the original plan. Shortly after, cars and SUVs filled the parking lot of Classic Customs.

"We brought home the trophy and $50,000 again, thanks to Cyclone and the boys. Everybody that attended the show can take off tomorrow since it's so late, and I'll see you Monday morning, on time. If anybody hears from Cyclone, give me a call ASAP." The crew began packing away the gear so they could head home. He returned to the Humvee and walked Lillian to the garage to retrieve her scooter. "It was a pleasure to have had you. I hope you look at motorcycles a little differently now. I know I was preoccupied today but if you would let me show you a much nicer time tomorrow I would be honored."

"That sounds good." She replied.

"You're probably tired and in need of a hot shower so with that I bid you a good night." He kissed the top of her hand. "Oh, and true to my word you can pick up your Mustang Monday morning at 9:00am sharp."

Lillian started the BMW scooter and jumped on the highway traveling at 80 mph the entire trip. When she reached the San Fernando Valley the familiar neighborhood was quiet as usual. Each house was spaced apart giving home owners ample privacy. The dark clothing she had chosen for the bike show offered perfect cover in the night. She pulled the quiet scooter off the road into a line of bushes, killed the engine and removed a pouch from the bike's saddlebag before running along the tree line, approaching the house she had visited early with the Eastside Restoration work truck in the driveway.

From her position, low in the bush adjacent to the drive, Lillian could hear the faint sound of music playing and the even, rumble of an approaching Chevy motor block. The '64 Impala slowly made its way down the street past driveways filled with Range Rovers, Porches and Honda Mini vans. Diablo pulled into his driveway and took a long drag from his Newport before laying his head back against the headrest.

From the look of his approach one could assume the driver maybe had a little too much to drink and was pacing himself to avoid an accident. Lillian figured too many beers at the event. She raised the crossbow, aligning it with his tempo and squeezed... A fraction of a second before applying the right amount of pressure to launch her arrow, a women's head popped up from his lap like a jack-in-the-box.

Oh shit, he was getting some head while he was driving. Lillian let out a sigh of relief. Suddenly the head disappeared as quickly as it had appeared. Diablo took another deep pull on his cigarette as his body jerked violently making Nadia think he was about to cum. She began working harder hoping he would finish because her neck was getting tired from blowing him during the entire trip home.

I hope he don't think I'm sitting around waiting for him to finish fucking off.

"Ah, come on Diablo. What's the matter?" she complained when she felt him going soft in her mouth. "Come on baby, don't you like it." She asked, raising her head. The first instinct to scream was quickly over run by the desire to flee. Panicking, she fumbled for the door latch trying not to look at the arrow protruding from Diablo's head. Nadia finally got the door opened and spilled to the flooring crawling like a scattering ant. When she reached the glass edge she got up and hauled ass.

The moment Nadia broke and ran, Lillian jetted from cover and snatched the red, gas can from aback the jeep she spotted earlier. With a twist of the cap she tossed the 5 gallon jug into the open car door and Diablo's lap. The fumes from the gasoline raced to meet with the tip of the lit cigarette he had been smoking moments before his demise. **Swish.** The car went up in flames illuminating the quiet neighborhood.

Lillian followed the tree line back to her bike and headed back to the highway. She watched the glowing fire disappear in her rear view as she sped the fast bike towards downtown. She couldn't wait to shower and hit the sack. *I missed Renee, all day. I wonder how her day went.*

Renee was fast asleep on the sofa when she arrived, television still on at full level. Gun shots, tires screeching and explosions met Lillian at the door. She turned off the TV and smiled at a sleeping Renee, evidence of her day all over the table. *Donuts and cereal for breakfast, Lunch, hamburger and French fries, chili dog, chocolate milkshake. Chips, candy bar, more chips. Dinner, let's see. Steak and potatoes, mac and cheese, no veggies. A strawberry milkshake, soda... coke, no root beer. More candy.*

Being away from Renee all day made Lillian realize how much she was becoming attached to the child. *When all this is over we're moving to Florida somewhere close to Mom. A nice quiet neighborhood like a real family.*

Lewis drove all the way home attempting to conceal his smile, still finding it hard to believe their baby girl was going to her high school prom. It seemed it was just yesterday they were taking her to Chuck E Cheese to play. He caught his wife's eye recognizing the same admiration he shared for their daughter. Renee knew that her parents really loved each other from the way they held hands at home and treated one other with respect. She hoped when she was grown she'd find a man who would treat her like a queen. Her mom Lillian was a MD and her father ran a very successful Business Consultant for a major firm.

"Thank you for giving me such a beautiful child and a wonderful wife." He leaned over and kissed her lips softly. Renee watched from the back seat in slow motion as their lips came together... The sound from the collision was deafening! As lips came together with lips, so did metal on metal, causing their car to explode into a fiery ball.

The percussion from the blast shook Lillian from her sleep. She awakened sweating and shaking. The family in her dream never saw the truck that T-boned them killing everyone including the truck driver instantly.

She looked over to see that Renee had climbed into bed with her sometime during the night. A fleeting feeling to pack up and leave LA, now quickly passed. The dream had made her uneasy thinking about Lewis and the family that should have been. Dismissing all doubt, she planned on leaving Monday morning after everything was taken care of. Lillian put her arm around Renee and drifted off, back to sleep.

*****

Osiris was up bright and early after hearing the news about Diablo's murder. He was convinced that something bad had happened to Cyclone at the fairgrounds. Not knowing exactly who to blame, he decided to retaliate against all natural enemies of Sons of Samoan. He had called together all factions of his gang and gave the green light for a fire fight.

"Brothers, those foolish enough to come after us will pay with their lives and the lives of their families. I, the Big Triple O.G, sanction a hit on every O.G from the three top crews in the Latino Nation. I want the Big Boy from Playboy Blood Gang hit. That nigga Damian from Englewood and BK from BTK in China Town.

Everyone present knew Osiris' statement about being the Big Triple O.G could only mean one thing... Kisona was dead. Osiris' cell phone rang before he could continue. The look on his face said, more bad news. He hung up genuinely upset. "Fuck! I knew it. We've been played. This shit's been started. They found Cyclone's body at the fairgrounds behind the lavatories at the picnic area we used to go to years back. Somebody stabbed his brains out. That was his wife."

There was an angry murmur about the room as each member felt that they were under silent attack. These were the crew leaders and neighborhood shot callers, war chiefs and shooters. At the conclusion of the meeting they all were preparing for all-out war. Osiris was always the one promoting peace for profit, frowning down on senseless killings because it interfered with cash flow and made the police upset. But this silent attack changed the game,"

And although it may be like killing a mosquito with a shot gun it will send a message for years to come. Don't fuck with Sons of Samoan.

The men filed out, heading to their controlled zone to put power moves into play and prepare for war in the streets. Each knowing what was to come ahead, some on the way to get their families out of harm's way.

Once every one had departed, Osiris grasp his face with both hands and let out a low howl. "Damn. I can't believe I got caught slipping like this." He banged his fist on the desk. Then called Rook who had spent the night at the shop. "Listen to me close."

"What's wrong?" Rook could hear the seriousness in Osiris' voice.

"I need you to bring the RV to my house in Hidden Hills. Back it up beyond the carports on the eastside of the property and leave the keys in the glass dish on the mantle in the foyer. Do you understand? This is extremely important."

"I understand. I been holding down the shop all night watching the security monitors like a hawk, The RV's locked up tight. I got'cha."

"There's a lot of things going on I can't really go into but things are gonna get hot for a minute. I need everybody to lay low, cease all movement stay in SOS zones."

"We warring with somebody?"

"We're warring with everybody as of tonight. After you drop off the RV go lay up over Lucinda's for a few days until shit cools down."

"Damn, Osiris at least let me put in some work on some clowns. I don't want to go hide in some pussy like a pussy."

"Chill Rook. What you fail to realize is that I put in all the work so you don't have to. I want you to be smarter, Remember, Chess instead of Checkers. A boss. How many fuckers you think I trust to do what you're doing for me now?"

"That's true."

"I'll talk to you later. I'm going to lay up in some pussy and you better believe I'm no pussy. Ever heard of the President going to Afghanistan to shoot guns? Hell no! That pussy is called, Out-of-harms-way, tonight."

"Of course you're right again." Right then he realized he was being groomed for something else. *Fuckin' boss.* He hung up feeling he had a new purpose. A quick check of camera #8 found all well with the RV. He pulled out a blunt and lit the tip, drawing in the smoke slow and steady. *Boss Bitch.*

Osiris hung up and called Lillian's cell.
"Hello."
"Ever heard of Hidden Valley?"
"No, but I'm sure I can find it with proper directions."

He gave her the address, although she knew exactly where to go. Lillian pulled up to the huge two level home and parked her bike in the front driveway between several cars, some under covers. As she made her way around to the front entrance she surveyed the area noting the privacy fence surrounding the property.

The purple, leather, mini skirt and six inch black, patent-leather pumps and net stockings made her look commanding and alluring at the same time. He opened the door wearing slippers, a robe and lounge pants.

One look and he knew she came to play. Seductively, she entered his home casting a sexual hologram in her wake. Osiris was ready for some good loving after all the pressures of the week. He was really digging Lillian and was even hoping to replace Precious with this goddess. After declining a drink, she followed him up a rounding, white marble staircase to his master bedroom. The huge, round, medieval style, bed boasted four coliseum type bedpost and a platform sculpted in polished copper. The room looked like a king's sex lair.

Osiris removed his robe and tossed it aside. It seemed to take forever as it floated across the room landing on a nearby lazy boy chair.

His huge frame loomed before her making her feel tiny and vulnerable momentarily. Without warning he grabbed her, tossing her over his shoulder like a cave man before tossing her onto the bed.

Oh shit. "Hey wait. Let me get on top. I'll give you a good massage before we play..."

Osiris shifted to his back placing her atop his chest. Lillian began rubbing his neck, shoulders and chest until he begun to relax and loosen up. "No rush, big man. I like to take my time. Do it right." She whispered seductively. His chest rose as she ran her fingers across his nipples. She could feel the bulge in his lounge pants making her anxious. Slowly she let her hands ease towards the ice pick in her garter. He suddenly reached for her breast, pulling one free, he pinched her nipple hard.

"Ouch. Yeah, like it like that." Lillian was hopping he didn't pinch her again. But then he squeezed so hard you'd think he was milking a cow. Before the next pinch could come one hand was on the handle of her knife and the other on his nipple.

With the speed of lightning she raised the ice pick and drove it straight into his left nipple to the hilt. Osiris couldn't fathom the sudden burst of pain he was experiencing in his chest. However, the response was surely instinctive. Instead of grabbing his chest and gasping for air, Lillian found herself flying backwards through the air before landing atop a dresser with blood leaking from the back of her head.

She tried to shake it off but couldn't move fast enough to avoid being snatched up and pounded to the head several times before being tossed across the other side of the room. Osiris was grunting and holding his chest in pain. He took a gurgling breath and stumble towards her before tripping and falling to the floor on his face. Lillian climbed to her feet scanning the room for the ice pick as Osiris struggled to get back to his feet. He propped one arm on the bed's copper platform and attempted to pull his big body from the floor. On her feet now, Lillian ran past, only to have him grab one of her legs and pull her back to the ground. She fought trying to get free but was no match for the big man. He snaked his hands to her neck intending to choke her until her eyes popped out. Just as he got a good grip she started kicking a flailing, determined to get free. The pain in his chest was almost unbearable and affected the amount of pressure he was able to apply to her neck. Still Lillian was finding it hard to breath. She could feel herself getting light headed. Images of her mother, Renee, her father and Lewis came to her as she drifted into blackness.

A voice came to her in the darkness. *Don't give up! Fight, fight, fight!*

Lillian raised her fist and blindly swung downward until it made impact with a solid thud. Again she raised a feeble hand and struck again and again. Again and again, until she could feel air entering her lungs. She raised her fist and struck over and over, when finally Osiris' let out a gust of wind as he regurgitated nearly a gallon of blood in several violent spasms before lying dead on the medieval style carpet.

Lillian got up covered in blood and stumbled to her feet. She left a bloody foot trail on her way out of the room. As she reached the top of the white marble stairs she heard someone come into the front door downstairs. Panicking, she ran back down the hall into Osiris' room hoping to find a gun or anything to defend herself. A set of floor to ceiling windows at the end on the room caught her eye. She was happy to find one opened, leading to a balcony. She ran along the balcony climbing onto the lower roof level, heading towards the eastside of the property. When she reached the roof of the carports she ran along the wall until she reached the edge, jumping atop an RV before climbing down to the ground. Before she knew it she was pushing her bike down the driveway. When she thought no one could hear she started it and sped away cautiously.

Rook locked up the office before going into the shop to get the RV. He hit the switch, raising the huge garage door before starting the engine. After pulling into traffic, he searched the radio for something relaxing to listen to during the hour drive to Hidden Valley.

When he arrived at the house he noticed the BMW bike parked in front of the three car garage and smiled. *Osiris must be knee deep in that ass by now.* Rook had plans on spending the rest of the day in some pussy. *Can't wait to get to Lucinda's. I need a beer and a blunt.* He backed the RV beyond the carports on the east of the house like Osiris had told him. *As much as he's been talking about this new bitch we might not hear from him for a while, might rent a space in that pussy.* As he approached the house he heard a muffled thud and the faint sound of a woman shrieking. *He must be giving her the big body treatment.* He tried to imagine the nearly 300lb man moving fluidly in the bed. Must like fucking a rhino.

Rook entered his code into the front door keypad and went inside. After placing the RV keys in the dish as instructed he headed towards the kitchen to grab a sandwich and six pack of beer before he headed off.

On the way from the kitchen he heard another thud that sounded like it came from the front balcony level. He glanced out of the window but saw nothing suspicious. Rook opened the door to leave before a strong urge came over him to take a peek. He shut the door and headed towards the rounded white, marble stairs feeling like a cat burglar. *Let's see how fine this bitch is, got my big homey's nose wide open.*

He placed his ear against the door listening for sounds of sex. *Did he bust a nut already? Three minute king. Wait until I confront him about this. He's always saying I fuck like a jack rabbit.*

Needing more details to settle his curiosity, Rook slowly turned the knob, carefully inching it opened until he could see into the room thru a slit in the door. The bed was empty, looking untouched. He cracked the door a little more and scanned the big room from side to side noticing something on the floor beyond the chaise lounge.

"What the...?" A thick dark red stain on the carpet caught his eye as he stepped into the room. "Osiris." He called as he approached to investigate. Rook froze in place, eyes wide in panic. "Osiris!" He ran, kneeling down. "Osiris." He began shaking Osiris' prone body in disbelief. "No-no-no!" Rook felt like he was just hit with a ton of bricks. This was epic failure on his part, knowing he had stopped taking his shadowing job serious long ago.

Lillian was trying to put as much distance as she could between the person who had come into the house and herself. She watched the rear view mirrors as she weaved her way through traffic, deciding it was time to leave LA, now.

She issued a sigh of relief when saw her exit up ahead glad to have made it back in one piece. Just as she pulled into the hotel parking lot her cell phone rang.

"Hello."
"What time are you coming back, I miss you..."

"Renee, listen. Quickly, pack everything! We're leaving now. I'm pulling up as we speak. Hurry please."

Renee could hear the urgency in her voice so as soon as she hung up the phone she begin speed packing. She knew Lillian was taking care of some type of business during their trip but had no idea what was going on.

Lillian whipped the bike into an empty spot and ran over the meridian and across the lawn towards the hotels canopy. As she reached the front entrance she suddenly remembered she had Valet Park the minivan and headed to the valet window.

"I'm checking out and I'd like my car brought up. It's a frost green Dodge, Caravan." She searched her brain frantically trying to remember where she put the ticket. Lillian saw the attendant staring at her shirt, almost forgetting about her blood stained clothes.

"Just show me some ID and your room key and..."

Lillian turned and headed towards the elevator now conscious of her disheveled appearance. Glad to get on an empty elevator car, she thought about what to tell Renee about all the blood.

When she got to the room, Renee had everything packed and ready to go. "Let me jump in the shower real fast. Did you get everything?"

"Yes." Renee didn't ask any questions. Lillian had saved her life and whatever was going on she would stick with her until the end. "Do you need me to do anything else?" She asked thru the bathroom door.

"Run down to the valet window and showed them the room card and my ID please." Renee removed Lillian plastic key and driver's license from her purse. The name on the ID said Katrina Whitfield. Without asking any questions she did as she was asked.

Moments later Lillian emerged from the bathroom, hair in a ponytail, wearing jeans and sneakers, looking like a completely different person. "Something came up so we're cutting our trip short one day." The urgency she felt earlier was beginning to subside. Now safe, at an unknown location, she begin to wonder if it was a cleaning lady back at Osiris'. *Nobody came after me. I guess it's the relief of a job being completed.* The bruising on her ear, jaw and lumps on her head were an instant reminder of how close she had come to messing up. Looking across the room at Renee, suddenly had her evaluating her decision to continue her crusade. There were others marked for death from Snookie's book, but Renee had come into her life and now things were forming differently and priorities were shifting.

"Are you okay?" Renee asked noticing the bruises on Lillian's face.

"I'm fine honey. Let's boogie." They loaded their bags and suitcases on a trolley and headed to the car.

Lillian could see her Caravan through the lobby window just as they exited the elevator. They rolled the heavy cart across the thick carpeted floor to their waiting vehicle. A bell hop commandeered the trolley and began loading their luggage. With all the shopping that had taken place they were leaving with three times as much as stuff as they had arrived with.

After tipping the valet, Lillian walked around the van, checked the rear hatch lock then the side door before handing the bell hop a twenty dollar bill. Just as she turned to get into the van a police cruiser pulled up. Renee watched from the passenger mirror as the officer waved her over.

"Excuse me ma'am but I'm responding to a call from the hotel about a woman covered in blood who was in a hurry to leave." He noticed the bruises on her face as he approached her. "Is there a problem?"

"No sir. No problems at all."
"Is that your vehicle?" He nodded towards the minivan.
"Yes. It's a rental."
"May I see some ID, please?"
"Ah, sure officer. It's in my purse."

He escorted her back to her minivan and stood back as she fished through her bag for her license. He waved at Renee when he noticed her visual inquiries.

"This is just formal. Since there was a call made. I have to follow up with dispatch that I made contact with all parties. There doesn't seem to be anything wrong here. People see stuff and come up with their own scenarios in their heads so we have to figure things out. I mean you clearly have some injuries to your face but if you're covering up for some bastard hitting on you there's really nothing I can do unless it occurs publicly or you point him out."

She handed him her license and followed him back towards the front of his cruiser as he begin jotting down something on a clipboard while giving advice about domestic abuse and scumbag woman beaters. Lillian issued a sigh of relief when he handed her back her license and appeared to be getting back into his car before coming back.

"You know, some women are afraid to come forth because there's no one to watch their backs when the police are not around. But if you ever feel you need a friend. Someone you can call if this problem continues, here's my card." He handed her a business card before giving her his best Super-Commando, Dave smile.

Lillian smiled politely and took the card. "Thank you."

*****

Rook was shaking with rage. Thinking under pressure surely wasn't one of his attributes. Looking down at Osiris' dead body was like being in a drug induced haze, laced with fury.

Suddenly the image of the pretty girl... Lollipop. Popped into his head. Then shit began clicking and falling into place. "Fucking bitch!" Oh my god. I can't believe..." He bolted out the room taking the marble stairs three at a time, remembering he had to leave his motorcycle back at Classic Customs when he brought over the RV. He glanced at the spot where the BMW scooter had been parked before running back inside for the RV keys.

Rook hit the coded sequence on the RV's media console, releasing the mechanical draw holding the Uzi machine gun. He whipped the big vehicle out of the driveway and headed towards the highway's entrance ramp.

Once he hit the highway he floored it making the big engine roar in protest. Rook had tunnel vision. His mind focused on thing... The RV sped along the fast lane slowing down only to pass in any available lane.

A man in a sanitation truck cursed as the RV weaved pass. *Shit! Where are the California Highway Patrol when you need them? If I go 5 miles over the speed limit I'd get pulled over for sure.*

Rook remembered the exit was approaching. He could see the Hyatt Regency Hotel from the highway as he exited. Anxious and excited he barreled along the service road roughly navigating a series of turns leading to the Hotel's drive, tires screeching on each corner. From about 100 yards away he could see the minivan she was driving the day he followed her from the shop.

His face was in a twisted ball of evil as he mashed the pedal, speeding straight ahead. "Ah-ah-ah!"

Lillian looked back to see what all the commotion was about as she headed to her vehicle. Before she knew it the RV was at the tail end of the police cruiser. Fire from the nozzle of Rook's Uzi shot from the RV's open door as officer Keller went down in a hail of bullets. Lillian ran to the passenger door, grabbing Renee by the hand just as a fleet of hot slugs peppered the Caravan. Glass shattering and bullets flying sent a group of nearby guest scurrying to get back inside the hotel lobby. There were people running everywhere.

Rook slammed on the brakes causing the huge RV to come to a screeching halt beyond the hotel's drive. He jumped out and ran back towards the fleeing crowd.

"Freeze and drop your weapon," was all the security guard could say before the machinegun blew his chest cavities out. He did the jerk dance backwards before plopping back onto his shredded guts and quickly bleeding out.

He entered the lobby, scanning the area for Lillian's figure. A surprised family exiting the elevator screamed in terror as he sprayed a barrage of bullets at a fleeing Renee and Lillian. With Renee firmly by the hand, she cornered the gift shop, feeling the bullets breeze by as they shattered the store glass. Lillian knew that the corridor looped back around to eastside of the lobby where he was just shooting from.

Lillian ran cautiously along the corridor wall, shielding Renee best she could. As she reached center point she realized that the glass wall had a vintage point of the elevator station. Employees, customers and guest were cowering behind counters and tables. Lillian peeped thru the glass wall beyond the elevator area and lobby and could see a police car pulling up out front just as another group of people exited the elevator closest to the glass wall.

"Come on." They sprung out heading towards the other side when the deafening sound of the Uzi reported. **Rat a tat-tat, Rat a tat-tat.**

The entire wall of glass came raining down on everybody. The guest exiting the elevator were pushed back into the adjourning corridor as Lillian and Renee attempted to make the way past.

With no regard for human life, Rook was intent on killing Lillian even if a family of innocent tourist stood in his way. With his target still in sight beyond the crowd he fired mid-level, almost chopping a teenage girl in half as she raised her tennis racquet in defense. The rapid fire sent everyone flying violently against the opposite wall, crashing to the floor in a heap. Rook continued to fire.

Blak-Blak... Blak!

Two of the three shots hit Rook high in the chest spinning him 360 degrees before laying him out flat. The first officer to arrive on the scene of the "Shots fired" call, kicked Rook's Uzi across the lobby before violently cuffing the downed perpetrator.

During the shooting melee, Lillian struggled to get out from beneath the heap of bodies, some screaming and crying. There was blood everywhere as she pushed people aside trying to get to Renee. "Renee!' She screamed, pulling at her wrist. Her hand was limp. "Renee-Renee!" A man lying close by howled in agony when he noticed his daughter's bullet riddled body oozing blood. Lillian could see the hole in the side of Renee's head and screamed.

"Oh, No-no-no-no-no-no-no-no-no-no-no."

People were getting up fleeing, mostly trying to make it out of the hotel. Men, women and children crying, trying to locate separated loved ones, were moving about.

Lillian finally pulled Renee free to find her not responsive. She fell to her knees and held her, weeping violently. As people were exiting, more police were arriving, running into the oncoming crowd.

The assistant manager who had called the cops after being alerted by the valet attendant, watched the entire thing unfold. He had decided to stand by just in case he had to fill out a report when the RV came barreling down firing like crazy. He was sure without a doubt that the shooter was after the woman he had complained about because after the cop was shot he watched, from a crouched position behind the counter, while the young Latino looking man bypassed everyone stalking the pretty young woman and girl into the building.

"Excuse me officer." He alerted a tactical commander about what he knew as he led them to the area where he had observed Lillian last. "Apparently the teenager was hit.
The woman's in the corridor behind the elevators crying her heart out. Earlier she showed up covered in blood and checked out suddenly when she had paid up until Monday. The glass wall is shot out and she's right."

The spot where Lillian had been caressing Renee was empty. "She was right there." The officer stepped through the shattered wall and immediately saw the carnage caused by the man with the Uzi. At least two dead and several wounded from what he could see. The prone figure of a young black teen could be seen a ways down the corridor like someone tried to carry her around to safety. He radioed in. "Need a medical response team..."

So much was going on that it was hours before any focus came upon the abandoned RV... That no one could locate.

Chapter Nineteen

Guilt

Lillian couldn't remember how long she had driven or exactly when she had made it home. The trance-like state took over her body during her bid to escape while dealing with the death of Renee. The overwhelming numbness left no room for tears as she regained consciousness, realizing she was laying on the floor just beyond the front door where she must have collapsed. The first thoughts of Renee sent a gush of guilt straight thru the chambers of her heart as she became flush with anger, and then hate. Most of it was aimed at herself for putting Renee in the position to be shot.

Still finding it hard to believe the outcome of the events in California, she sat up, noticing the RV keys, still in her hand. She began to recall Renee's final moments vividly, and the shots she was sure was coming from the police. That's when she attempted to carry Renee but the weight of her lifeless body was too much for Lillian and the police were headed her way. As Lillian made her way around the eastside of the corridor she headed out of the lobby blending with all of the other screaming guest. Police cars blocking her minivan caused her to continue past, along the roadway where she stumbled upon the running RV. Exiting from the south end of the parking lot she traveled along the service road, heart pounding like a bass drum, until she reached the highway and drove nonstop until she made it home.

Devastated and exhausted, she broke down on the floor and passed out. The curtains were drawn tight but she could tell it was daytime by the rods of sunrays peeking into the shadows. The clock on the wall indicated she had been asleep approximately 13 hours after the two day drive from California. She tried to clear her head as she got up and looked out of her window at the huge RV outside.

First I need to get rid of this thing, then try to get some info on Renee. Lillian headed to the shower before dressing to leave. The first stop was an auto/RV storage facility where people stored camping homes during the off season. She paid up for a year then returned home to make some phone calls.

Lillian spent the entire day on the phone without one bite to eat, trying to gather as much information as possible about the shooting and the victims. The internet had several different accounts of the events and death toll. One site reported two teens and adult killed, another reported six dead. The information she received on the phone was bland at best and she was beginning to realize that the only way to find out anything was to return.

Not only did she leave Renee behind, she reflected, but the minivan full of their effects and Snookie's Brown Leather Book. Lillian decided not to return to work. *There is no way I can deal with the rudeness right now. I might get completely off on someone.*

When she finished brain-storming, Lillian hit the refrigerator, finding one of Renee's favorite Grandma's chicken-stuffed pot pies in the freezer. The house was extremely quiet and lonely without Renee. Looking at all of her things lying around gave Lillian a sense of isolation, void of love and hope.

Although Lillian knew the sooner she could return to Los Angeles the better, but, suddenly, the next name on the list from the Brown Leather Book appeared in her head as clear as day. She couldn't remember any of the others following, but the name and address in Eagle, Colorado remained on her brain until she fell asleep. When she awakened, the plan was already formed. It was like she was driven to complete the last known task in the book.

Being without Renee was like the eerie after-tones of Lewis' death. Right now she just wanted to do something to fix the situation, anything. If only magic was for real... She would bring her fairytale family together. Lewis, Lillian and Renee. She sat at the kitchen table for hours deep in thought always ending up cursing her decision to take Renee to California. She couldn't figure out how they had found her at the hotel when she had been careful in her movements, or so she thought.

After what happened to Renee, there's no way I can just go back to work like nothing happened. What am I going to do? Sit around the house and cry? I need to be moving around. I refuse to shut down before I totally destroy these clowns. If Lillian wasn't so pretty and smart... At this moment she could have been mistaken for a lice infested, bag lady twitching on a park bench. She was crazy with revenge.

Chapter Twenty

Elliot

The plane landed in Eagle, Colorado at 10:44 am. Lillian rolled her suitcase across the airport's waiting area to the entrance in search of a shuttle van to her hotel. The ID and other fictitious paper work she had used to rent cars and hotels were most likely in the hands of the police in Los Angeles. So she had to be very careful about how she handled things from now on.

She arrived outside to discover the shuttle was full. "Wow. Just my luck."

Honk-honk.

Lillian turned to see a black town car approaching. "Need a car service Ma'am?" A young, handsome, brown-skinned man asked.

"I was told you guys were on strike."

"That's contracted airport service. I own my own car. Where are you headed?"

Lillian scanned his face trying to get a read on a personally type. On first glance he seemed okay. *He is definitely very handsome.* "Hi I'm Katrina. I'm going to be in town for only a couple of days on business and was looking for a quiet place to check in, also I was wondering if I can kind of have you on standby call. I have no idea how to get around..."

He smiled, sensing something different about the pretty, young woman. Eagle, Colorado was a quiet city not far from Denver. Population 48,996. Only six blacks were registered during the last census report.

Elliot Brown had come to Eagle from the Aurora section of Denver three years ago to drive for the airport car service. His girlfriend, Sandra joined him months later and they rented an apartment in a nice complex with a swimming pool and exercise room. Elliot went about hustling, during extra shifts and booking side jobs in hopes of saving up for one of the newer Lincoln, Town Cars. It wasn't long before Sandra became bored with the calmness of Eagle and hightailed it back to the Colfax club scene and her ex-boyfriend Kebob. Elliot had dated a few times, deciding to focus on his work and saving money.

"I hope you have a reservation somewhere because everything is booked up pretty solid. Are you here for the Business Convention?" He asked.

"I, ah. Well my assistant was supposed to make reservations but things got hectic... I was hoping I could find something once I got here."

"Here is a list of all the lodging in Eagle. Maybe you'll luck up." He smiled. "I was supposed to leave for Long Beach yesterday to visit family but decided to hang around for the convention rush. With the airport service striking, there was a spike in private car calls. To be completely honest with you I was on my way to park my car in long term when I saw you miss the last shuttle. You would have been waiting for hours."

Lillian was on the phone with the fourth hotel as she listened to the driver talk on. "No-o!" She moaned as she was told a replacement for a no show was just filled. "I guess you were right." She dialed a few others getting the same result. "Thank you for picking me up. I couldn't have handled the wait after my long flight."

"Sure, no problem. I'm Elliot." He made eye contact with her in the rear view mirror.

"Yeah, that's my last name." She blurted it out before she realized she had given her real name.

"Nice to meet you Miss Katrina Elliot."

Lillian silently cursed her slip up and changed the subject. "I'm here also for the convention so I really need to find accommodations. I'll pay you for your time if you can help me find a place before you head off." Lillian had become relaxed by Elliot's handsomeness and genuine smile.

"I don't want to further delay your trip."

"Actually I'm surprising my parents. We talk all the time on the phone but it's been almost a year since I saw them." As if on cue, his cell phone rang. "Excuse me." He held up his hand politely. "Afternoon, Mom. Me, I'm fine, had turkey bacon, wheat toast and a big bowl of oatmeal. I'm actually driving a client to her destination. Okay, I'll see you soon, I mean talk to you soon. Yes, Ma'am. Love you, too. Goodbye." Elliot apologized to Lillian for the interrupting.

"I see you made a slip and almost told her you were coming."

"Wow. I sure did. I'm not good at keeping secrets, so don't tell me nothing." He joked. "Let's find you a hotel."

Lillian could tell Elliot was attracted to her by the way he glanced her way and needed someone to help her get around the town. "Is there any way we can stop and grab something real quick? I'm starved."

"I know a popular diner in town that has pretty good food. It's on the way to the Motel Mile, a string of motels along the pike." Lillian knew she should have made better arrangements but losing everything in California had her at a disadvantage. Elliot drove past a mile of motels, all with no-vacancy signs posted before pulling into the restaurant parking lot. "I just realized I'm due for a meal myself." He rubbed his flat belly in jest.

Elliot suddenly found himself sitting across the table from this beautiful young woman, not knowing how to interject a compliment without seeming inappropriately flirtatious.

"I think it was cute. The conversation with your mother. Or was that staged?"

He grabbed his chest to fain being hurt. "I would never do that. Here, want to talk to her yourself?" Before she could say no, the phone was already on speaker ringing.

"Yes, son?" An elderly woman's voice asked. "Did you forget to tell me something?"

"No, Mom. Somebody wanted to talk to you."

Lillian was waving her hands frantically and shaking her head. "No." She whispered. "I was just playing. I believe you."

One look at his (I know you ain't gon' dis my momma) face and she spoke into the phone. "Hello Ma'am."

"Well hello, young lady. What's your name?"
Lillian almost hated lying to the nice woman. "My name is Katrina."

"That's nice. You must be a good friend of Elliot's because he's never let me talk to any of his friends before."

"Really?"
"Well, you sound special. I hope to meet you some day."

"Thank you Ma'am. I hope to meet you also, one day." The women shared a few more kind words before saying goodbye. Lillian was reminded of her sweet mother and instantly took a liking to Elliot as he appeared more and more likable. They sat for thirty minutes talking after their plates were empty before realizing they were supposed to be looking for a hotel.

"Hey I just wanted to make the offer, even if you decline. I know I just met you and you don't really know me, but I have a trusting side to me that may get me in trouble one day. I sense something trustworthy about you, plus I have nothing to steal but some furniture... What I'm saying is, if you want to stay at my place while I'm visiting in California, you're welcome to. I'll only be gone three days and you can feed the cat and the fish, and water my Jesus plants."

"You have a cat and fish?"
"Ah, yeah."

Lillian smiled in agreement. Looks like things would work out after all. *If I can get him to loan me the car, too, that would be great.* In the back of her mind she knew that things could change in a heartbeat if Elliot turned out to be a creep and she had to protect herself with lethal force.

Elliot pulled out chairs and opened doors like a perfect gentlemen. The type that grew up in a household watching his father still courting his mother with kindly gestures years into their marriage.

Lillian was glad to see that Elliot wasn't taking her to a shack on the ridge. He lived in a nice one room bungalow in a quiet, modern area fifteen minutes from everything. There was a white Durango, SUV and an old Honda motorcycle in the driveway.

"I ride a little." Lillian said as they approached the front door. "Actually, it was just a fast scooter."

"I toll around on this old Honda that one of my neighbors gave me before he passed away. Thing runs good as the day it was purchased, he used to say..."

Elliot's place was nicely furnished, nothing flashy besides the fabric sectional and flat screen TV. Everything was clean and neat, like the place was barely used.

"I wouldn't say I'm a neat freak, I just like to keep things in order."

"I like a man who cleans up." Lillian replied. Truth is, at this point she didn't know what type of man she liked. "It's nice and comfortable. No girlfriend?" *Inquiring minds want to know.*

Elliot wound up telling her everything about his past situation, glad to be able to talk to someone and get it off his chest. Lillian also shared some things, staying close to the subject of family. They ordered Chinese food later in the day. Somehow the newly acquainted friends spent hours talking to each other before the moonlight ambushed the sun, holding it for ransom until the following day.

Elliot had insisted Lillian take his bed while he crashed on the sofa. The night was uneventful as far as any attempts by Elliot to get in her panties. He remained respectful the entire time.

Lillian stared into the darkness, reminding herself why she was there. There was something potentially distracting in the mist. The adrenaline rush she normally got leading up to a mission was lukewarm at best. Missing was the burning desire to swoop down and wipe the world clean of all evil. The name on her list seemed less menacing than the others.

Benjamin Steinberg was the owner of the Four Seasons Resort. The venue where the Business Convention is being held tomorrow. Lillian slipped the small caliber gun inside the pillowcase before dozing off.

Lillian could feel the heat from his breath against her cheek making the fine hairs at the nape of her neck quiver. Closing her eyes, she couldn't recall such a soothing sensation. She could feel herself purring like a kitten as a lustful fog crept over her body. He bent down, placing a kiss gently on her forehead that seemed to linger forever.

Lillian awakened to the sun's rays licking her pretty face, as she took in her first deep breath of the morning. She could feel an invisible pressure of lips on her forehead like she had just been kissed. The first thing she did was check for her pistol, wishing she hadn't crashed that hard.

"Shit!" She cursed when she saw it was 10:40 already. Jumping up, she called out to Elliot with no response. The note on the counter explained everything.

Morning, Katrina.

Didn't want to wake you from sleeping like an angel. Caught the first flight, will be back Sunday. The keys to the Durango are on the kitchen table and there's food if you decide to prepare something. He left a few contact numbers. I left you a little map of the town to help you get around. The Business Convention is at the Four Seasons Resort on Brighten Rd.

PS. I have a confession. Don't want to seem like a pervert or something but I kissed your forehead before I left. I don't know why I did it... Anyway, I know the Convention ends on Sunday but I was hoping you were there when I return.

Elliot

Lillian touched the spot where she felt the invisible lips and realized he must have left his phantom impression on her. She didn't know how she should respond to someone liking her. Someone who she liked back. *I didn't come here to meet anybody... Or maybe I did.*

The killer instinct that had accompanied her on her last missions failed to kick in. Instead she found herself wanting to talk more over dinner and replay the phantom kiss in her mind over and over.

Lillian showered and dressed in business attire before firing up Elliot's SUV and heading to the Four Seasons Resort. Once she reached the huge compound, she parked amid other SUV's, exited with her attaché case and entered the building.

"Avian Price from Walcott Incorporated to see Mr. Steinberg." She approached the young, pretty, blonde receptionist, all business.

The young woman quickly verified her appointment before sending her to Steinberg's office and returning to the online game she was playing. Lillian felt surprisingly calm as she walked through the plush resort.

"Come in." Steinberg responded to the firm knock at the door, failing to conceal the look of surprise when he saw a black woman enter. "Ah, Walcott... Ah, Mrs. Price. I'm sorry I was under the impression..."

"I was white?"

"Well yeah, and a man. I'm familiar with an Alvin Price. Still, I didn't know Walcott had any black employees"

Lillian sat in the chair across from him and placed her attaché case on his $10,000 desk, releasing both clasps. She took Steinberg to be in his early forties with an air of confidence from being entitled and wealthy.

"They don't."

Still not aware of any pending danger, he looked at the pretty, professionally dressed woman waiting for her to deliver the punch line.

The hole at the tip of the silencer made the gun look like a cannon pointed at his forehead. Drama was something he knew nothing directly about and his belly became queasy. Now he realized that in his tidy world a black face, man or woman should have raised alarm. He suddenly thought about his pretty, blue eyed, brunette wife Viola and two children back at the house. The blonde receptionist he'd been fucking since she started working for him last year even crossed his mind. *Fucking blonde whore probably sent me up!*

"Listen close Mr. Benjamin Steinberg III, and let's get some business situated. This is a big business convention, correct!"

"Yes." He nearly whispered.

"I'm here as a result of your relationship with one-New York-Snookie."

Hearing the name made things worst in his mind. Knowing death was nearing he sighed in fear as the warm stream of urine soaked his gray slacks and $2,600 office chair.

"We checked to make sure the family was in good health because we are concerned about our people. 13446 Bridgeview Heights. That's where the nice dog house sits on the southwest part of the backyard."

"Please don't hurt my family. They don't know anything. I swear I was going to contact New York, I just... Look I have all of the money, I-I kept it safe. I was waiting to hear something."

"I came here to kill you before giving my crew the word to do the same with your family because you're a lowlife, drug-dealing piece of scum, acting like you're the pillar of the community. So the only way you live to see another second is if you send every dime you owe plus five million of your own money to the address on this card." She handed him an index card. "You have 48 hours. If you try to do anything different, a hit team will move on your pretty wife and you will be exposed as an international, narcotics distributor. We will not relent until the money has arrived at its destination. Do you understand?"

"Yea- Yes ma'am."

Lillian closed the case and quietly left the building, half expecting a security guard to come running out, weapon drawn. But her exit was as quiet as her entry. The receptionist had even bid her a good day.

"You too, sweetie."

Lillian drove back to Elliot's, wanting to relax in the comfortable bungalow. The reaction she got from Benjamin Steinberg was so far, satisfactory. Maybe not killing him was her subconscious plan in the beginning and meeting someone like Elliot fit in the scheme of things. Her intentions were to leave immediately following contact with Steinberg, but Elliot's note was tugging at her along with her growing curiosity. Never imagining being in a relationship since Lewis, she occupied her life with hate and vengeance.

The short amount of time she spent in Eagle had toned her brewing anger down to a minimum, bringing forth more positive vibes. She put on an old Sade CD and stripped down to her underwear, while singing along. "Is it a crime?" She harmonized as she fed the fish and water his plants. The cat continued to spy Lillian from a distance as if she were there to take its place.

After searching the refrigerator, she prepared herself a Red Snapper, wild rice and buttered squash meal, washing it down with some white wine from Elliot's kitchen rack. She also had some sliced peaches and two flutes of fruit wine.

Lillian grabbed a picture frame, holding it closer, admiring Elliot's features and neat brush waves. The music continued softly in the back ground as she glided around looking at his personal affects. She peeped in his closet to find everything neat and orderly. Mostly department store suits and a few pairs of black work shoes. The cosmetics and cologne was arranged neatly on his dresser. *Is he so organized? I need to get my life in order.*

She laid back on his bed and spread her arms out, liking the feel of the sheets on her skin. The wine had her relaxed and before she knew it she was in la-la land.

Lillian felt the bullets whiz past her head as she turned the corner headed towards the parking lot. Elliot was surprised to see her running in her heels at full speed. The gunshots didn't register until it was too late. Just as she reached the door she saw Elliot's brains flying from the gaping hole in his head. He never knew what hit him. Lillian screamed in horror as he slump forward, deader than Lewis. The security pursued her to the Durango, emptying his firearm into her back as she held Elliot's lifeless head in her arms.

The force from the shells were powerful enough to blow her out of her sleep, upright in bed. The disturbing images took a few seconds to dissolve from her head before she realized it was a bad dream.

After relieving her kidneys, she opened Elliot's laptop and accessed the internet searching for anything about the incident at the Hyatt-Central Plaza Hotel. There was a small article about a man in custody for the shooting who was listed in critical condition. Still nothing about Renee. Lillian began pacing, deep in thought. The clock on the table read 5:45 am. She dialed the contact number Elliot left behind.

"Hello, Elliot."
"Katrina? What's wrong? Did anything happen?"

"Oh no, I just awaken from a wild dream. Guest I was tired from running around taking care of business. Anyway, I was calling because... Well my business is finished here and..."

"I was hoping to see you again." He interrupted. What was only a second or so felt like an eternity as he waited for a response.

"I have some business in Los Angeles so I would like to meet you in Long Beach afterwards, and meet your Mom also, of course."

Elliot breathe a sigh of relief. *Yes, thank you lord. I knew if I was patient I'd meet someone nice. Wow.* "I'd like that but it looks like I'll have to extend my stay. My mother will love that, so when are you leaving?"

"First flight out." Lillian hadn't officially quit her Job and decided to keep her options opened. Meeting Elliot had changed a lot of things in her mind. "I should be in Long Beach in two days."

"Can't wait."
"Thanks for the kiss."

Elliot hung up the phone with a smile on his face. He knew she didn't want him for his money because it was obvious he was a hardworking man with barely twenty thousand in the bank. He stopped in front of the mirror on his way to the bathroom tightening his rock hard abs. "It's got to be this handsome face because she hasn't had the chance to see all this." He joked with himself.

Truthfully, Elliot had found it hard to deal with being abandoned but refused to chase Sandra back to the hood. He dated only a few times before deciding the available Caucasian dating pool wasn't for him, especially after a high profile basketball star was accused of raping a white woman who had two other men's semen in her panties. The incident occurred at the Four Seasons Resort owned by Benjamin Steinberg.

He had a good feeling about this new mysterious woman who he happened upon at the airport. Being as trusting as he was hasn't always worked out for Elliot but he was really hoping she was real. He dropped to the floor and did 50 pushups, just because.

Lillian caught the 8:15 am flight to LA and arrived at the motel, Super 8, three hours later. *No more flashy accommodations.* First thing she did was use the free Wi-Fi to get online in search of a motorcycle for sale by a private owner.

After meeting a seller at his home, she purchased a used Kawasaki for five grand and drove straight to Classic Customs Restorations. The shop was quiet like on any other day as she sat waiting for the light to change. Her plans were to do a quick drive by of a few locations before checking into the location of Renee's remains.

Honk-Honk! "Hey."

Lillian glanced at the car honking aside her not recognizing the chubby girl trying to get her attention. Then, suddenly it came to her. Teuila, the girl at the desk. She was waving. "Hey, I thought that was you. When are you coming for your car?" She was all smiles.

Lillian quickly accessed the possibility that any suspicion of her involvement stopped with the man in the hospital in critical condition. "A lot of changes are being made and we need to find all the owners of the vehicle we have left over. I didn't have any further contact information on you but I still have the invoice. If you want to pay your balance you can do it now." Teulia was praying the woman wanted her car now because ever since to gang war started that killed Osiris, business had come to a halt and the women were trying to tie up all the loose ends their gangster Fathers, Uncles, and Brothers left behind.

"Actually. I was on my way to see you." She lied.

Teuila let out a sigh of relief, needing the money for the family. Lillian followed her into the parking lot, noticing that the nice girl had gained 20 lbs. since the last time they met. Teuila was chatty as ever as she searched her draw for Lillian's paperwork. "Let's see... your balance is $16,000."

Mistaking the look of calculating for hesitation, Teuila quickly added, "But I'll be willing to settle your account for $10,000. That's if you can pay today." She held her breath. "Come on, let's go see it." She got up and led Lillian down the hall to the shop doors. There were a few workers, nothing like before, making it was obvious the illegal part of the business had been the meat of Osiris' income.

The remaining crew represented the legal working employees that Teuila tried to hold on to, keeping the shop open. From the looks of things, it wouldn't be long because cash was an issue.

"See, it's beautiful."

Lillian had to admit it was a professional job. "Nice finish. Oh shit!" She was amazed at the custom work done on the interior. "Wow. Beautiful." She quickly imagined Renee behind the wheel. This would have been nice for her. "Okay. I'll take it today. Umm, I'll have to have a tow truck pick it up."

"So much is going on, I don't know if I can take it. In a few weeks, a group of uncles and cousin are coming over from Hawaii to take over everything. I'm so glad you're getting your car now because I don't know what they're gonna do. There's some big gang war going on and everybody's dying. Most of the families have already left LA."

Gang war, huh. Lillian reached in her purse and handed a thin stack of hundred dollar bills to Teuila. "That's $16,000, the full amount I owe.

"Thank you, don't worry, I'll have Chico move it to the lot. Go ahead, touch it. It's your new baby. Let me go get everything ready." She could hardly contain her excitement as she called for Chico to get moving. The tired old mechanic made his way towards the back of the shop to move the car, no security type, jumpsuits hanging around.

Lillian looked around the garage, noticing a walkout door next to the mechanical door. She disengaged the latch and disabled the safety lock. Towards the rear of the shop she could see a truck loaded with 50 gallon barrels of Ether and a room full of similar barrels beyond a gate.

"Hello, pretty lady." Chico greeted her more freely than he did during their first encounter.

She remembered his face. "Oh, hello. You showed me where to go last time I was here."

"Yes." He nodded, smiling like a Cheshire cat. "Everything bad now." He said in a heavy Spanish accent. "The Boss, gone." He made an unknown gesture.

"A truck will be coming to pick it up shortly." She handed him a 100 dollar bill, causing his eyes to light up like a street light.

"Mucho Gracias, Madam." Chico hadn't been paid since everything went crazy, which is the only reason he was still hanging around the shop. Teuila gave Lillian her receipt and a big hug before she left.

She called a private auto transport company and made arrangements to have the Classic Mustang shipped back to her home in Rhode Island before going downtown to the vital records department to do some research, accessing recent death certificates issued during the time of the shootings. The only thing she could find concerning an adolescent for that time period involved a young Caucasian teen. She looked for unidentified body's even called the medical examiner's office looking for a tagged, Jane Doe with no luck. *Damn!*

*****

At 2:00 am, Lillian, dressed in all black clothing, headed back to Classic Custom Restorations and parked her bike in the last stall of the closed, Wimpy Burger's, walking across the light traffic onto the lot of the shop and around the back to the walk through door she had unlocked earlier. She entered and proceeded to the cargo truck in the rear. She quickly searched the key box until she located the truck keys.

"Bra'mmm- Bra'mmm." It started with a puff of black smoke. Lillian climbed out and took off jogging until she reached the front, hitting the button to raise the huge garage door. As the chain rattled in protest, Lillian ran back to the truck and removed a giant pry bar from behind the seat and headed to the room filled will barrels. She began carefully prying lids from several containers until the room was filled with fumes, causing her to almost choke, before covering her nose with her hand.

The truck lurched forward as she mashed the gas. Once out of the garage she opened the main gate and drove into the parking lot before running back and grabbing a plastic gasoline jug she had noticed earlier. After dousing a twelve foot tower of tires she lit the receipt Teuila had given her earlier and tossed it towards the gas drenched tires before hitting the garage button and sprinting to the waiting vehicle.

She watched the side mirrors as the garage door descended, heavy, black smoke bellowing from the Goodyear rubber.

The explosion could be seen a mile away as Lillian continued to Hidden Valley. *Let's see them set up shop again at that place. By the time the replacement team gets here there won't be nothing left.*

*****

Osiris' mansion was dark and quiet. She drove along the far side were the RV had been parked when she had made her escape. Climbing atop the cargo truck, she pulled herself onto the carports and ran along the roof to the balcony she had hopped when Rook had arrived unexpectedly. She was relieved to find the floor-to-ceiling window in the corner still cracked opened. She navigated the dark room, finding the door leading to the hall and the white marble stairs. Lillian bypassed the living room towards the entrance to the 8 car garage. She hit the garage door and backed up almost completely against the far wall. Exiting the truck, she snatched the cover from one of Osiris' custom Harleys.

Kaboooooooooooooooooooooooooooooooooooooooooooooooooooom!

Lillian was almost three miles up the highway when the explosion lit up the night sky. She hit the throttle, thrusting the powerful motorcycle forward, seeming to have been shot from the blast in her wake. Before the last fire truck arrived, Lillian was already back at her Kawasaki headed for Long Beach, just 30 miles away.

"Hello."
"Good morning."
"Morning. Up early today."

"I wrapped up all my business during the day and was able to catch up on a little napping."

"So when should I expect you?"
"Oh, it won't be long."

"Really, well let me hop in the shower and put some clothes on..."
"I was hopping you'd let me in first."

"Hold up. Where are you?" Elliot went to the curtain and headed to the front door after seeing her motorcycle in the driveway of his mother's house.

They hugged like an old couple being reunited. Lillian liked the way he made her feel. He took a step back and took a good look. "Now that's a look I could get used to." Admiring her curvaceous figure in the all black bike gear. "Wow! You weren't kidding when you said you ride. What's that, a KZ900? My old Honda is like a 250cc, ha-ha."

She led him by the hand. "Let me put some shoes on." He protested. Lillian continued towards the bike. "You trust me?" She asked. He issued a sparkling smile and followed like a good chap.

"Wow. This is amazing." Elliot exclaimed as he held on tight, clueless and shoeless in lounge pants and a tank top. Being pinned against her body was the best place to be for him at this moment. Wherever she was taking him, he was a willing participant her co-conspirator.

*****

The shower seemed to lubricate her face as she felt the warm stream navigating her curves, irrigating her burning insides. What could have been nothing but pure lust was building rapidly. The curtained opened like she was impatiently anticipating. As brave as she had been in her quest for revenge the thoughts of intimacy created butterflies in her fluttering heart.

Elliot stood momentarily watching the water create a waterfall effect over her erect nipples. His enlarged penis was pointing straight ahead like a flag pole waiting to be draped. As he stepped forward he had to force his dick down to get skin to skin with Lillian, letting it pop up between her legs. She felt its thickness as it protruded from the rear. Like riding on a seesaw, in slow motion, she stimulated her growing clit as he kissed her deeply, applying just right amount of suction on her tongue. He made his way down her neck leaving a tongue trail across both nipples as he sucked each one rock-candy-hard. She shivered during the short trip along her belly on the way to her waiting pussy lips. Oral contact, launched Lillian into a series of orgasms as he sucked the juices as if nectar of the Gods.

She grabbed his head only to momentarily slow down his face's pace because she couldn't control the cum flow. Her legs seemed to barely be able to hold her up as she shook uncontrollably.

"Ohhhhhhhhhhhhhhhhhhhhhhhhhhhhhhhh, oh-oh-oh, Ouuuuuuuu!"

Lillian led him to the bed by his dick and climb atop carefully inserting the head as she inched downward. Wet as she was, she was even tighter. Before this very moment sex meant absolutely nothing to her and her inexperience was obvious to Elliot so he was happy to be gentle until he was able to enter her partially, eventually working the tight pussy into a oscillating cum machine.

Lillian wanted to feel every thrust pumping upward to meet his downward strokes. His balls created a slapping sound as they banged against her ass hole. Cum leaking down onto the sheets caused a puddle to form. "Oh god!" She screamed.

Like a well-oiled machine, Elliot delivered shock waves after waves of pleasure to Lillian's purring Kitty Kat. The two made love for hours eventually collapsing in each other's arms.

Chapter Twenty One

Putting together the pieces

Detective Reyes slammed down the phone. "That little fucker! If he makes me come find him I'm gonna find a reason to hold him for 48 hours." He took a big swig of coffee. "Damn, where's the sugar?" He got up and returned with the sugar jar, pouring way too much.

"Whoa, Willie Wonka, chill on the sugar. Remember I have to work with your already hyper ass." His partner jokingly, complained as she entered the station. Priscilla Gaiety came from a family of correction officers. Her father was a Captain at Lompoc and most of the men in her family worked in one of the different prisons throughout California. Priscilla was always a tomboy and challenged her brothers at every stage even if it meant fisticuffs. Some of the guys frowned down on her becoming a cop, however, they didn't necessarily want her to become a corrections officer either.

"Crooks don't take pretty cops seriously. You gotta be diked out with a razor cut on your cheek and a bullet hole in your ass." Her cousin would say.

"Shut up. I remember when we were little. I used to slam your ass." She knew that always got to him. "I bet you took me serious then?"

"Ah I slipped. I was a scrawny thing. Don't try it now though."
She laughed so loud he turned red. "I slipped." She mimicked.
"Bitch!" He left with an attitude.

Priscilla had brunette hair, a firm athletic built with a good sense of humor and likable attitude. She had eight years under her belt and a number of merits and accommodations for outstanding service. She and her partner of two years, Billy Reyes had been assigned the case involving the hotel shootings. "It's hard to believe that someone with no criminal history would just shoot up the Hyatt Hotel for no reason." He assessed. They were still putting the pieces together, having learned nothing about the shooters identity or the whereabouts' of the mystery RV.

However, they were waiting on information to come back from New York concerning the identification, weapons, paperwork and other personal affects recovered from the Dodge minivan. The woman who had been driving the minivan and checked in under the name Katrina Whitfield was being sought. Another problem they had was trying to identify the teen who was with this person of interest when she was gunned down.

Reyes dropped a cardboard box filled with evidence collected from the scene. "You can get started since you like to read so much. I'm going to get some real coffee and have a smoke. You want donuts?" Reyes hated writing reports and doing depositions. Kicking down doors and slapping cuffs on bad guys was his niche. Having a strong policemen's intuition that hasn't always been on point had been a problem for him in his earlier years on the force. Reprimanded on several occasions for being hotheaded and many times overreacting, he eventually transferred from Newark, NJ, PD to anti-crime unit in Los Angeles. After 8 years on the force. the two years he had been partners with Prissy were the most commendations he had earned in the prior 6 years. He liked that they worked good together. She did most of the pen work and brain storming and he did the storming in to seal the deal. Even he was the first to admit that some of his important findings that led to big arrest had come from her energy.

By the time he had returned with the coffee and snacks, Prissy had made some type of connection. Several other detectives were gathered around her desk giving their input and comments.

"Hurry up with the coffee, buddy, and you might have to go back for popcorn. This is surely going to be an action-packed drama." Detective Bradley stated as he accepted his black coffee.

"Don't you have a case to work?" Reyes made it clear he wanted some space. "Cases to work?" He eyed the other men as they took their coffee and donuts getting the message fully. The small crowd dispersed. "I got you tea with lemon and a brand muffin." He gave Priscilla her cup.

"Thanks. Hey, look at the names highlighted in this book. It's like a ledger or something. And look, the last highlighted information is for Osiris, Classic Custom Restorations. Hey, detective Bradley." She shouted across the room "Didn't you just get an inquiry from Hidden Hills PD about a homicide, ah, Osiris Classic Custom...?"

"Did you say Classic Custom Restorations?" Another detective stood up looking over his partition. "I'm working an arson case that hit my desk this morning. The place was burnt to the ground, entire square block. Boom in the middle of the morning. Fire Marshals report stated the place was filled with Ether."

Bradley and detective returned to Priscilla's desk. "I got a call from their homicide division. The owner of a restoration shop in our division was found slain in his home by his maid. There is definitely some connection between the murder and arson." They all agreed. A return call to the Hidden Hills homicide division enlighten the case even more when they discovered that Osiris' mansion had been burnt to the ground less than an hour after his shop.

"He had a mansion in Hidden Hills?" An officer asked.

"Okay let's start with this guy Osiris. I want to know everything about him and anybody associated." The captain ordered Priscilla, Reyes and the addition three officers assigned to the case. "The surveillance recordings arrived a few minutes ago so we'll all have time to view the footage to determine exactly what happened. Priscilla, you're lead detective on this one."

"Detective Gaiety." A young detective called to Priscilla. "You have a call on the line from a detective Josh Flemings in New York, homicide."

She rushed to take the call. "Hello. Detective Gaiety speaking."

"Hello, this is detective Josh Flemings. You submitted an N.C.I.C for a Katrina Whitfield concerning a homicide in your county. Well I was the detective that worked the Whitfield murders. Her boyfriend, a drug kingpin by the name of John Peterson, aka Snookie, was convicted and is serving two life sentences, at one of our fine concrete and steel accommodations here in the state of New York. So what is your interest?"

Priscilla quickly explained about the woman in possession of Katrina Whitfield's driver's license and credit cards and everything about her case.

"Fax me over the driver's license photo to compare with a New York, DMV picture." Flemings had an idea.

"I'll do it right now." She faxed the photo immediately after hanging up then returned just in time to see the first surveillance shots of Lillian and Renee checking in the Hyatt hotel. "That's her right there." She held up the driver's license. "Pretty little thing here with the guns and ice picks, and phony ID was definitely our shooters target. I guarantee they're somehow connected to this Osiris." They watched as Rook gunned down the police officer outside before pursuing Lillian and Renee into the hotel, firing like a madman before being dropped by L.A.P.D. "See there," Priscilla pointed out another shot. "Our pretty little friend used the RV to make her escape." They watched Lillian frantically running from the hotel along the walkway before stumbling upon the RV and taking off. "Can you see that tag?"

"Yeah GHS-7442."

"Put out a BOLO immediately. Also contact each state and run an N.C.I.C on each name corresponding with that state highlighted in the Brown, Leather Ledger from the suspect's minivan. That's South Beach, Miami- Dallas, Texas and Chicago, Illinois. We already have New York on board but because this thing involves so many states outside of our jurisdiction we may have to bring in the F.B.I."

Priscilla spent the next two hours making phone inquiries including re-interviewing the hotel manager while Reyes shot balled up sheet of paper into the trashcan.

"You missed more than you've made." She looked up for a moment.
"You haven't even been watching."
She gestured towards the pile on the floor. "If you make it in, I'll pay for Italian delivery. You miss, you buy, and I want a piece of cake from the diner for dessert."

"Oh yeah? Yeah-yeah." Reyes pretended to dribble the balled up sheet of paper. "Uh, cross over." He faked a shake like he made a brake to the 3 point line then launched an overhead hook shot. The balled up incident report soared across the room, spinning like a paper moon.

Priscilla was already digging inside her purse for her wallet as the paper made a beeline to the waste basket.

"Swoosh! Make that a Pastrami melt, fries, large Coke and a slice of that carrot cake from the diner."

"Ah, be quiet. That's what I get. I should have known you'd perform for food." The faxed machine running a long form, caught her attention before she could finish her comment. "That's gotta be it." She looked up with excitement in her eyes. "Looks like we have a female assassin on the loose. Every last subject highlighted in the Ledger has been a recent murder, all were international drug kingpins. Surprisingly there were witnesses. Employees at the Blue Lagoon in South Beach, described our girl as the suspect who poisoned the club owner, a Rafael Mignon."

"A bartender shot in the rear of a bar in Chicago trying to help is employer also describes our suspect. The victim's brother was killed at his home shortly after and a woman present said a black female had hit his car then shot him when he went to investigate."

"Then there's the murder of this pimp guy in Texas, Bone, killed along with an associate. A few of Bones' girls describes our girl, yet again. The report says they were arrested with her in some type of sweep. Shit! She was arrested!" Priscilla was ecstatic.

"Gary." She called another detective on the case. "Pull everything you can find on the Osiris murder and cross check other counties for any associates of Osiris recently murdered."

She immediately got on the phone with authorities in Texas attempting to locate an arrest record of her suspect. Priscilla was trying to figure out the motivation behind this young and apparently very dangerous girl's actions.

The men she had dealt with were very rich and dangerous, yet they all were sent to meet their maker... Curiosity merged with admiration and even though she intended to catch her and put her away for the rest of her life, she was gaining combat-respect for Lillian.

Another call from Detective Josh Flemings was all she needed to lay the foundation of her pending apprehension of a female killer. "I love you detective." She thanked him. "Please let me buy you lunch one day."

"Sure thing. Whenever you're in the city, look me up. Glad I could be of some assistance."

"Maybe sooner than you think. Thanks again, Detective Flemings. Bye."

"Okay everybody! We have a positive identification on our suspect. The subjects name is Lillian Elliot. The ID and credits cards were obtained by information she used from her deceased cousin, a Katrina Whitfield making the circumstances of that case questionable. The mother of Katrina Whitfield identified our suspect as her sister's daughter. She stated they had lived in Rhode Island all of their life until a couple of years ago she heard her sister relocated somewhere in Florida, said they're not close and she doesn't have a new address. "

She held up an 8X10 photo of Lillian. "So our target has no prior arrest...Other than the one we're looking into in Dallas. Run copies and send them to all relevant locations. We have to assume that she's going after the remaining names in the book. Reyes, contact law enforcement in Eagle, Colorado and the other cities on the list." Priscilla took a deep breath before picking up the phone and dialing her counterparts at the Federal Bureau of Investigation.

Chapter Twenty Two

Finding Love

Lillian sat across from Elliot at the dinner table full of food and family waiting for his mother to return to the table. Elliot had already fed his father in the master bedroom to avoid too many trips up and down the stairs. His younger brother, David was also visiting from college with his girlfriend. An aunt and uncle had come by for dinner with three well behaved children who referred to Lillian as Elliot's fiancée, which made her blush.

"So Katrina, are you from Colorado originally?" Mrs. Brown asked.

Lillian smiled, contemplating her next words carefully. She really liked Elliot and his family and felt bad about having to perpetrate lies. "No ma'am. I was just there on work related business. My family is originally from Rhode Island, but my Mother recently moved to Florida to live."

"What kind of work do you do?"
"Mom, come on, stop interrogating the woman?" Elliot begged.

"Hey, she did the same to Tamera?" David laughed. "Right baby." His girlfriend shook her head in agreement before shooting Lillian a knowing look. David was being courted by several NBA scouts in preparation for the upcoming draft having acquired his early basketball skills from Elliot.

"You all know how I am. I think Katrina's a very nice young lady and I like her a lot already. I hope she and Elliot settle down together. Now yawl leave me be and eat. The roast reminded Lillian of her own mother's cooking, on a bed of baby carrots."

"Thanks Mrs. Brown. I can't wait to enjoy your cooking."
"Well dig in honey. Elliot, give her one of those buttered rolls."

Lillian also had some of Mrs. Brown's onion greens and mashed potatoes, topped off with a huge piece of chocolate cake. The family seemed close knit, making her wish Renee could be there to enjoy all the good food.

"So are you ready to go pro obi?" Elliot joked with his brother.

"Don't start the obi stuff, and I'm ready." David took a big swig of his iced tea. "Thinking about South Beach."

"Miami obi? I feel you but I might have to take you to the courts and remind you where you got your skills."

"I wouldn't want to embarrass you in front of your honey so I respectfully decline, but you guys can come up to see me play next month."

"Depending on Katrina's and my schedule, I'll let you know."

Lillian sat listening to the family's chit-chatter, thinking that she wouldn't mind becoming a member of this warm tub-of-love. She smiled at Elliot, admiring the closeness he shared with his parents. After dinner, Elliot borrowed his younger brother's Volvo to show Lillian around, even riding through the poverty stricken neighborhood his parents had worked so hard to get out of. She was learning more about him and sharing less about herself. She felt since Elliot wasn't part of any scheme she was embarking on and she genuinely liked him, she decided to start being more honest.

"Elliot. I have something to tell you."
"You're a mirage? Am I dreaming?"
"Seriously, listen, honey."
He detected the seriousness in her voice and was all ears.

"When we first meant I was being careful and protective when I said my name was Katrina but the truth is my name is really Lillian. I felt so bad introducing myself to your mom as Katrina, but I told the truth about everything else."

Elliot smiled, un-offended. "So your last name isn't Elliot?"

"Oh no, I mean yes. Elliot is really my last name. It's just when I told it to you it slipped because you said Elliot first, you know?"

They caught the last movie at the Lowes Theater before retiring to the hotel room for a night of heated and passionate sex.

Lillian lie awake rethinking her entire situation, trying to figure out how she could put all her past demons to rest and settle down with Elliot, happily ever after like her parents and his.

After a morning of nonstop fucking, Elliot was sound asleep and snoring lightly. Lillian knew since there was a three hour time difference between California and New York the fresh business day had begun and someone should be available to take her call. Someone picked up on the first ring.

"Hello, and good morning. You have reached the Covenant House of New York. How may I help you?" A pleasant sounding woman answered.

"Hello Ma'am. My name is Viola Steinberg and I'm calling because my husband made a donation to your agency. I just wanted to verify that you are in receipt of the funds. We think the work you guys have been doing since 1972 is great and since you're privately funded, we know you depend on donations."

"Thank you. Everyone here works so hard to provide a safe haven for the young and helpless by giving loving care and vital services to homeless, abandoned, abused, trafficked and exploited children. I can check the arrival of any donations as soon as the computer powers up. Okay, what is the origin state the donation was sent from?"

"Colorado, Eagle."
"Let's see... Oh my god!"
"Is everything alright, ma'am?"

"Yes, but this says 15 million. Madam, I don't know what to say... Thank you." Breathing heavily. "This is a shock. Last week we had to make several cuts and had no idea about the coming months..."

Lillian got a good feeling inside as she listened to the gratefulness in the woman's voice. "Thanks ma'am. Have a great day." She hung up just as she heard the woman calling the director to the phone. It felt better making Benjamin Steinberg pay forward than it did killing all the others.

She left the bathroom feeling refreshed and eased back into bed with Elliot snuggling close enough to feel his breath on her neck. The heat from her body caused him to stir until all of him was awake. She could feel his rock hardness pressing against her.

"Is this how you wake up every morning?"

They skipped breakfast and picked up where they had left off, making love until lunch time. Lillian hadn't had this much sex in all her years and she was quickly, falling in love.

Chapter Twenty Three

ABC boys

The case directive came directly from FBI Headquarters in Washington, DC. J. Edgar Hoover, building. Two special agents both from different jurisdictions were assigned to the case.

Agent Daniel Garrabrissi had recently began investigating Bone for human trafficking in Texas and had heard the name New York, Snookie on a few occasions from some of the rescued women and teens who had agreed to inform on Bone before he was killed. A 16 year veteran, Garrabrissi headed the human trafficking, especially dealing with exploited children and has been responsible for saving thousands from being sold as sex slaves and arresting their abusers.

Alan Gregory, the only African American agent in his branch back in Atlantic City, New Jersey had six years with the bureau, making an impressive collection of high profile arrest in a short period of time. Having no brothers or sisters growing up made him a target for neighborhood bullies in Newark, NJ and so joining the FBI was always a secret dream he had, while on the ground being jumped. Being from the hood and blending in thoroughly in thug gear allowed him to infiltrate some of the more violent ghetto drug organizations and gangs. He closed the folder after reading its entire contents, catching up to speed.

Agent Garrabrissi did an overview of the accumulated evidence before them. "Lillian Elliot turns out to have been a flight attendant with no prior criminal history before this string of gangland style hits on some of the most wealthy and dangerous drug kingpins in the country. We can coordinate her travel schedule with most if not all of the locations involved even the murder of a drug trafficker in Miami named Miguel Cosine at an airport hotel even though his name appears nowhere in the Ledger. Surveillance cameras have our girl leaving the room with a briefcase.

"Maybe the Cosine thing was something personal outside of her list." Agent Gregory suggested.

"The flight manifesto puts him on a flight she worked the evening of his murder so this becomes their point of contact." Garrabrissi continued. "The shootings at the Hyatt in California was an unexpected occurrence, where the teen was shot and so it ended the killing spree. Still no identification on that young victim yet. Authorities in Colorado reported no incidents concerning the next intended target on her list. We have surveillance video from several different agencies, witnesses and loads of physical evidence. This girl was motivated by blind but calculating rage. She never even had a traffic citation before all this."

"So we have her for the murder of Cosine in Miami, looks like it could be the first one. Then there's Mignon in South Beach, cocaine poisoning. That was clever. I read that report twice." Agent Gregory stated matter-of-factly. "Um, the Chamber brothers in Chicago. The Pimp in Dallas and his associate, and Osiris and half the S.O.S."

"We can probably attach her to Osiris' death and about two or three of his men but the resulting gang war can be attributed to wiping out the bulk of their organization." Garrabrissi reached for the last piece to the puzzle; a huge box from the New York State Prosecutors Office filled with every piece of evidence used to convict John Peterson, aka New York, Snookie of two counts of murder in the death of Katrina Whitfield and her lover. "This is going to be the key." He took the Brown Leather Ledger and tossed it amongst Snookie's files. "When it's clear we'll find that this book belongs with Peterson's stuff. The question is, how the hell did Lillian Elliot get it and if she got it from Snookie, why is he still alive?"

"Looks like revenge. I mean Katrina was her first cousin and she did assume her identification during the murders." Agent Gregory added.

After quickly scanning over the New Jersey and New York arrest reports, he knew something was fishy. "The evidence in this case was overwhelming. This guy who had been acting with impunity, meticulously building a drug empire that spanned from coast to coast, yet he murders two people and leaves all the evidence for the police to conveniently find. Maybe Mr. Snookie can do the impossible and explain away his DNA. Anyway, he is the key to the Elliot woman and this entire mess." Garrabrissi surmised.

Chapter Twenty Four

A Deal with the Devil

The Maximum Security prison in Dannemora, NY looked like a huge concentration camp from the outside. Clinton Correctional Facility is the largest and third oldest of New York's 70 penitentiaries at 153 yrs. old, being called New York's "Little Siberia." The state prison, almost 400 miles from New York City is close to the Canadian border and is said to only endure two seasons; winter and July. Meaning other than July it's rather fucking nippy.

Some of the most dangerous criminals are housed there, having a high security level for various, hideous behavior. Murders, lifers and everything in-between make up the demographics of this subculture. Prison society, much like the outside world operates on a system of money and power, only the power comes before the money inside. You can be rich in prison but without the power you can become the victim. The power structure incorporates the tariffs and fee's on imported and exported goods in addition to controlling the internal operations of the prison. Gambling, and extortion are part of the equilibrium which keeps the system moving like a well-oiled machine.

Snookie was well known throughout New York, because of his kingpin status but he was hardly a shot caller at Clinton. As a matter of fact he had been approached by a cell-block-click looking to press him for some extortion money but instead of strapping-up and going to war he opted to make a separate arrangement with some young cats from Harlem to have his back. Of course he was smart enough to make it look like he had built a little crew from the hood but truth is he had his last few contacts on the side putting money on their inmate accounts weekly. Loyalty, was for the commissary money and Snookie knew he could trust no one with his life like he had trusted the people who had taken money, drugs and material assets since his incarceration.

His arrest was based on the murder charges, however there was no evidence to go after his drug assets but he had lost a lot of things to the game; Money owed before his arrest, drugs deals in limbo, various members taking off in fear of pending indictments with large amounts of dope & money and out-of-state associates cutting off ties in fear of the future involvement of the DEA. Within two years of his incarceration the empire that he has amassed was crumbling. In all Snookie relied on three people to handle his outside business, probably because they depended on him to maintain their living circumstances. He had spent a fortune on his trial and was spending a fortune on his appeal. The money going out but not coming in for years was beginning to take its toll on the cash he had readily available. He had maybe two to three years at his current rate of spending. The 32 year finance agreement with the bank concerning two homes imploded leaving him in debt on the legal end, however like a carrot being dangled before the rabbits face but forever kept from his reach, he dreamed almost every night about the wall full of money that he could never tell anybody about back on Sugar Hill in Harlem.

*****

Agents Garrabrissi and Gregory sat patiently in the prison visiting room waiting for their infamous subject to arrive.

"Don't they have better visiting areas for the lawyers..?" Alan complained. "It's dim as hell in here." He spotted a cockroach scurrying across the floor. "He's on his way to the stewpot just in time for diner."

Both men carried two accordion type briefcases on their way in, looking like appeal attorneys on the eve of their client's execution date. Everything about Snookie's case and the following events were summarized within.

The outer metal door opened with a heavy, metallic, clink before slamming shut. "He comes our boy." Another metal door opened and closed before a Correction Officer appeared at the gate with an inmate wearing a drab, grey, prison jumpsuit.

"They didn't let him put on his gators and silk shirt before he came." Garrabrissi joked as Snookie stood by, looking confused.

"You're not my appeal attorneys."

"We're better than appeal attorneys." Garrabrissi responded.

He looked at the four, stuffed briefcases at their feet before checking their suits. Lawyers and Agents definitely had a different style. "I don't have nothing to say to the DEA."

"We are not DEA, we're FBI." Alan replied.

"Just as bad." Snookie turned to the guard. "Get me the fuck out of here!"

"We don't think you killed Katrina Whitfield and this Carlton guy." Garrabrissi added causing Snookie to stop in his tracks. Since you've been cooling off in here things have been going on. "Have a seat please." Snookie took a seat across from the two eager agents. "Innocent people never stop proclaiming their innocence. Tell us about your involvement with Lillian Elliot and how she is connected to this entire situation."

"I've been telling everybody for the longest. I was set up. The Judge wouldn't even let my lawyer mention an alternative suspect. This Lillian bitch came to me... She-she must have stolen the used condoms from the wastebasket after we had sex."

Garrabrissi looked at agent Gregory and smiled. "Explain away his DNA." He responded. "Judging from her subsequent work, she could have killed him as well."

Gregory turned to Snookie. "Why kill her own cousin?"

The hesitation in his response gave him enough time to re-route his answer. "I think they had some falling out years ago over money or something..."

Garrabrissi sat back in his chair and stared hard at the convicted murderer with distain. "Listen real close because life changing decisions are about to be put on the table for only a short period of time so first let me warn you this! We know shit you don't know. The briefcases on the floor are just a few copies of the files we have on this case. We have Katrina Whitfield's diaries!

You have a lot of fill in info concerning our case. We can clear you of these two homicides, however. You would have to enter into an agreement with the Federal Prosecutors office stating that you will be forthcoming and completely honest about information involving your past drug constituents. I have been instructed by Department of Justice to place the following deal on the table for a fourth of an hour so you have 15 minutes to decide. In testifying against Lillian Elliot and any other subjects involved in this interstate conspiracy the state murder cases against you disappear, however you have to plead guilty to the murder of Lewis Armstrong. At the conclusion of Lillian's conviction the two life sentences will be converted into a flat fifteen to be served in federal custody and you'll get credit for timed already served. You do the math."

Wow, my way back to the streets. Snookie's mind was racing as fast as his heart was pounding. *I wonder how much they know about anybody else.* At this point he wasn't motivated to protect anyone, especially those that had jumped ship, robbing him blind in the process. "Where do I sign?"

Snookie started from the beginning back when he was serving crack hand-to-hand on the block. Like an actor giving the details of his life for a movie he recalled his exploits vividly. After a week of straight lawyer visits other inmates began to become suspicious only to have their suspicions confirmed by a C.O, that Snookie was talking to the feds. The next series of meetings took place at a federal detention center in Brooklyn where he was subsequently transferred. The agents only began to speak about Lillian's other murders when the subject of his interstate drug connections came up.

The news of Lillian's activities made Snookie do a double head shake that left him stuck, with his mouth wide open. "Whoa! Who did what?" He thought he was hearing things. The idea of her killing any of the men mentioned was impossible for him to digest. "And you said Osiris too?" He was going through some things realizing how smart Lillian had turned out, making him feel like a total sucker. He prayed for the day he could catch up with her, receiving new motivation to help the feds take her down.

Snookie fell into a deep stage of recollection giving up every single person who he had ever dealt with and all known associates. He admitted to supplying Bone with underage girls for years as well as his involvement with each of Lillian's targets and the remaining names in the Ledger.

Garrabrissi despised Snookie for setting this all into motion with his perverted fetishes for underage girls. He watched the sick man eating from a Styrofoam container purchased by one of the agents, wishing he had told somebody to add a lump of dog shit to the order.

"Enjoying your steak and fries?" He asked sarcastically. "Let's get one thing straight, Peterson. I think you're a real fucked up dude and if it were up to me you'd be castrated, so don't get the illusion that we're buddies because I joke around with you sometimes."

"Well don't think I'm your friend because I helped you with your case." Snookie responded before taking a bite of garlic bread.

"So to be exact, Lillian killed her cousin, Katrina, and set you up for the murders before murdering your drug connections because she was set up to be raped. Correct?"

"Correct."

"I like this girl. She's got more heart than most of the guys in this prison, including you." Agent Gregory said.

Trying to belittle Snookie was useless because he had navigated the surface of the ground many times on his belly like a serpent during his climb to the top of the game. He had no conscious and no problem being super, selfish because when he was young he heard someone say "Self-preservation is the first law of nature", and adopted it as his slogan.

Back in his cell he sat on his bunk feeling redeemed. He had long ago come to the conclusion that it was Lillian who had hit his safe house in New Jersey for almost two million after setting him up. No one knew about it and the home had an A-one security system. *She got me for my black planner when she stole the condom with my semen and somehow deciphered the codes finding my Brown, Leather Book at the house with the cash. That little bitch turned out to be a beast. Oh my god she was able to kill Osiris and the others. I created a fucking monster.*

For a split second he was even feeling a little safe behind bars out of Lillian's reach before his ego kicked in fueling his false bravado. *Nah, fuck that! Bitch knew better to fuck with me that's why she put me in here. I'll be free one day. Fifteen years is a whole lot better than two life sentences, is right, Agent Garrabrissi.*

Chapter Twenty Five
Lady luck

Lucinda answered her cell phone on the first ring. "Hello."

"Hey cuz, they're moving him tomorrow to some FED hospital. I heard some of the nurses talking. I put everything in the gym bag. Hurry while the shift manager's at lunch. The rest of the bitches are lazy as hell and the cop mainly stays in the four man room watching the other detainees because one of them is very loud and disrespectful to staff. They don't even watch him closely because he's in a coma but I swear he responded when I told him you were coming for him.

Lucinda's cousin Lanett worked at the hospital where Rook was being held and kept her abreast of his condition. She sped the entire drive, anxious to see him even if he couldn't speak to her at the moment.

The county hospital was not the most modern or cleanest. It was huge and not so organized. Lucinda changed into the nurse's uniform before entering the employees entrance, flashing the ID Lanett had provided for her. She noticed how hectic the waiting room was and traveled unchallenged into the detainee ward, catching her cousin's eye immediately.

Lanett motioned towards Rook's room and proceeded to distract the assistant at the desk while Lucinda entered. She flew across the room and hugged his face before quickly removing the IV. The gurney banged against the door as her small frame summoned the strength of 10 emergency service technicians. She took a quick look at the ID tag on her shirt before heading towards the nurse's station.

"Where is John Doe going? And where's his police escort?" The nurse's aide inquired. "I know they said that one was dangerous."

"He's being transferred in the morning." Lanett looked at the chart in her hands. "I guess they're doing a follow up for the discharge." Lucinda nodded politely as she breezed past the hospital, security, officer, never having saw a cop. The orange lines on the floor led her to the emergency room service entrance where a waiting ambulance driven by her uncle and ex-boyfriend whisked them away.

Chapter Twenty Six

Round Up

Law enforcement from 23 different agencies were preparing to effect raids in several different cities across the United States on over 200 suspects, secretly indicted and on the FBI's wanted list. Any past associates of Snookie and his organization from high level to the low end where rounded up and charged under the R.I.C.O law

Businesses, land, homes, bank accounts, planes, cars, boats, jewelry, drugs and money were seized. It was one of the biggest coordinated efforts in recent history. Agents Garrabrissi and Gregory were big dogs on the case having amassed a wealth of information from their informant.

Every last, known location was hit hard and fast during the early morning when everyone is presumed to be sleeping. Federal task force implemented the use of heavy military equipment to gain entry into some of the fortress like homes. Tanks were used to overrun privacy gates and storage units, making the raid seem more like a Russian, invasion.

When the smoke cleared more indictments dropped as a result of deals made with snitches trying to lessen their culpability, causing the government to focus on a few overseas targets. Another piece of welcomed information was the identity of the hotel shooter at the hospital confirmed by a cooperating, member of S.O.S. Agent Gregory had put in the paperwork to have Rook transferred to a prison hospital to be processed and finger printed.

"A cousin of Osiris. Atini Faamoana, a.k.a Rook. His father is supposed to be one of the founders of the group and was recently stabbed to death in prison. Kid has no criminal record but our snitch says he was more like a little brother to Osiris. Have somebody find his school records."

"That explains why he went after our girl with an Uzi. She murdered his big brother." Gregory assessed. "Whacked the 'Big Homie.'"

"I'm beginning to like Lillian Elliot more and more." Garrabrissi admitted just as the phone rang." Agent Gregory watched as the look on his face turned from admiration to shock. "Say fucking what?" The news about Rook's escape caught him off guard.

Chapter Twenty Seven

Making Plans

The more time they spent together, the more Lillian wanted to be with Elliot. The last few days had been so peaceful in total contrast to the previous months. She wanted to be in his loving arms forever...

"Elliot, I was wondering if you would come back to Rhode Island with me to see if you like it. Maybe we can get a nice place together, you know?"

He gave her a tight hug acknowledging his rapidly, building feelings. "I want to be with you Lillian. I've been so happy and relaxed lately, it's been a lot of stress relief, not that my life was so complicated..."

"I have some money in the bank that my father left me when he passed away. If you don't like Rhode Island we could find someplace in Florida. My mother moved out there a few years back and when I visited, I really liked the peacefulness."

"I have a little something saved up too." Speaking proudly of the $18,958 he had in the bank. "I'm my own boss so we can make it happen. I could obtain a license to operate, maybe get a few more cars in the future and hire some drivers." He explored the possibilities. It was all music to Lillian's ears.

Lillian's stomach tightened momentarily as she was about to tell what she felt was a necessary lie. "When I return to Rhode Island, my plans are to resign from my job as chief financial advisor at the airlines because the position keeps me on the road like the trip that brought me to Eagle. I'm looking into a supervisory position with an organization that's helps at risk teens."

"That's very humbling. I wish there was some way I could help." Elliot felt like he'd hit the jackpot in this emotional game of love.

"Would it be alright if I left my bike here at your mom's?"

"No problem, but we better lock it up good because her and my father still like to ride." He joked.

*****

They decided to rent an SUV for the long ride across the country hoping to do a little sightseeing and sexing along the way. Elliot drove the white Lexus truck most of the trip while Lillian sang with her feet on the dash. They stopped to eat at several different places and even stopped at two motels to fuck, turning a normally 48 hour drive into three days.

"This is a nice quiet neighborhood." Elliot commented as they turned onto Lillian's Street. "On the left, right here." She pointed to her home as she prepared to exit for a good stretch.

"Nice Mercedes." Elliot admired the powder blue Benz.

"I've had it for a while now." At this point, Lillian really didn't care if it was a Toyota, Camry.

"It looks brand new." He added as he began unloading the SUV. "It's nice here, sort of like Eagle but not as cold and lonely."

"What's under the cover?"

"That's a '65 fully customized mustang. It belonged to my little sister that recently passed away." A cold feeling ran through her as she read the stamp on the car cover. *Classic Custom Restorations.*

This was the first mention of a younger sister and right then Elliot realized there was a lot he had to learn about his new love. "I'm sorry to hear that."

They spent most of the day in each other's arms before Lillian cooked Elliot a fabulous diner and fed him dessert from the sweet nectar between her legs. They slow grinded to soft music and talked about their future together. The plan was to buy a three bedroom house in Florida within the next 6 months, not far from her mother, get married and have a few children. It seemed like life was just beginning for Lillian, and, not surprisingly, Elliot shared the same feelings.

*****

Lillian showered and dressed, preparing a quick breakfast for Elliot on her way out of the door. She planned on officially resigning from her job and returning her equipment and uniforms.

Her appointment with the same real estate agency that had found her mother's home in Florida and subsequently sold the old home in Rhode Island, was later in the afternoon. There were so many beautiful houses in Florida that she wanted to go online with Elliot to find something comfortable but modest.

Thoughts of the past days with Elliot and the upcoming search for a new home had Lillian beaming with hope. There was only one person she wanted to say goodbye to at work, having kept to herself for the most part. When she pulled her Benz her into the employee's parking lot the nice, elderly woman she wanted to see before she left was just pulling up also.

"Hello Lillian, back from a long vacation." Mrs. Crafton said as she approached Lillian with a hug. "Things are crazy around here, and they hired a lot of new people within the last couple of days. I never seen them hire that many people that fast in all my years..."
"Actually I'm turning in my heels and cap. I wanted to say goodbye before I left." She gave her coworker another hug.

"Oh my. Must be a man."

Lillian blushed at the assumption. "I might be getting married in the near future."

"I knew it. See, being in the air... Is like being on the road for a trucker. Now if love has its way... It's time to anchor down. Congratulations. You deserve to be happy. I told my husband how sweet you are, helping me when it's so busy. Well... Take good care of yourself." The women headed into the building side by side.

Lillian went directly to the general management office looking for a crew chief. "Hey, Sandra." She stopped a familiar face walking by. "Can you page Margaret? I need to turn in my equipment and sign off on my contact."

"Oh. Sure. How have you been?"

"Just coming off vacation. Ah, just decided the constant movement was a little too much."

"I know what you mean, that's why I stay grounded. I have to give it to you guys. After a while, all airports look the same. You know, I could check you off and take your stuff. Just put it here."

Lillian sat the satchel on the desk and thanked Sandra for everything. She left the office heading to the admissions center to drop off her ID and keycards. After dropping the items off, she headed to the escalator on her way back to her car. She shook her head, trying curb the images of her riding Elliot's dick like the rodeo. *The man has turned me into a damned nymphomaniac or something.*

As she ascended on the moving, metal stairs, she reminded herself to get rid of the Classic Custom Restoring cover on the Mustang, not wanting anything to remind her of the past. A dark haired, Caucasian woman standing at the top of the escalator, almost blocking her passage was looking behind Lillian like she was expecting her husband to come up.

"Excuse me." Lillian politely stepped around the woman.

"Ah, hey there!" The woman called out. In a hurry to get home, Lillian barely turned, until she heard her name.

"Are you by any chance, Lillian Elliot?"

Having just quit, she figured the lady for one of the new management, employees Mrs. Crafton had spoken about. That's until the gold detectives badge gleamed under the bright airport lighting. Still not sure of what was going on, Lillian answered professionally. "Yes ma'am, how may I assist you?"

"You can start by lying face down on the floor with your arms spread wide. Now!" The Glock was aimed at the bridge of Lillian's nose. Agents appeared from everywhere. "My name is officer Priscilla Gaiety, part of a special federal task force put together just for you, pretty lady."

Lillian complied with the police officers demands, lying faced down. Priscilla slapped the cuffs on her and snatched her to her feet. "Lot of people would like to talk to you, but not before we have a little chat first."

Lillian's heart was thumping in her chest not knowing what to expect. Getting caught had never been in the equation. She was flushed with that numbing feeling of reality sinking in. A thousand scenes from her life flashed rapidly across her mind as if she was traveling thru a wormhole at a million miles per hour.

Once she was seated in the black Suburban, between two huge agents, she could see another group of agents congregating out front, realizing that almost every person she had greeted or returned a smile to, had been FBI. At the same time that Lillian was thinking to herself that Agent looked like a person not to be fucked with, Prissy was thinking to herself that her killer looked like she couldn't harm a fly.

Lillian put her head back, crying silently inside, thinking about Elliot at home alone, waiting for her to return.

Chapter Twenty Eight

Right to Remain Silent

Lillian was transported to a warehouse in Brooklyn, NY used to secure high profile prisoners for interrogation and debriefing. The ride in shackles and cuffs made it much worst causing her back to seize. She tried to shift to a better position, to no avail. By the time she arrived at the FED building all she wanted to do was lie on the floor to take the pressure off of her aching body.

Prissy arrived in a separate vehicle and removed Lillian from the holding cell. "You know what they say, the guilty always sleep it off the minute they realize they're caught and it's basically over for them." She poked at the exhausted looking woman lying on the cold, concrete floor. "Sorry to wake you from your slumber sleeping beauty but we have to go talk a little. They're going to be finger printing you and a whole bunch of other stuff. Do you need to use it first? As you can see there are no toilets or sinks in these cages. You will be moved to one of the women's federal detention centers later."

She followed the detective who had come all the way from Los Angeles to talk to her, across the dimly lit warehouse. After using the restroom, they made a series of turns until they entered an office. "Have a seat. Want a soda or something?" A few agents, eager to get a peek at the pretty, woman assassin, glanced into the interview room on the walk by.

Lillian sat quietly, watching the detective's eyes as her lips moved. She was deep in her own thoughts as she tried to figure the process she was about to go though. Would there be a bail? When could she call her mother and Elliot? The room was cold and uncomfortable causing her to fold her arms.

Prissy looked up from a stack of papers. "As a formality, I have to read you your rights. You have to right to remain silent..."

Lillian was concerned, Elliot would be worried when she didn't return. The idea of never seeing him again crossed her mind. Since Lewis' death she always seemed to lose the people she loved, some way or another, she reflected. Crying wasn't the answer. She took a deep breath and put her big girl panties back on. As her posture straightened, she realized she would have to prepare herself for a different type of war. A battle with the United States, Attorney's Office. Before Prissy could ask the first question, she was interrupted.

"I am inclined to preserve my constitutional rights by refusing to make any post, arrest statements without the assistance of Counsel of my choice." Lillian said, somehow remembering the spiel from one of the crimes shows she had watched in the past.

Prissy tried another angle. "I'm just concerned about a few things that happened in California. I need closure of my local situations that occurred because of all this... The big boys are out holding a press conference, all about your arrest. It's getting national coverage so right now as we speak your picture is plastered across every television set in the United States. When they get finished tooting their horns, they're focusing on you. I hope to be on a plane headed west by then. The case against you is iron clad. I have a box of security footage that places you at every location where you killed someone. The Hyatt footage showing you and a young girl fleeing the shooter. We need to ID this girl. You need to talk to me before Agents Garrabrissi and Gregory arrive with the federal, drama."

Lillian fought off a load of gloom as she thought about her mother seeing her on the news charged with these heinous crimes. The disappointment and shame that her daughter caused. *Like back when they thought I willingly got pregnant and caught an STD. I didn't make it to medical school, but look mom, I'm going to prison.*

Lillian, refusing to answer any questions, was the same response that the ABC boys got when they finally showed up. Even after being subjected to several, uncomfortable hours in the cage between attempts to question her, she said nothing. After 48 hours, they let her finally make a phone call. The first person she called was her mother who luckily hadn't seen the news coverage about the case. The next call was a little harder. Elliot may not attempt to try to understand what was going on. *Then again, who would?*

Eventually, Lillian was moved to the Brooklyn Federal Detention Center where she was re-fingerprinted and photographed, left in a holding cell for four hours before being fed stale sandwiches and warm milk. She was stripped, searched, and given a drab, grey jumpsuit to wear with the option to donate her clothes or mail them home. Only after a busload of inmates returned from court was she allowed to be placed in a housing area.

She was escorted with a group of grumpy woman who had been up since 5:00 am preparing for a long day in court, being shackled and transported in a caged bus to sit in concrete holding cells, eating boloney and cheese with a cup of sour Kool-Aid. Some had received lengthy sentences and judging from the looks on everybody's faces they just wanted to get back to their cells to crash, same as Lillian. The day's events had her emotionally drained.

It seemed like she had just curled up under the rickety, wool, blanket and went to sleep in the cold, dull, center when the heavy metal door popped open. She could hear an officer calling inmates names as other cell doors opened.

"Elliot, court!"

Lillian sat up with her arms folded feeling cold and alone. The sleep was more like a blackout, devoid of schemes and dreams. Nothing came to her during the night's slumber that could help her navigate her present predicament, not one bright idea. Walking in a line of shackled prisoners along the quiet jail corridor seemed like the dream. She couldn't bring herself to eat the sausage and biscuit they had served on the way out of the housing block. A warm cup of watered down orange juice was all she could stomach.

Once on the bus some of the other inmates begin to loosen up, talking amongst themselves about their cases. Lillian kept quiet contemplating her fate. She had seen plenty of court situations on TV but couldn't separate the facts from the fiction.

The streets surrounding the courthouse were lined with news vans with huge reception antennas pointing into the sky. There were reporters and police milling about in wait. The moment the bus pulled up everything went digital. Cameramen were scrabbling getting SD cards ready and everything else needed to get that perfect shot.

"Damn, somebody important must be in court today. Look at all those reporters and cops." A heavyset woman charged with armed robbery said as the bus pulled into an underground garage at the Federal Court House.

The prisoners were hustled off of the bus into the dark garage before exiting thru a big metal door to the fenced walk way leading to the courts. As soon as they emerged, a group of reporters rushed the fence.

"There she is!"
"Lillian Elliot are you a serial killer?"

"Lillian are you some type of hit man, well... hit woman?" The reporter corrected herself.

"Miss Elliot, can you tell us why you did this?"

The questions were flying from all directions. Lillian held her head down, shielding her face with her mane. She hadn't figured she'd be under such scrutiny and wasn't sure how to respond. By now the other inmates were beginning to realize the quiet, pretty girl they brought in yesterday was big news, some hoping she would take some of the light off of their cases. "I hope she got my judge." One of the girls said. "Then my case won't look like shit, might give me probation."

Lillian was relieved when they entered the building and the big, metal door closed behind them shutting off all the chaos & noise from the shouting news people. "Damn girl, what did you do?" Another girl asked, really not expecting a response from the quiet woman. In the holding cell, everybody gave Lillian her space, figuring she had bigger problems.

Two hours went by before a court officer begin to call names. Four hours later with a few only more inmates left, she still hadn't been called. Inmates who had been seen where placed in a different cell awaiting early transportation back to the jail. Lillian figured she'd be on the late bus back like the inmates that had arrived when she was in the reception pen last night.

"Lillian Elliot."

Lillian headed toward the bars when she heard her name. "Right here, I'm Lillian."

A tall, well dressed, black man with a shiny briefcase appeared around the corner. He smiled showing a set of even, white teeth, his cologne emitting a scent in direct contrast to the scent of urine and unwashed pussies lingering in the cell house.

"Hello. My name is Maurice Cooper and I have been retained by your husband Elliot."

After getting the call from Lillian, Elliot had his bank send a wire transfer, using his savings to hire a lawyer. Because the case was so high profile, it took $20,000 just to retain the federal lawyer. He recalled Lillian, saying she had some money in the bank so he figured she would be able to handle the rest.

"Miss Elliot, these are some very serious charges that carry the death penalty under federal law if the Department of Justice chooses to seek it. So I must tell you up front, it's very intricate. I've spent the last thirty minutes or so going over your arrest report. It's vague so I'll motion for discovery, meanwhile, you'll have to fill in the blanks. Get ready, they'll be calling you in a minute. See you in the courtroom, just answer yes sir or no sir, in a clear voice if questioned by the court." He exited the way he came.

Lillian felt some type of relief, having talked to someone who seemed to know what to do. She smiled and grabbed her face as she exhaled deeply. Elliot wasted no time coming to her aid, instead of hightailing it back to Eagle, Colorado, glad to be away from a maniac.

A court officer came for her. "Stand right here. When I open the door keep your hands by your sides and have a seat next to your attorney."

Entering the court was like walking into a monkey cage as all the spectators waited to see a trick or two. She stared straight ahead and took her seat. "They're reading the charges, taking a plea and contemplating bail. It's just formality."

Lillian caught the evil eye of the federal prosecutor assigned to the case. She looked like one of those vindictive, white chicks with power to wield and something to prove. Patricia Chernoff's grandfather was the U.S Attorney in the Eastern District of New York and Patricia was as fierce in her quest to prosecute criminals. In her 8 years she enjoyed a 100% conviction rate. Many people secretly disliked her courtroom arrogance but kissed her ass as a way to cope. This was just another case to knock down to her, that's until she saw Lillian face to face.

Sneaky little, black bitch. Patricia didn't necessarily like black people but disliked black women more. On a professional level she tolerated them but in more than a few instances she pushed the envelope to convict an "innocent" to support her theory about a case. In the beginning, the few who knew about her overzealous ways were on board until she began acting, over the years, like she was the greatest thing since summer's eve douche and doing things by the book, when she was a cheater. As far as Lillian's lawyer was concerned, she hadn't worked with him before and disregarder him as just another nigger-shyster working both sides of the fence.

If she had her way she would make sure this time next year that Lillian was spending the rest of her life in federal prison. The judge kept a sharp eye on the defendant having glanced at the serious charges in his files.

"Has the US Attorney's office secured an indictment?" He inquired.

"Today we are entering indictments for murder in the deaths of Katrina Whitfield and Carlton Wycliffe as well as tampering with evidence and several other offenses. Also there will be amended indictments as to the multiple charges of murder concerning the assassinations of several, high level, international, drug kingpins in various locations around the country prompting several counts for violating the Hobbs act. Also we motion to deny bail. Defendant is a threat to society and a flight risk."

"Defense counsel?"
"Your honor, my client as no prior record. She has been employed..."

"Bail denied! One of these counts is enough to sustain a denial but the defendant has several."

Maurice was prepared for a hard way to go over here in the Eastern District Court, where the judges had a reputation for favoring the government's account. He knew the only way to survive out here was to be in possession of full knowledge of the law. Some hard-strung judges would rather have a decision reversed by an appellant court rather than subside. Judging from this judge's attitude and the lead prosecutor's reputation he knew they were in for a fight. He wanted to smack the smirk from the prosecutors face only he was taught never to hit a woman. The look on everybody's faces were readable, like they were saying: *We're a team working together against niggers and outsiders and you are both.* Evident even on the court reporter's face, probably the judge's niece.

Lillian followed her lawyer to the podium. "Head high and speak clearly." He whispered.

"Ms. Elliot how do you plea in the cases against you?"
"Not guilty." Her lawyer nodded affirmatively. "Sir." She added.

The judge continued writing without looking up before addressing the prosecutor. "Okay, when do you want to come back...?"

"Excuse me, Your Honor." Maurice interrupted, not missing the look of distain on the judge's face. "At this time, I'm making a notice and motion in accordance with local Rule 3, Federal rules of Criminal Procedure 16., the Constitutional requirements under Brady vs. Maryland, United States vs. Agurs and States vs. Bagley and Agency, asking the government to furnish discovery, inspection and the right to copies of all items deemed appropriate by the court, reasonable and necessary to the preparation of the case. This request for discover and inspection relates to items in the possession, custody and control of the United States Attorney as well as all federal, state and city agencies or governmental entities over which has control or liaison to obtain, access to material possessed by such agency or entity. In addition to motion for discovery, I submit this memorandum in support of the defendant's motion to preserve the right to suppress any physical evidence against her in a subsequent trial. If possible, I'd like to receive a copy of the complaint, information and indictment at this time."

The judge rolled his eyes slowly shuffling his head in the direction of the prosecutor's table. "Any objections from the government?"

"No, you're Honor." Patricia answered.
"Okay, defense motions granted. Next court date in 32 days."
"Thank you, Your Honor." She agreed.

Maurice turned to his client. "I will come to see you in the holding cell. I need you to tell me some things about the case real fast for a press release of our own."

Lillian nodded before feeling the court officer's hand on her arm. "This way." Leading her towards the holding cell door. Just as she was about to enter something told her to raise her head, just in time to see Elliot wave quickly from the third row. She smiled and disappeared inside, feeling conscious about being seen in the baggy, prison jumpsuit and flimsy, jail sandals.

243

The Daily News front page read INDICTED with a photo of Lillian taken at the courthouse during her walk of shame. The story was front page news and running on TV stations across the country.

The New York Times, having obtained information from a confidential source, who reports, Lillian Elliot was a victim of rape as a child and later exacted revenge against her attackers. The portions about being molested as a child were grasped upon by several woman's groups, opposing violence against women and children. Suddenly there were people showing support for the defendant as a victim of sexual abuse. The paper reported on the illegal activities of the all the victims, making it easy to sympathize with the young woman who had never committed a crime in her life before this incident.

After getting some advice from his wife who was a floating-paralegal at several law offices including a big law firm in Atlanta, Georgia, Maurice decided to give an interview to GQ magazine, hoping to find more people sympathetic to what his client had gone though at such a young age.

The interview with GQ was powerful, causing them to write Lillian Elliot up like a crime story, vigilante. They spent the best part of the article detailing the criminal histories of the victims which included murders, trafficking, kidnapping and a slew of other crimes. It was apparent that someone in the editing department saw Lillian as a sort of hero and went about uncovering negative information about the victims while making Lillian seem like the answer to modern law enforcement.

Maurice lay awake thinking about the high profile case he was handling. Being a fairly good judge of character, he didn't take Lillian to be the sociopath the police and media was portraying her to be. He had seen cases were a defendant engages undesirable, mainly criminal, behavior in direct contrast to their character and actions in the past. After speaking with her briefly at the jail he came to understand, as she explained the reason for her actions. Having admitted guilt to Maurice didn't make him not want to help. However, he knew clearing her of Katrina's murder would be an important factor because a jury may find some way to rationalize the death of the dealers and killers, but a young relative will hit too close to home.

"Anything I can help with?" Maurice's wife Gwen placed her book on the nightstand. She could see her husband was deep in ponder. "Having a lawyer's block?"

"Very funny. But I'm trying to figure out the best way to go about my defense. You see the climate is such that people can now pray for such a person in the mist of the rise in crime over the years. My client who has no criminal record, not ever a traffic ticket, murders a bunch of hardcore criminals all over the country. The only unmoving problem is the murder of her cousin that she claims she didn't commit and I believe her." Maurice explained everything he was told about the case to his wife who often researched cases he worked. Her ability to find landmark cases to support her client's motions were impeccable. She listening inventively, scanning cases in her head that met the criteria.

"That Snookie is a real piece of shit. She should have ended it by killing his ass."

Maurice looked at his wife and knew she meant every word. "Ah." He continued not really one for violence, even being around real criminals at work. I need to check to see if the boyfriend, victim had any arrest in the Virgin Islands."

"Bam! Got it." Gwen hopped up. "Follow me baby, listen. The subsequent, amended indictment will include the murders, by way of interstate travel, of victims in various other states, thus creating the nexus for federal intervention, however what gives the F.E.D.S jurisdiction over the Whitfield girls death? The answer is venue. I will look up cases on jurisdiction of the feds to prosecute local, intrastate crimes.

The interstate murders can obviously be connected by the references in the hit book you have copies of, but if Katrina Whitfield and Carlton Wycliffe aren't noted as targets, then the connection is blurred. That doesn't mean the state can't convict."

"Forget fighting the cousin's murder charges. Get rid of them." Maurice just looked at his wife and shook his head. "Damn you're so smart. I'm so glad I married you." He joked.

"Oh, you married me for my brain?"

"That and something else." He grabbed her and kissed her gently on the side of her face."

"What's the matter, my breath stank?"
He kissed her lips before they made passionate love.

Chapter Twenty Nine

Reality Sinks In

The women's facility at the federal lock up was overcrowded so some women were being housed in one side of the male dorm area, separated by a metal door. There was a diverse inmate population because lots of foreign drug mules arrested at one of the New York airports found themselves here as well many other non-black, female, federal lawbreakers.

The story ran on the news regularly making Lillian infamous at the jail, however upon first glance she could easily be mistaken as timid. Sitting at a table watching a T.V with no sound she assumed all the people with ear buds on were tuned in on a TV channel or something. She couldn't wait for Thursday, her scheduled visiting day to come around so she could explain everything to Elliot herself.

She was scheduled to see a counselor later who would orientate her about the jail, fill out her visiting forms and phone list and give her a code that one of the other girls said she needed to use the phone.

"You have to prepay all your calls." The girl had said. With no money on her account Lillian looked towards a visit. Seeing Elliot in the courtroom was a good sign but the knot that had been in the pit of her stomach since walking behind the gates was quivering at the thought of losing him now. As she continuously pondered her predicament, seeing no way to get around it. To her she was perfecting the motions of her deeds, however she had left a trail of evidence that began to emerge after the incident at the Hyatt hotel in Los Angeles. It finally begin to sink in that she was in real, deep, shit. The only way to be with Elliot was to somehow win this case. *There's no fucking way.* She thought about the things she had done. *I'm finished.*

Later that day she was called to see the counselor, a nosey old woman who asked too many personal questions. Lillian pretended to listen hoping she would hurry up issuing some allotted items and her phone pin code.

"Here is your rulebook, acknowledgement form and some other papers, let's see. Okay this is your cell location, 26. That's at the rear of the unit by the phones, and this is a copy of your inmate account records." She glanced at the balance." Looks like I won't have to give you toothpaste and soap every week. Somebody out there cares about you." She concluded her interview. "Okay, Ms. Elliot stay out of trouble."

Lillian took a quick look at her account balance. $500. *Thank you Elliot.* She made a beeline to the phone area. There were three phones against the wall, two were occupied and one was empty. She put in her pin number and waited impatiently as the operator alerted the person on the other line that this was a prepaid call from a federal, correctional facility. The sound of Elliot's voice was enough to make her weak in the knees.

"Are you alright honey?" The concern in his voice was real. He didn't know the true story but he knew there was no way Lillian could have done the things they are saying she did… Without good reason, anyway. The empty spot that threatened to consume his heart was willing him to pray for her innocence and to be back in his arms.

"I'm sorry, Elliot. I didn't mean to put you through this…"
"Don't worry, I'm here for you, Lillian."

That was all she needed to hear. Suddenly the pressure in the pit of her stomach begin to subside. "Thanks for paying the lawyer and putting money on my inmate account. I miss you so much already…"

Click!
Lillian looked up to see a fat hand holding down the button.
"Bitch I don't care who you are. You must be ready to bring it if you think your using the Latin phone."

Only then did Lillian notice the long lines on the other two phones. "My bad. I didn't know there were special phones."

A group of women standing with the fat woman, named Carmen began chattering in Spanish. "Well you know now, honey. But check this out since I see you have money to make calls why don't you hook me and my people up too. As a matter of fact I need you to call your little boyfriend or whoever it was that you were talking to on my phone and have them put $200 on my account." The woman finished her sentence with a mean snarl.

"How much?" Lillian asked.

"Two!"

The receiver struck the bully on the bridge of her nose, with lightning speed, breaking it instantly and spraying blood everywhere. The second blow caught her in the top of the head on the way down to the floor.

"Two to go." She gently placed the receiver in its cradle and calmly walked toward the group of shocked women causing them to move aside and let her past. From then on that was the only phone Lillian was seen using.

The following day she was called for a legal visit. An escort officer attempted to engage her in small talk but quickly got the message when she got no response to any of her three questions. Lillian could see her lawyer sitting beyond the wired glass next to a pretty black woman and sighed in relief.

"Good morning Lillian." Maurice stood to shake her hand. "I want to introduce you to my lovely wife, Gwen and most trusted legal, research, technician. She is helping me with your case and found some very helpful legal notes to help us along with this thing." The women exchanged polite nods. "Again I cannot downplay the seriousness of this matter, nor can I guarantee a favorable decision but I will promise to give it all I've got. We have copies of a lot of the evidence that the prosecution intends to use so we need to spend the afternoon going over each item to determine the foundation of our defense. Also here is a copy of a motion to suppress any and all evidence that the Government intends to use concerning the murders of Katrina Whitfield and Carlton Wycliffe because they lack nexus as does the actually homicides themselves. The FEDS are attempting to clump the New York murders with the drug murders as a convenience to their case but there not federal. I'll file this in the morning so that means a hearing sometime next month. Understand everything?"

"Yes." Lillian responded as she accepted the motion.

"I don't want to discuss money at this time but we have to establish a pay schedule."

"Yeah, that's fine. I'm expecting a visit from Elliot tomorrow. I'll have him bring you the balance then..."

"Oh, no. I didn't mean you have to pay everything, of course not, say six, or ten thousand?"

"I'd prefer to get you paid so that you'll have all the recourses to proceed, also I know I owe you win or lose." She shared a look of respect from the beautiful, well dressed woman looking like a black queen sitting next to her king. Being out of her element had Lillian feeling a little lost but the woman sitting across from her gave her a returning sense of emotional strength.

Gwen smiled at Lillian. "I just want you to know that I don't judge you. The bigger picture is we as a society bare responsibility for our youth. We mold them at every point in their existence and, all, have the chance... Parents, teachers, coaches, neighborhoods, preachers, aunts, uncles, cousins... To touch these children's lives and provide them with the knowledge to become who they become."

Lillian nodded in understanding. *Gwen was saying that if Snookie had raped me, killed Lewis and fucked up my life then I may have done the same thing. At least somebody understands.*

Thursday finally arrived and Lillian found herself both anxious and nervous. A few of the girls were up early preparing for their visits, trying to look as sexy as possible in the baggy, beige prison uniforms. Lillian was housed in a two person cell with a young, black girl named Pam who had just been sentenced to 20 years for narcotics conspiracy, just for putting rental cars in her name for her boyfriend who was transporting drugs across the state lines.

"You look good. I wish I was going on a visit, I'd wear a bed sheet if I had to." Pam assured Lillian.

"Thanks. Hey would you do me a favor and give the canteen officer my commissary list if I'm on a visit when they pick them up? I'll get you fifteen bucks worth of stuff."

"For real? Thanks. I got you." Pam had no one looking out for her in the streets, so any help was appreciated.

"Elliot visit." An officer called down the unit.
"Don't worry, go ahead. I'll make up your bed."
"Thanks." Lillian trotted out of the cell.

Lillian's heart was beating like a school girl meeting her crush for the first time. The trek to the visiting room seemed to take forever. When she finally entered the visiting room, Elliot sat in a corner chair waiting patiently. He smiled when he saw her approach. Beyond the bad choice of clothing, he saw nothing but the beautiful girl that made him pick up and move to the east coast.

They kissed and hugged until the officer motioned for them to separate. Elliot had read the stories of Lillian's ordeal as a child and felt he had to get to know more about her. He couldn't imagine himself doing a fraction of the things she was being accused of even during his gang banging days as a teen. Lillian looked him in the eyes and told him that she had nothing to do with her cousin's Katrina's death even though she knew in the back of her mind she had planned on sending the double crossing bitch to meet her maker. Their love for each other was evident even without a single touch.

"Oh, Elliot I need you to pay off the lawyer for me."
Elliot listened careful while calculating the balance.
"I received some good news from him today and he's filing a motion..."
"Are you sure you want to pay him everything up front?"
"Yes, and I want to give you back the money you spent."

Lillian looked her man in the eyes, seeing realness and told him where she had hid the 1.7 million in her house. For the first time she told him everything about Lewis' death and her life after she returned from her trip to Harlem. Understanding and compassionate, he gave her the moral support she needed. "Whatever you need me to do, don't hesitate to ask. No matter what. I'm part of your support system, down until the world stops spinning." They spent the rest of the visit laughing and stealing kisses. When the officer waved, indicating that their visit was over they tried to suck each other's tongues off before departing.

*****

Day's turned into weeks and weeks into months. It took 60 days for the courts to schedule a hearing concerning her motion to dismiss the New York charges. The judge, after being urged by prosecutor Chernoff denied the request, at first causing Maurice to walk a petition into the Office of the Clerk, Appellant Court, It was sent back to the Eastern district with an ORDER to review. The judge, with more to worry about than Patricia Chernoff, now that it was under judicial, scrutiny eventually scheduled a hearing date, but during the month Patricia was scheduled to take her two weeks leave. He knew from the past that Patricia could be a real bitch sometimes. Aside from being overbearing and the granddaughter of the Attorney General, she was in possession of some very compromising information about the judge.

Lillian stayed busy re-reading all the letters from Elliot and her mother. Her cellmate, Pam had a collection of urban, paperback books, left to her by an inmate that went home on bail.

"You should read one of these hood books, they're very interesting. I read this book by Junius Russell." She handed Lillian a book, smiling like she had just found a cure for cancer.

Lillian looked at the cover. "SHE KNOWS." She turned it over and read the synopsis. It caught her attention because the description of a girl name Sharice mirrored some of the things she and other young, unguided teens go through. "I'll read this one."

She started reading that evening and continued on into the morning hours, not able to put the book down until she was finished. Faint sounds of gates opening could be heard in the distance as the first indication of life stirred in the quiet jail. Laying back on her bunk, she reflected on some of the things she had read in "SHE KNOWS" and thought about her predicament. Adversity, prevails only if you let it, without a fight the outcome is predetermined. With the weight of Junius' book on her mind her eyelids begin to get heavy until she could be heard snoring lightly.

"Elliot- Elliot!" The officer shouted in the doorway of her cell door. She was in such a stage of sleep that she hadn't heard the heavy door open, even after the C.O had screamed her name several times.

Lillian popped up looking around confused, not knowing where she was at first until the drab cell and screaming C.O begin to come into focus. Pam was at the head of her bed trying to shake her awake. "I been calling your name."

"Court! Let's go. You already missed the feed tray. I've been calling you for 20 minutes. Thought you'd be up and dressed by now. Let's go!"

Lillian hopped up and tried to speed brush her teeth and hair, doing the best she could before running from her cell to line up with the other inmates at the gate.

"Okay, move out. Straight line to the elevators." The court, escort officer ordered.

She had become so engrossed in the book she forgot she had to be up early in the morning for the hearing. The ride to the federal court building was uneventful except for the normal chatter between inmates. The word had spread about Lillian smashing in Carmen's face and putting her in the infirmary. One of the counselor's house snitches revealed that it was Lillian who had done it but Mrs. Krum was so fed up with Carmen's bullying she just giggled inside instead of reporting it to the disciplinary officer.

Maurice was waiting for her when she arrived, seeming to be in a good mood. He couldn't wait for her to sit down. "Good news. A different prosecutor is handling the hearing. Mrs. Chernoff is on vacation or something anyway the judge may be impartial without pressure from her so that's a plus." He tapped his briefcase.
"I have a solid, legal argument. The prosecutor filling in is another hard ass but he's strictly by the book and that's what our motion is about, text-book-law."

Lillian paid close attention to his every word, trying to follow all the legal terms. The court officer arrived to escort Lillian to the defense table. "I'll will see you inside." Maurice liked to snack on cashews during the day and usually kept a small pack in his jacket pocket. He headed up the corridor to hit up the vending machine before a long day of legal arguments.
Federal prosecutor, William Forbes, Patricia Chernoff's fill in for the hearing, whisked passed Maurice on his way to the courtroom without acknowledging the black attorney. He carried an air of confidence as he gaited up to his assistant as if this were a game of golf. They shared a long laugh before disappearing inside the big courtroom doors.

Maurice popped a few nuts in his mouth before going inside. Forbes looked up momentary as he entered and approached Lillian's side. "He looks meaner than the lady prosecutor." Lillian whispered.

The judge entered and everyone stood upon direction of the court officer. Lillian quickly scanned the faces of the judge and other people busied with her complicated situation. The skinny, brunette stenographer shot her a distasteful look before continuing to record the proceedings.

"Your Honor, I apologize. This was a last minute thing. I received copies of everything just yesterday evening. I am slightly familiar with the case but not of the pleading so if I can just have a few..." Forbes said as he scanned through the file.

"Of course. Take your time." The judge would rather deal with Forbes any day over Patricia, not having to worry about being asked to bend the law a little or dismiss a motion without even looking at it. He was aware that the defendant's attorney probably paid attention in law school and wasn't asking for any favors. "You can use this time to talk privately with your client if you like." The judge tried to seem impartial to the defense as he addressed Maurice.

Maurice nodded in affirmation before turning his chair towards his client and talking in conspiring tones. A smile opened up on Lillian's face after looking at what Maurice had saw.

Prosecutor Forbes, only a page into Maurice's motion, had the sickest look on his face aside from turning beat red. Being a practitioner in the field of legal motions, upon reviewing the first argument he instantly realized this wasn't going to be a routine day.

This was the point that Maurice caught his eye, confirming the validity of his work. He then told Lillian, look at his face after reading our motion, causing her to smile.

When Forbes completed the document, he became upset, having been set up to receive a blemish on his near perfect record. He took another peep at the black attorney he had regarded as just another sap. The legal arguments were concrete, being supported by recent Supreme Court rulings. His mind was racing a 100 miles an hour. *Maybe he can't speak as well as he can write.* "At this time, Your Honor, the government is ready to hear the defense."

Maurice stood after concluding the conversation with his client. "You're Honor." He acknowledged the judge and government. "Prosecutor Forbes." Briefly glancing in his direction, he began. "The basis of my motion is dealing with venue, what forum has the legal right to host... State and city or federal entities. Murder, is a quintessential example of a crime traditionally considered within the U.S fundamental power of the state..."

The moment Maurice began to speak Forbes shook his head, mentally already packing his briefcase to leave.

"In certain instances the Department of Justice can prosecute if the crimes in question share a nexus, being directly involved with a federal violation for example the government's information provides nothing to establish, 18 U.S.C 1951, The Hobbs Act in the case of Katrina Whitfield and Carlton Wycliffe, concerning interstate travel in the commission of robbery or extortion, nor 18. U.S.C 2261A- Interstate stalking, nor in the perpetration of any federal crime... Meaning the federal government lacks jurisdiction to pursue said venue... Also the most important point I'd like to make is that John Peterson was convicted by a jury of his peers in that matter and is presently in prison for the rest of his natural life!"

Prosecutor Forbes without saying a word, got up from his chair and walked out of the courtroom. The Judge knew what was going on was a result of the changes he had made but he wanted to fly straight knowing this was one of those cases that could come back and bite you on the ass if not handled legally.

His wife, who didn't normally get into his legal business, had fallen into support of the defendant and had been badgering him to let her go. He had gotten information that scores of women groups were planning on occupying the courthouse by the hundreds in support on the defendant. "I hear by dismiss the murder charges in connection with the deaths of Katrina Whitfield and Carlton."

Maurice stood up smiling and touched his client's shoulder. "I have to catch a flight in two hours. I'll come visit Friday." He quickly left.

Lillian could feel the eyes on the back of her head and slowly turned to see Elliot sitting there with an easy smile on his face. He mouthed the words, "I love you," before placing two fingers on his lips and touching his heart. She mouthed, I love you too. Before being escorted back into cell housing area to be transported back to jail.

*****

By the time Lillian arrived back at the jail she was emotionally exhausted, having gone over several scenarios in her head about the possible outcome of her case. She wasn't fooling herself into thinking she hadn't fucked up... Covering her tracks should have been as simple as completing the task and escaping from the scene but in reality, no movie or TV program can properly teach you how to circumvent all the forensic and electronic evidence left behind. Her confidence in her attorney was quickly building, liking the way he handled himself in court today. She thought about the words of encouragement she had gotten from his wife.

"I collected your mail." Pam hopped from her bunk as Lillian entered the cell.

"Thanks, I'm tired as hell, my butt is sore from sitting on them hard seats all day, especially the metal benches in the holding pens."

"I feel you. How did things go?"

Lillian smiled at her new friend. "They dismissed two of the charges."

"That's good." Pam said genuinely as she gave Lillian three letters, two from Elliot and one from her mom. She smiled knowing Elliot couldn't wait for the first letter to arrive before writing another one. The one from her mom was noticeably thicker than the previous ones. She sat on her bunk and tore it opened.

"Dear Lillian, First of all I want you to know that I love you with all my heart and since finding out the details of your situation, I have been struggling with the guilt I have for not trusting you and being there for you when you needed us the most. Finding the exact words isn't easy... Just to imagine what you went through... I had no idea, and to think that you did something intentionally... You father, he always said that there was something... He did give you the benefit of the doubt, he held fast... Me, I thought you, well, the way we brought you up. Honey I'm sorry."

Lillian could see the dried tear stains on certain portions of the letter.

She continued reading her mother's words feeling the pressure of years of unrest being released from her heart. Not being able to tell her parents about what had happen as a child put a heavy burden on her mentally. Eventually her whole life became defined by what had occurred. The incident destroyed her mother's trust and as Lillian struggled through school and life the disappointment she felt from her parents battered her self-esteem... Until she began getting revenge. Right then she realized that she needed to do what she had done. The capture and court appearances had her feeling belittled and filled with self-pity. She read the rest of her mother's scribe before laying on her back, staring at the wall. A calmness set in as she breathe deliberately. Each breath seemed to slowly inflate the ball of courage she had summoned when she went on a cross country, killing spree. The battle today was just the beginning of a full, fledged war with the government. Deep thought turned into dreams as she slipped into slumber after a long day in hell.

Maurice arranged for Lillian to be assessed by a psychiatrist and she was subsequently given an evaluation consistent with post, dramatic stress, disorder linked to her rape and witnessing the murder of her childhood boyfriend, Lewis Armstrong. The defense case relied mostly on character witnesses and psychological evidence. He was hoping to convince the jury that this girl with a squeaky clean past, should be forgiven for several, violent homicides. He shook his head, knowing it was likely that she could lose and receive multiple, life sentences. The prosecution was going to have a ball with all the physical and forensic evidence they had against her. He continued to prepare for the trial, just two days away.

Chapter Thirty

Jury of Your Peers

Lillian sat next to Maurice at the defendant's table listening to him go over some last minute changes when the door used by staff and the judge opened abruptly. Patricia Chernoff entered the court with the look of hell fire on her face. An eerie chill filled the air as she made her way to the prosecutor's table. Her cold, evil eyes were trained on Maurice and his client, radiating pure hate. The judge tried his best to bury his head in a stack of papers, feeling a chill under has black robe.

"Let's skip all the bullshit and get to the meat of the case!" Patricia snarled at the judge causing him to swallow the lump in his throat. "Bring him out."

The door slung open to find Snookie standing there dressed in all white in contrast to his dark skin. He smiled showing an even row of white teeth. "Thought you'd never see me again, huh." He uttered as he took the witness stand. Maurice just got up shaking his head and walked out of the courtroom. Lillian observed everyone smiling and chattering during the proceedings like she wasn't even there.

Guilty-guilty-guilty-guilty-guilty-guilty-guilty-guilty-guilty-guilty-guilty- guilty-guilty-guilty-guilty-guilty-guilty-guilty-guilty-guilty-guilty.

"Lillian Elliot, I hereby sentence to you death under the federal statute..." The judge slammed the gavel so hard splinters of wood went flying.

"Wait!" Lillian shouted. "I thought there was supposed to be a jury..." Kicking and screaming all the way to the holding cell.

He was waiting for her... Patricia made sure. "You owe me for my DNA, Lillian" Snookie stared blankly ahead speaking in monotone. "I did you a favor when I gave you some of this dick. Made you a woman and you repay me by setting me up. Well, I've already took care of your momma."

Lillian eyes opened buck wide with the mention of her mother. "That's right!"

She lurched at him but he was too fast, grabbing her by the neck until he secured a tight grip. Lillian fought to get loose, striking him about the chest and face. With a twisted grin on his face he tightened his grip until the veins in his arms were bulging. Slowly, Lillian sank to the floor as the life was choked from her body. Her head hit the concrete floor with a thud.

Lillian jumped up gasping for air. She was startled by the C.O standing in her cell." "You alright Elliot?" Realizing she had a bad dream, she shook her head affirming. "You're on the list for court, let's go."

She climbed out of bed, touching her neck as she prepared to brush her teeth. Lillian had become used to the routine after five and a half months of court appearances and lawyer visits. Today she would be selecting a jury. Maurice tried to explain how important the make-up of the jury was. "A jury of your peers is right! People who can relate to your plight, not a bunch of people who just see black's everyday on the news involved in negative events. Sometimes this process takes more than a week to get it right."

Lillian was the first case called. She hopped up quickly, happy not to be sitting on the cold, hard, steel bench for hours before seeing the judge. Maurice was already in the court. We have a big jury pool to select from and a limited amount of challenges to the government's selections as well as choices of our own. If we can secure at least two, black, middleclass, hardworking women over 55 years of age we'll have an anchor, meaning a potential hold out if things aren't quite going in our favor. Mature independent black women won't allow themselves to be persuaded to shift their beliefs even under pressure. Strong headed, strong willed with eyes that can see... Hearts that can feel... And a strong moral compass."

The jury selection process took two and a half days. Lillian realized how important it was after seeing the government dismiss three witnesses that Maurice said would have been the greatest asset to her case. They were able to dismiss three of the government's witnesses too but Lillian stilled felt like she had lost some ground. They did get two African Americans and a Latino juror.

The black woman was a 49-year-old insurance agent with no children, the black man was 38-year-old, probation officer and the Latino woman an executive for a large investment firm in Manhattan. The rest of the jury could be described as Caucasian and not being too happy with the over whelming, senseless crime going on most of the time with a black face connected to it. A few old enough to remember the slave trade and curse its passing.

As Lillian's trial date grew closer articles appeared in papers. Even Time Magazine did a story on the woman vigilante and the growing crowd of supporters rallying outside of the courthouse, packing the courtrooms. Lillian felt loved at times, even when there had been just a handful of people outside the court building, shouting "Free Lillian!"

Chapter Thirty One

Trial

Today the streets and courthouse were filled with spectators, Lillian supporters, reporters and police. Lillian sat nervously waiting for Maurice to come to the holding cell to give her some last minute words of encouragement. For some reason she felt extra cold today. The metal door creaking as it opened, interrupted her thoughts as she nearly ran to meet him at the gate.

"Did my mother make it?" She stopped short when she saw Patricia's cold eyes staring through her.

"I wanted to make sure you weren't back here throwing a party about the charges that were dismissed when I was gone. I've been in touch with the Westchester District Attorney's Office and they will be filing in state court, however, by the time I'm finished with you over here, any time they have for you won't make a difference. You see, I'm going to slowly pick apart the good girl, gone bad theories by showing the jury just how cold and calculating you really are. You can expect to never see the light of day again." Patricia, turn to leave. "Have a nice, new life."

Lillian had met her glaze with unmoving eyes, showing no bravado, nor fear. The cold chill seemed to disappear just as the scent of Maurice's cologne hit her nostrils. The metal door opened and her lawyer entered planked by his wife and two other smart looking young men. "Good morning."

"Good morning, Lillian." The entire group greeted her. "This my wife's brother, June. He's in his fourth year law, Harvard, and this is my assistant Dorsey. The cavalry is here."

All Lillian could do was smile.

"Lillian, the power of the lord is yours to wield in the mist of evil and oppression. It is the strength we have within to withstand the pitfalls and life's negative installments. Summon the strength as you have in the past against your rapist his representatives..." Dorsey was also a pastor in the church.

"Oh yeah." Gwen chimed in. "Your mother arrived yesterday. I picked her up from the airport myself and brought her over to our home. I made a lovely diner, although she insisted on helping. We talked about the case and laughed a little. She's a very, lovely woman and will make a great character witness. I could see the sincerity in her eyes when she spoke of your childhood." She smiled. "Um, Elliot picked her up early this morning after breakfast so she's in the witness room." She handed Lillian a brown bag. "Elliot picked this out for you to wear."

"Thanks guys. I feel like family in a way... I hate that I got my mother involved in all this mess. I just want say how much I appreciate you all for making me feel this way." Lillian eyes watered. "Thanks for the books, too Gwen. I understand the law much better now."

"That's what we are here for, now, let's get ready for war." Maurice chanted on the way to the courtroom. After they left she quickly dressed in the business outfit she had been wearing when she first met Elliot. She felt good in her own clothes and said a silent prayer. Minutes later a court officer came for her.

*****

Lillian didn't remember the courtroom being so big before realizing she was in a totally different court. She was so preoccupied in thought she didn't recall making a left instead of a right. Her heels tapped loudly as she made her way to the defense table, feeling all eyes on her. She managed to look over at the jury politely as she leaned in close to address Maurice. "This place is so big it looks like a cathedral. Who's on trial, King Arthur?" The place was packed from wall to wall.

"Big case. Had to turn down a bunch of request for interviews. Don't want to give none of these media outlets the opportunity to exploit the case with my blessings. The prosecution has mounds of stuff on their evidence desk. I'm not sure if they even gave me all of that stuff."

Patricia, with just one assistant at the prosecution table, made her way back and forth between him and a shelf filled with boxes and crates of physical evidence several times, looking somewhat unprepared. During a quick inventory of the evidence her assistant realized the box containing all of the video evidence was missing.

Suddenly, she could see it in her mind on the counter next to boxes of copy paper, where she had left it. "Damn!" She quickly grabbed her cell phone and called the office. "Hello."

"Hello, Federal Pros…"
"Quickly! Who is this?" She demanded.

Frazier thought the office was rid of Attila the Hun for the day. *What does she want now? I thought she had the big case.*

"Hey, Patricia. What's going…?"
"Shut up listen! My box."
"Box?"

"My video evidence. I left on the counter, near the copy room, by some boxes."

Frazier moved the receiver away from his ear to stop from hearing her irritating voice. "Anybody seen Patricia's box? Oh, shit." He whispered the last part.

Prosecutor Forbes, was on his way out of the copy room just as Frazier called out about the evidence box. "Hmm, this must it." He grabbed the box on his way out of the office at same time Frazier got up to take a look. *I don't see no fucking box. She must be losing her fucking mind, Fucking bitch.* "No, I don't see no box."

"What! That's absurd." She almost shouted in the court. "I'm sending someone down to find it."

Forbes was only about 30 minutes away from the court house. He could drop the box off and be home in time to catch his girlfriend before she left for work. *A quickie before my afternoon case would make the day.* Forbes notice a trash truck making its way along the street and pulled over a few blocks up to a dumpster. He got out tossed Patricia's box of video evidence inside and pulled a few feet ahead until he watched the truck make its stop and load. "Let's see how you maneuver around this." Prosecutor Forbes wanted to give her a hard time because she hadn't warned him about the frivolous case that attributed to the non-favorable, hearing-ruling on his record. Never having gone against the law in the past, he felt good sticking it to the office witch.

The only other recourse was to ask the defense for copies of their copies, only problem was Patricia called herself playing the withholding game with the defense, waiting for the last minute to produce the videos, right after the defense complained to the judge during the commencement of trial. That usually gave her some extra time during the copying process to insert trial data in her laptop. "Damn." She cursed knowing this time her tactic had backfired. Gaining her composure she summoned her game face.

Maurice didn't skip a beat. He knew something was awry, then it dawned on him. He stood to address the judge "Your Honor, may I approach the bench, as well as the government?"

The judge looked up from his paperwork and waited for Patricia's nod of approval. "Approach."

Maurice was already complaining about not receiving all of evidence before she made it to the bench. "Hold your horses. I just realized a box of videos were left behind. Someone is in route to retrieve it as we speak." She spat at them both.

"Whatever evidence you intend to use in trial must be..." He cut his words under her glare.

"I need a legal course?"
"Okay, it's noted."

The lawyers returned to their tables.

Judge Joseph Brenner address the court. "Now will commence here in the Eastern District of New York the trial of Lillian Elliot for violations of the federal statues of the United States of America, including murder in the first degree. You the jury will listen carefully to all the evidence presented by both parties and at the conclusion of this trial, make an intelligent assessment of the story, either finding the defendant innocent or guilty of the charges beyond a reasonable doubt. The prosecution shall present their case first and wrap up with the final summation."

Patricia stood up. Head held high, closing in on the jury, mostly the elder, whites. "Good morning ladies and gentlemen, productive citizens of this great country we share.

We find ourselves here this morning to serve a purpose, to make a difference in the process we all are afforded as hard working Americans to weed out the misfits that make of society and our country one of the most violent in history. We all bare responsibility for our actions. Have you ever heard the expression, SHIT HAPPENS? Well it does, and we as humans must deal with shit, formidably but responsibly. I have in the past heard psychologists say that because Billy was abused and molested, he is not liable for acting out, by going into a school filled with children and executing innocent people. Not to say to you that whatever happened to Billy isn't terrible, but then I have to show you hundreds, no, thousands, of cases where victims of even worst abuse, went on to become productive citizens. Some of you may know such a person. Of course we all want to strike back when were done wrong, hurt the person back but in America when you seek such vengeance as Lillian Elliot, it can only be called murder. In her case, premeditated murder! She used her job as a flight attendant to facilitate her crimes. Shame on her." She pivoted on her heels and headed back to the prosecution table, looking majestic in her pinstriped suit.

Maurice stood up looking courtroom polished in his dark, blue, Brooks Brother's suit and black wingtip shoes. He removed his jacket displaying his athletic form in the tight vest and walked over to the jury box. Even the old woman who didn't really care for blacks admitted that he was a very, handsome young man. *And smart looking too.*

"Hello ladies, and gentlemen. My name is Maurice and today we find ourselves here because like the prosecutor so boldly put it. Shit happens. Now I take that to mean... Or let's say it's a meaner version of saying, no use crying over spilled milk. As we view crime on the news on a regular bases we tend to become desensitized to violence. Some of us that is... However, some of us can never get used to the nonsense, to the senselessness. Shit happens and it happens to us, you. Good, hardworking citizens. It happens to our children and the elderly... A criminal is a criminal, usually partaking in a pattern of criminal activity early on... When the smoke clears, you will find that my Client, Lillian Elliot, a woman who never received so much as much a traffic ticket was the victim of a despicable crime that would ripped the innocence from any child, and when you hear about all of the men involved, you'll all agree. Thank you for your time." Never breaking eye contact with the jury, Maurice bowed and returned to his chair.

"The prosecution shall state their case." The judge announced.

"The government calls agent Garrabrissi of the FBI." Agent Garrabrissi spent the next hour laying the foundation of the government's case starting from the beginning with the murder of drug dealer Cosine in Miami to all the other murders leading to California. He made Lillian out to be a very, organized and dangerous assassin. When asked, the defense declined to cross examine, not wanting to reiterate the negative connotations.

Detectives from Miami, South Beach, Chicago, Dallas, Texas and California spent the entire day highlighting the evidence for the prosecution concerning their different cases, each describing the results of violent homicides. Police photos and other evidence was paraded in front of the jury for cause and effect. Some could not bear the sight of the aftermath. More than a few of the jury felt that it would have taken an army to cause the damage Lillian had was accused of. She was being scrutinized heavily by all of the jurors as the government continued to demonize her. Maurice kept his questioning of the officers to a bland minimum not wanting them to repeat something bad the jury had already heard and saving the important question for the so called eye witnesses. He had explained to Lillian earlier. "Police who are not eye witnesses themselves to a crime provide second hand information so why not wait to grill their source after their statements are solidified by the court." The day crept by and court was adjourned until the following morning.

*****

Day two, still no video evidence, Maurice called the first detective from Miami for re-cross examination because he was the last to be contacted by the FEDS, at first they hadn't made the connection. "Officer, before you were contacted by the FBI, had you ever heard my client's name?"

"No, sir."

"Did your department recover any fingerprint evidence involving my client?"

"No, sir."

"Did your department recover any video evidence involving my client?"

"Ah, yes, sir."

Maurice knew something was going on with the video and decided to play a hunch. He faked being uninformed by looking down at his paperwork. "I don't have any video on my evidence list. Did you view this video personally?"

"Well, ah, no. One of the detectives in charge of those things took care of that while I was out in the field picking up dead bodies and chasing leads."

"And the victim, Miguel Cosine. What was his occupation?"

The detective took a breather before answering. "He turned out be a high ranking boss in the Columbian drug cartel."

"Well don't these people play dangerous? Can you rule out a rival dealer?"

"Ah, not really. Hey, the FEDS contacted me told me the suspect could have been involved in my case we pulled the video and here I am..."

"No further questions." Maurice sat down.

Patricia jumped up. "Re-direct! Officer after being contacted about the suspect what measures did you take to prove that she was indeed in Miami during the murder."

"I personally checked her schedule at the airport which showed she had arrived on the same flight as our victim." He recalled.

"Thank you officer. No more questions." Patricia returned to her seat, breast sweating beneath her blouse.

The next to be cross examined by Maurice was the only one of Mignon body guards to agree to assist the police. He had already identified Lillian as the female at the table with Mignon when he was killed at the Blue Lagoon in South Beach, during direct testimony.

"So in your capacity as a body guard you keep watch on your employee, Mignon at all times correct?

"Yes."
"Were you watching him closely on that night?"
"Yes But he asked for a few feet to talk business."
"But still you kept a watchful eye?"
"Yes."
"Was Mignon doing any drugs?"
"Yes."
"What kind?"
"Cocaine."
"Did he get the cocaine from Ms. Elliot?"
"No he did not."
"Is this the first time you observed your boss doing drugs?"
"No, he did coke on a regular basis."
"Now! At any time did you observe my client doing drugs?"
"No."
"Did Mignon give her his drugs to hold?"
"No."
"So let me get this straight. You never took your eyes off of Mignon?"
"Correct."
"Thank you, no more questions."

The Chicago case seemed to come apart quicker when the police testified that one of their witnesses, James Pratt had been killed in a subsequent bar shootout and wouldn't be able to make an appearance from the graveyard in time for trial to identify Lillian as Ronald's killer. Also the woman that was in bed with Stanley Chamber's when he was shot by a woman that hit his car in the middle of the morning was too far away to make a positive ID. Maurice was able to get the police to admit that the Chamber brothers were two of the most feared drug dealers and murderers in Chicago. "That area of Chicago is known to have a very high crime rate, correct?"

"Yes."
"Have the Chamber brothers ever been charged with murder?"
"Yes, Stanley Chambers, on more than one occasion."
"Any enemies?"
"Yes."

"I conclude, Maurice took a seat."

Patricia barked. "Officer what measure did you take to make sure Lillian Elliot was in town during the Chamber brothers execution?"

"A check of her schedule shows she arrived at the O'Hare airport on flight 470 from JFK."

Patricia looked at the jury as if to say c'mon stupid. "Nothing further." She looked at the defense table as if to say, not a chance.

Patricia focused in on the Dallas, murders of Bone and his accomplice where Lillian had been arrested and finger printed for impersonating an officer. "Detective, what are your duties at Dallas, PD?"

"I'm with the vice unit specifically, anti-crime. We were during a sweep when I noticed the defendant walking across the parking lot dressed in prostitute attire and approached her to proposition her for a date. In order to make an arrest the hooker must quote a price, the conversation is recorded via 2way and the subject is arrested by another team. However I was told by the defendant that if I didn't leave I would be taken in but when I asked, "Are you a cop?" She replied, "Now be a nice boy before I call for back up." The defendant was captured in the sweep and charged with impersonation but the DA said her threatening to call for back up could have meant calling a pimp. When asked about being a cop if she would have said yes, she would not have been released without bond."

"But it was clear that she wasn't there to turn any tricks, correct?" Patricia asked.

"Absolutely not. She had no intention of doing a date with me. She even threatened to take my red pickup."

"Do you think she knew you were a cop, that's why she turned down a date?"

"The normal response is to walk away or start asking questions of their own, like. "Are you a cop? Let me see your cock? Here touch my tits. Some will even cite entire disclaimers right on the spot. But acting like a cop to the cops, Nah. She just stopped short of saying the wrong thing."

"Officer would you, for the court, make a positive identification of the defendant?"

He pointed directly to Lillian who had been listening closely. "It was the defendant Lillian Elliot, who was arrested and finger printed under the alias Sandra Collins."

The homicide detectives who handled the Bone murders coincided the incidents with Lillian's time in Texas. Although there were no witnesses to the actual shooting a cooperating witness working with police at the time stated the defendant had been recruited by Bone to work as his prostitute."

Maurice asked a few simple questions before moving on. "Detective would you take a look at the mug shot of the defendant?" He complied. "Do you know what prostitute attire is?"

"Well I'm in robbery and homicide but I'm sure it means, practically nothing, a thong and some real, tall boots."

"And what does it look like my client is wearing in her mug shot?"

"Ah." He shrugged, not really seeing the relevance. "Some type of dress."

"That's right, a sun dress."

"Objection! You're Honor. The description of the defendant given during her arrest was by a totally different officer. Asking the wrong officer undermines the prosecutions right to get the story explained accurately. Using my witness to insinuated a vice officer lied is objectionable and I think its misleading the jury."

On redirect of the vice officer, Patricia was able to clear things up. "What exactly was the defendant wearing when you approached her?"

"A white G-string outfit and some type of white boots, I think. Her entire tail was all out for the world to see."

"Well can you explain why in this police photo she's dressed like she just came from church?"

He took a good look. "Why sure, the girls carry cover-up clothes in their purses in case they find themselves in front of a judge that don't rightly take to a bunch of naked girls disrupting the court. Some judges will send them back, won't call the case till the next day and they better be fully dressed."

"Thank you, officer." Smirking at Maurice. "Nice try." She mouthed, silently. A look at the clock meant another day coming to a close.

*****

Third day, the crowd of spectators and Lillian supports still showed up in droves, carrying signs and chanting. Police barriers kept everyone on either side of the main entrance. The noise intensified as Lillian's transportation bus pulled into the underground garage. She waved during the fence-walk on the way to the court tunnel.

Free Lillian- Free Lillian, Victim's Rights, do it Right!

"I think the poor girl deserves a freaking medal. Are you kidding me?" An Italian woman was telling a news reporter just outside the courthouse.

"All rise." The court officer ordered as the judge entered. Everybody complied except Patricia. She sat pondering about the disappearance of her video evidence. Not that I really need them, I'm doing great. *But they came up during testimony so not having them isn't a good look...*

Everybody at the defense table looked refreshed and ready to go. Lillian's spirits were lifted by the supporters on her way in. Gwen and the other team members had an early breakfast, preparing for today's battle. Maurice even got in ten sets, 50 repetitions of pushups and 200 crunches before court. His business gray suit fit impeccable as all his clothing did when he was before the court perfecting his craft.

Patricia called her first witness of the day after taking a giant swig of coffee. "Please identify yourself for the court."

"Detective Priscilla Gaiety of the Los Angeles Police Department Robbery and Homicide. I'm also the arresting officer."

"Can you briefly explain how you became involved with this case?"

"It all began when I was called in to investigate a mass shooting at a four star hotel in downtown, Los Angeles..."

Priscilla recalled the entire story about the shootout and finding the Brown Leather Ledger containing the hit list along with a cache of incriminating evidence. "There was fake ID, weapons and other paperwork." She explained how she begin connecting the dots as information poured in from other police agencies. The suspect was subsequently connected to the murders of Osiris, a high ranking member of the Sons of Samoan, one of the most dangerous, illegal, enterprises in the country, and two of his lieutenants. His multimillion dollar mansion was then burned to the ground as well as one of his restoration buildings. It was some fire the place was filled with Ether. Boom!" A few old women jumped in their seats when she made the loud sound including one of the jurors. "After contacting every department about my findings, I called the FBI." She continued, smiling to herself.

"Officer Gaiety, have you ever saw the defendant before the arrest at the airport?"

"Well, not in person. After viewing the video footage of the hotel shooting, we observed her along with a young teen who was one of the victims. It appears they were in the process of checking out..."

The mention of Renee saddened Lillian and she tried to let it wash over before showing any signs of weakness. Visions of her running through the hotel with Renee firmly by the hand flashed across her mind as she tried to listen to the rest of the testimony. Maurice reached over and patted her shoulder without saying a word.

"Are you 100% the defendant was on the video?"
"Yes, 100%."
"In Los Angeles during the time of the Osiris murders?"
"Yes."
"The shooter was shot by police and is presently in a coma..."
"Well, we don't know."
"Excuse me officer."

"The shooter had no record or fingerprints on file and apparently someone helped him escape from the trauma unit before we could move him to the prison hospital. We know he's a relative of Osiris."

Patricia hated to be hearing something about her case for the first time from someone on the witness stand. She concluded her questioning, cursing silently for letting her witness complete her sentence.

Maurice approached the witness. "Officer Gaiety, are there any witnesses to the murders of Osiris or any of his crew members?"

"No, no eye witnesses."
"Was any DNA from the crimes connected to the defendant?"
"No there wasn't."

"Are there any video surveillance from the victims residence of my client?"

"Any DNA or ballistic evidence concerning the items found inside of this Dodge minivan?

"No sir. There has been talk of surveillance video but the jury is yet to see any. Officer would you please tell the jury what my client was doing in these videos."

"She was running."
"Running? What, running track? Running errands?"
"She was fleeing."

"That's right officer! She was running for her life and the life of Renee." Maurice walked back to his chair and sat down. "Several people were shot that day. Anyone of them could have been the target." Continuing from his chair. "Without these videos everyone keeps talking about we'll never be sure!" He sighed, making eye contact with the jury. He had observed more than a few cringe during testimony about the violence and when viewing crime scene photos. "Nothing further, Your Honor."

After a parade of witness from foot patrol cops to the medical examiner's office the prosecution planned on calling their final witness, Special Agent Garrabrissi. "This is basically your case, special agent. What I need you to do is give the jury a jolt of understanding about federal crimes and how they are prosecuted by the government."

Garrabrissi went on for almost 50 minutes, non-stop explaining why the crimes Lillian were being charged with were federal offenses. He made strong points about the pattern of the defendants travel schedule and the locations of the crimes. Gave a certified, psychological analysis on the defendant admitting her behavior was only the result of her past trauma but she was in his mind, no doubt, 100% the killer.

Using the Brown Leather Ledger he connected all of the homicides together like a puzzle right before the jury's eyes. "This hit book came from the defendants, Dodge, Caravan in California were the last incident occurred the only reason the next victim in Colorado wasn't killed is because by then the defendant figured she was good as caught, deciding to run and hide instead."

Patricia stood, satisfied she had made her point. "The prosecution rest."

The judge banged his gavel. It's getting pretty late. Let's stop here. See you the same time tomorrow morning.

Maurice looked down at the witness list puzzled. The prosecution had neglected to call two of their witnesses. He scanned the list. *Benjamin Steinberg and Jonathon Peterson.* His mind began processing the info until he thought he had a plan, deciding to sleep on it.

That evening he stayed up in bed, papers scattered about going over the Whitfield murders even though they had been dismissed. Gwen put down her book. "What's up?"

He shifted some papers around. "It's obvious she scratched Peterson because the Whitfield murders were dropped and he would have been a difficult witness for the prosecutor to gloss over with Katrina Whitfield's diary in evidence. I'm thinking Benjamin Steinberg, allegedly the next victim was taken off the list because he could have possibly made our girl look good."

"Why because she didn't kill him?"
"No, because she extorted him instead."
"I don't see how that would help."
"It's where she directed him to send the money."
"Where?"
"To the Covenant House for displaced teens."
"Oh, I see. So why don't you call them as defense witnesses?"

"How could I? When they don't appear on my list and it's too late to submit an amendment."

Gwen slid from her side of the bed and begin riffling through her leather carrying case.

"I just filed a brief involving a recent Supreme Court case where the prosecution called witness from the defense list who the defense had decided not to call. The lawyer argued against it but the judge sided with the prosecution. He appealed it and the appellant court affirmed. So that means it works for both sides. I'll note the case so you can argue it with the judge if he decides to bend for the wicked witch of the Eastern District." She joked about Patricia.

"I'm still contemplating calling Peterson but he started the entire thing. We have to let the jury know exactly what Lillian went through." They kissed before wrapping up the legal work and going to sleep. "Love you."

Day four. Lillian's dream team filed in the courtroom together looking like a well-dressed, crew of bank robbers coming to stick up the case. Lillian imagined their briefcases being filled with special, get-out-of-jail-free weapons.

Patricia looked up momentarily to snarl before whispering to her assistant who was by now sick and tire of being the brunt of his bosses growing attitude. "They're all looking smug this morning. Think they have their frivolous cases ready for the trash bin." She hissed. "They only have a hand full of witness if that many. This shouldn't take long."

The judge greeted the jury and court before announcing continuance of the defense's case. Maurice stood, sharp as a tack as always. His infant blue, Egyptian cotton, Prada jacket, over malt chocolate shirt and slacks caught the attention of many wandering eyes. The dodo brown, Gucci slip-on's tapped lightly on the floor as he approached center stage. He made pleasant, eye contact with everyone including Patricia, supporting case in hand. "Your Honor, the defense calls the first witness, John "Snookie" Peterson."

"It took a minute for the words to sink in, however, when they did, Patricia's expression changed from bad to worst. She jump from her seat knocking a stack of folders to the floor. "Objection! Ob-motherfucking-jection!"

The judge turned beet red causing a few spectators to laugh out loud. There was a mixed reaction from the jury, even more confused when the judge called a recess.

In the judge's chambers, Patricia's voice was a little higher than allowed when addressing a judge. "There is no way!" Patricia shouted hoping to incite some influence over the judge, knowing in the back of her mind that one of the prosecutor's in her very office had been the one who had won the Supreme Court decision, allowing witnesses on either side to be called by either party after being notified of that party's intent to testify.

Maurice as a courtesy, handed the judge his case file. "Take two hours. I'll cross reference some decisions." Patricia cursed, sensing her loss of pressure on the judge. She realized he was more afraid of any judicial review concerning his conduct in such a high profile case.

The jury was sent to the deliberation room for coffee and donuts, while the defense stayed put, feeling okay about the climate in the courtroom. Gwen Giggled. "Did you see the dragon lady's response when you called her witness?

"Priceless." Gwen's brother June responded. "I thought she was about to have an aneurism." They laughed enjoying the prosecution's response.

Two hours later the judge called the lawyers back into his chambers. He could barely look Patricia in the eyes. "Ah, upon further review I find that the request by the defense is supported by recent case law. So as per, Supreme Court ruling, witnesses need be, included as a witness in the said proceedings by either party to withstand review of the court."

Patricia quickly evaluated the footage lost by the judge's decision. If she had it her way, Snookie would have never been in the equation but he was the only one to explain away the DNA evidence used during his conviction. The dismissal of the Whitfield case eliminated him as a witness. She was aware of the lasting response any jury would receive after hearing his offensive, story.

"Your Honor, this witness won't be available today. He is at the Manhattan House of Detention preparing to testify in an array of trials coming up. We can have him brought over tomorrow. I don't see why we can't proceed with the defenses other witnesses in the meanwhile."

"Um, your honor the defense would also like to call another witness on the list. A Benjamin Steinberg."

Patricia frowned wondering where Maurice was going with this tactic. *Calling prosecution witnesses can also dirty his case a tad bit more...* This particular witness was recently expedited from Denver under a RICO conspiracy indictment. He is also a cooperating witness for the prosecution so that affords us the right to confer with him beforehand. We can have him available tomorrow at, let's say midday."

"Acceptable?" The judge seemed bored.

Maurice nodded and exited the judge's chambers. "Damn. What's with you?" She poked at the judge without insinuating he should be ruling in her favor or reminding him that she had sometime on him.

"Listen Patricia, You're gonna have to go by the book on this one. The defense is not just here for a check and he has a history of getting favorable decisions from the appeals court meaning he has one hell of a paralegal that allows him to file so quickly. I'm just a few years short of retirement. Let's not rock the boat. The evidence you displayed already is enough to convict the defendant ten times without any funny business. Get your witnesses here before the defenses submits a writ of habeas corpus."

Patricia sucked her teeth and stormed out. *Calling my witness will strengthen my case under the Hobbs act, traveling in interstate with the intention to rob or extort. They think showing the jury that she was compassionate by not killing Steinberg will help. However, after killing several people it's definitely too little, too late.*

Maurice gave his team the wink on the way out letting them know everything was good. After the judge and prosecutor entered the court returned to order as spectators shuffled to regain their seats after grabbing a bite to eat or taking a quick smoke break.

"The defense calls a character witness, Mrs. Laura Elliot." Lillian sat up straight at the sound of her mother's name. Laura made her way to the witness stand. After being sworn in she panned the audience spotting Elliot sitting two rows behind the defense table. She issued a warm smile after making eye contact with her daughter.

"Mrs. Elliot would you give us some background on your family?" Laura started from the very beginning, explaining about how she and her husband met, joy about the birth of their only child.

Laura surely made a connection with the jury familiar with family issues. She told the jury how they had built a successful business while raising their extremely smart child, eventually getting to the part about the business trip that required their daughter to be left behind, visiting family in New York. "That was the turning point." Laura explained everything about Lillian's subsequent behavior and the sudden decline, academically. Painfully, recalling her daughter's downward spiral, Laura wiped the tears forming in her eyes.

"Can you explain to the court about some of Lillian's early academic, accomplishments?" He handed Laura a folder containing copies of Lillian's report cards, certificates, trophies and medals she had provided to him. Laura spent almost two hours testifying. Finally the jury was able to get a view into the life of the defendant giving her a human face. It was evident that Lillian had been through something terrible judging from the sudden change in her life after the summer in Harlem. Slowly, Maurice created a picture of an innocent child, traumatized by something that had occurred to her young mind. When Laura concluded her testimony, Maurice could feel the humanization as the jury softened their frowns caused by all the talk of murder and mayhem.

"What happened to this young child was horrible. You will hear testimony that she was brutally beaten, raped. Also you will hear that a close friend of hers was executed right in front of her before she was threatened with the murder of her parents if she ever told anyone."

"Objection your honor! There was nothing entered into evident about a rape and murder!"

The judge looked at her like she was stupid, tired of her playing dumb. The jury hadn't heard it yet but she knew it was on the way to their ears when Snookie was called to testify.

Truthfully, the jury's response to Laura's testimony made her a bit nervous, now that the jury was seeing the defendant as a person because when that occurs there is at least one jury who asked themselves; what would I have done? Once you have just one person comparing the defendant's situation to other possibilities...

"And we have yet to see a surveillance video of my client." Maurice added deciding to play a little dumb himself. "If they even exist."

Patricia gave him the evil eye. On cross examination, Patricia had to be careful with a witness so likable to the jury.

"Mrs. Elliot did your daughter at any time tell you that she had been raped?"

"No she didn't."
"Did she ever tell your husband that she had been raped?"
"No, she didn't."
"Was she sexually active before visiting, New York?"
"Ah, no."
"Are you sure, I mean how could you really know?"
"We kept a close eye..."
"So maybe once she got a little freedom she lost control."

Laura shook her head slowly, knowing she had entertained the same thing and now knowing what really happened to her baby, hearing it from the prosecutor made her feel guilty for not giving Lillian the benefit of the doubt. "Lillian was one of the most respectfully and well behaved children I have ever known."

"Yeah, as long as she was under your thumb. As soon as she..."

"Objection, Your Honor, the prosecution is attempting to undermine the defendant's testimony by leading scenarios."

"Will the prosecution stop leading the witness with unfounded statements?" The judge felt good correcting Patricia, knowing he would have let everything slide in her favor in the past.

"Mrs. Elliot when did you move from Rhode Island to Florida?"
"It's been over three years now."
"How many times would you say your daughter came to visit?"
"A few about three or four."

"Did she drive or fly."
"I think she flew."

"As a flight attendant she had the ability to fly almost anywhere, correct?"

"I'm not sure of the policy."
"But you do admit she had unlimited access to the sky?"
"I'm not sure."
"Places like South Beach, Chicago, Texas, and California…"

"Objection your honor! Leading to scenarios!"
"No further questions." She sat down confidently.

All Lillian could do was sit quietly while Laura was being grilled. At one point she imagined attacking Patricia for trying to give her mother a hard time.

Maurice called the psychologist who had evaluated Lillian on three different occasions. "Doctor, can you explain your findings in regard to Ms. Elliot?" For an entire four hours the defense and prosecutor went back and forth arguing the witnesses points to the jury. Basically the psychologist was saying that the incident caused a mental reaction from the defendant that overtime festered into a ball of overwhelming, hatred and psychological arrest. "The defendant then becomes un-responsible for their actions, wholly, attributed to psychosis. The under lining reaction to post-dramatic disorder."

Patricia stayed on the attack, prolonging the witnesses stay on the stand. Maurice was confidant the jury had grasp the important parts of the testimony and hoped it sank in good. Patricia spent the rest of the time questioning the doctor's credentials and trying to down play his expertise.

Eventually the day had come to an end. Everyone, the defense, prosecution, judge, court employees, spectators and supporters had the same thing on their minds after a long day of boring testimony… Rest and sex, however, Lillian and Elliot would have to reserve the sex part for a brighter day. Before taking Lillian back to her cell the court officer allowed her to stop and hug Elliot as he leaned over the divider.

*****

Friday the courtroom filled with well rested people some, having taken the edge off with a drink of liquor and some with an evening of love making. Maurice and Gwen, feeling refreshed after going at it before bed floated into the room followed by June and Dorsey who looked like they both had gotten a little bit of pussy themselves last night. Truth is, June had gotten some from his girlfriend Amy and Dorsey got bent over by his undercover lover, Trevor.

Lillian and Elliot where probably the only two people that went un-fucked last night, besides Patricia, the dragon-lady-of-sex and the judge whose wife was pissed that he hadn't let the nice lady on trial go yet. "They raped that poor girl. What if it was our daughter?" She had said.

At this point the movements where routine as everything fell into place. The judge sat back not too happy about having been shunned by his wife about this case. He blandly addressed the court, thinking how tired he had become of the routine of his life. "Defense will pick up on direct, calling prosecution witness John Peterson."

Patricia shot the judge a salty look. *Fucking jerk doesn't have to tell the jury that Peterson is a prosecution witness. Just let the defense fucking, call him.* She had Snookie brought in super early to go over his testimony. "I was beginning to think that you guys forgot about me." He entered, all smiles. "Been seeing the trial coverage on TV and I was wondering when you'd come for me."

"Mr. Peterson, there has been a change of plans."

Snookie's mood shifted knowing that *change of plans* usually meant some type of problem. "What's that mean, something wrong?"

The federal judge throughout the Whitfield murders so you won't be testifying in that case, however, the subsequent indictments are standing and so you will have a long journey as far as those trials are concern. Actually, you were called by the defense in their attempts to use you to clean up their client. Try to answer yes and no, without elaboration on anything too long. Understand?" She hated the sight of Snookie and thought him to represent the scum of the earth like the she-devil at the defense table that she intended to put away for the rest of her life.

"So what about my deal?"

"What about it?"

"Does everything still stand as it was?"

"Sure." Patricia assured him with a double nod. "Make sure you keep it short and sweet today." She wished she could hold his head in a vat of acid and watch his face melt away.

Snookie needed to hear her say that his deal was still on the table, knowing he was getting ready to prepare to testify in a stream of upcoming cases that could take well over three years to complete.

After supplying information to the government about all his past associates he now had to testify against every last one of them. The government had agreed to allow him to testify with a black hood over his head and an assigned name for his protection.

Snookie walked to the witness stand like he was being seated at the steakhouse for dinner, adjusting the collar of the white, suit-shirt they had given him to wear.

Maurice approached the witness stand. "Would you please identify yourself to the jury?"

"My name is Jonathon Peterson."

"Mr. Peterson, where do you live?"

"I'm from uptown, New York but I moved to Fort Lee, New Jersey."

"No, I mean your address today."

Snookie frowned before answering. I'm presently incarcerated at the Manhattan, Detention Center."

"To be clear you're in prison, correct?"

"Yes."

"Can you tell the jury, for how long?"

"I have two life sentences." Reaction from the courtroom was surprise. "For a crime I didn't commit," he quickly added.

"Did you have a trial on these issues?"
"Yes."
"Did a jury, like these wonderful folks, find you guilty?"
"Objection! The defense is pandering to the jury." Patricia belted.
"Aren't they wonderful people?"

"Objection, sustained. "Drop the jury compliments and continue please."

"Mr. Peterson, what was your conviction for, please?"
"Two counts of murder?"

"That's right and, is it correct that one of the victims was your girlfriend, Katrina Whitfield, who is in fact the defendant's first cousin?"

"Yes."

"And the other, a young man whom Ms. Whitfield was alleged to be sexually involved with."

Snookie shrugged his shoulders. "I-I don't know anything about that. I've never met the cat in my life." Patricia shot him a look that said, too much talking. "Yes or No." She mouthed as he took a look in her direction.

For Lillian it was all like a movie gone haywire. Here before her was the man who started everything. Images of Lewis kept popping up in her head. His smile and the way he spoke about life. "*When I get my degree...* She remembered the day they had gone to the museum and Lewis knew everything about dinosaurs, even the exact times of their existence. The last image to cross her mind was the loud bang right before his brains were splattered on her face. She looked at Snookie, seeming content and realized she should have blew is brains out when she had the chance. The hand on her shoulder startled her until she realized it was Gwen consoling her. "Everything's gonna be fine."

"Mr. Peterson. Who owned the house, Katrina Whitfield was murder at?"

"It was her place. She..."
"Whose name is on the deed?
"It was in the name of a front person, but I owned it."

"Do you know the defendant, Ms. Elliot?"
"Yes."
"And can you tell the court how you met the defendant?"
"It was though her cousin Katrina."
"What were the circumstances surrounding this meeting?"

"I was throwing a big party at my place in Jersey and she came with Kat, I mean, Katrina."

"How old was Katrina?"
"I-I, don't know. I never asked."
"How about 15 or 16?"
Snookie shrugged. "Could be. These girls lie so much..."

"So now, you have these two underage girls at your mansion in Fort Lee, New Jersey." Maurice peeped at his file. "Who is Lewis?"

"He was like a little brother to me. I kind of raised him, his mother was a crack head in my neighborhood. Kid had spunk." Caught up in the interview, Snookie began recalling different instances when he and Lewis were together.

"Were Lewis and Lillian seeing each other? You know, boyfriend and girlfriend?"

"Well, see Lewis was like the shy type with chicks. He and the little redbone went to the movies once or twice but... To be truthful people were starting to think Lewis was kind of, you know? Funny. Always talking about saving himself for marriage like some old fashion broad or something." The moment Snookie looked up Patricia was mouthing to him to shut the fuck up. "They liked each other but nothing serious."

"Is this the first time you saw Ms. Elliot, at the party?"

"Ah, I did see her one other time during Harlem Week, the day I met her cousin, Kat."

"Mr. Peterson, are you a pedophile?"
"Objection!"
"Overruled. The witness may respond."
"No."
"Snookie! Do you have penchant for underage girls?"

"I- we- sometimes they..."

"Did you have Katrina lure the defendant to your house by telling her Lewis would be there when in fact he was keeping watch over his sick mother who was in Harlem hospital dying?"

"I think I asked was she coming."
"Isn't it true you paid Ms. Whitfield $500 to bring her there?"
Snookie shrugged. "Answer yes or no." The judge ordered.
"I always gave Kat money."
"Mr. Peterson, are you aware that Katrina kept a diary?"
"I am now."

"So did you give her $500 to lure the defendant, a 15-year-old child to your home in New Jersey?"

"Yes."

Snookie was an instant icon of hate in the eyes of the jury. The more he spoke the more he sank. At this point he didn't give a fuck what anybody thought of him. He was working towards one goal and that was freedom. He would admit to raping and killing 20 nuns right now as long as his deal with the government was still in place. "I'll admit I had a little back then, liking young girls, but I'm planning on getting help while I'm inside, plus I don't feel those urges anymore." He went on to tell how he spiked Lillian's soda and sexual assaulted her along with a few of his boys. "Lewis popped up. He didn't know she was there. I tried to stop him from coming in the room but he must have recognized her in the dark because he went crazy and attacked me. I-I must have lost it."

"Then what happened?"
"I've already admitted to the government. I shot him."
"Where?"
"In the head."
"Where was the defendant?"
"She was lying on the bed in a pool of blood."

The jury gasped, during the gory description. "And then what happened?"

"Katrina convinced me that the cousin wouldn't snitch so I made a decision to let her live."

285

"What happened to Lewis?"
"We buried him in the woods on City Island."

Lillian fought to control the tears threatening to run down her face, to no avail. Gwen was right on cue with the Kleenex. Elliot sitting one row behind the defense silently cried during Snookie's testimony, feeling the hurt and pain for his woman. The spectators were certainly moved by all the emotional drama also. Patricia? Furious at all the soap opera shit, she wanted to convict both Lillian and Snookie as a team...

"Mr. Peterson, do you know a Gail Davis?"
Snookie thought hard before saying no.
"Rosanna Hill?"
"Ah, no."
"Karen Rogers?"
"No."
"Angela Scott?'
'No."
"Liana Frazier?"
"Nah."

"Cynthia Ross, Sophia Love, Brenda Williams, Sandra Atkins, Latisha Grant, Paula Higgins, Alicia Brown, Roxanne Gilbert, Tamera Dixon, Marsha Evans... Maurice read off a list of 198 names of young girls documented in Katrina Whitfield's diary. "Girls she admitted procuring at your direction so that you could satisfy your sick, twisted, perversions. Sadist! These girls had no names to you, they were just pieces of flesh to you."

"Objection. The defense is not a psychiatrist therefore not in the position to make any mental analysis."

"Sustained."

Maurice continued. "Mr. Peterson do you know an International, drug kingpin by the name of Rafael Mignon?"

"Yes. He is a past associate of mine."

"How about Ronald and Stanley Chambers. Killers and drug kingpins from Chicago?"

"Yes. Ronald worked for me in New York, back in the days"

"Harold Johnson, aka Bone, Texas? Yeah Dallas?"

"Yes."

"Osiris, triple O.G, S.O.S gang in California?"

"Uh-huh."

"If the prosecution is right and my client committed all the offenses, alleged then it would be correct to say that as a result of your **sick, sexual, deviations** and the terrible things you did to this innocent child... That an almost billion dollar, ruthless, international drug enterprise was brought down to the ground, and that you!, an admitted, child molester, drug dealer and killer and all your constituents, spread out all over the country, criminal organizations were all neutralized by an 150 lb. female. A victim of molestation at your hands to be passed around to your boys. The downfall of a dynasty? More like reason for celebration!"

"Objection!" Patricia popped up again.

Some spectators clapped in agreement before being shushed by the court officers. Patricia declined to cross examine, wanting this witness to go away immediately. If she had it her way, any deal he thought was in place would go away. *Do you think the government is gonna let you back out on the streets just like that?* Patricia knew that when Katrina and Carlton's murders were dismissed that it effected the terms of the agreement the government had entered into with Snookie because it stated specifically "Assistance in the prosecution of Lillian Elliot and others." Being called as a defense witness didn't help his matter one bit. Sure he would receive some benefit from the trials he was preparing to testify in, but as far as the government was concerned he was disposable. Patricia shot darts at his back as he exited the courtroom on the way back to MDC.

She planned on using the next witness, Benjamin Steinberg to support the Hobbs Act violations. (Traveling interstate to effect a robbery or extortion scheme.) While the defense intends to show that the defendant is an angel because she didn't blow Steinberg's brains all over the walls of his office. *Problem for the defense is the jury already heard what the defendant is capable of.*

"The defense calls Benjamin Steinberg."

Steinberg took the stand looking like he should have been seated at the prosecution table.

Maurice questioned him about his relationship with Snookie and his connection with the drug organization as well as the agreement he entered into with the government to snitch on his friends. He answered all the questions in a professional manner as if it was an important business meeting.

"Mr. Steinberg can you tell the court about any contact you had with the defendant?'

Patricia cupped her hand over her nose and mouth. *Go ahead, do my job for me.*

"Well, it was during the business convention which was being held at my facility, the Four Season Resort. One morning she popped up in my office and put a gun to my face."

"Well, did she pull the trigger?"
"No, she didn't."
"What she do?"

"Well, she told me that she knew about my connections with Mr. Peterson, well--Snookie and that if I didn't send the money that was owed to Snookie, plus another 15 million of my money to a location in New York, she would return and cause harm to me and my family."

"Did you send the money?"
"Yes."
"How much?"
"15 million."

There was an audible gasp in the court. Maurice paused to let the amount sink in with the jury. "The drug business must be very lucrative." He added.

"Mr. Steinberg, exactly where were you directed to send this money?"
"To a place called the Covenant House."

Another gasp from the audience and a few scattered claps from people with knowledge of the Covenant House in New York.

"Do you know what the Covenant House is?"

"Ah. A-Um, like a center for at risk, or displaced, teens in New York City."

Suddenly a few more claps ensued eventually causing a large portion of the crowd to begin clapping, loudly, disrupting the court. The judge waited patiently for the court officers to regain control while Patricia sat stone faced. Maurice turned and sat down in a huddle with his team.

"No cross." Patricia leaned in towards her assist. "We still got them. I didn't have to cross examine Steinberg because ole Maurice already established that his client traveled to Denver to extort the witness. I don't care if she had him send the money to save babies in Africa, its extortion, period."

Maurice decided not to put Lillian on the stand because he felt her mother had represented an aspect of her daughter that he wanted to stick with the jury, not his client being riddled with incriminating questions by Patricia.

"We'll knock off for the day and hear closing arguments Monday morning." The judge banged his gavel before disappearing in his chambers. Some of the spectators were chanting Lillian's name as they filed out of the court building. Just before entering the door to the cell block, Lillian paused long enough at the divider to give Elliot a good, tongue kissing. Maurice shook his hand. "We're working." Elliot nodded in agreement. "You guys are doing a great job."

*****

Monday with a packed courtroom, closing arguments begin. June stood up having remained quiet during most of the proceedings. He approached the jury calmly, looking young and educated in a brown, three piece suit with a bow tie. "Good morning, ladies and gentlemen of the jury. My name is Junius Walters and I'm a Jr. Attorney with the firm. Today I will be giving the final, defense statements... Making direct eye contact, he continued. The two words I'd like to impose upon you today are accountability and justifiable. We all recognize the accountability that everyone shares concerning their actions and behavior. However, in certain situations, extenuating, circumstances occur that were unforeseen by law makers, while measuring the *intent* factor, concerning criminal behavior. For example a person abandoned, left without food to die in the dessert who happens upon his perpetrator's campsite and steals food to survive is nowhere near the same as the bandit that overtakes a campsite, robbing the food and supplies for personal gain. Which is somewhat like this matter. As you've heard from the psychologist, significant changes took place mentally in the defendant after she was raped and beaten as a child. Ms. Elliot is nothing like the bandit in the night but more like the abandon soul stealing from her oppressors to survive. No way, no how, will I ever try to insult your intelligence by downplaying murder. But some of you are Mothers, fathers, grandparents, aunts and uncles. Now tell me what if Lillian were your child. Who would protect her from people like Mr. Peterson, who as you heard, made a career out of abusing young girls. It didn't stop with Lillian or her young cousin, Katrina who is no longer on this earth because of people like Snookie. You heard the facts, that Lillian Elliot never having jay walked, or got a traffic ticket... to the extreme, serial murder. Attribute that to something. Nobody wakes up and says today I will kill people for no apparent reason. The sickness festered until it developed into hatred and vengeance. The victims, all bad people, lived daily in the mist of danger. No video to support human testimony which has proven to be somewhat flawed, no accurate eye witnesses. I think the only one to show up said she was too far away... However, regardless of any inconsistencies on either side, the bottom line is what would you have done? We heard straight from the horse's mouth how he and his crew raped a 15 year old child and murdered her very first boyfriend right in front of her, leaving her terribly scarred for life, while they went on to live their criminal lives. When will this nightmare that began years ago end for this poor woman? You heard her dear mother and the things she'd been through as well. You heard all about the so called victims. These were soldiers of misfortune peddling dope and elevating the body count all over the country. Lillian's life was destroyed by these people... Please vote to send Ms. Elliot home today. Thank You."

Patricia wasted no time taking front center. "Hello, ladies and gentlemen. As you already know my name is Prosecutor Patricia Chernoff and I like to thank you for being here as an obligation to your civil duties. We have a criminal system like no other and our country is predicated on law and order. Homicide is the highest level of crime a person can commit. You've heard testimony and saw evidence of the viciousness of these murders. The defense would have you believe their client is an angel but I warn you don't get caught up in all the rhetoric in the mist of all these dead people. It takes a devil to commit such acts. I have a saying that if you're trying to convict the devil, you may have to go to hell to find witnesses. Somebody like Peterson, no matter how disgusting and vile, exist in the sublevel of this subculture and therefore can provide insight. Murder is murder no matter how you slice it. The grown Lillian Elliot maliciously took the life of several human beings. Regardless if they were fishermen or drug dealers no one has the right to end their lives. Just think how much disregard for life it takes to kill someone with an ice pick or slice someone's throat. This woman is no hero! She must be punished for her actions. Letting a killer of this magnitude go free would send the wrong message, like cosigning wholesale murder. We as law abiding Americans bear the burden of establishing the guilt or innocence of our citizens using this courtroom as a forum. The facts have been stated and Lillian Elliot is no exception to the laws of this land. So I ask that you not let justice allude you and come back with a guilty on all counts. I speak for the preservation of law and order. Thank You." Patricia headed back to her table, head held high.

The judge spent twenty minutes instructing the jury before sending them to deliberate. Patricia got up without saying a word to anyone and disappeared thru the staff entrance.

Maurice bowed his head with his hands on Gwen's and Lillian shoulder while June said a quick prayer. Lillian turned to wave at Elliot who was smiling from ear to ear. He kissed the tip of his two fingers and placed them on his heart. Lillian felt a good chill run down her spine causing her nipples to get hard.

The defendant was required to wait out the verdict in the holding cell and Lillian begin to feel the pressure, barely an hour into her wait.

*****

Back in the jury room the appointed jury foreman named Bill started by asking one question. "After listening to all the testimony, how many of you at this point would vote to convict?"

Bob Shivery, a white, 57-year-old business man was the first to raise his hand. "I feel bad about what happened to her but killing all those people was wrong."

He was followed by Bill the 59-year-old jury foreman, Jed, a 44-year-old restaurant manager, Joseph, a 32-year-old graphic designer, Calvin a 67-year-old Greyhound bus driver, Evelyn, a 28-year-old hair dresser, Roger, a 60-year-old racist, and Gary, a 38-year-old probation officer, the other black juror out of the two to vote to convict.

"Looks like 8 for convict."
"How many not to convict?'

A 49-year-old black insurance agent named Brenda Potts raised her hand quickly, followed by 35-year-old Linda Hernández, and the only Caucasian to vote no, Martha Prude, a 49-year-old socialite from Manhattan.

"And three not to convict. I guess we have one undecided." 24-year-old Amy Shultz raised her hand. "I just need to hear more about you guys' opinion. I had to cover my eyes during some of the pictures."

"Okay." Bill started. "This thing is clear cut to me. Them there boys raped that girl and killed her boyfriend so this is a classic case of revenge. Now I'll admit, I got all caught up in feeling sorry for that girl for what those cowards did, but there was just too much time between the rape and all those murders. She planned and executed those people, and that's illegal, point blank."

All of the original yes jurors agreed. "Look," the black probation officer said, speaking mainly to the other black juror. "This has nothing to do with race. I work around criminals all day and they come in all shapes, sizes and colors. I don't know if everybody was listening to the same case I heard but I was horrified at some the things I saw and wouldn't want a person like that running around on the same earth as me."

After three hours of arguing, everybody was holding their positions except 24-year-old Amy who decided to change her vote to convict.

Brenda Potts spoke up. "I come from a rough place where people like this Snookie rule the neighborhood, taking advantage of the community. Pure scum who keep their feet on peoples neck. Standing up against these thugs, impossible when the police can't even get them in order. Somebody like Lillian is not a shock to me in this day and time and not soon enough if you asked me. After what she's been through, no! I don't want to see her go to prison. That's just me."

"But you think she did it?" Evelyn asked. "That's not how the law works. She's a killer and deserves to be in prison."

Brenda ignored the hair dresser. "Anyway, let your daughters have to grow up around stuff like that. I bet you'd see things differently then."

"The fuckers are the scourge of the earth. This girl did the world a freaking favor so let's cut the bull and make this a short day." Martha Prude barked. "And why am I the only white person who sees that?

Roger interrupted. "I've been around for a long time and I tell you we can't let scum like this exist on earth alongside of good white people. All those critters shooting and killing each other. We need to put them all on a barge and send them back too..."

"Okay, people." The foreman interrupted, although he agreed with Roger.

"Well me, I like to look at a person's underling intentions. No innocent citizens were harmed and Lillian only had a bone to pick with a certain group of people. That last guy Benjamin Steinberg she could have easily shot him or took the money for herself." Linda Hernandez was a 35-year-old registered nurse from East Harlem.

"I've always heard the road to hell is paved with good intention but I don't think any of hers were good. I hope we all can see that so we can get back to regular life." Jed said.

They argued back and forth for the remainder of the day with 9 voting to convict against, Brenda, Linda and Martha holding out. With no decision made they were due back tomorrow to continue deliberating.

Lillian spent a sleepless night back at the jail even though Maurice had told her it was a good sign they were arguing the issues. They had rushed her out so fast she didn't get a chance to kiss Elliot before leaving.

The following day Lillian was brought in early just to sit in the holding pen all day. Maurice showed up a few times to smuggle her some home cooked food stored in Tupperware containers.

"Thanks." She quickly demolished Gwen's wings with macaroni & cheese.

"No problem. I'll come for you when there's a verdict."

Lillian nodded and tried to find a comfortable position to sit on her butt. Time went on and towards the end of the day the jury sent a note telling the judge they couldn't agree on a verdict. The judge ordered them back yet another day.

The next morning Lillian snacked on cashews, Maurice had given her as she waited and waited. Lunch came and went then Lillian was finally called into the courtroom. There was a hush as the spectators and lawyers waited for the judge to announce a verdict. Entire news stations were on alert.

After everyone was seated the judge made his announcement. "The jury is hopelessly deadlocked. I've ordered them to come to a conclusion on several occasions. In the past days there was a vote of 9 to convict with three hold outs. Today they are hopelessly dead locked with a vote of 11 to convict and one holdout. Therefore, I declare this a mistrial."

Patricia jumped up and slammed her files on the table. "Bullshit!" The court irrupted like it was a not guilty verdict. "Order-order." The judge shouted.

Maurice didn't skip a beat. "Your Honor, in the mist of said ruling and the extended period of time involved in the prosecution preparing for a retrial it's in the interest of all parties that my client be granted bail. I had prepared a bail package that I would like to present to the court. It contains two property deeds and four personal signatures for $200,000 each. Including my wife's and my own."

The judge looked over at the Prosecution table, only to find the assistant Avery looking defeated.

"Any objections to the defendant's bail package?"

"Ah, no-no objections." This was the only decision Avery had made during the entire trial.

"Bail granted."

Everybody was all smiles. "They should have your paper work done in an hour. They'll bring your thru the front gate when you're ready."

"Thanks." She hugged them all, glad that she wasn't on her way to prison for life, yet. Laura almost hopped the divider getting to her daughter. "God is good." Lillian returned the hug, not wanting to explain to her mother that they would most likely retry her again. "Where is Elliot?" Lillian turned towards the spot he usually sat.

"He was right next to me a minute ago. Probably went to the bathroom." They hugged again before Lillian was taken to be processed for release.

Chapter Thirty Two

Free as a Bird

Maurice had volunteered to drive Lillian and her mother home when Elliot couldn't be found. "Thanks again." She was grateful for Maurice and Gwen. The three hour ride to Rhode Island was quiet as each passenger pondered the day's just past. Laura had to be awakened once they had arrived. The first thing Lillian saw was the Classic Customs Restoration insignia on the mustangs car cover. Her Benz that Elliot had been using to get back and forth was parked in its spot in the driveway. *Maybe he wants to surprise me in his birthday suit.* "You better let me go in first Mom." She found the door unlocked and peeped inside. "Elliot. I have mother with me." She called out before opening the door. The place was dark and quiet. "Boy I'm so tired. I think I'll have myself a nap before I start cooking." Laura headed to the guestroom while Lillian headed to her room. "Elliot." She continued to call as she hit the light switch. A knot formed in her stomach as she noticed the empty spot where Elliot's suitcase once were. All his cosmetics and clothes were missing also. Lillian was puzzled. Then suddenly she ran to the closet and began pulling out everything until she could remove the heavy trunk from against the closet wall. She pulled the wall of fake sheetrock down and stood, staring at the empty space where she had hid the million and change she had taken from Snookie. There are no words to describe how she felt. The money wasn't even the issue. She thought, matter of fact, she prayed every night to be home with her man but instead he took the money and ran. Lillian collapsed face first on her bed and wept.

Chapter Thirty Three

Making a Difference

Within days of her release, Lillian begin making arrangements to proceed with her vision. First thing she did was hire a reputable, law firm to act as an executor concerning the distribution of her sponsorship. Then she took time to research different organizations that provided programs and shelter for at risk teens. When she was finished she had selected several locations around the country in poverty stricken areas and composed a list of 20, in cities like Philadelphia, Chicago, Detroit, Atlanta, Newark, Gary Indiana, Dallas, Houston, Washington D.C, St. Louis, New Orleans, Little Rock, Cleveland, Baltimore, Vegas, Denver, Wichita, Oklahoma City, Long Beach and Los Angeles.

Lillian made a graph and wrote specific instructions concerning a pay schedule for each organization. *Sponsor shall remain anonymous.*

Maurice greeted Lillian as she entered his office. "You look great. I guess it feels good to be rocking your own clothes instead of that jailhouse gear."

"You're right about that." Lillian sighed. Just thinking about it made her stomach tense. She had taken a few moments in the mirror before leaving her home this morning, glad to be free. She took a seat and crossed her leg. "So how fast do you think the government will re-file?"

"There's no telling with Patricia. Could be anywhere from 90 days to a year or more..."

"I'd like to keep you on retainer for the criminal trial in addition to our other business."

"Well, that's great. Since the research and case law is already done the billing will be for hearing and court appearances. The fee will be a fraction of the cost from the first trial."

"I think you guys did a wonderful job and feel that the fee was well earned so I'd like to pay for your services in advance." Lillian reached in her shoulder bag and handed Maurice a large, manila envelope stuffed with $200,000 cash. He leaned back in his seat. "Wow." Was all he said.

She pulled out a folder and handed him some paperwork. "The 20 locations are not government funded and rely on private donations to exist. Many are struggling and flat broke. I've researched the more legit locations and would like the funds to be distributed as such."

Maurice begin reading the forms. "One million dollars to each of the 20 organizations to be allotted at the rate of $100,000 a year for a period of ten years, which is a grand total of 20 million. The executor shall receive a ten percent commission and bare such duties accordingly, to be paid from a different fund. "Whoa." Maurice breathe as he calculated 10% of 20 million.

After leaving her lawyers office, she drove uptown to Harlem to a location she had found doing her research. She was scheduled to meet with a structural engineer to determine if the abandoned storefront was safe enough to build on. The building was an entire block long but had been abandoned for over a year. The city wanted 2 million for it, and it was in a good location in uptown Harlem, not far from the Apollo Theater. After getting the okay from the engineer and paying his $600 fee, she had her lawyer broker the deal and hired a construction crew to begin renovation.

After careful thought she had calculated how much it would cost to get the center up and running. She envisioned the neighborhood with a place to be nurtured and taught extra skills, have free food provided and neighborhood awareness programs... Lillian's mind was racing, thinking of all the possibilities. Children laughing and playing on the playground and learning computer skills in the same building. Five million was put into place for what is to be called RENEE'S HOME, for disadvantaged and abused children like Renee to find a place for help. Once the project was up and running, Lillian planned on overseeing the center personally so that they could assist as many teens as possible.

Lillian called her Mom on her way home. "Hey Mom, I'm driving in from the city, would you like me to pick up something on the way?"

"You know, I always wondered if that vegetable store over there where your Aunt Barbra lives was still there, if so, would you stop by and grab two full bushels of turnip greens and some red potatoes."

"Got it. See you in a few hours." Lillian headed towards the vegetable store, mind on a few things at one time. When she reached the area where she had spent the summer with Katrina, images of Lewis popped up in her head. *That's the store where he called me Lollipop.* Lillian pulled her Mercedes over in front of a fire hydrant with her flashers on and ran inside the store real fast. She emerged with a brown bag full of animal shaped lollipops, the kind she used to like as a child. A few blocks away, she parked legally and went inside the vegetable store to grab her mother's items.

Lillian found herself singing along with the radio on the long drive to Rhode Island, like she and Renee used to do. She was shocked when one of Renee's favorite songs came on, right on cue.

"Loving you, is easy cause you beautiful... Every day of my life, is filled with loving you. La-la-la La-la, La-la-la La-la, La-la-la La-la, La-la-la-la. Do-do-do-di-do-do... Ahhhhhhhhhhhhhhhhhhhhhhhhhhhhhhhhhhhhhhh."

She experienced an array of emotions during the ride home, even having passing thoughts of Elliot. Twenty five of the 30 million that had come from Osiris' drug organization was already making its way back into the communities across the United States helping needy children. Lillian planned on dedicating her life to this cause, making the Harlem center, RENEE'S HOUSE a landmark center like the Covenant House, downtown. The remaining five million was weighing down her trunk as she pulled onto her quiet street. *What a long day. I'm pooped and can't wait for momma to put a real meal together.*

Lillian whipped the Mercedes into the drive next to the Mustang and again cursed herself for not remember to get rid of that damned Classic Custom car cover. *As soon as I unload the car I'm coming back out to roll that thing up and put it in somebody's dumpster.*

She began collecting the groceries, opening up one of the lollipops and putting into her mouth. "Uh-huh." She could hear her mother's voice in the back of her head saying, *never eat candy before dinner, it will spoil your appetite.* She decided to chew it before going into the house, feeling like a kid again.

Lillian felt her mother approach the car before she saw her and quickly turned to swallow the remaining pieces of lollipop before speaking. "Hey momma, I picked up those turnip greens and some..."

The single blast barked like a Great Dane, piecing the silence of the quiet neighborhood. Lillian didn't even have time to scream before the military styled ammunition tore her face away as her brains exited the side of her head. Without hesitation, Rook opened the door and snatched Lillian out onto the ground before getting behind the wheel, slamming in reverse and peeling off in a cloud of tire smoke.

It took a while before confused neighbors connected the ruckus outside to an actual event, having never before witnessed a crime in this district. The reaction was pure shock as they approached the body of the pretty young, well dressed woman lying next to a bag of turnip greens and animal lollipops. An elderly woman could be heard over the gasps and screams. "Looks like they carjacked the poor girl."

"Revenge belongs to no one, regardless of its easy access. Those who utilize it will be surprise to find that is perpetually, exclusive, only to itself." Author Junius Russell

Linda Hernandez sat down on her couch and kicked off her shoes after a long day at the office. She picked up the remote and turned on the TV before heading to take a quick shower on her way to have dinner with a friend. As she stepped out of her skirt, a face on the screen caught her eye. Grabbing the remote quickly, she turned up the volume and sat back down on the couch shocked as the news gave the gruesome details of Lillian's murder. A sudden feeling of sadness mixed with guilt ran through her... Being the remaining holdout she had held fast, even when the other two jurors had given in and eventually voted to convict, it was her who refused to budge, even if it took weeks more of deliberating. All the testimony about the killings troubled Linda as well, but somewhere along the trial she got stuck on the defendant's **intent** like one of the lawyers had said. When Linda was young she found herself on the streets when her mother overdosed on heroin and her father got life in prison for murder. It was a cold, dark experience. She had to have what's called survival sex for a few nights of sleep here and there. One grown man took her to a dark corner under a trestle to sell her body. She was able to escape by begging the driver of the first car she got in to take her somewhere safe... He took her to the **Covenant House** and dropped her off.

THE END

COMING SOON from JUNIUS RUSSELL

LUCKY (revenge 2)

NAW'LINS

THE MILKMAN

SHANAUTICA

MR POLITE

TASTE OF LIFE

BAD TO DA BONE

WWW.PlanetPoliteEnt.com

www.ingramcontent.com/pod-product-compliance
Lightning Source LLC
Chambersburg PA
CBHW062126170626
46813CB00002B/579